BLACK WOLF
SILVER FOX

Katrina Joyner

Black Wolf, .Silver Fox
Joyner, Katrina

Third edition; second edition edited by Timothy Belcher
ISBN: 978-1-944322-03-8

Published via the Writers of the Apocalypse
www.apocalypsewriters.com

Black Wolf, Silver Fox isn't my best story. I broke a lot of guidelines when I wrote it, ones that I realize now should have been listened to in order to get a more cohesive story. It took me ten years to edit, rewrite and produce.

Despite it's failings, I am in love with at least one of the characters in the way that authors can't help but to fall in love with their creations. From time to time I will reopen this book and look at the pages, to remind myself of what happens within. I've had a sequel start on it for years now - and someday I swear I'm going to find the time to finish it. If life will allow it.

I thank you for giving this book a chance, and I hope you enjoy.

Black Wolf, Silver Fox

Katrina Joyner

www.apocalypsewriters.com

CHAPTER ONE
"ARAMINA"

The moon hung full and bright over the thick canopy of the forest. Shafts of moonlight pierced the leaves to fall in dappled shades of grey onto the ground. Occasionally, there was a swish as underbrush was carefully moved aside to allow the passage of some nocturnal beast. Otherwise, the air was deadly quiet as if the entire world were waiting.

The black one ran silently through the trees, dodging the pale moonlight as if it were poison. She paused and sniffed to test the air and get her bearings. The moon called her onward. Through the trees and underbrush, she rushed, across streamlets and pale meadows.

The cries of her brethren followed as she loped along. They sang of family, kinship, and togetherness. They were the things she turned her back on now as other memories moved restlessly in her mind. Her ripped left ear throbbed: a warning from the pack leader. It would probably scar and serve as a permanent reminder.

Suddenly, a clearing burst out of the trees. Not wanting to step out of the forest and be exposed, the black one halted and whined. Indecisively, she paced back and forth in the shadows.

She could hear a familiar, flapping sound in distance. It's presence nagged at her, although she only acknowledged it with a flick of her good ear. Her pacing slowed then halted altogether as it grew louder. To herself, she growled a low warning before setting paw into the clearing before her.

Something that looked like an old rag appeared suddenly in a nearby patch of moonlight. It circled the black one like trash caught in a whirlwind, dizzying her senses. Finally, it stopped flying to land in the clearing before her. She lowered her ears, crouched in place, and whined again. Her tail hung limply between her tensed legs.

Either a flying bat or an old cloak—it was difficult to tell—it fluttered once by way of threat. Then it changed, lengthened, and gained mass until a handsome elf stood in its place. His green eyes sparkled above a sharp-toothed grin.

"Aramina," said he, "leaving so soon?" His grin mocked her. He had killed with those teeth; it was a matter of pride for him. Unimpressed, the she made a sound that might have been a snort.

"Come now," he said soothingly. "You and I are above this beastly behavior."

Suddenly at ease, she sat and scratched her ears. Let him carry on the conversation by himself, her attitude seemed to say. Her unwelcome companion ignored the insult. Laughing, he crouched before her to wait. Clouds moved slowly past the moon, marking time.

It was a very long time before the elf got bored enough to try again. "Shall we sit here all night?" Again the black one growled, and then she barked softly. She stood, circled a time or two, then faced her adversary. The elf leaned back, his smile widening as he watched her change. Similar to the one he had just undertaken, her emergence was deliberately slow. The first thing she did when done was to toss her long, black hair and narrow one eye.

Shadowed by the night, her deep brown eyes glittered like obsidian. With a voice like a deep howl, she said, "Speak, and be quick."

"You've been feral too long," the elf said calculatingly. "Where are your manners?"

"I don't have time for manners." She stood naked, for she had long ago dispensed with such trivial things. The chill in the air made her shiver. It would only get colder before dawn, but she preferred not to think about that.

The elf sighed. How like her: business before pleasure. "Where are you going?" he asked unenthusiastically. They both knew the answer.

Aramina looked past him toward the moonlit clearing. "Gredber," she said slowly, as if she found speaking to be painful, "what is it you want?"

Gredber continued to smile, but now the expression looked sad somehow. He shook his head, freeing a brown cowlick into his eyes. Aramina had found that painfully attractive ages ago, but now she could barely remember why or even how they met.

That was the price of immortality. One could forget and never learn from their mistakes or go insane from the burden of memory. Aramina had been happy living with the pack and feeling the bliss of pure wildness. If Gredber's occasional visits did not remind her that she was more than a mere lupine, she would have forgotten herself forever.

That would be too easy, she thought with narrowing eyes. Gredber was waiting, watching her warily. The choices she made tonight would affect him as much as her. Regardless of that responsibility, she intended to plunge onward. She was not the naive girl of long ago and would no longer sacrifice time for another's comfort. Of all people, Gredber should know that.

"Let me pass," Aramina snapped.

Chin high, she took a step forward. Their shoulders brushed each other. He gripped her arm suddenly and jerked her back in one violent motion. She gasped in pain, ducking a little to protect her ears. Involuntarily her eyes met his and locked. Then, shamefully, Aramina looked away and toward the ground.

Angrily, Gredber pushed her away. "Go then," he said, his voice choked with pain and anger. "I won't stop you."

Something fluttered, swept upward, and touched her cheek. By the time Aramina dared to look up, Gredber was gone back to the wood. Her pack had fallen silent; everything was quiet again but for the soft crunch of leaves under her feet as she timidly walked forward. Aramina rubbed her cheek where Gredber had kissed her.

When the moonlight hit her naked flesh, it set her aglow as if she were a goddess. Around her, the darkness held back as if it knew how unreachable she truly were. Her eyes remained focused on the clearing's center, a dark area the moonlight could not touch. There as an ancient altar there. It was made from piled weathered stones and was stained dark with the blood of countless sacrifices.

Three rings of weathered stones, each marked with sigils of forgotten spirits, surrounded it. Aramina could not remember what the sigils were for, or who they named, except one. She paused when she reached the first ring of stones and touched it with a single finger. "Mine," she whispered.

Her heart hammered in her chest. It was a long time before she could bring herself to step over the first ring and into this unholy, yet somehow sacred, place. The second ring of stones was even harder to cross, as if something pushed her back. Aramina held her breath when she stepped over the third and final ring. With the altar now just feet away, her soul shuddered.

Mortal eyes could not see the energy that flicked over the darkest part of the center. She smelled the energy in the same way she saw it. For an instant, she could not think of how to react. Then, she remembered as if instinct needed only the excuse to come alive. Her knees buckled, and she sank to the ground. Pressing her face to the earth, she touched the altar base with sweaty fingertips. A shock run up her arms and sent spasms to her toes. Atop the altar, a bright flame burst mysteriously to life, chasing away the shadows.

Inwardly Aramina groaned as her every nerve was set on fire. To acknowledge this torture was to forfeit her life, and she could not do that yet. She bit her lip, tasted blood, and stayed perfectly still, even when a spark jumped from the fire and burned a hole in her wrist.

Rise, a deep voice commanded. It came from everywhere; the ground, the trees, even her mind. She obeyed, resisting the urge to brush off her soiled knees. The flame flickered before her, capturing her gaze and holding it. Something invaded her soul, read it, then withdrew. Although she had expected and almost welcomed it, she still felt raped. Revulsion tightened her stomach.

Speak, said the voice.

"Lord," the fey said before choking. She swallowed, but a moment passed before she found her voice again. "I would ask a boon for your loyal servant."

Ask.

"I want to go home," she said as quickly as she dared. "At least for two seasons—"

Silence! The air crackled with the command. Despite herself, Aramina flinched and awaited her punishment. The air was pregnant with expectancy.

You may go, the rumbling voice said after a while. *It pleases me that you do.*

"Lord?" Hope filled Aramina's eyes and moistened them with unshed tears.

I have an errand for you. Your companions will await...

Aramina nodded her head dutifully and bowed again. Within her mind, the voice methodically explained. Memories, left slumbering for ages, rose screaming to the top of her mind. Helpless, Aramina could only watch history replay behind her eyes...

The city gates were shattered by the siege engines, and fire rampaged through most of the area. The few survivors fled but were efficiently hunted down and exterminated. Their heads were severed and placed on pikes outside the walls.

One young woman - a fey creature of alluring dimensions - did not flee. The temple which had been her home for most of her life was now burning to a cinder right before her eyes. She stood fascinated while it crumbled inward, devouring itself in its death throes. There would be nothing left except fine ash when it was over.

Winds whipped at her torn, sooty acolyte's robes, pulling it around her legs. Shaking a triumphant fist toward the blaze, she laughed a high, crazy note before turning away. That was when she saw the ancient priest, who watched with sad eyes as he leaned on his staff. Apparently, he had been there a while.

"Join the fun, Old Man," she said playfully. She traced her hips with her hands, stretched, and pulled her hair up. "You could use the excitement."

The priest shook his head slowly. "It is enough," said he, "to watch the damage you have done."

She laughed again, but this time her mirth had a lower note to it. "Yes, I thought so, too." Coyly, she approached him. He did not back away nor show any sign of malice toward her, not even when she kissed his breast. Disappointed, she pulled away from him.

"You aren't mad at me?" she pouted, childishly putting her hands behind her back.

The old elf responded, "You were so full of promise," as if he spoke to an errant child and there were no fires around them.

"Promise?" she shrieked suddenly, spreading her legs apart and bringing up two fists. "What do you know of promise? You dined while I starved, scrubbing the floors with my bare hands! The only promise you filled was that of humiliation!"

"I am sorry for what the others did to you. It was out of my hands and beyond my knowledge."

"You saw me every day!" Her face was a mask of fury framed by the fire. "Every day you walked by, too intent on your own inner peace to see the suffering it caused!" She crouched.

"We saved your life," the old priest said.

"You used me," the woman hissed.

"I wish," said the old elf as he stood a little taller and leaned a bit less on his staff, "that it had not come to this."

With a shout and a flick of his wrist, he reached towards her. He was quicker than she expected, but she jumped out of reach just as his hands, glowing with white-hot flame, groped for her face. She cracked his chin with her fist, and he staggered back, flailing wildly. His pinky grazed her cheek, burning it. She howled in pain, backing away while he regained his senses.

They feinted: a slow dance in which she circled and he shifted only to watch. With a new howl, she changed form and rushed him. His form matched hers and two wolves, white on black, clashed in a rage of snapping teeth. Rolling over each other, tearing any flesh within reach, they hit the temple steps. Kicking legs scattered glowing embers.

The black wolf somehow managed to clamp her teeth on the white wolf's inner thigh. Yelping, the white wolf broke free with a twist and scampered to get away. The black one latched to his ankle and held tightly. She tried to get a better grip, but slipped. The white one twisted loose, snarled, and ripped into her front leg.

She bit his nose, tasted blood, and limped back when her leg was released. The two faced each other, snarling, for the briefest of moments. Then the black one leapt.

The white wolf dodged but slipped on some cooling embers and missed his footing. The black one was on him instantly. They rolled until the white wolf lay on his back. The impact knocked the breath from the aging werewolf. While he was stunned, the black one tore his throat. Hot blood sprayed into her eyes, and she knew that she had won. The black one's warbling howl sang victoriously across the burning wreckage.

Warily, three elves and a dwarf approached from up a nearby street. The black one barked at them, content to scratch one ear while she waited. When she was within reach, the leader scratched her ear. He was a charming elf with tousled brown hair. His sparkling green eyes studied the body of the white wolf as it slowly lost its transformation to again become the high priest.

"Well done, Aramina," he said. The black one harruphed, wagging her tail. "If a little dishonorably accomplished."

The black one's eyes were full of mischief. However it was done, the job was complete. And what was honor between her and her enemies but a lie?

CHAPTER TWO
"EAHN"

The sun was hot for spring, but Eahn knew he could manage. He had just two more rows to sow before turning his attention to butchering a hog. His wife could make a grand dinner from it this evening and days to come if he kept the predators from the larder. He paused in his sowing to wipe his brow.

Three men on horseback topped a distant hill to be silhouetted by the morning sun. Eahn frowned, sensing that these were no ordinary guests. There was a feel about them that was wholly familiar, but he could not remember just what it was. Scratching his chin, he watched them as they approached.

When they were close enough for Eahn to see the sunlight flash off their golden hair, he took precautionary measures. His old sword, lovingly cleaned and oiled, was hidden nearby in the barn. He made way to get it and did not feel better until it was in hand. Then, he leaned casually against the barn door, sword tip to earth, and chewed a bit of grass.

When they were near enough to make out their faces, they reigned their horses in. One put his hand up, palm out, in a gesture of peace.

"Well," Eahn spat, "you're here. Now what do you want?" Elves, these riders were, and therefore a danger. Eahn dealt better with dwarves than elves, even though he was elven himself. Dwarves were forward with their intentions and usually a good deal more honest. Elves, especially mages, were something else entirely.

"You are Eahn the Northern Thorn?" asked the peacemaker.

"Maybe," Eahn said, drawling the world out for all it was worth. Casually, he pointed his sword tip to each elf. "Who wants to know?"

"Lord Eahn," the rider said, making a half bow in his perch. It looked ludicrous. "We have ridden a long way to find you. It concerns The Five."

"The five what?" asked Eahn suspiciously.

The rider opened his mouth to speak, but a gesture from one of his companions stilled his tongue. The other rider urged his horse up a step, leaned forward, and grinned. He was feet away from Eahn, who did not appreciate the intimacy. "Eahn," said he, "don't make our lives more difficult than it is. We're not here to arrest you for treason, or burn you, or whatever else you might imagine."

"No?" The sword whistled when Eahn gave it an experimental swing. Clearly unimpressed, the riders exchanged a single glance. "Is that because of what happened the last time Cnos Fada sent someone for me? Which makes me wonder. What was the reaction in court when they received the pieces?"

The second rider chuckled to himself, then dismounted. Immediately, Eahn struck the earth with his sword. Lifting it into a guard stance, he held himself ready while the sword rang a high-pitched tone. The air stood still while the sound faded.

"I am Handfast," the second rider said. He stepped closer and ignored Eahn's shift of balance. "I came with a message from Moirfenn. MacKegan summons you, Eahn the Northern Thorn, upon the very geis that holds your spirit."

Eahn, entirely against his will, suddenly remembered... Aramina. The first thing he had to remember out of the entire ordeal had to be the dark were-creature. Annoyed, Eahn resisted the urge to kick the nearest object. Not that the elf standing before him would not have looked better sporting a few bruises.

Eahn lowered his sword and sighed. "Well," he muttered.

His three visitors waited patiently. Eahn gazed into the horizon, still remembering, and frowned. The hills were beginning to show color with the first flowers of spring. Eahn had no flocks to keep them grazed. Picket would love those hills and have a jolly time trampling them. And... there was someone else. Not a companion, but someone who liked flowers. Someone who *really* liked flowers.

Someone he should be wary of. Eahn could just taste the memory.

Eahn's eyes flicked back to Handfast and stayed. "I remember you," he said harshly. Handfast had fought alongside Eahn years ago. The elf still had that whiplash scar across one arm. His sleeve was rolled up, as if to proudly display the blemish.

"I thought you might," Handfast said with a trace of a grin. "Now, shall we talk business?"

The sun set unnoticed outside. Handfast's companions, Maguire and Neolch, sat near Eahn's fireplace after a hearty supper of ham and early greens. Sulking at the table, Eahn kept his thoughts to himself. His guests were sent from his master in Moirfenn, and this meant nothing but bad news. Anyone from Moirfenn was bad news, although Handfast could be trusted to a certain degree. Then there came a point in which Eahn found himself not trusting the elf at all. Not that he trusted any elf, including himself.

The servants had been sent to their quarters, and Eahn's wife was ordered upstairs. The dinner mess could be cleaned in the morning, he had told her. She had obeyed without argument, obedient little thing that she was. Eahn felt a glow of affection in her direction, and spat into the fire to cover it. He glared once again at Handfast.

Handfast ignored Eahn's barely concealed malice. Without touching it, he stirred his spoon around in his empty bowl. The atma made little sparks off the utensil, which was wood, but otherwise did no harm. Eahn disdained such frivolous uses of magical gifts, and Handfast knew it. The faster the spoon moved, the more irritated Eahn looked. It was rather amusing.

Maguire and Neolch were hired swords and not concerned with any discussion other than their own. They played sticks and bones in the corner, alternately cursing and accusing each other of cheating. Eahn was more annoyed with them than Handfast's mischievous activity.

Eahn flicked his fingers, wasting a precious bit of atma, and the spoon flew from the bowl. It bounced into the fireplace where it promptly caught on fire. A log popped and sparks jumped. Handfast chuckled, leaning back and drinking his glass of mead. Maguire mumbled something faintly murderous to Neolch in the background.

"What if," Eahn said casually, continuing a conversation they had begun during dinner, "I refuse to do this?" The things Handfast had told him this night were not agreeable, not in the least. Eahn knew better, but the thought of killing his two guests and hiding the bodies were not far from his mind.

Handfast snorted with mirth. "As if you would dare," he said. "I think what you should be asking is where to go first."

"All right then," Eahn said in his slow drawl. "Where? Do I meet them there or wait?"

"Nebhirrlos," Handfast said. "And wait for the others to arrive, if you are first." He set his cup, now empty, down on the table. There was more mead – indeed, an entire barrel nearby – but he felt too lazy to get it. Eahn would surely not, and the wife and servants were banished from sight. Apparently, Eahn sought to protect his family from the dangerous intruders. Handfast was only annoyed that he was forced to serve himself under another's roof. This smacked against all rules of etiquette and hospitality, not that Eahn had been anything but surly and impossible to deal with.

"There is a Sanctuary House there," Handfast continued, pushing the cup a little away. "The Priestess will be waiting for you there. She knows what to do and is already on her way."

Eahn remembered Nebhirrlos. There had been much blood, and even Aramina the Priestess had been quite... shaken. A pleasant memory indeed, he reflected as he fought to keep from smiling. "Have you nothing further to tell me?" he asked.

"Of course not," Handfast snapped. "I know only what you need to know for now. Have a little common sense. MacKegan would not trust even you with the details, if it were not necessary."

"I suppose you will not be accompanying me." It was not a question, merely an observance of fact. Handfast nodded affirmatively.

Eahn stared into the flames a while longer, listening to Maguire and Neolch play. Or rather, argue. They seemed to take much pleasure in their personal conflict. "To sleep then," Eahn said. "I should start early tomorrow. What shall you do, my friend?"

"Wait here," Handfast said calmly. "I'm under orders to protect your wife, should you fail."

Eahn went cold inside and resisted the urge to look up the stairs.

***

His wife clung long to his embrace before he mounted their best horse to leave. He leaned down from the saddle and patted her bulging stomach before whispering into her ear, "I will be back before my son comes. I promise you that, my Joalie."

She flashed her bravest smile and said, "You best be back before your daughter arrives. I wouldn't want her to greet the world without your strong arms to protect her."

Eahn nodded, letting her win their argument this one time, and flicked the reins. Too soon, Joalie was a waving figure swallowed by dust. Somewhere in the house, Handfast and his crew drank his mead and argued over dice. Eahn wanted to burn the house down and carry Joalie away, but he knew better than to try.

How long has it been? Eahn wondered to himself as his horse's hooves plodded patiently down the road. Memories of settling down to make his own stead were always clouded, ,as if they were only a dream. Time did that, as well as simply not wanting to remember. One thing was irrefutable: he had been given that land for a reason.

One obvious reason was that it was close to a break in the veil. Eahn chewed a piece of grass, spitting to the side occasionally. How convenient to place a valued servant so near a doorway to Éire, where the mortals dwelt. And then MacKegan seemingly had forgotten him, which had led Eahn to believe he was no longer in use.

If MacKegan had wanted Eahn to do something through the veil, the reason was lost forever, especially in light of this new task, whatever it may be. Eahn knew better than to question MacKegan's sanity; the elf was merely fickle. It was his way, and thus far MacKegan had won an entire kingdom merely by deciding he wanted to rule.

All of Fion's rulers did the most peculiar things, as if they trusted to blind luck and foolishness to keep a country sound. It had worked for generations, but Eahn sometimes felt that even luck such as that could not hold out forever. MacKegan was an old fool, and sooner or later it would be his downfall.

Yet, even mortals flocked to MacKegan's banner. Eahn could not stand the creatures and wished MacKegan would either kill them or send them home. Their atma was weak. They bred like flies and died quickly. Their fascination for Eahn's people, and the divine fire within, drew them like moths to light or repulsed them just as strongly. Eahn had participated in dozens of sluagh rides, mainly to patrol his borders, and witnessed the mortal people's ways first hand. He did not wholly approve of them.

Eahn found them to be crude-mouthed and sometimes brutal, even when compared to crueler breeds of two-leg. They were almost completely without honor. The bravest mortals had the tendency to swarm over the land, like ants, and dig without the slightest thought for the local inhabitants.

Their music could be delightful, and occasionally a mortal bard had the ability to play a sprightly tune. But overall, the lure of enchanted gold always became too strong. Twice Eahn had to dodge attempts on his life. By mortals!

Thieving, lying, filthy mortals.

Not that mortals were the only dishonest creatures in the world. The most honest person Eahn had ever known was the mage, Raori. Raori could stretch the truth or lead you to believe false by omitting certain facts and letting you make your own conclusions, but not once did he ever truly lie. No, he was not like the Priestess, whose every breath was questionable to Eahn's ears. Reminded of other things he had long ago forgotten, he spat out his piece of grass and scowled.

He camped that evening near the highway leading to Nebhirrlos. He kept his fire small; the last thing he wanted was to be found, and firelight was a giveaway in the dark. Chewing a bit of dried meat, he sat staring into the tiny flames blankly. Then, he noticed that he was being watched.

His observer was a young elf standing on a nearby hill like a statue against the oncoming night. Eahn considered the silhouette a moment, blew out noisily, and got to his feet. It would be inhospitable not to invite this stranger to share his fire. He waved his arms once, then he sat down again.

The youth bounded down the hill enthusiastically and slid to a deep bow at Eahn's feet. A harp case, hung from his right shoulder with a worn leather band, slid forward and made a musical bump against his knee. "Oenghus, at your service," he declared breathlessly. He stood with a flourish and pushed the case back to its proper place.

Eahn grunted and resettled by the fire. He did not care for formal introductions. Confused, the bard waited just long enough to be sure Eahn would not be introducing himself. Then, he also sat by the fire. Eahn handed him a bit of cheese and dried meat.

"Your mother either had a sense of humor or a good sense of character," Eahn observed while the youth ate his meal, "to have named you after the god of mischief."

Oenghus grinned fleetingly. "Yes, my mother does like to stay entertained." He swallowed his last bit of cheese and reached for the waterskin which lay near his foot. "What do they call you?"

The waterskin was passed to Eahn, who switched it for a full skin of wine. Wine Eahn had no trouble sharing with company, but there were occasional times that good drinking water was more precious than gold. The youth grinned his pleasure at the change in the spread, thinking himself honored.

"My name is Eahn."

Oenghus' eyes grew wide. "Surely not the Northern Thorn?" he whispered with awe. "A pleasure, Lord! To think that I, a lowly bard, would be graced with the hospitality of one of Moirfenn's greatest heroes!" He shook his head in wonderment.

"I did not say I was the Northern Thorn," Eahn said, scowling. "Eahn is a common enough name."

"Oh yes, Lord," Oenghus said agreeably. His eyes lit with a twinkle. At least, he did not press the subject.

The wineskin was passed between themselves during the following silence. Oenghus idly poked a stick in the fire to keep it burning. He was smiling to himself. Eahn ignored him while he oiled his sword. When the skin started to go limp, Eahn packed it away.

"Where are you bound?" Oenghus asked as if to break the silence. Bored with the fire, he turned to his pack and began to unpack his sleeping furs. Intent on his work, he only heard Eahn spit into the fire. His furs were mangy-looking and probably had fleas. Eahn forbore wasting atma to charm any such pests away from his person.

"To see an old friend," Eahn said after a brief pause.

"Ah," Oenghus said knowingly. He began to pick up rocks, large and small, to throw them into the darkness. "Uncomfortable things," he muttered to himself while he worked. When he had thrown what he felt was enough, he spread his furs on the ground. "That should do."

Amused, Eahn watched until his guest was finished. "My guest asks me questions," he said once Oenghus was completely settled, "but offers nothing concerning himself. Where are you going?"

"Wherever suits me," the bard said with an airy wave of his hand. "I was thinking Nebhirrlos. The people there love a good tale as much as anywhere else."

"Of course," Eahn said, faintly annoyed. The last thing he wanted was to be tracked by a faithless bard. "How very convenient."

"From there I might go to Cnos Fada," Oenghus said. "Then usually I just go straight to the temple in Tech Danaan to gather more news. Bound to stay there," he yawned mightily, "for months." He closed his eyes and shifted until he was comfortable.

Oenghus was asleep almost immediately and snored faintly. Quietly Eahn spit to the side. It did not bother Eahn that the boy did not offer to take first watch. His carelessness was his own business. When Eahn wanted to get some sleep, he would set protection spells around the camp and be secure.

What bothered him was that Oenghus was going to the exact same destination. The last thing he wanted on this trip was a companion. In this case, the last thing he wanted was someone who knew his face.

In much the same way as he had done before with Handfast, he pondered killing the boy. After a while, he rejected the notion. It was far too much work. He would wait to see what developed later.

To Eahn's relief, his fears were unfounded. Oenghus, when he woke the next morning, industriously packed his belongings. Refusing Eahn's offer of breakfast, he plead that he did not want to waste the morning. Marching straight away with only a jaunty wave of farewell, the bard was gone before Eahn had his horse saddled. The farmer was glad to see him go and bade him good riddance.

Rain clouds hung low in the sky, making the air gloomy and heavy with rain. It drizzled at the best of times, and rain fell in sheets of blinding silver at the worst. If Eahn did not have to hurry to Nebhirrlos, he would have found shelter to wait it out.

Afraid water would get into his bags, he skipped lunch and barely allowed his horse to rest. The bags were waterproofed by oil, and he refused to waste atma to reinforce it. Water ran in rivulets down his neck and back. Those tiny streams joined to make bigger ones that ran down his saddle and to his horse's legs. The horse snorted to itself, shaking its mane, and trudged along in the mud.

Evening had deepened into soft gloom before the rains finally lightened up. Eahn camped at a crossroads and made his fire beneath the weathered wooden marker. It was hard to keep the wood lit given that it was drenched. In the end Eahn was forced to resort to atma to set the wood on fire. The enchanted flames glowed greenly over the area but offered little warmth. Miserable, Eahn shivered in his cloak and thought of his warm house and Joalie.

"Hai!" someone shouted in the gloom. Eahn reflexively grabbed his sword. "Hai!" they shouted again.

It was Oenghus, dripping wet but looking none the worse for wear. He emerged from the darkness and rain to stand just beyond Eahn's camp and grin. For the briefest of moments, Eahn was reminded of a hopeful mongrel begging for scraps.

Eahn considered the situation. He could turn the bard away, or he could allow him by the fire. When Oenghus sneezed, the decision was made. Before long, the youth was huddled by the fire. The last of the wine warmed their bellies. Oenghus sneezed again.

"I'm glad I found you," Oenghus said through chattering teeth.

"Looking for me were you?" Eahn asked suspiciously. He had not put his sword away, although the rain was sure to rust it.

"No," Oenghus said with a chuckle. "It's just that a bard is a sorry sight in the rain with no fire to warm himself with. I'm sure to catch a cold." Mournfully he sniffled, as if to say he had caught one already. "Even a green fire with little warmth is welcome. My poor harp! I can only hope I mended that hole in her case well enough to keep her dry."

Eahn did not respond, turning instead to the difficult task of drying his sword enough to put it away. He could put the fire out; it made no sense to keep it except as light against the darkness that surrounded them. But, he did not. His companion obviously appreciated the fire as he curled himself into a sodden ball as close to the flame as he safely could. With misgivings, Eahn settled to sleep after Oenghus was snoring, his sword nearby.

A boot by his hand startled him awake. With a yell, he grabbed his sword, rolled and crouched into a defensive position. Oenghus, whose boot it was, stood dumbfounded, staring at Eahn with eyes round as coins. It was late morning, and Eahn had overslept.

"I was just," the youth stammered, "I was just going to wake you before I left."

Eahn forced himself to relax and lower his sword. He ran his fingers through his beard, feeling foolish. "My apologies," he muttered. "Twas a reflex."

The bard nodded solemnly, stepping back a pace. "I wouldn't let it be known that I had frightened the Northern Thorn from his sleep." Eahn snarled. "I wanted to give you this," the bard squeaked, offering a golden medallion strung on leather.

"Why?" Eahn said, trying to keep the edge out of his voice. The bard shyly handed it over, took another step backward and readjusted the strap to his harp case.

It was a simple disk, no larger than the palm of a woman's hand, engraved with a swan. Someone had used it for a tool and left the edges slightly battered. The leather, slipped through a worn hole, looked fairly new. There was no inscription.

"You were kind to me, for one thing," Oenghus said. "Because, I don't know. You're the one to take it." His voice trailed lamely away. At Eahn's questioning glance, Oenghus grinned. "Give it to your woman friend," he said, "in Nebhirrlos."

"Wait!" Eahn demanded as the bard turned to go. "I never said I was going to–!"

"Don't forget!" Oenghus cried as he strode away. "Give it to her when you see her!"

Eahn cursed as Oenghus strode further, yet further away. The lad was walking impossibly fast. Eahn followed a few steps then stopped. He had not time to go chasing after a bard, medallion or no. It would have to wait.

Later, when the monotony of riding grew unbearable, he removed the medallion from its place in his saddlebags to examine it further. Tracing the swan with his fingers and using atma to see things his eyes could not, his world was the inside of this metal thing for an instant. The sounds around him, even the horse's ungainly plodding, faded away.

He sensed nothing about the medallion; not a faint odor of magic. Eahn refused to carry a cursed thing all the way to Nebhirrlos, but if the medallion were such a thing, it was well concealed. He considered throwing it away, but thought again. The Priestess might find some use for it, and perhaps it was cursed. The Priestess more than deserved it, if so.

The faint rush of water reached his ears. Somewhere in the trees, at the end of the road he traveled, would be an arm of the River Nosloraug. Beyond by about a two-day ride lay Nebhirrlos.

CHAPTER THREE
"RAORI"

H is brain was pounding mercilessly against his skull when Raori opened his eyes and struggled to bring his world into focus. Someone groaned. He realized it was himself.

Something was pushing him down and holding him to the ground. He tried to push against whatever it was, but he was stuck fast. After a second of struggling, he lost his temper. The backlash of his brief fury slammed it across the room to shatter against the wall. Raori winced as the sound amplified the already resounding throb in his brain and realized that he had just splintered a good table. Now he would have to pay for it.

Picking himself up off the floor, his hand brushed an empty bottle and sent it rolling. Another groan emerged. Holding his head in one hand, he surveyed the situation.

He stood in what had been a tavern only a few hours ago. All of the furniture, now that the table had met its abrupt end, was destroyed. Broken glass was everywhere, twinkling in the morning light. The building was missing one wall and smelled of scorched flesh.

Oh.

A grin cracked his face, causing his lips to burn. The table be dammed, he would have to pay for the entire building. With pride. He had caused this: a beautifully rendered fiasco starting with accusations about a girl he did not even know. It had been so easy to get the fight started. All without uttering a single lie.

That would teach old Febis. Next time the tavern's owner saw Raori, he would look the other way and mind his manners. If Raori again heard the old man speaking ill of MacKegan or anything to do with The Five even remotely, he would do worse.

Dropping to one knee in the midst of the rubbish, Raori immediately offered thanks to BileEll, the shining god. Then, a little guiltily, he offered a second prayer to the god of mischief. A breeze brushed his cheek, affirming his prayers. He could not tell from which god it came, but he would lay bets on the latter.

He was filthy, but his head hurt too much to make an effort to magic the dirt away. Grime, ripped shirt, sore muscles and all, Raori stepped out of the ruined tavern. The town was surprisingly busy that morning. Raori seldom got up before noon, and he could not comprehend the need to do so. If it had been left to him, the place would be little better than a ghost town.

Fortunately, it was not up to him. Bread was being baked, wives made their way to buy eggs and butter, and children shrieked happily. Raori dodged a toddler, nodded cordially to his mother, and scowled at her back.

"Stupid woman," Raori muttered under his breath. Children were rare enough these days without some woman allowing her child to be murdered under foot. Not that Raori would ever do such a thing, but there were those who would.

Home jutted against the rising sun sharply, and welcome. Gratefully, Raori slipped inside. Moire greeted him, holding a cup of warm milk, and took his cloak. He stood by the door and sipped the beverage slowly. It settled sharply against the lump in his stomach.

"Master," Moire said nervously, "you have visitors."

Raori grunted. "You mean, I had visitors and you sent them away."

Moire blinked for a moment. She was dutiful, for a mortal, but sometimes got details confused. He supposed it had been a difficult transition for her. One moment she was picking flowers on a hill in Éire, the next being borne away in a sluagh ride.

He had bought her intending to set her free, but she refused to go. Why go home, she said, when years, even centuries, may have passed for her there? The quality of life was better in Fion, too. She preferred to take her chances among her kidnappers and appeared grateful.

Raori had found himself stuck with a servant he truly did not want. He gave her some tasks to earn her keep but insisted on doing most things himself. Being raised on a small farm with eight siblings had tempered Raori into independence – and allowed him to appreciate the finer things in life, like not having to share a bed.

Moire was still blinking stupidly. "Do you mean, you want me to send them away?" she asked.

Raori sighed.

"Yes, Moire," he said. "I'm for bed. Tell them to come back this evening."

"I would, Master," she said hurriedly, placing a brave hand on his chest to stay him from leaving. "Truly, I would. But, Milord, they seem important."

Everyone who came to see Raori was important. He did not encourage friendships, other than those made years ago, and those people had forgotten him by now. Raori could not forget, even when he tried. The ability had always escaped him, even from childhood.

Drunken nights and late mornings helped temporarily. With Moire standing before him, unwittingly forcing him to think and remember, Raori almost regretted what he had done to the tavern.

Moire was waiting for him to say something. Her eyes were targeted on his lips. She had clasped her hands in front, as if she regretted touching him. Raori felt obliged.

"How important?" he asked, raking his fingers through his hair.

"Very," Moire said, as expected. She pointed to a side room. The door was closed.

Raori considered first the closed door, then the stairs leading to his bedroom. Then the closed door. The stairs were winning the debate.

"They bear the mark," Moire said in a wide-eyed whisper.

His attention tumbled down the stairs and back to Moire. "What mark?" he demanded.

"Like yours," she said. "I know you don't like anyone to see it, but you get careless once in a while, if you don't mind my saying. In the bath," her face reddened, "when I bring your fresh clothes is usually when I get a look."

Fear suddenly gripped him. His guests, it seemed, were also Marked. He could almost forget when, but he was sure the last time he had been visited was after he had settled in Boynaan. He remembered.

Blast it.

Before he could change his mind, Raori strode bravely into the side room. Three figures rose from their seats to greet him. Moire had taken good care of them while Raori was away; they each had a goblet. A half-eaten loaf of bread sat on one of their best plates on a little table.

Raori took a breath to demand their business. Then he saw the Mark on each of their cheeks. Sorcerers. The demand dwindled into an inward sigh. As adept as Raori was in the manipulation of atma, these men could beat him without blinking.

"Raori MacGuinnan?" asked the oldest of them. The question was unnecessary. They knew who he was.

A lie formulated on the tip of his tongue. "Yes," Raori said, belatedly giving each of them a short bow. "My lords."

"We've had a little trouble finding you," said another of them. He was dressed in dark black and wore a cloak trimmed in gold. "You were not in Boynaan."

The inward sigh became a lump in his throat. "No, my lords," Raori said slowly. "I had some trouble and was forced to move."

"Trying to forget, eh?" asked the old one. He cackled.

When Raori did not answer, the third elf stepped forward. He was young and tanned from the weather. Flashing a friendly grin, he said, "You know as well as any of us the price of forgetfulness. And that it is... impossible for practitioners of magic to do so." He clapped Raori's shoulder. "You should feel proud. We're too few."

Raori bravely did not wince. Even his toes ached from the blow. "May I ask," he said through clenched teeth, "why you have come?"

The old one grunted. "Why else? To get you."

The one in black said, "We've an errand for you. Sadly, we had to waste some time looking for you. Now you're going to be late."

"They can wait for him in Nebhirrlos," the young one said. "He can travel four times faster than they. He'll probably be there early."

"Think you so?" the old one said. He peered at Raori knowingly and said, "Well, boy? Over that hangover enough to ride a ley line where you need to go? I'm telling you, Leahr," he turned to the one in black, "go find another one for this. Raori will never do."

Raori wondered what he would never do for and hoped they might find someone else who would do better.

The one addressed as Leahr frowned. "Moirfenn wants him specifically. He knows the others, remembers more than they will, and has tremendous talent."

"Too bad he doesn't use it," the old one said.

"I agree with Leahr," the young one said. He flashed another grin at Raori.

"The others are waiting in Nebhirrlos?" Raori, several sentences behind, managed to ask. His mind's eye flicked over long gone events, lingering at some and trying to ignore others. Mostly, a woman's face haunted his inner vision and taunted him with smirking kisses. If ever there was someone he would like to forget, it was her.

The three nodded in unison. "There is a Sanctuary near there," Leahr said. "They will be waiting for you."

"Why Nebhirrlos?" Raori constructed a mental map of the land and pursed his lips in thought. Cnos Fada, the last city to remain standing against Moirfenn, was closer to his home by several days. "It would be easier if I just met them at Cnos Fada."

"You will obey orders," the old man snapped. Raori jumped and immediately lowered his eyes to the floor. In a gentler tone, the old man continued, "You've a mission, my boy. MacKegan wants someone dead and it's you five to do it. Meet them in Nebhirrlos." He handed Raori a small scroll sealed with MacKegan's waxen mark.

"Yes, my lords," he mumbled. His headache was trying to get worse. All he wanted to do was get some sleep.

"Be there by the end of the week," Leahr said with what he must have thought was a reasonable tone. "If what Skagg says is true and you won't use the ley lines, I suggest you leave now." Raori refrained from mentioning that few used the ley lines anymore, with good reason.

Leahr and the old one left the room without further word. The young one started to follow, thought about it, and lingered behind. He watched the other two covertly until they were out of earshot.

His boyish grin would have been infectious at another time. "Don't worry about those two," he said. "They're harmless."

Raori had never heard of a harmless sorcerer, but he nodded anyway. The elf chuckled. "My name is Aes. It's a pleasure to meet you." He touched the Mark on his cheek, and his grin faltered for a brief moment. "I grew up listening to stories of how you and the others burned the temple. I took this Mark wanting to be like you."

Raori refused to feel guilty. If the young man's illusions were destroyed by meeting the real thing, so be it. He said, "You seem to have done very well for yourself."

"Better than you?" He laughed easily. Narrowing his eyes, he looked around suspiciously and whispered, "I just want to know one thing, if you don't mind my asking."

"What?"

"To be honest, I cannot decide just who I've heard the most about in court; you or that wolf woman. It's rumored you two had a thing going." The young sorcerer chuckled. "I wonder, though. Is the Priestess as beautiful as they say? I find it hard to believe, but you can tell me." And he grinned, wickedly and narrow-eyed, like an embittered sprite about to rendezvous with disaster.

"Beautiful cannot begin to describe her," Raori said softly. Visions of the very thing he had been striving to forget resurfaced in his mind. He swallowed, fighting for control, and won.

Aes was watching him closely. He still grinned, this time with disarming charm. A twinkle came to his eye.

"I said before that I know all about you," Aes said after a moment. His boyish charm faded, revealing deadly malice.

"You have no love for Moirfenn. Said MacKegan was 'too dishonorable,' am I right?"

For the second time that day, Raori was tempted to lie. It was not that he would not. He simply could not. When he tried, he did so badly. So, he settled for nodding his head.

"Moirfenn wants you to do this errand. Who knows, it may put us in a position to wipe out Cnos Fada entirely." Raori's face remained wooden. Aes snorted. "I've worked very hard to get where I am. Be successful, and I don't just stand to benefit. You do."

There was nothing this young man had to offer that would tempt Raori. Raori could be happy in a kobold's den while he was fed and comfortable. He said nothing.

"If you, for any reason, have a sudden change of heart and decide to fail," Aes went on quietly, "then don't expect any mercy. We found you here. Not even Tech Danaan has the atma to keep us out."

Raori nodded cautiously.

"Turn against us, Raori, and I will kill the Priestess."

Helplessness flooded Raori. Satisfied, Aes walked away. At the door, he paused and said, "I think it's ironic. She would let me kill her, if it would get you to behave." He left Raori alone with his misery, but not without a final say. "Her loyalty is astounding."

Raori sent Moire into town to barter for supplies immediately. While she was gone, he read the scroll twice, ripped it apart, and kicked the nearest table. Then he set about inspecting and repairing his horse's tack and sharpening his sword.

So, it was a prince they were to kill. Raori found the task typical and unpleasant. MacKegan had managed to drive out the royal family and claim Fion for his own centuries ago. Why destroy some harmless boy? Raori forced himself to put his frustration and bewilderment aside. Most times, one could not fathom the resolve behind MacKegan's actions. He wondered if even MacKegan knew what he was doing at times.

The house was quiet, except for the soft scraping of his sword against the whetstone. Raori worked in his bedchamber where the light graced the floor with the afternoon sun. Downstairs, wood scraped on wood as someone, most likely Moire, entered the house via the front door. Raori ignored it, content with his work.

The sword was sharp, had been for years, but the sounds it made were soothing. One could fall into a pleasant momentum; swipe, swipe, swipe... The blacksmith Duinn had taught Raori how to sharpen his weapon with a tiny whetstone like this one. It was dwarven magic Raori wove into his blade as he worked; spells to strengthen and assure victory. His mind was thankfully numb from the exercise.

Moire entered timidly. Her eyes, red and puffy from crying, made her look like an owl. "I got all you asked for," she sniffled. "I'll pack the rest you need, Master, and you just rest. There will be plenty of time to get started after noon."

"Thank you," Raori said, not breaking his rhythm. Moire fled the room, weeping loudly.

When Raori could delay no longer, he saddled his horse, packing it with only a small sack of food and his sword. His other tools, magical pebbles and bits of colored sand, were tucked safely in a little satchel at his waist. He mounted slowly. Moire stood below him, holding the reins, and choked back her sobs.

"Moire," Raori said, "I'm setting you free now."

"I know," she said miserably. "But I don't know what I'll do with myself."

"I could send you back to Éire."

She shook her head. "What good would it do me to be there? I've been here since I was a little girl. This place is all I know."

An uncomfortable silence stood between them. Raori broke it with, "Close up the house. Tomorrow morning, I want you to go north. About a day's walk from here is a stead owned by a man named Leanehus. Tell him that I had to take a trip south and would ask for him to give you employment. At least, until I return." He smiled boyishly. "I'll send word when I do."

Moire nodded dutifully. She knew not to expect him back.

Raori leaned down as far as he could go to whisper, "Don't mention my birthmark! Not to anyone! They'll get the wrong impression, and you'll be killed." He so desperately wanted to tell her the price of such a burden: to serve MacKegan with no choice, to feel the angry stares of people you conquered as you passed by on the street. Few would do it, but there was the chance Moire could be the victim of someone's misplaced hatred.

Moire said, "I knew that mark was something horrible. But I never said a word about it. For your sake."

Their eyes met: mortal into elf. A deep moment passed. "You've been a good servant, Moire," Raori said finally. "I hate to leave you."

"I hate to lose you," Moire whispered, stepping back. Raori's horse was galloping away before the sentence had completely left her lips. She watched him go until he was no longer in sight.

CHAPTER FOUR
"PICKET"

The spotted stallion reared his challenge to the wind and thundered down the sloping hills of Éire. He skirted around a small circle of stones and skidded to the bottom of a hill. With no effort, he topped another rise and stopped running.

He stood, unconsciously posing, and turned his gaze to the next hill. His nostrils flared, his back legs quivered, but he stood his ground. Someone was approaching. Their black cloaks billowed in the wind, the flapping sounds touching the horse's delicate ears.

They were sorcerers, these travelers across the stallion's domain. One was young, seeming almost too young to wear MacKegan's mark on his cheek. The other was too old and leaned on his staff for support as he struggled to climb the grassy slope. The stallion dipped his head, snorted, and resolutely met them at the bottom of the hill. The three regarded each other silently.

"Cuiddal Cernach?" asked the old one. The horse shook his head and started to graze, a docile nag that never knew the freedom of the wild. He walked away a few steps from the old man, one eye watching him warily.

"No sense in trying to trick us," snorted the young one. "We know you're no normal horse. For one thing, a normal horse would not stand there grazing like an idiot."

"Silence, Aes," the old one snapped. "Fool." The horse lifted his chin high while still chewing a bit of clover. His ears swiveled independently. "I don't suppose you would grace us with a little conversation, Cuiddal?"

The horse reared, then bucked. His sharp hooves came dangerously close to the young sorcerer's nose, but the two watched this without flinching. Suddenly the horse stood on his hind legs, pawed the air, and the naked man stood before them.

His red hair was spotted with gray, even though the slightly hostile face that regarded them was youthful. Freckles covered his skin heavily, like fleas on a sick mongrel. He was clean-shaven, and he had a long nose. Only his eyes gave him away, for they remained equine and gleamed at the elves mischievously.

"Thunder, man!" Aes exclaimed. He discarded his cloak to place it around the pooka's shoulders. "At least have the decency to appear dressed!"

Cuiddal shook his head, scratched his shoulder where the freckles grouped into an hourglass shape, and settled into the cloak. His entire demeanor said he could care less if he was clothed or not. "'Tis my nature to change and not the fabric I wear," he said

"We did not come here to discuss the theories of lycanthropy," the old one muttered impatiently.

Aes looked properly reprimanded. "Cuiddal," he said, "Moirfenn needs you to come back to Fion."

If Cuiddal had still been a stallion, he would have challenged the sorcerers immediately. Instead he shook his head with a snort. "It was our bargain," he said, "that I would not be called upon again. If MacKegan wants my services, he must bring me to him." The set of his jaw indicated that such an act would be impossible, if not fatal.

"You mean, you would not be called upon while you were not in Moirfenn," the old one said. "MacKegan still holds a part of you, creature. Don't forget that."

"This is not Moirfenn," the pooka said with a whinnying laugh. "This is the mortal realm. And that part of me may not yet be free, but it is not a tether. Not here. Not in the mortal realm."

"Skagg," Aes said, turning to the other, "is this true?"

Skagg sighed heavily and scratched the earth with his staff. "I'm afraid so," he said. "It's stone magic, young one, and a solid spell at that. When MacKegan captured this one with the Sight Stone, he was lucky to keep the creature as long as he did. I'm not sure how 'twas only this little bargain that held him this long. That's MacKegan's secret." The horse-man rumbled something. "And yours, of course. Yours."

Aes scratched his chin, musing. "Clever," he said. "I thought the Sight Stone's charm only worked a short while; a full cycle of the moon or some such. And you say this pooka has been MacKegan's for time out of time? By something so simple as leave to go outside of Fion?"

"Aye," Skagg said. "Geis, my boy. Something you've yet to learn about."

Cuiddal grinned broadly. He knew he was safe from MacKegan while living in the green hills he now called home. MacKegan could very well renew that hated charm in Fion, but this was Éire... and few rules from across the veil applied here. The prolonged vassalage of Cuiddal was not one of them.

"Then," said Aes somberly, "I'm sorry, Cuiddal."

His hand was too swift for the eye to catch, but Cuiddal thought it grabbed something from one of the sorcerer's pouches. Something powdery and glittery hit him in the face. He sneezed, coughed, and tried to shake it off. His form wavered a moment and the man remained. Dizziness brought him to his knees.

"Let's hurry," Skagg said. The two sorcerers grabbed each of Cuiddal's arms and began to drag him. The old one's hands gripped Cuiddal's arm with surprising strength. The pooka's protest came out as a choked whinny.

They dragged Cuiddal to the small ring of stones, lay him down within, and spoke three words. The world dissolved around, then it reformed. Before the pooka knew it, he lay in the sparse grass of Fion. Already, he could feel the unwelcome chains of MacKegan's curse settling over his hide. Cuiddal rolled to his knees.

"Welcome home," Aes said, helping Cuiddal to unsteady feet. He made a pass in front of Cuiddal's eyes, whispered a word, and stepped back. As the spell lifted, the pooka's control returned. He aimed a glare at both of the sorcerers. In his equine form, his ears would have been flat against his head. Only one thing held him back from murdering these two, and that was MacKegan's sudden awareness of his return. He could almost feel the ancient lord sit up suddenly in his throne and take notice. If Cuiddal acted against these two, MacKegan would punish him severely.

Geis and stone magic. The pooka clamped his teeth in displeasure.

"Now that you're here," Skagg said smugly, ignoring Cuiddal's blatant anger, "you should consider what Moirfenn has in mind for you."

As quickly as it had come, Cuiddal's anger vanished. He grinned, shifting his feet much in the way horses do when they've stood still for too long. "Fair enough," he said easily. He wore a disarming smile. "What is it this time?"

"For now," Skagg said, "you'll go to Nebhirrlos, the Sanctuary, and meet the others."

"The others? The others?" Cuiddal's face was blank. "What others?"

The sorcerers exchanged a glance. "He doesn't remember, yet," said Skagg. "He may need a guide."

Aes shook his head. "All he needs is a reminder." He reached into the little satchel again. His hand emerged covered with the sparkling dust.

Cuiddal backed away, half turning his back toward the young sorcerer. He nodded his head in alarm. "What is the dust for?" he demanded. "I'm here, wherever here is. In Fion. Moirfenn definitely. I will keep the bargain."

"It's not to harm you," Aes said. He blew the dust from his palm onto Cuiddal, who stood there and blinked stupidly. "It will help you remember, Picket."

The pooka was hit with a new wave of confusion, which he tried to brush off with the dust. His hands moved quickly, and he snorted. "I don't like this stuff. Makes you sneeze. Why did you call me Picket?" The pooka blinked. His hands slowed to a stop. The sorcerers grinned in spite of themselves.

"They called me Picket," Cuiddal said, answering his own question. "Picket is I."

"And who are they?" Aes asked dubiously. He crossed his arms and quirked a grin.

"The Priestess," said the pooka, "Eahn, Raori, and Duinn. The rest of the Five." His voice held a note of awe, as if he could not believe that he ever knew them. His snort broke the spell. "You say go to Nebhirrlos?"

Without waiting for an answer, Picket changed back into a horse. First, he snorted into Aes' face. Then, he spurred away. A few pebbles scattered, striking Aes, in his rush. The stallion reared his challenge a few feet away from them before galloping north.

Skagg cackled while Aes brushed himself off. "He has good aim."

Aes was unperturbed. "I wish he had waited so we could tell him to get the last one on his way. Now we'll have to do it." He closed his satchel and then looked around. His brow furrowed. "He took my cloak, too."

***

Picket ran for the sheer joy of it. It was what he did best, and it was when pookas felt the most free. The hills passed quickly under his rumbling hooves. He jumped a fence, scattering the sheep within, and galloped to the other side of the field.

He stopped running and paced the fence a minute. It was a perfectly innocent structure. There were no protective wards placed along it. It was not too high, nor even painted to enhance it unnatural existence. Nothing about it should have caught the attention of any fairy, but it had caught Picket's.

For a moment, it looked like he was going to forget about the fence and keep going. He pawed at the bottom railing indecisively, then he walked away. Stopping after five steps, he looked back at the fence.

He could not resist.

Running back, he jumped over it lightly, faced his hindquarters to it, and kicked. And kicked. When kicking got boring, he pranced. On their own, Boards flew off of the fence and landed randomly all over the field. When Picket grew tired of that, he carefully pawed the railing until that, too, fell apart.

When he was done, the sheep had scattered. Most stayed together in a clump that steadily grazed farther and farther away. Picket snorted, turned, and resumed his journey. He wanted to stay and watch the shepherd's reaction when the damage was discovered, but there was no time.

In the past, he would run a ley line and made it to Nebhirrlos in an hour. He could not remember why, but the prospect filled him with dread. One sentence lodged itself into his mind. *Once, we were six.*

A vast forest loomed in the distance. It started suddenly and was edged with hazel, hawthorn, and oak. Picket did not relish the idea of fighting his way through the primeval undergrowth. Fortunately, there was a small river that cut a straight path through it and beyond. So, he forded the river.

The currents were strong, but his atma – the all-source of magic – gave him strength to fight back. Fey creatures such as he were more atma than flesh, and the strength of their magic seemed boundless. It was Picket's nature that gave him the seeming of a mortal body, that and MacKegan's hold over his soul.

Once on the other side and on dry land, Picket shook himself dry (and free of that memory). He kicked in the river's general direction. Nothing happened, so he assumed the river god was away or ignoring him.

With no sport to be found along the river, he resumed his journey with double speed. He could be in Nebhirrlos in two days, provided he took no detours. He might even beat the others. But... what fun would that be? It had been a long time since he was home. One might as well make the most of it.

The trees thinned out as the terrain fell away to cultivated lands. Ploughed fields passed him by. He galloped by someone's house and was gone before the children knew what kicked their pigskin ball on to the roof. The cows lowed when he passed about a mile away and paused only to knock down another fence.

Darkness began to fall. He relished the night, but he had been running all day and was tired. He found a small clutch of oak trees of the road and used them as a makeshift stable. At first he tried sleeping in his man form, but it was uncomfortable and cold. The tree roots dug into his back, and the sorcerer's cloak was a pitiful shield against the night air. Settling for four legs and a warm hide, he spent the night grazing in his sleep...

The Five had gathered beneath the full moon to discuss their future. It was weeks after they had proven themselves to the Lord of Moirfenn by burning the temple and ransacking the city. Raori was late, as always, but when he arrived he had someone with him.

Picket had excellent night sight, especially in his natural form. He grazed nearby, cocking his ears to listen, and watched the pretty girl who shyly clung to Raori's arm. She would not need an hourglass on her shoulder if she joined their group, he decided. The shape of her body was hourglass enough.

"This is Leannahn," Raori said, giving her a slight push to present her. "She used to live in the temple with Aramina and myself."

Now, what's wrong with Aramina? Picket wondered. The werewolf sat to the side with her head lowered. Was she afraid, or did she feel threatened?

"I wanted to cheer," Leannahn said, "when the temple started burning. I hated it there."

"You're free now," Eahn said, puzzlement coloring his tone. "I'm glad for you. What would you want with us?"

"To join you," the young woman said. Her pointed chin trembled, but her eyes were steady. "I can be a big advantage."

"Oh?" Duinn leaned his burly frame forward. He was dwarven stock, an audacious breed, and did not trust easily. "What could you, a mere slip of girl, do for us? Can you cook?"

"Cook?" the woman demanded incredulously. She sniffed. "Does this one cook for you?" She gestured to Aramina. "Is that what she is to you? A cook?"

Raori looked uncomfortable, glancing sidelong as Aramina visibly bristled. "We take turns cooking."

"Except for Duinn," Aramina murmured. It was the first thing she had said all evening. "Dwarven fare is not very palatable."

"Say that," Duinn said, flashing a sharp grin, "in the field with sword in hand. My halberd and I could convince you that my cooking is worth eating."

"All right," Aramina said. She returned his grin. "Let's go. Maybe your halberd can tenderize the meat into chewable chunks, too."

"Wait," Eahn said. He blew through his nose noisily. "Be serious, you two. We haven't settled this matter with the girl yet."

Leannahn said, "I can do more than cook. I was about to take the Rite of Blue Passage before... the burning."

Admiration took the power of speech away from the others. Anyone qualified to take the Rite of Blue Passage were talented indeed. It was no wonder Aramina was not comfortable with this strange girl in their midst. Picket lifted his head and nuzzled Aramina in the ear. He nickered.

"Picket likes her," Aramina translated grudgingly. "That's one vote to her favor."

"And me," Raori said. His sly glance in Aramina's direction hinted that Leannahn was not there to enhance the group in any way. His affair with Aramina, lately peppered with disinterest on her part, had been a continuing drama for a year now. If Picket were any judge of men – and he was, but a terrible one – then Leannahn's pretty looks were at the heart of the matter.

Aramina refused even to look Leannahn's way. Picket could safely bet Raori's ploy had failed. Or perhaps it had worked, but not the way Raori would have preferred.

Duinn grunted. He never voted for anything. That was for people who liked responsibility, he always said. All eyes turned to Eahn.

"Very well," he said slowly. "She can travel with us to Moirfenn, and we'll ask the lord. If she proves herself along the way it will be easier."

Leannahn broke into a happy grin. "I will," she promised. "You will be very surprised at what I can do."

CHAPTER FIVE
"DUINN"

The mountain was home to dwarves, who mined and lived there like ants in a rocky anthill. Their city, tunneled miles within the mountain, was a network of roads and rooms all lit by torch or magic. There were chambers within so old, they were all but forgotten, and new ones begun daily. Dwarves loved to build, so it was told, and many lords sought the dwarves' industry.

Where there were dwarves, there was a forge where the hammering sounded. The musical sound of hammers rang throughout the mountain constantly. There was a language within that steady beat; thrums of warning or echoes of reassurance. Old ones called it the mountain's heartbeat. It lulled babies to sleep, comforted the heartbroken, and kept time for many songs. To the dwarf smiths, no sound was sweeter.

Duinn was accustomed to the hammers. How could he not be, raised with them as he was? There was something in them that bothered him; something incorporeal or absent. It rang a half-note in his soul when he stopped to listen. So, to forget his melancholy, he joined the music with a hammer of his own, pounding metal in his tiny forge near his home.

He brought his hammer down with a ringing blow. The shapeless lump of metal held between his tongs would have become a sword, if the mood struck at the critical time. Right now it was Duinn's outlet for frustration. Each ringing blow distorted it further, and he had only begun to beat it. He could always recycle it later, if the bar became ruined, by remelting it with the rest of the ore it came from. For now, the rhythm of hammer to metal filled his time.

Several blows later, Duinn realized he was being watched and had been for some time. Straightening his back, feeling his bones crack, he turned and saw two elves. Wrapped deep in their cloaks, their faces peered out from within the enshrouded hoods. At least they showed proper respect, dwarf fashion, by letting him turn in his own time. A smith could be wounded if interrupted at the wrong time. In turn, an intruder could be hurt more, depending on the infraction.

These elves knew their manners, and good for them. Still, elves meant business, usually trouble. The sight disturbed him.

"I'm not supposing you want a sword made?" Duinn asked with fading hope. The hourglass marks on the elves' cheeks leapt from the shadows, as if screaming an advertisement.

Smiling, the elves shook their heads. The younger of the two stepped forward and bowed deeply. Duinn scowled with recognition. A business call indeed.

"Master Duinn," the elf said. "A pleasure, as always."

"Yes, Aes," Duinn snapped impatiently. "Enough formality. What is it this time?"

"'Formality,' he calls it," the young one laughed. "How like him. I'll be brief, then. Duinn, Moirfenn has called your comrades to Nebhirrlos." He laughed again.

"What in Éire and Fion could be found in Nebhirrlos?" the dwarf demanded incredulously. He scratched his beard, realized he still held the tongs, and lay them on a nearby anvil.

"There is a matter of the new king," the other elf said quietly from the doorway.

"What care I for kings?" Duinn asked with a grunt. "The tribes rule themselves with or without a king, even in the palace to the north. If MacKegan is worried, he shouldn't be. No one recognized the royal line anymore, no more than I do. It would take something more than a claim to kingship to get them to do so." Dismissing the matter, Duinn turned back to his anvil and the cooling piece of metal.

"You would be wise to remember," Aes said sharply, "your required services. You were not released."

"Aye, I know it," Duinn said. He returned the metal to the fire in disgust. There it would melt, and he would reclaim it later. "The way I see it, I have done more than my share for Moirfenn. Let a younger spirit break his back this time."

The elves exchanged a glance. "Leahr?" Aes asked with a rising eyebrow. The other stepped toward Duinn, paused, and slowly raised his hand.

The dwarf could ignore it at first. The pain emanating from the Mark on his shoulder merely pulsed. He turned to choose another bar. The pulsation became a pounding throb. His breath grew shallow.

"Enough!" Duinn gasped. The pain stopped suddenly. He was on the floor with no memory of when, or how, he fell. Irritation blackened his brow, but his mind he kept to himself. He was too weak to do more than lay there, like a beaten mongrel.

"Nebhirrlos," Aes said. "Don't forget. Meet them at the Sanctuary."

Duinn nodded weakly. He did not bother getting up again. A black boot came down by his hands. "And do not fail this time," the voice of Leahr said. "We can do worse if need be. Get up and listen while I explain."

***

He traveled light, down into the bowels of the mountain. Underground highways that had been built for generations crisscrossed not only his mountain, but miles around the area and even into other mountains. It was like a giant ant mound, dwarves often said proudly if called upon to talk about their homes to strangers. He walked them, making good time. Before long he came to the deepest areas that were mostly deserted.

These places had once been bustling mines, but the ores were mostly gone. Whispers of dark things that lurked in the shadows, waiting for a good supper, sometimes were told around family dinners and gatherings. Duinn paid them no head as he continued.

He turned into an old mine shaft where the darkness was very deep. He required no torch, being a creature of the dark, but still he stumbled occasionally over scattered debris. At one point, he tripped on a fallen timber and fell face first up against a skull. Pausing long enough to pay quiet respects (and apologize to any spirit that might be listening), he sighed and moved on. Perhaps he could return to give the remains better honor later.

The darkness went on forever. He stopped only to eat and rest, sleeping with his back against the wall and his halberd across his knees. Two days, according to his senses, passed in this manner before reaching the end. The mine's exit was a small crack in the mountain side with a boulder half blocking the way.

One thing more dwarves shared with ants was their strength. If Duinn chose to, he could push a boulder out of the way easily. He pushed against this one, but it was stuck tight against the mountainside. Undaunted, Duinn dug his way out, using his hands to clear away rubble and push at the boulder until it went crashing down loudly. Duinn crawled outside, not even winded.

It had been years since he had been above ground. He almost did not recognize the place. The exit had let Duinn out in the foothills with the mountain a lurking beast behind him. In the distance, a worn ring of stones stood on a barren hilltop. They marked a ley line, if Duinn's memory was correct, and promised an easy avenue to his destination. Hoisting his pack on one shoulder, he walked to it. This did not promise to be a pleasant task, but there was no other option. Duinn did not know enough about the terrain to make his way by foot, nor did he care to learn the hard way.

The stones were weathered and cracked in various places, but this was hardly a testimony to their performance. Duinn's magical senses were very weak, but he thought he felt some power within them. In his opinion, elven magic was unreliable at the best of times. He could invoke the ley line in the traditional manner, elf magic, or his own. He stood a moment, plotting which choice might be the most effective.

Touching each stone, he stepped around the circle in the prescribed matter. Elves liked their circles, and much of their magic was based on intricate knot works and various themes involving round dimensions. It was all silly nonsense to the dwarf, who preferred straight lines and clean angles. He walked the circle five times, then two more. There was a flicker of light, the only reaction. The stones were almost dead.

Duinn had suspected he would have to resort to dwarven magic. If dwarves built the ley lines - which they did not but if they had - the stones would still work. He was willing to bet they'd even work as if finished just an hour ago. Elves were a silly lot. They built the ancient roads in a frenzy of enterprise and, once they were done, almost forgot about them. To be sure, there was probably some clan of elves somewhere who still knew how to make and repair these structures. Duinn knew not where and held no interest in finding them.

He settled in the middle of the circle with his pack still in hand, making himself comfortable and even pausing to groom his beard with a quick rake of the fingers. Once settled, he closed his eyes and, slipping into a light meditative state, began to mutter. The words came slow and haltingly at first, but as he gained confidence his memory improved. He shouted the final word, and the stones began to vibrate.

Pure light sliced into his brain, split his nerves wide open, and carried him into the sky. *How can the elves stand this?* he thought. Opening his eyes only brought misery, but he forced himself to look.

He was standing in the ley line. It glowed under his feet (funny how he could not remember standing up), looking like a bright ribbon tapering off in the distance. It forked up ahead with each turning a subtle difference in color to mark where they went. Like a sleeper in a dream, he knew the way he had to go. He started to walk.

A gentle hand reached out of the light and touched his shoulder. Duinn froze in dread. He had been expecting this, true, but he still felt nervous.

She emerged from the light, smiling. Thankfully, she withdrew her hand and backed a couple of steps away. Her pointed chin, those blossom cheeks — they were all as Duinn remembered, if a bit whitened by the illumination around them.

She had not aged, but specters did not know time the way physical folk did. Not that any of the Six, Duinn's age-old companions, knew old age first hand. They all remained young, as was their choice. Duinn never regretted it.

"I thought I was forgotten," the ghost said.

"I could not," Duinn said, letting a touch of regret tinge his voice. "Perhaps the others, but they cannot help what they are."

"I know," the specter said miserably. "Raori would not have forgotten, though."

Duinn privately reasoned that any elf with a memory of stone would be utterly miserable. "What have you seen?" he asked past the urge to run away from her, for all she had been once a dear friend. "Does no one pass through the lines these days?"

"Oh," she waved a hand. It was a familiar gesture, but made eerie by the trails her hand left in the air. "A sorcerer or two will pass occasionally. I do not bother them."

"No one else," Duinn mused to himself. "Where do they go?"

"Some to Moirfenn. Most to Tech Danaan. The traffic grows less and less these days."

Duinn digested the information calmly. The ones going to Moirfenn were not important. Moirfenn naturally got a lot of traffic as lords sent envoys to pay Moirfenn's tribute or, to their folly, ask a boon. And Tech Danaan, the isle of the land's most holy temple, served hundreds of pilgrims every season. There was nothing unusual in that.

"Duinn," the specter said in a quailing voice. She edged forward a pace, then stopped at the dwarf's look of warning. "Do you think that maybe you could find a way to set me free?"

He gave the ghost an appraising glance. Her eyes were full of hope, as if he were some savior sent by the gods. It was an effort not to agree. "I'm truly sorry, " he said. "If I do find a way, I will help you. You have my word."

Anger flashed across her features. Her hands balled into fists and shook. Looking down, she said, "If that is what I must take as payment for my help, then so be it."

What help? Duinn opened his mouth to speak, but his mind was blank. There was nothing to do but continue his journey, and so he did. Reluctantly, he cast a final look over his shoulder as he walked away. The woman watched him go. She looked like she was crying, although her tears were not real.

Later, Duinn opened his eyes to a different circle of stones. He was sitting as if he had never moved. His legs ached like they had walked miles without rest.

The wind was fierce and tangled his hair into his beard. Duinn ignored it as he turned around, getting his bearings. This place was familiar, but ages of change made known things alien and strange things familiar. Resolutely he shouldered his pack and began to walk.

The highway greeted him like an old friend. He walked until he came to a marker, read it, then angrily turned the other way. An hour at best was lost by his misdirection and now he would have to hurry if he wanted to reach shelter before sundown. He hoped there would be mead, at least, when he finally got to where he was going.

The Sanctuary House seemed to come out of nowhere as it sprang from the gloom of late evening. Duinn stared at it suspiciously for a long moment. Dogs barked at him from the doorway. A plump elf woman waved him in merrily.

"We don't see many of your clan," she said conversationally as Duinn crossed the threshold. He lay his halberd in the corner where guests were required to leave their weaponry. There were a couple of swords and three daggers. This meant the house had a few guests to force Duinn into unwanted conversation. This, he did not like. All he wanted to talk about was a fresh mug of ale.

He got that, and a plate of forest roots with gravy, ham, and peas. Devouring the meal in a corner of the house's room, he barely looked up when the door opened to admit another visitor.

The newcomer was a red-haired man with freckles visible even in the dim light. Duinn chewed thoughtfully on his ham and watched the man settle by the fire. The stranger did not seem to notice Duinn, or he was simply ignoring him. The woman brought the stranger a goblet of mead before whisking away.

There was no denying a certain animosity between the pair. Duinn's glare glittered in the firelight. The newcomer drank his mead calmly, casting the occasional return look at the dwarf. Finally, Duinn decided to make the first move.

When the woman, Residhnne, collected his plate, Duinn stumped to the fire. Red-hair did not look up. Duinn cleared his throat. The newcomer ignored him as he took a final, deep drink from his goblet.

At last, Red-hair turned his eyes to Duinn. He started to smile, then adopted a serious expression. It made his face look longer than it was. "Well," he said.

"Thought you'd be first this time, eh?" Duinn asked.

Red-hair snorted. "Perhaps they told you before they dragged me here," he said. "Gave you a head start?"

Duinn chuckled. "No, Picket. I don't think so. You're getting slow. You're spending too much time with the mares. Maybe you're no better than a mare yourself."

They glared at each other. The fire crackled in a background of silence. Then, as by some unspoken command, they burst out laughing. Duinn patted the pooka's shoulders and settled down beside him.

"Any word of the others, fairy man?" Duinn asked. Residhnne, who had been nervously watching the exchange, brought them a new pitcher of ale.

"Nay," Picket said. "Then again, I haven't asked. I've spent my time in Éire." He grinned lopsidedly. "With the mares," he continued just as Duinn was taking another drink.

Duinn's new fit of laughter forced ale through his nose and into the fire. "Gods, man," Duinn finally choked, dabbing at his burning nostrils with one sleeve. "Leave off, you're ruining the ale."

Picket nodded in good horse fashion. He drank his ale more of courtesy than anything. The stuff never did anything to him. Few fairies had any problem with alcohol. Often he wondered about the fascination for getting drunk, when all one did afterward was lament the deed.

"The elves said to wait," Picket complained. "I hope it isn't too long."

"You know the Priestess will be along," Duinn said. "And Eahn. It's blasted Raori that's the slow one. We might have to wait for weeks."

"Would that not be a good thing?"

"The bluidy coward refuses to use the ley lines," Duinn grumbled.

"I don't blame him. Did you?"

"Yes." Duinn rumbled the word into his chest. "We have no time for the nonsense. Not at all. We've a king to catch, my fey one. Bad enough we'll be walking all over hill and vale just looking for him, let alone wasting time on some seven day trip just to get ourselves together."

Picket snorted into his drink. "Politics," said he. "Things were simpler when we lived by our clans and nothing more."

"Aye. A fight was a fight in which your brothers stood by you."

"Death was a quick thing," Picket mused. "Honorable. Mares had a stallion to be proud of."

Duinn grunted. "Women sang proudly of fallen heroes. We made weapons that wanted only for blood." Picket reached back and scratched his right shoulder. It made Duinn acutely aware of the Mark on his own shoulder. "When we died," Duinn went on, "it was forever. We passed into the next realm easily. Only the highest of us lived immortal, and by their choice."

Picket swirled the ale around in his mug. In a regrettable tone, he added, "The ale was much better, too."

"What do you know of ale, you flea-bitten animal?" Duinn roared. "Can't even get decently drunk and he complains of the flavor!"

Innocent eyes regarded Duinn for a solemn moment. "'Tis true," Picket said. "By my mother's mane, this ale is watered down. No taste at all."

Duinn downed his drink in one gulp. Waving his mug, he shouted, "Residhnne, lass! Get over here with the ale! The best I've had in years!"

Residhnne obeyed, chuckling to herself as she went about her business. Duinn drank six more pitchers before he passed out. Picket, who had watched the dwarf's antics impassively, stealthily crept for the door.

He was incredibly fond of Duinn, but there were times when a pooka just did not want to be bothered. "I'll be back before he wakes," Picket whispered to Residhnne. She smiled, yawned, and blinked eyes heavy with sleep. Picket disappeared by the third blink, but she was not surprised. Pookas were that way.

She tucked a blanket around Duinn and went to bed. Somewhere in the distance, a stallion screamed. It sounded angry. Residhnne locked her bedroom door....

"A test," said Duinn to the five faces before him. "An easy one, I think. Before we meet the lord tomorrow."

The six companions were lodged at Jurbhean City in Moirfenn. At dawn they were to approach their lord, Chulain MacKegan, in his keep and speak of Leannahn. The subject of the impending encounter was not feeling cooperative.

"I have burned three cottages, crossed the veil and stolen twenty babies for many families, and robbed two temples of their treasure," Leannahn said bitterly. "I refuse to do more!"

Picket's chuckle sounded like a rumble in a long throat. "Now lass," he said. "Those were just practice."

Leannahn's eyes grew round with rage. She opened her mouth to speak and found Duinn's hand covering it. The dwarf, standing on the room's only bed, nearly lost his balance in the process. Leannahn jerked away, ignoring him as he fell to the floor, and turned her face to the wall.

"Never mind that horse," the dwarf said, picking himself up with as much dignity as he could. "One last test will not harm anything."

Aramina giggled in the corner. Although nothing was said between the two girls, she obviously enjoyed Leannahn's discomfort. Leannahn haughtily tossed her hair, making it a point not to look at the other.

"If she thinks she has done enough to please MacKegan," Eahn said, "then let her alone. It isn't the deeds that he appraises."

To Aramina's obvious disappointment, the band decided to go to Moirfenn before sunrise. Leannahn was not forced to anything more. The werewolf sulked all the way to their lord's gates, before which they arrived just as the sun topped the horizon.

The gates stood open and the guards ignored them as they passed. Picket had chosen to be a horse that day, and he bore Leannahn majestically. During the short time Leannahn had been with them, he had spent more and more time in her company. Duinn did not agree with the two growing as close as they were, but he never protested aloud. The same went for Aramina, who spurned Raori's advances constantly. The dwarf knew she was restrained only by the occasional presence of Gredber, who held her to his heart like a dragon's hoard. Raori often wished that Gredber would disappear and leave Aramina to him alone.

Gredber had been brought into the picture at MacKegan's behest; something about an old favor that MacKegan owed. The wily elf only came around occasionally; Gredber was no more a member of the team than strangers living across the sea. But he had taken a liking to Aramina, who played at loving him only when Raori was around. It was no secret that Aramina hated the elf, and she often echoed gruesome sentiments of what she would like to do to his person.

Their lord met them in his dining hall. He was at late breakfast and suggested his servants join him. They did so warily, sniffing their food before tasting it. The master ignored their seeming lack of courtesy: It was a sign of wisdom in his eyes.

When the meal was almost finished, MacKegan regarded Leannahn with eyes red-rimmed and blazing like lamps in the darkness. "How did you fall in with these five, Niece?" he asked.

"Niece!?" Duinn's familiar roar cut across the room. He stood, a formidable gesture despite his lack of height, and faced Leannahn. "You never said you were his flaming niece!"

The lord's eyes were cool as he leaned back to appraise his minions. Aramina was beside Duinn quickly, firmly pushing her teammate down into his chair. Leannahn looked amused, while Raori, Picket, and Eahn were stone still with caution and fear.

"How very clever, my dear," the lord said to Leannahn. "They never knew."

Leannahn sniffed. "It protected my backside," she said. "How could I know to trust these ruffians?" Haughtily, she drank from her goblet.

When everyone, including Aramina, protested indignantly, Chulain laughed. His laughter rang like bells. Everyone grew quiet and respectfully waited for him to finish. "Well spoken," he said, dabbing his eyes with a white cloth. "I think you have represented our clan wonderfully. Well done. Well done."

Leannahn, looking pleased, returned to her meal in silence. The others were not as willing to do so.

"Lord," Eahn said, "your niece asked to join our band. We had thought to let her, but knowing she is your relative, we cannot put her into danger."

"Aye," said Raori, obviously fighting not to stutter. "T'would be unforgivable if she were to be hurt, Lord."

Their master drank deeply from his goblet as he pondered the statement. "Eahn," the lord said, "are you not one of my most prized servants?"

"Yes, Lord," Eahn said in some confusion. "But--"

"And is loyalty why you would now reject my niece's offer?"

"Only in regard of her safety," Eahn said, his confidence wavering.

"I see." Another pause of contemplation. "I would never place a member of my family in danger," Chulain announced. "As I have no children, the role of heir falls to Leannahn." Leannahn jumped, then beamed. "It would be unthinkable to put her into danger. Why, if she were to be killed–"

It was Leannahn's turn to be indignant. "Uncle, that is unfair! How can I prove myself worthy of you, of the realm, if I am kept indoors like, like... a pet?"

"Indeed," the master agreed too easily for his servants' comfort. "You're right, my dear. I would not expect anyone in Moirfenn to follow an untried warrior. You must be worthy of my seat should the day come that you would assume it. What do you think, Duinn?"

Duinn felt an unaccustomed flush creep past his neck. "Lord MacKegan," he said slowly, "she should surely join us. So far we have put her to some petty tasks, to test her mettle, but if you had something important for us to do..." He could feel the astonished glances around him. Grimly, he stuffed food in his mouth and chewed slowly.

"A task it is then," Chulain said without hesitation. "I know the very thing. Retrieve for me the spear Birgha of Allen, which is now in the mortal realm."

"Too easy!" Picket proclaimed proudly.

"If it were so easy," Chulain said, "then it would already have been done. Know that the spear is guarded by the magic of Vighn MacFhion, who was raised by his father to hate us."

Duinn kept his own counsel, even when Eahn asked what use Birgha would be put to. Doubts about facing a spiteful sorcerer, even a mortal one, assuaged his mind. If Chulain truly wanted the spear, he would have had it by now. The entire business seemed bad.

It was too convenient, all of it. Chulain had this planned. But why? Duinn had decided ages ago that Chulain MacKegan was quite mad, although to what extent he could not tell. The lord seemed to have no single agenda. His mind followed twisted paths that snakes feared to travel. Most likely, there was no reasoning behind Chulain's desire for the spear. It was there, and that was enough for Chulain.

After Chulain retired for the night, the Five (now Six) drank more wine and discussed a strategy for claiming the spear. Leannahn sniffed haughtily and often, declaring it an easy victory. The others exchanged uneasy glances.

"We all know my uncle is insane," Leannahn said. "This Vighn is not a threat to us."

"Yes, your uncle is eccentric," Raori agreed diplomatically. "However, he's not a fool. Do not take this business lightly, Leannahn. It could mean your death. You wanted a serious task, now you have it. We should treat it that way."

Leannahn only smiled as she sipped her wine.

CHAPTER SIX
"SILVER FOX"

Finnbhear the Silver Fox, Lord of Cnos Midhea, Keeper of the Bard's Seal, Practicer of Magic and current Protector of Bodb Derg, sat in his garden, frustrated over his roses.

His roses were his pride. No gardener tended them save himself. Clipping them, watching them bloom, even procuring fresh manure to feed them was his special delight. They, in a sense, were his children.

This love of horticulture was his mother's breeding, although Finnbhear did not know it. She had been the great granddaughter of a wood nymph who forsook immortality for love. Finnbhear was the finishing result: hazel-eyed, silver-haired, and gentle. He was also ferocious when necessary and solid in his beliefs.

With a great sigh, he brushed the soil from his leggings and stood. The roses would have to wait. This morning he would embark on a journey to escort the Crown Prince to Cnos Fada, where the prince's friend (and only surviving family), Chonnall, waited. There, Bodb would be crowned king.

Then all the trouble will begin, Finnbhear mused. Bodb's succession meant hope for the scattered loyalists who aspired to win their land back. Although the north was not as under MacKegan's thumb as the south, it still knew the harsh lash of his whip. The annual alone left barely enough food for people to live on. Most spiritual practices had gone underground while the new religion - temple-born and government maintained - flourished with Moirfenn's guidance. Even traffic between Fion and the other realms was limited.

Tech Danaan, the island temple north of Cnos Fada, was the only other place free from Moirfenn. This was only because MacKegan's power could not pierce the walls and magical wards tended constantly by the acolytes who dwelt there. Full scale sieges used to be common around the walls of the temple, but MacKegan had given up and withdrawn. The temple's maintained neutrality gave the conquering lord an excuse to keep his distance, and so far a tentative peace held even when the rightful crown prince was born within its walls.

The young prince had grown up near the temple, Finnbhear knew, but then moved mysteriously north towards the mountains. It was said the lad had narrowly escaped no less than ten attempts on his life once MacKegan learned he, and his family, lived. In each attempt, someone had died to protect him. That, the Silver Fox acknowledged bitterly, was why the boy now had no family.

There would be another attempt on Bodb's life, surely. Although the young prince did not seem a threat to Chulain

MacKegan, the south's master would not pass up this opportunity to finish what he had started. MacKegan was insane and liable to do anything, but he was also predictable to a small degree. Bodb Derg's life was in danger.

Which was why he, Finnbhear, had been hired to ride with the young elf to Cnos Fada. Finnbhear was not keen on the idea, but Bodb's supporters had argued convincingly that with Finnbhear the Silver Fox, hero of many battles and stories, by the new king's side nothing could go wrong. The Silver Fox had his doubts, but the gold was plentiful enough to keep his mouth shut.

"Hai, Finnbhear," a voice said from the back door. It was Mohg Deagan, Finnbhear's partner in this venture. He was girded in leather armor, belted with his sword, and holding his helmet. The latter object was beaten from years of abuse, but recently shined. "Come on, old man. Bodb wants us to leave now."

"Aye," Finnbhear said with weary sigh. He was getting too old for this. The thought was uncomfortable, but true. Even tree-bred elves grew old and died. It just took longer for it to happen.

The thought also reminded Finnbhear of something, or someone, but he could not quite nudge the memory awake. Dismissing it as unimportant, he followed his friend to the front of his home where the young prince was waiting. Bodb Derg sat his horse like a champion on the pathway by the front door of Finnbhear's small cottage. The expression he wore was a mask of nervous tension. The mood was bleeding to his horse, which snorted and pawed the ground. Two other mounts snorted to each other just behind the prince, as if to say how ridiculous the young were in this day and age.

Finnbhear felt a mixture of pity and amusement at this boy child. He barely looked ready for such an adventure, as young as he was. But then again, who ever was ready? Finnbhear's own life of venture began at an even earlier age. The troll who had unwillingly participated was still looking for its tail, it was said. The Silver Fox chuckled softly, careful to keep his mirth to himself.

Finnbhear swung into the saddle of his grey gelding and looked to the house. His servants, all humans who had entered his service willingly, hurriedly ran from the house to see their master away. They thought it attracted bad luck if even the smallest babe missed saying farewell. All of them, down to the smallest babe or most ancient gaffer, lined up and tossed shamrock to the earth for luck.

Gods knew Finnbhear needed all the help he could get. He thanked them heartily and promised to return quickly. With cheerful farewells caroling behind, the threesome rode away. It as almost as if they were going to the fair rather than treading dangerously through wilderness and MacKegan's lands. Bodb rode between Finnbhear and Mohg. His mare was skittish, but Bodb controlled her with an iron hand. Finnbhear wondered what that meant for Cnos Fada. Indeed he wondered what it could mean for Fion, should things go that far.

They rode in silence for the first couple of hours. Mohg was more concerned with the ground than anything. Bodb seemed too shy, or arrogant, to make small talk.

"I remember," Finnbhear said when the silence grew unbearable, "my first trip to Cnos Fada."

Startled glances met his eyes. "Are you sorcerer as well as a warrior?" Bodb asked. His somber face was not built for shock, but he conveyed it well. "I thought only those who practiced atma went to visit the Moonstone."

Finnbhear laughed. The mental image he had of the Moonstone, a fallen star revered by the denizens of Cnos Fada, always made him smile. "No," said he. "There are some things too pleasant to forget. Or too important. And besides, my liege, the Moonstone is in Tech Danaan. Without it, the wards around the island would fail."

"It must be very powerful," mused prince.

"Aye," Finnbhear agreed, mind dwelling on the past. "The atma in it practically glows, it's so strong, and those who touch it are said to be cleansed from darkness of any kind. I've never seen it, of course. Cnos Fada is the furthest north I've been when not on a war campaign."

Mohg snorted. "You were a child then."

"I was grown." Finnbhear's lips tried to smile. "Barely. There was a girl, an acolyte. Sweet little thing. Just my age, too."

The trio fell back into silence. Mohg concentrated on sitting his horse. Bodb worried about his future. Finnbhear dwelt in the past, recalling the face of his first love.

It seemed to him that grass was greener then. The sky was clear during his entire visit to Cnos Fada (although privately he knew memory overlooked the bad weather). The girl had been an elusive figure at best times, a solid creature with haunted eyes at the very end. She was always so sad and he, gallant soldier on his first assignment, had wanted to rescue her.

That was long ago, and she was dead. Finnbhear had lived a long time, longer than most. Few elves were left with immortality in their minds. Although it could be waked in them at any moment, one out of every hundred had the desire. Finnbhear himself had decided long ago to die gracefully.

They camped that evening on a hill off the road. The grassland lay flat around them and afforded no protection for would-be ambushers. Most of Fion's terrain was a strange mixture of grassland with forests cropping up in thick to sparse clumps. Common folk avoided the forests out of respect for the fae, fairies and creatures of older magic, that were said to dwell within. Finnbhear hoped to use that superstition to their advantage and cross the woodlands in relative secrecy.

The night was uncharacteristically warm for the season. On nights like this, Finnbhear liked to play the silver flute he kept beneath his shirt. Stealth stole those joys from him now, although he was tempted to play it anyway. He consoled himself with thoughts of the journey's end. Their fire was small and smokeless, thanks to Mohg's skill, and dinner was dried meat. Surprisingly, Bodb did not complain about their meager fare. Finnbhear had expected worse.

The morning smelled of rain. Breaking camp quickly, they guided their horses through the hills and thickening forest. The road, abandoned, disappeared behind them. As the sun climbed in the sky, the day grew uncomfortably hot. Bodb unlaced his shirt and mopped his brow with a sleeve, but otherwise never said a word. Finnbhear and Mohg only muttered occasional comments to themselves. They reached a river by noon, just as storm clouds darkened the horizon and sent cooling breezes their way.

The water current was not too strong for the companions to cross. The horses were snorting and dripping on the other side in minutes. Bodb stripped, laying his clothes on the ground to dry. He stretched lazily on a boulder and closed his eyes happily. Mohg and Finnbhear were preferred to dry with their clothes on, which made setting up camp uncomfortable..

A movement caught Finnbhear's eye while he rummaged through the saddlebags for lunch. Pretending not to notice, he pulled out the sack of herbs and dried meat. Mohg was at the river drawing water in an old pot. Bodb left his boulder to warm his backside at the fire. With obvious reluctance, he slipped into his shirt and leggings. His boots he left where they lay.

Finnbhear blinked. There it was again: a flicker of black leaping from one bush to another. He surveyed the plain around them, noting that vegetation gave way to grass and Bodb's single boulder. It was not a good place to defend oneself.

Mohg returned with the water. Satisfied that his work was done for the evening, he sat opposite Bodb to enjoy the fire. Finnbhear put herbs in the pot, some of the meat, and watched it thoughtfully. By unspoken consent, Mohg and Bodb unrolled their bedding and began to settle in for the night.

"A fresh rabbit would be wonderful," Finnbhear said. "It would make our food last longer, too."

Bodb stood gallantly. "I will hunt for it," he offered.

Mohg grunted. "No," he said with his customary scowl. "You're to stay here with us." Bodb whined like a little boy, but sat back down.

"Too bad," Finnbhear said. "But you're right."

He saw the black shadow again while he was on first watch that night. When he investigated by casually strolling nearby, he saw nothing. Cursing his imagination, he turned away and then noticed the freshly killed rabbit at his feet.

A predator, he decided while skinning the rabbit by the dying fire. It killed the rabbit, and he had frightened it off. Lucky for him. Only, why would a predator hunt so close to their camp? It made better sense that a predator would hunt elsewhere. Maybe it was a scavenger, and it came seeking scraps. The rabbit escaped a hunter and died near their camp, and Finnbhear was lucky he had frightened the scavenger away.

Bodb took second watch when the moon, heavy and full, was high in the sky. Finnbhear slept heavily and dreamed of rabbits being chased by the night.

Mohg's boot prodding his leg scattered the dreams. Finnbhear opened his eyes to the dim light of early morning. "You should have let me take my watch," Mohg growled. "And look at ye, sleeping like a baby. Aren't you supposed to be protecting the prince?"

"Bodb took second watch," Finnbhear said, sitting up and scratching his head. "It was his responsibility. I protect him, but I won't baby him. The lad's to be king." Groggily he stood, prepared to berate Bodb for falling asleep.

Within moments, they realized Bodb was nowhere to be found. "Blast it!" Mohg cursed, pointing out the prince's boot prints leading out of camp and along the river. "Young boys and their fancies!" He followed them at his fastest walk, pushing violently against any foliage that chanced in the way.

"What was the scamp thinking?" Finnbhear asked the air as he followed the rugged elf. He berated himself severely for allowing the boy to watch the camp alone.

They followed the tracks down river where the brush was thick and almost impenetrable. Finnbhear winced every time Mohg snapped a branch or ripped a plant out by its roots as he made his own path after the boy. If the fae took insult, they would all three be in for serious trouble. Continuously, he glanced around and offered apology. Mohg apologized for nothing, not even his muttered threats toward the prince's life. At least, Finnbhear prayed silently, let not the boy hear that.

Twice, they thought they had lost the trail, and privately Finnbhear despaired that the boy was gone. Reliable Mohg always found it again just when Finnbhear felt panic rising in his throat. The sun climbed high in the sky.

When they finally found Bodb, the sun had just passed its zenith. Bodb did not notice them at first, even though they both clamored from the brush. The prince was lying on his stomach and leaning over a small rocky outcropping to look into a clear pool below it.

"I could do that," he said thoughtfully, "but I don't see where it would do you any good."

He went silent as if listening to something. Finnbhear and Mohg exchanged a look of dread. Had the young prince stumbled into a fairy glamour or lost his senses entirely? Signaling for Mohg to stay put, Finnbhear crept quietly forward.

"I'm sorry," Bodb said to the pool. "I have a little trouble believing a creature of your clan can have an interest in helping another."

Finnbhear was almost to the rock. Bodb said with a laugh, "No need to be insulted! I was only speaking truth. And your kind appreciates the truth, do you not? Three times and three times over?"

Finnbhear carefully slid onto the rock near Bodb and prepared to grab him away from danger. Bodb glanced up slightly and slowly motioned for Finnbhear to stay still. Then Finnbhear noticed the tiny voice coming from the pool.

"--looks so pitiful," the voice said. It sounded like the trickle of water in a stream. "She stands at the gate and wails. It disturbs my children."

"How did she get trapped there?" Bodb asked, sounding as if he were barely interested. "She might belong there. I'm not sure if I should tamper with the delicate balance of something like this, especially if there be a life involved."

"No," the voice said. Finnbhear edged further forward, trying to crane his head for a peek beyond the rock. "It was an accident, she's not meant to be there. So sad, so sad." There was tiny splash, as if the water were slapped with a tail. "She disturbs my children." The voice sounded irritated.

"I suppose I might take a look," Bodb said thoughtfully.

"Would you?" The voice sounded hopeful. "She disturbs my children ever so much." The water splashed again.

"I'll go right now," the prince said candidly, pointedly ignoring the Silver Fox.

"Its up the old trail there, to your left," the voice said. "Please hurry. Nightfall will be here, and my children will be disturbed again!"

Bodb slowly scooted off the rock. Finnbhear followed him, muttering under his breath. "Quiet," Bodb admonished him. "She might still be around, listening. No doubt she knows you two are here. If I hadn't agreed to help her, who knows what she might have done to either one of us. Now, hush."

Finnbhear considered doing quite the opposite. Then he remembered that this child of command was about to be king. Sulkily, he followed Bodb away from the pool. Mohg fell in step behind them, glaring at the ground. When the pool was out of sight, Bodb stopped walking and sighed.

"You can yell at me now," he said without turning around.

Mohg chuckled. Finnbhear opened his mouth, but found that all the anger had been replaced with curiosity. "What was that?" he asked.

"A sprite, of course," Bodb said and resumed walking. Not toward camp, Finnbhear noticed, but further away. "An asrai, I think. She called me, pleading for help. I thought it was about something important, not a noisy neighbor."

It was an old trail they followed. Leading away from the river and into wild land, it ended with the familiar ring of stones that marked the gate to an old ley line. Finnbhear did not neglect to observe the decay of the place. The rocks were chipped as if they had been attacked, although it obviously happened years ago. He did not recognize the place, which he thought strange. In his years, he thought he had been to every gate the ley lines had to offer.

"This is it," Bodb said, stating the obvious. He touched each of the stones in the formulae used to invoke the gate. Something flickered, but nothing happened.

"Broken," Mohg said. "Damn shame. We could use it to get to Cnos Fada."

"No," Bodb said. "She doesn't want us to see her."

"Who?" Finnbhear demanded, then suddenly turned to Mohg. "And you know we don't dare use the ley gate. Chulain would have us in an instant, and woe to our hides if he does."

"The noisy neighbor," Bodb answered Finnbhear's first question as Mohg kicked one of the founding stones in vexation. "The asrai was not very specific in who she was, only that she had once been an elf. And now her spirit is trapped here, in the stones."

Neither of the other men had a comment to that. For a while, Bodb continued to putter around the stones. Still nothing happened. Finally the prince gave up.

"Well, I took a look," Bodb said on the way back to camp.

"For nothing," Mohg said. "Now we'll have to camp by the river another night."

"The sprite won't bother me again," Bodb said with a wry smile. "She already knows I can't be drowned."

For the first time Finnbhear noticed the state of Bodb's clothes, as if they had dried while being worn. After yesterday's meticulousness, Finnbhear did not figure Bodb went for a swim fully dressed. The prince did not seem to mind the wrinkled state of his attire, for good or bad.

The late spring night was chilly. The other day's promise of rain, renewed, loomed over them in the shape of grey clouds. It sprinkled occasionally, but otherwise the sky withheld its downpour. Finnbhear expected a deluge at any second, and hoped it would wait just another day.

"We need shelter," Mohg said, casting an accusing eye to Bodb. The prince sniffed, refusing to be blamed for the delay.

"Never mind," Finnbhear said. "We're here."

"A little rain won't hurt you," Bodb said. "You could use a bath."

"I'd rather need a bath than smarts," Mohg said. "Or common sense." He was sharpening a knife. With each stroke against the whetstone, he managed to convey the feeling that he meant the knife for Bodb.

"It's a good thing I've got intelligence to spare," Bodb said casually. "Or you'd be in real trouble."

Finnbhear smiled to himself when Mohg stabbed the knife into the ground. Mohg would never let an insult contest get out of hand, but he could make you wonder. "Keep them," Mohg said. "Any less, and you'll never live to be a man."

Bodb snorted. "Maybe I don't want to, if the women are more interested in cleanliness."

Mohg grunted. "If you're talking about that sprite, boy, then keep her and welcome. I've plenty of real women who appreciate a man's hard labor."

"Labor? What do you do all day except ride that horse? If you can call it riding."

Inwardly Finnbhear sighed when Mohg's mouth wagged as he tried to think of a response. He grabbed his cloak and walked to the edge of camp. An insult contest with Mohg could last all night, and Bodb obviously had no intentions of losing. Finnbhear would take first watch again.

His watch passed uneventfully, with not even a shadow to tease his eyes.

CHAPTER SEVEN
"FOUR OUT OF FIVE"

Mohg was correct when he assumed the old gate was broken. It was not broken in the sense that it would never work again, however, but like a stream clogged with branches. Deep within the essence charged to keep the line alive, something else writhed to be free.

That night, a spark flickered within the gate and jumped from stone to stone. An observant eye might have noticed that the spark was repeating the formulae Bodb tried earlier. The only eye available to watch the eerie display was the asrai, who came there by means of an underground stream that surfaced nearby. She knew what was happening. Irritably, she slapped her tail in the mud.

Like the sun, the gate filled with light. The sprite winced; her eyes were not made to withstand the intensity. A figure stepped forward, shrouded by the light, looked around in disappointment, then started to cry. Before long her sobs became the customary wails of the hilltop.

The asrai grumbled to herself as she slipped back downstream to her pool. Her children would hear the noise and surely be disturbed. Drastic measures must be taken to silence the gate spirit, and soon.

***

Briskly, Raori strode through the front door, into the Sanctuary, and looked around. A bard was tuning his harp in the corner. A familiar redheaded figure stood nearby, studying the strings as a matter of course. The housekeeper was outside, presumably tending to his horse after admonishing him for riding the poor animal almost into the ground. There was to be no one else.

The redhead looked up. "Raori," he cried jovially. "Finally here!" With long strides, he thumped his way to the mage. His boots shed dust with every step.

The two clasped forearms briefly. "Where is everyone else?" Raori asked. "Don't tell me they're the late ones for once!"

Picket laughed and shook his head vigorously. "Everyone else is still asleep, bored to tears from waiting for you." The pooka scratched his woolen shirt over the shoulder. It smelled musky and faintly of death. He probably stole it from some unfortunate's grave. That was his habit when human shape was a long term necessity. Not that Raori found reason to complain. The dead certainly did not need it, and clothing could get expensive. "Hai, I've been walking circles down here. If not for the bard over there, I think I might have run screaming mad into the wild!"

Raori scowled, eliciting more laughter from the pooka. It was infectious, as always. "We can't expect anything different from you," the mage said after a mirthful explosion.

The housekeeper appeared, holding a pitcher of ale and a small mug. "I've let the help take your horse, sir, as I knew you'd be needing something to drink after such a hard trip. The critter is exhausted, but she'll make it," she said. She handed Raori the mug and filled it to the brim. Mouth watering, Raori watched the brown liquid swirl around in his cup, thinking it was the most beautiful thing in the world. "Begging your pardon, but does this reunion mean your company will be departing soon?"

Picket snorted in remembered fashion. "Unfortunately no," he said. "Unless our last friend arrives today."

"Ah," said Residhnne, nodding. "I'm sure they'll be along shortly. Until then, I'll be thinking of supper; the house is quite full with you!" She smiled, patting a stray hair back into place, and withdrew.

"Who is missing?" Raori asked, watching the housekeeper's hips sway as she walked away. He tasted his cool mug of ale gratefully. No other beverage did justice this early in the morning.

"The Priestess," Picket replied. His dark eyes watched Raori steadily.

Raori was careful not to betray himself. "Finally," he said into his cup, "someone later than I. Our Northern Thorn must be crazy with impatience."

"Rightly so," Picket murmured. "The rightful king of Fion goes to Cnos Fada to be crowned. It is our job to stop him."

"Stop him how?" Raori asked incredulously, voicing what he had been mulling over the entire journey to the Sanctuary House. "He must have an army at his tail, mages and access to the treasures of the House of Danaan as well!"

Even as he said it, Raori knew that was not the case. The Clan of Danaan had been conquered long ago with many of their treasures lost. The only treasure recovered, albeit briefly, had been the bloodthirsty Spear of Birgha.

Picket shrugged, using all of his body to do so. A heavy step on the stairs dragged their attention upward. Duinn, followed by an alert Eahn, had come down for a late breakfast. Residhnne, reappearing from the other room, whisked to attention professionally, promising eggs and bacon if someone would raid the chicken house. The bard left to do the chore, not without giving the company a strange glance.

The latecomers greeted Raori with nods, followed by shouts to Residhnne for fresh ale. The housekeeper bustled her way to the back, reminding Raori of Moire in her industriousness, and left the four men alone in the room.

"I thought," Duinn said to Raori with his usual lack of tact, "the Priestess would be with you. Did you two have a fight, or have you seen her at all?"

"She's chasing rabbits somewhere," Picket said as though he envied her with all of his being. Residhnne returned, holding a pitcher full of Raori's favorite breakfast beverage, and refilled Raori's mug.

"Sounds like her," Eahn said once he, too, had a full mug of ale in hand.

Raori buried his face in his mug of ale. If the drink could do him any favors, he'd be properly forgetful before the day was over. Eahn was inclined to follow Raori's example and downed two mugs before the bard was back carrying a basketful of eggs.

Residhnne crowed in delight. "That's the most those hens have ever given this place," she said. She gave the bard a kiss on the cheek and left him blushing.

Eahn noticed the bard for the first time. "How long have you been here?" he demanded so suddenly that his companions jumped.

The bard's pleased grin faltered. "I came this morning," he said. "You were still asleep."

"You know this fellow?" Picket asked. He thumped the bard's back like an old friend. "Talented, this one. Plays an excellent tune!"

The bard, who was none other than Oenghus, smiled ruefully. "You haven't heard me play, yet," he said.

Eahn was not to be distracted. He thrust his hand under his shirt and brought out a medallion. "Take this thing," he spat. "Give it to her yourself. The last thing I want is a case of mistaken identity. Or bad luck." He thrust the thing in the bard's direction.

Oenghus blinked at it, as if he could not remember what it was. "You'll be seeing her before I will," he said, slowly. "I hardly think she'll think it a token of your love." But, he accepted the medallion hesitantly.

"Who are you talking about?" Picket asked. "What's going on?"

"He never said," Eahn grumbled. "But who else, do you think? This bard, here," Eahn jutted his chin in Oenghus' direction, "shared camp with me a few nights ago. Gave me this medallion, saying it was for some woman I knew."

"Your wife?" Duinn asked with uplifted eyebrows.

"No," Oenghus said with a laugh. "Although I'm sure your wife is pretty," he said quickly at Eahn's darkening expression. "I meant it for your companion. If she gets here."

Eahn spat. "How do you know my wife?" The question came out dangerously. Picket grinned and stamped a foot.

"The Priestess?" Raori asked in spite of his inner resolve, forgetting his ale long enough to focus on the bard. "You know her?"

"How do you know my wife, bard?"

Oenghus' expression was serious. "I know the Priestess as well as anyone. I've watched her grow, you might say." Wisely, he ignored Eahn's question. Brow furrowed in thunder, Eahn let the matter drop.

Picket expressed awe with wide eyes and the impression of ears facing forward. "An old friend?" he asked in a whisper. His black eyes glinted. "An ally?"

"I don't choose sides," the bard said simply. As an afterthought, "Leastwise, not the way you have."

"Will," Raori said haltingly, "you be staying here for very long? She's late, but she'll be along. I'm sure of it."

Oenghus searched the ceiling. "I go on in the morning," he said. "I've got to get to Cnos Fada."

The companions looked at one another. Only Raori was unsure what the suspicious glance between Duinn and Eahn meant. Picket pondered thoughts of his own. Judging by his expression, they meant small trouble.

"Give the medallion to me. I'll give it to her," Raori said impulsively. Eahn spat again. Duinn only grunted.

"Yes!" Picket said a little too eagerly. "Give it to him. Yes, yes." He nodded his head happily.

His smile returned as Oenghus handed the medallion to Raori. "She'll know who it's from." Without another word, he returned to his spot by the fire, took up his instrument, and proceeded to play softly to himself. The tune was an old one and beautiful. Oenghus made it sound like two cats fighting in the bushes.

It started to rain, which happened frequently at that time of a year. Oenghus fell asleep in his chair while listening to the rhythm of the rain on the rooftop. His lute had fallen to the floor with a twang and lay just a foot from the fire. Eahn wanted to feed it to the fire, but Picket would not let him. The companions waited until the bard started to snore then gathered in a small huddle for a whispered conference.

"Give the thing back to the bard," Eahn whispered heatedly to Raori. "It's bad luck, or worse."

Raori shook his head. Picket snorted, agreeing. "I can figure out what it's for," the pooka offered. "It might be something important for her. Or even us. You know how things go with her..."

"Is he from Moirfenn?" Raori queried, changing the topic by expressing his inner fears.

Four pairs of eyes watched the sleeping elf. The bard remained oblivious to the sudden wary suspicion, lost in dreams as he was. "He's no bard," Duinn said. "Did you listen to him play?"

"He plays wonderfully," Picket said loyally.

"Only you would think so."

"Quiet!" Eahn hissed, for their voices had started to get loud. "I say we leave now. We may have waited too long already. And, Raori, you throw that medallion in a hole somewhere! It's no good, I tell you!"

"But the Priestess," Raori protested.

"She can catch up," Eahn said. "She's not helpless. This will not be the first time we've had to leave someone, especially her, behind. I can't say it will be the last. And the last thing she needs is a bit of jewelry to slow her down."

"I promised the bard I would give it to her," Raori muttered as the crew went upstairs to pack Eahn's and Duinn's bags.

"Fine, then," Eahn muttered back. "Just keep it, and yourself, far from me. When the curse that's on it hits, I want to be out of range."

They saddled their mounts, one of which was Picket, and left when the rain had slackened to a drizzle. Raori privately lamented that Eahn would not let him bring at least a small keg of ale, but he supposed he was lucky to get away with the amulet. Duinn scowled and gripped Picket's mane with a death grip. Eahn's thoughts were with Joalie.

Dawn: Raori listened while the others discussed their mission, comparing what they knew while they ate leftover soup from last night. It was all basically what had been said in the letter the sorcerers had given him. Bodb Derg's coronation had to be stopped. With the north's last king gone, Moirfenn would never worry about losing power again.

Or so the excuse went. Raori knew what MacKegan really wanted was the satisfaction of wiping the prince's family, the Danaans, out completely. Maybe the kinglet planned to strike back against Moirfenn, maybe he did not. The boy had nothing to back him: The treasures of his house, which had once made his family a formidable force, were gone. Most families remotely sympathetic to his cause would be too afraid to lift a finger in his direction. And MacKegan held Fion in his clutches.

Wet mornings always made Raori sneeze. Desperately he tried to control it as they rode. No one cared about Raori's discomfort, which was just as well. Each were equally miserable, except for Picket who minced under Duinn jovially.

Raori soon noticed that ever so often the dwarf swatted himself. It did not take long to realize that this always happened when the pooka twitched his tail.

"Blasted insects," Duinn muttered viciously, slapping his arms. He turned to Raori and Eahn. "Why is it you two aren't plagued with the little beasts?"

Eahn's thoughts were still with his wife, and he did not hear. "Dwarf must be a delicacy," Raori suggested, biting his lip and fighting to look serious. The pebbles under Picket's feet were actually dancing along with them. Duinn slapped himself again. Raori noticed that a particular pink pebble had disappeared from the ground.

Picket turned to Raori and blinked his eyes in a slow, sleepy way. His mincing slowed to the sedate pace of the other horses, who appreciated it. He twitched his tail again. Duinn cursed.

"How much farther to Cnos Fada, Eahn?" Raori asked, turning his attention away from the dwarf before he burst into gales of laughter.

Eahn, pulled from his reverie, let his breath out in a slow way. "Days," he said. "What we should do is find Bodb, who won't be on the main road, and stop him from getting there. The lad won't be taking the ley lines, I'm sure of it. No one takes those much anymore." He turned to Raori.

Raori noticed that everyone else was looking at him as well. "What?" he asked. "You want me to cast a location spell for him?"

"Obviously," Duinn drawled. "If not that, what use are you to us except to eat all of the food?"

Picket snorted in mirth. Something stung Raori's cheek, but he knew not to swat at it. He stopped his horse, glared at the pooka, and dismounted.

With the others behind him, faithfully waiting, Raori opened his little pouch and pulled out a quartz crystal. It was a small one, but it did the job. If there was one thing Raori had learned through the years, it was intent that made the magic and not the props. Raori fingered the crystal a minute as he allowed his mind to wander of memories of the Priestess. He had her to thank for that bit of wisdom, as well as other things that set him apart from others of his class. The mage half-smiled, feeling bittersweet.

Props were nothing but objects, stepping stones for amateurs to learn with like an infant grabs his mother's hands while learning to walk. Raori's crystal may have been small, and cracked, but it worked greater magic than ever his teachers had tried to create. He had seen the mightiest men tremble with a mere flick of a finger. With a crystal like this, Raori could own the world if that was what he chose. He had become, against all odds, a better wizard than his teachers thought him capable of.

But that wasn't that what he wanted? Greater power, and the will to show them that he was more than a clumsy boy?

He breathed on his crystal, closed his eyes, and waited.

He thought about Bodb Derg, the prince of Fion and heir to the throne. Where was he? For that matter, who was he with? The spell took hold and tugged at his mind. His inner vision pictured an old ley gate, with three figures walking away from it.

The gate reminded Raori of the past and then to thoughts of the Priestess. The memory of her scent tantalized him. *Careful, Raori,* he thought to himself. *Stray thoughts, stray thoughts... You'll twist the spell!* He forced the Priestess out of his mind and turned back to the prince.

Without warning, the vision changed, but only slightly. He still saw the gate, now further in the background, and the three figures. Close to him was a patch of bushes where something moved. Curiously, Raori concentrated on that, wondering what lay hidden within. The bushes parted, and the spy crept forward.

To Raori's surprise it was a wolf-dog, crouched and watching the elves. Its tail wagged slightly. The figures passed by, not noticing it.

The crystal tugged at Raori's hand. With satisfaction he noticed that it was glowing a pale yellow. He remounted his horse, ignoring his companions' impatient questions, and turned it in the direction the stone had shown.

"I think The Priestess is with them," he said to the others. Without waiting, he nudged his horse into motion. The others scrambled to get mounted, complaining loudly. Raori let them complain, even as he heard Duinn thunder curses when more pebbles bounced in his direction. They would catch up soon enough, and he dare not lose the spell.

"How do you know she's with them?" Eahn asked suspiciously when his horse drew abreast with Raori's. "If that traitor is working with them–"

"She's not with them," Raori said with a scowl. "And I'm not sure anyway." He gave an account of what he had seen.

Eahn was silent for a while. Behind them, Picket pranced in the mud puddles. Raori glanced back once and quickly had to look forward again lest he lost his concentration. The dwarf was covered in splatters from the mud. He looked like a short golem.

"Leave off that, you twisted creature!" Duinn shouted when a particularly deep puddle splashed into his beard. The pooka whinnied mischievously but slowed his pace. Duinn's grip on Picket's mane relaxed slightly. Raori kicked his horse into a trot to put some distance between himself and the pair.

Just in time, for without warning, the pooka frog-hopped into another puddle. The dwarf almost fell off, but Picket knew how to keep his rider. Muddy water went everywhere, landing on everyone and everything except Raori. The mage laughed, despite himself, and had to struggle to regain the spell's image.

"Blast it!" the dwarf cried. "Black-hearted, double-dealing, muck-ridden, hag-loving creature! Let me down, I say!"

The pooka stopped short, standing like any dumb animal who never turned a trick on its rider. Even Eahn chuckled as the dwarf tangled his feet in the stirrups and fell to the ground, flat on his back. Picket flicked his ears and shook his head. His snort sounded like stifled laughter. Duinn stood and tried to brush the mud off. The looks he gave the pooka could have fried eggs.

"I'll ride him," Eahn said through his laughter. "That is, if you would be so kind, Picket."

***

"That way," Raori said, pointing the direction. The sun was starting to sink, but Eahn judged they still had time before having to stop. Picket, of course, had excellent night vision. He could travel until dawn, if he chose to. But the other, more mortal mounts would surely perish from exhaustion if the company made the attempt.

The horses snorted to one another and continued to walk slowly. Even Picket looked tired. The mud on his legs was dry and had attracted flies. Duinn said it served him right when the pooka wanted to stop and brush himself off. With a grim smile, Eahn had denied a halt.

Sometimes when Raori concentrated on the stone he could see the three men, and at other times he saw the wolf in the distance. He guessed that the younger of the three was Bodb. The oldest of them, a silver-haired elf, seemed familiar, but his identity remained elusive. No matter how Raori aimed the spell, he could not get a clear vision of the third elf's face.

"Time to stop for one night," Eahn said, his voice breaking into the silence. Picket's legs froze immediately. Eahn had barely dismounted before the pooka changed form, casting off the bridle and saddle in disgust.

"What will the mares think of you now?" Duinn asked. He helped the pooka brush the mud from his legs.

"Likely they wouldn't," Picket muttered.

Raori left his horse to Eahn's care. Usually Eahn would have protested, but this time it was necessary. The youth-like wizard found a spot away from the others and concentrated on his stone. He had to keep contact with Bodb's company constantly. If he lost the link, he might not be able to reestablish it. His only chance was to stay awake through the night. Fortunately, a mage was trained for just such an emergency. And even if he had never been taught the trick of conserving energy while learning beneath his masters, serving MacKegan made up for any lack.

Once again, he asked himself: Wasn't that what he wanted? To be the best?

CHAPTER EIGHT
"BLACK AND SILVER"

Finnbhear shifted in his saddle. It was a futile attempt to relieve the pain from his saddle sores, but he tried anyway. A fly landed on his nose, avoided his swat, and flew for better pastures. He wished he were home, bathing in hot water and listening to his musician play the lyre. At least, he reflected further, he could sneak a tune or two on his flute. They were far enough from the road now that something like that would not endanger them, for all the flute had come from the fey folk and was magic.

MacKegan was listening for that flute to play, Finnbhear knew, but this deep in the woods, fey magic was common. A small tune could do no harm, but he kept it tucked away out of sight.

The Silver Fox snorted to himself, shaking his head. He was being a silly old man for even worrying over such a small matter. The trees around them were oppressive, and that was what he was supposed to be concentrating on. Bodb and Mohg were investigating an abandoned hovel they found in an overgrown patch of grass. That left Finnbhear to wait outside and guard. It was not the way he wanted to spend the afternoon. Then again, this entire process of traveling through the wilderness seemed silly. Traveling the ley lines were not an option due to the danger of being captured or murdered by any other assorted evils that lurked in those gleaming passageways, but surely there was a better way to do this. Surely, the boy could afford a better guard than two, old elves.

Only slightly coated in cobwebs and dust, Bodb emerged from the building. His smile smacked of satisfaction, as if he had discovered Viking treasure. "Seems safe enough," he announced. "There's room for the horses."

"It took you two long enough," Finnbhear grumbled. Gratefully he dismounted, pausing to crack his back before leading his horse inside. The horse stumbled on a fallen timber but otherwise was content with her new surroundings. Mohg was already tending to a small fire in the floor beneath the window. Bodb did not enter immediately. When he did, he sat by the door and peered outside constantly.

Dinner was rabbit, another gift found on the edge of camp that evening. Finnbhear was getting tired of rabbit, but he never turned a free meal down. "Eat now, for you may go hungry tomorrow," his mother had once said. He had been a small boy at the time, but it was right after his father's death.

Memories from that time were always crystal clear, burned into his memory like fresh brands.

When night had almost fallen completely, a wolf howled somewhere outside. Finnbhear was sure it was the same wolf that had been following them. It surely was a lycanthrope, not a true wolf at all. Why it shadowed them was mysterious, but not worrisome. Finnbhear was used to this sort of treatment – the gifts and escort – from denizens of the forest. When he was a boy, he had even managed to befriend a brown lad, a wild type of fey prone to tricks and thievery. The silver flute he carried close to his breast was a gift from that friend.

Finnbhear was sure that if the wolf wanted to harm the prince, it would be doing more than leaving rabbits on the doorstep. It would have attacked by now.

Bodb had already curled up in a corner with his travel blankets rolled for a pillow. His soft snores rumbled in the darkness, ignored by his escort who sat on opposite sides of the fire. Mohg chewed a rabbit leg thoughtfully. Finnbhear asked him for his thoughts.

"We should have taken that ley line," the gruff elf said. "Leaving from home was dangerous, aye, because Moirfenn would have captured us for sure. But that other ley line is forgotten." Rip, chew, swallow. "Gettin' tired of rabbit. Don't trust that wolf."

"You eat it quick enough," Finnbhear commented. "As for the ley line, you yourself said it was broken. By that spirit, or whatever it was. We might have run into worse trouble than Moirfenn. Besides," and he jerked his chin in the prince's direction, "it's not what he wants."

"The lad makes no sense," Mohg mumbled, unsure if the prince were really sleeping. "Have ye ever seen such a mellow prince? He seems more content to float through life than anything else. A king must be made of sterner stuff than that."

"Well, that's not for us to decide," Finnbhear said, nodding. "He'll become king or die trying. I admire that much in him. I wouldn't do it."

"Aye," Mohg said with a low chuckle. "There's less freedom in that position than for any slave in the entire realm." The fire crackled between them for a moment. "I'll take first watch," Mohg grunted. "That wolf is out there."

Finnbhear chuckled. "You, take watch first for once? No." He stood, discarding his cloak. "I'll take the first watch as usual. I'm quite used to it. Get some sleep. If the wolf were going to do something, it would have happened by now."

"Fattening us up for the kill," Mohg muttered, but he obeyed.

Finnbhear waited until Mohg's snores sawed in time with Bodb's, then he stepped outside. He started to unlace his shirt but thought better of it. The wolf howled again.

It was a questing howl. Finnbhear was not fluent in the language of wolves, but he understood a call when he heard one. He hesitated near the door with one hand on the rotting frame. Another howl echoed through the trees. Caught between the need to go and the need to stay, Finnbhear scanned the darkness with narrowed eyes.

If there was a chance to rub noses with their unlikely caretaker, this was it. This was more than a matter of mere curiosity, the Silver Fox told himself. He was obligated to the wolf for the meals he had shared with his companions. Supposing it were the fey who guided and protected him on this trip, things could turn dangerously bad if they were insulted. The fey were famous for their fickle nature, and the last thing Finnbhear wanted was to wake up dead the next morning.

Bodb and Mohg were safe inside. To ensure that, Finnbhear scratched a few warding signs on the door posts. With a resigned sigh, he then crouched on all fours and concentrated. A liquid light covered him, molded into him, and the silver fox streaked away.

Always with the change from man to animal, Finnbhear became drunk with the heightened sense of smell and hearing. He chased a mouse, yipping at it, then followed the smell of water until he came to a small pool at the base of a tree. After he drank his fill, he cocked his ears and listened.

The wolf had fallen silent while he played in the leaves and shadows, but that did not mean it was not out there. Finnbhear considered the shack, now farther away than it should be. He should not have gone so far. He had acted foolishly.

Slipping from bush to bush, he made his way back to Bodb and Mohg as quickly as he dared. The feeling that he was being watched made the hair on his spine raise up. Perhaps it was only an owl, but he trotted faster anyway. The shack was not much farther.

The wolf exploded out of nowhere. It barked, a deeper and richer sound than that of a dog. Cocking its head to measure Finnbhear up, it then dashed away. At first, Finnbhear jumped back in alarm but when the wolf ran, he ran after it. Their flight was frenzied as the fox struggled to keep up with his larger counterpart.

What began in earnest became a game. The wolf danced around him, nipping at his heels, and laughing in almost human fashion. Finnbhear could only retaliate with a few nips of his own and a yip or two for the feel of it. It was an odd sight, the fox and wolf running along side by side.

It was not a true wolf, as Finnbhear had suspected. For all intents and purposes, the lupine's form was wolfen, but a discerning eye could see dog in that shape, even in the flash of bushy tail that slapped Finnbhear's back when he slowed. It was a familiar shape that ran beside the fox, and Finnbhear knew he was enjoying himself too much.

It ended when the wolf-dog rolled suddenly in the leaves and lay on the ground. Finnbhear, feeling winded and glad for the rest, flopped down beside it.

Suddenly *she* was there. Finnbhear leapt to his feet, startled by the sudden change. The woman merely smiled at him with a faintly lupine grin. Her black hair covered her naked breasts but not the rest of her body. Despite himself, Finnbhear felt embarrassed.

He changed back to himself and took off his shirt. "Here," he said, offering it to the woman. "It's chilly tonight."

She accepted the shirt, slipping it over her head and shaking her hair free. Shadows hid parts of her face, but she looked achingly familiar. The smile faded as she leaned forward, touching his cheek with a delicate hand. Finnbhear realized he had been scratched.

"It's nothing," he said in the face of her concern. He gently pushed her hand away and sat back to consider this stranger. She, in turn, considered him.

What did she see? Finnbhear could not see his shadow in her eyes; her face was half-hidden in darkness. Her eyes glittered like hard diamonds from those dark depths, and her breasts heaved as her lungs strove to replenish her body. She smirked. Something in the gesture brought the chill in the air running up his naked back and sent the hair on his head standing on end. This woman was neither fey nor elf; Finnbhear could not tell who, if anyone, she would be aligned to.

"We could sit here all night," Finnbhear said when the moon had begun to sink. He was guiltily aware that his watch was more than over. Mohg may or may not have woke up on his own. Finnbhear hoped he had not. The last thing he wanted to do was tell Mohg about this woman or anything to do her.

To his surprise, the woman said, "We can go. I promise not to disappear... for now." Her voice had a sultry quality to it. It fit.

They walked back to the shack as humans. Covertly Finnbhear watched her as they went. Her eyes were on the ground and never seemed to turn to him, though he had the feeling that she watched him just as much as he her.

She was better at it.

They reached the house, and suddenly the woman was not with him anymore. The wolf-dog bounded to the door, turned three times, and settled down to sleep. Finnbhear stared at her for a minute, remembered Mohg, and woke his partner even though there was no point to it. The werewolf was obviously guarding them in her fashion. Finnbhear almost mentioned her to Mohg, but thought better of it when he noticed that she had disappeared from her place by the door. Mohg did not seem to realize the night was half gone, and that suited Finnbhear fine.

Someone tripped over Finnbhear that morning and cursed soundly. As consciousness became reality, the cursing continued. Mohg was outside and upset.

"Go on now, you beast!" the scruffy elf was shouting. Sunlight seared Finnbhear's sight when he stepped out. He blinked, barely making out the werewolf dancing just out of reach of Mohg's sword. Mohg swung at it and continued his black litany. Finnbhear staggered toward him.

"Leave her alone," Finnbhear said, grabbing Mohg's arm. "She's harmless."

"The blasted creature stole my breakfast!" Mohg shouted. He shrugged Finnbhear's hand off and took another swipe at the wolf-dog.

"As many rabbits as she fed us for supper," Finnbhear said, "I think you can spare her a bit of breakfast."

The wolf-dog barked, apparently agreeing with Finnbhear, and dodged another swipe of Mohg's sword.

"So that's who's been following us," Bodb said, stepping quietly beside Finnbhear.

Finnbhear looked sidelong at the boy. Mellow prince, indeed. The lad always knew more than he should, yet rarely was inclined to share that knowledge with anyone else. Finnbhear was not so sure that was a healthy sign in one so young . Even for an elf.

"She's harmless," Finnbhear said again. "She might even be fey." The last he added lamely, half-hoping Mohg would take the hint and stop fighting with her.

"A wolf, harmless?" Mohg incredulously sheathed his sword. "Huh. May my mother be human first!"

The wolf-dog lay back her ears and growled.

"You might want to apologize," Bodb said in amusement. "She seems to have taken insult. Please, do not think that I agree with him, sweet lady," the prince said to the wolf. "This brute is ill-mannered and ungrateful. Your rabbits have warmed my nights, and I thank you."

Mohg muttered something to himself and turned away. The look on his face was a mix of anger and amusement. The wolf-dog's ears were still back. Finnbhear approached her cautiously. Her neck was stiff when he petted her, but at least her ears came up.

Finnbhear wondered how much Bodb knew. Did he know the wolf was enchanted? Not that it was not obvious. Most beasts had some sort of enchantment about them, especially in Fion. He still could not decide if she had come from the fey world or if she was something else altogether.

The youth, it seemed, had dismissed the matter and was packing his equipment. Mohg apparently had no suspicions, nor any cares, as he went about his business. Finnbhear decided to keep the secret, such as it was, to himself for now. If she really were a fey, she would take violent insult if Finnbhear spoke too soon.

Traveling again, Bodb rode beside Finnbhear and said nothing for most of the day. He had the air of someone who was waiting for something; an explanation perhaps. Finnbhear had not thought of a good one yet. The wolf-dog padded alongside his foot, panting happily like a docile dog, apparently oblivious to the tension between the three men. Mohg muttered darkly, glaring in her direction, but was far too used to Finnbhear's odd habits to protest louder than that.

The old general lived almost completely by instinct, which was more common in elves than not. Mohg's instinct was to trust his friend, which he did. He attempted to put Bodb's misgivings, if he had any, to rest with a stern look. The young prince ignored him.

Mutually, they instinctively agreed that Bodb's identity remain secret around the wolf-dog. When they found it necessary to speak, they omitted each other's names or substituted gestures for words. Occasionally, Mohg and Bodb traded insults, but the game always died when Bodb glanced at the werewolf. The prince did not seem disturbed by her presence, only wary. The wolf stared at him often with gleaming eyes and lolling tongue, as if the boy's discomfort were fine wine to be savored. Finnbhear sighed to himself, wondering if he should have chased her away.

By evening, they reached the end of the forest. It stopped abruptly, like a growing fence on the boundary of a wide plain of high grasses and stunted shrubbery. Finnbhear was glad to call a halt for the day. Bodb refused to dismount, looking around himself warily. "I don't think we should stop here," he said to Finnbhear.

"Nonsense," grunted Mohg as he worked at opening a saddlebag. "It's a perfect spot."

The wolf-dog whined anxiously. She slumped down so that she was hidden in the grass. Finnbhear decided that she was just nervous at being outside the protection of the trees. Not many fey were brave enough to venture beyond the forest. Bodb glanced at her. "Even your pet agrees with me," he said.

"There's another ley gate," Mohg said. He pointed over the grasslands where a structure of standing stones silhouetted the horizon. "Let's camp near it. The stones will give us protection, and we'll be drier come morning. If I wake up covered in dew one more time, I'll simply go mad."

The wolf-dog sneezed.

"Better we stay in the trees," Bodb said, "if we must stay here at all. You'll not escape the dew, my friend, except indoors."

"Aye, we'll build a hovel right here and live for a while. Moirfenn would never think to look for you at the edge of a forest, half-hidden by grass and dirt."

Finnbhear hissed softly, but the werewolf was scratching and seemed not to have heard Mohg's lapse of caution. Bodb grimaced, scanning the horizon with nervous eyes. "I just don't like it out there," he said finally.

"If we get ambushed in the night," Finnbhear said, "we can at least escape down the ley line. We can't do that, trapped in the trees." Prince or no, Finnbhear wanted to be near those stones by nightfall. The boy could make his own decisions when he was king.

"I still don't like it," the boy muttered.

They went to the ley gate anyway. It was in worse disrepair than the last, as happened when things fell into disuse. Finnbhear knew how to activate it, of course, and so did Mohg. Bodb too, which showed that his education was well rounded. But too many people had deemed the lines too dangerous to travel, or they simply could not activate the magic within.

Those who traveled the lines tended to disappear, or they were found later dead and often mutilated. Once upon a time, such mishaps were completely unheard of. Finnbhear could not remember how long ago it was, but he was sure it was within his lifetime.

Also, mortal blood ran through the elven race now. Many humans had been brought to Fion as lovers to elven counterparts, and Finnbhear blamed the problem on this fact. With them, the humans had brought their ways and their lack of magic. Finnbhear could Fion's present with his youth and see a marked difference. Their exotic mates had polluted the elves, and the ley lines were only one of many vanishing ancient ways.

The wolf-dog calmed down a little after they tethered the horses by the gate. Finnbhear sat next to her with his back against one of the stones. She lay her head in his lap. He scratched her ears with his eyes closed.

Suddenly the wolf-dog lifted her head. Her nostrils flared. From deep within her throat a growling emerged. It was a chilling sound.

"What's wrong with your pet?" Mohg asked.

"I don't know," Finnbhear said faintly. The werewolf leaped to all fours, grabbed Finnbhear's hand, and began to tug it. "Something is happening, at any rate. It's too bad I don't speak Wolf."

"Looks like she wants you inside the ring," Bodb observed. He reached down to touch the wolf-dog, but she released Finnbhear's hand to jump away. "Pretty smart for a dumb beast."

The wolf's hackles rose and she bared her teeth.

"You've insulted her," Finnbhear said. "As if Mohg weren't bad enough."

"She's not growling at me," Bodb said. He shaded his eyes with one hand and looked across the grassy fields around them.

The horses grunted between themselves, pulling at their tethers and stamping their feet nervously. Mohg stroked his horse's nose, whispering to it. "Something is nearby," the grisly elf said, stating the obvious. "Watch the horses."

The wolf-dog resumed tugging Finnbhear's hand. He let her lead him into the ring. Satisfied, she barked and dove at Mohg's horse. It whinnied and tried to bolt, but Mohg had its bridles firm in hand. Bodb ran to help him.

The wolf continued to dash at the horses. Mohg shouted at the wolf, kicking at her when she ran within range. The other horses danced in place, frightened. "She's trying to drive them into the ring," Bodb shouted over the commotion. "Let them go, Mohg! We're likely to get trampled, blast that cur!"

The beasts attacked.

Finnbhear felt them even before they emerged out of the grass as if from nowhere. His shouted warning came too late. Four beasts were on top of the horses, who squealed in pain and outrage, before the words reached his tongue. Tossed to one side, Mohg disappeared in the grass. Bodb ran to him, sword unsheathed. The wolf-dog ran into the ring.

Their tethers broke, and the horses launched into a desperate run with the creatures clinging to them like fleas. Finnbhear got the impression of skinny, fur-covered bodies and wicked teeth before they were too far way to see clearly. Then two more appeared and ran for him. His sword cleared its scabbard in the nick of time.

His first slash was clumsy but effective. The first beast went down with a moan and did not move again. Warned, the second beast circled him and watched with human eyes.

Intelligence gleamed within them as the beast plotted its next move.

The werewolf leaped from nowhere and crashed into the creature. A fierce battle erupted. The snapping of teeth chipped at the air. Someone was shouting in the background. Finnbhear forced himself to look away and saw Bodb, straddling something in the grass and facing off three of the creatures with only a knife. His sword lay discarded nearby, behind the beasts.

Damn the lad! They were supposed to be protecting him! Finnbhear got there just as one rushed in and grabbed Bodb's leg. The prince howled and stabbed with his knife. Finnbhear's sword impaled the creature neatly, then swung upward in time to catch another across the throat. The third creature wailed, dashing off after the horses. Mohg struggled up from the ground, cursing and threatening the fleeing beast.

Panting from his exertion, Finnbhear raced back to the werewolf. She sat primly next to a throatless body and seemed to be smiling. Mohg, with Bodb leaning on him for support, came up from behind.

"Fell beasts," Finnbhear said, prodding the body with his sword. The poor creatures had once been elves, but something had broken them inside, leaving them half between themselves and their animal counterparts for an insane eternity, Fell beasts were known to wander the wilderness of Fion in search of easy prey. Finnbhear could not help but shudder and turn away from the body before him. He noticed that the werewolf was also regarding the creature with very human loathing.

"Finnbhear," the prince panted, "I think it's time to explain about your beast. Don't get me wrong," he raised one hand, "I trust you, and after this I can honestly say I trust her. Still, this was just one attack on my life, and we know there will be others. I was going to wait to ask, but under the circumstances..."

"But these were Fell beasts, milord," Finnbhear protested. "They would have attacked any one caught alone out here."

"Finnbhear," the prince said by way of warning. "We left the safety of the trees against my wishes. We are also traveling to the old capital against my wishes... most of what I have done in my life has been against my wishes. I think I've had enough of that for one lifetime. Who is she?"

The wolf-dog whined and butted her head against Finnbhear's leg. "I'm sorry," Finnbhear said, kneeling down to caress her pelt, "but the prince wants to know. I think we all do."

The wolf swiveled to face Bodb and lowered her head. Her eyes, once so clear and trusting, had turned dangerous. She growled.

"I don't think your beast likes me," Bodb said, limping back and looking for shelter.

"No!" cried Finnbhear just as the werewolf leaped forward. Bodb raised his arm, a puny defense but enough to deflect the wolf's teeth from his throat. She latched on and held. Bodb cried out.

"Get off of him!" Mohg shouted, trying to bat the wolf-dog away. "I knew that beast was trouble!" He drew his dagger.

"Let him go!" Finnbhear cried, grabbing the werewolf's neck and pulling. "Let him go, or Mohg will kill you!"

Mohg lifted his hand for a killing thrust. Instantly the werewolf released Bodb and dropped to the ground. She backed away and found Finnbhear right behind her.

Trapped, but not ready to give up, she whirled back to Bodb. The young prince sensed her suicidal thoughts and shouted wildly. Finnbhear grabbed her and held. Mohg stepped forward, murder in his eyes.

Beneath Finnbhear's grip, fur disappeared into smooth flesh. Man and shifting lupine collapsed together with Finnbhear on top. The woman tried to wriggle free but Finnbhear held firm.

"I knew she was something like that," Bodb crowed triumphantly. "I thought she might be one of your fey folk, Finnbhear, but still I had my doubts."

"What in the realms were you thinking?" Mohg demanded of Finnbhear, gesturing at the woman with his dagger. "A werewolf, of all things! Did you honestly think she could be trusted?!?"

"As if you didn't already suspect her to be one," Finnbhear snapped back. "Have some common sense! No normal werewolf would have helped us the way she has."

"Silence," the prince commanded, glaring at both elves before turning back to the werewolf. Holding his arm to his chest, the prince leaned forward to get a good look at their prisoner. "Why did you attack me?"

With his trust betrayed so quickly, Finnbhear was not about to loosen his grip on the struggling form in his arms, no matter how much he came into contact with the more delicate portions of her flesh. He did let the woman sit up, but he continued to hold her. She tossed her hair from her eyes and glared at the prince. "Let me go," she said imperiously, kicking viciously.

"We might," Bodb said, motioning Finnbhear and Mohg to remain silent. "You helped us after all. But I want to know why you just tried to kill me."

"What does it matter?" Mohg muttered. "She made the attempt, now let's kill her and move on!" Bodb's withering glance silenced the elf.

The woman stopped struggling to raise her nose haughtily into the air, lips tight and eyes closed. Mohg moved to guard her rear, then made a hissing sound through his teeth. Finnbhear's eyebrows shot upward. He knew that sound, and it was not a promising one.

"Look at this," Mohg said, pointing. Bodb leaned around while Finnbhear craned his head to see. The woman resumed her struggling, screaming nonsense. It was all Finnbhear could do to keep his grip.

"Hold still!" Finnbhear said, wrapping his legs around her as well. Pinned, the woman wriggled and cursed. Bodb crouched, inspected her backside, then stood back up grinning.

"I was wondering when one of your kind would show up," Bodb said to her. "Too bad that Mark you wear is permanent. You were helping us until you were sure of who I was, weren't you? That can be the only explanation. She's Marked by Moirfenn, Finnbhear. See for yourself."

Smarting with betrayal, Finnbhear sighed and nodded to Mohg. "Get some rope," he said. "We'll tie her so she can't get loose regardless of the form she takes."

"You can't leave me here!" the woman screamed with sudden panic. "Not with the Feral Beasts abroad! I'll be killed!"

"Nay, lass," Mohg said as he scavenged among their scattered belongings until he found a suitable coil. "We wouldn't do that. Not right away, anyway."

They bound her wrists and ankles tightly, then wound the rope around her neck and secured her to one of the stones. She whimpered when they were through but otherwise said nothing. Bodb tended his wounds in silence. Finnbhear sat by the fire, brooding.

She had looked so familiar – and what with the gifts she had brought – that he had automatically assumed she was a friend. Finnbhear had grown accustomed to being taken care of by the magical denizens of the land. So much so, that he obviously took it for granted. His foolishness had almost gotten the prince killed. The others had trusted him enough to let him do it, which only added to his burden of guilt.

But she had defended them against the Fell beasts. And she had fed them nightly, saving them from having to eat the less palatable road tack they had in their bags. She had plenty of chances to kill the prince before now. Mark of Moirfenn or not, there was more to this wolflet than met the eye. The evidence said as much. Stabs of pity went through him when he saw how they had to truss her up. Like a pig.

It did not matter that the Mark of Moirfenn was on her shoulder. She had helped him and up until then had seemed friendly. The prince should have watched his tongue around her. He had insulted her twice, Mohg had attacked her with a sword, and now they expected her to be grateful for sharing their company. It was they who should be grateful to her.

He waited until Bodb and Mohg were asleep that night, then crouched next to her. "I don't understand," he whispered, not expecting an answer. "You helped us, you stayed near us... You had a thousand chances to kill the prince. Why try now, in the open like that? Who are you? Are you fey, or are you Moirfenn's servant? Could you be both?"

"I'm a friend," she said. "I helped you, didn't I? Untie me."

Temptation pulled at Finnbhear. "I could," he said thoughtfully, "but you would try to kill His Highness again. Like it or not, I've been contracted to protect him."

The woman looked away as if to say she might or might not attack, given certain circumstances. "Untie me," she said again.

Finnbhear almost reached for the ropes, then he realized what was happening. "Glamour," he hissed, feeling the spell break instantly. "No wonder we trusted you. It was part of your glamour spell!"

"You always were hard to trick that way, Silver Fox," the woman said. Her sharp-toothed grin flashed in the dark. She was still a shy creature, but now Finnbhear saw she was determined as well.

"Who are you?" Finnbhear demanded, clenching his fists before him.

"Don't you remember me?" She laughed barkingly. Mohg and Bodb stirred in their sleep but did not wake. Finnbhear searched her face for clues, but she obviously had said all she wanted. Closing her eyes, she tried to get comfortable and fall asleep.

Finnbhear crawled a short distance away and spent his watch trying to resurface memories of her face.

CHAPTER NINE
"PELT AND PRIDE"

With a crick in her neck and legs dead from lack of circulation, Aramina awoke. The early morning chilled her to the bone, and she could no longer ignore her discomfort. She wanted to complain but figured her three captors were not good listeners. Instead she settled for locking glares with Mohg, who obviously had never forgiven her that stolen breakfast.

"Morning," the prince said to her with an amiable grin. He approached with a bowl of stew between his hands. "Hungry?"

"Yes," Aramina admitted warily, thinking of all the rabbits she had caught to feed these three.

"Open wide," the prince said. He held up a spoon of stew and blew on it as if she were a small child. His blue eyes twinkled with amusement. She ignored it and dutifully let him spoon feed her.

"Now, girl," Mohg said, stomping his way to them and holding his naked sword. "We must decide what to do with you."

Trembling inside with terror, Aramina put on a brave face and looked the burly elf in the eyes once more. One glamour was broken, but there were other tricks to count on. She shifted against the stone, touching it with her fingers.

Bodb set the bowl down and made himself comfortable on the ground. "Might I inquire if you're the only one sent after me?" he asked mildly.

"Go ahead," Aramina said.

"But I might not expect an answer," Bodb said dryly. "I can assume then that you are alone, and if we kill you we'll have no more problems... for a few days at least."

"Oh, I'm alone." Aramina's smile suggested otherwise. "Except for you three."

Finnbhear sat by the dying fire, listening to the exchange. He muttered, "She's telling the truth, that much I can tell. But there's something she's not saying."

"Good, Silver Fox," Aramina crooned. "Can you read my mind and tell them what next?"

Finnbhear shook his head and continued to stare at the coals. Mohg fingered his sword after a long look at his partner. "I don't like this," he said to Bodb. "She's bewitched him. I knew it from the minute he brought her into the camp."

"You should have said something," Bodb quipped.

"Aye," Mohg said, cowed. "We were all bewitched. And poor Finnbhear is still trapped."

Bodb stared at Finnbhear. "No," he said slowly. "What enchantment there was is broken. I don't understand just how, but it is done."

Aramina tried to kick the prince, but the rope held her fast. "Are you going to kill me?" she demanded. "Get it over with then!" She spat at him angrily.

The prince laughed. It was infuriating. "We'll take you with us," he said. "You'll have to walk, of course, thanks to those beasts from yesterday."

"At least let me rub my arms and legs," she whined. "I'm numb all over."

At Bodb's consenting nod, Mohg released Aramina from the stone but kept the rope to her neck tied. She shook her legs first, rubbing her ankles, until she felt enough sensation to stand. Then she walked in circles around the camp.

"Hurry it up," Mohg growled.

"Let the others get ready while you're waiting," Aramina suggested. "It will be a while, I think, before I feel right. You owe me that much, after all those coneys you devoured. Now, don't you?"

There were other ways to skin a rabbit. She had been forced to play her hand early this time, but with the right resources she could gain another opportunity. Her plan just needed a bit of work.

She walked from stone to stone, touching each with the casual brush of her fingers. In her mind, she remembered her first days, days she had spent with Raori...

"It matters not how the spell is cast," Raori said, as if quoting. More than likely, he was. His memory was perfect. He was seated at a small table on an old barrel—his only furniture save for a small pallet of cloth in the corner—facing an old lamp. "So long as the intent is in your mind, the spell is as good as done. I can light this lamp by snapping my fingers," he snapped, and the lamp blazed into life, "and extinguish it the same way. I could also clap my hands, whistle–"

"Or hop on one foot?" Aramina said with a yawn.

Raori blinked, his concentration utterly broken. The lamp sputtered. "Oh," he said, "I didn't know you were there."

"Obviously," Aramina said dryly, leaning against the door frame to Raori's tiny room. Raori had only been staying in the temple a few moons. As far as she knew, Aramina was the only one he spoke with... outside of himself, it now seemed.

"I was just practicing methods," Raori said with a small blush. "I'm to be tested on the 'morrow. If only I had the Moonstone! My power would be strengthened a thousand fold, and I would never need a teacher again!" This last part he cried wistfully as he stood, stretching his arms to the ceiling.

"Hrm," Aramina said, fighting back a laugh. The lad could be so dramatic sometimes. "People keep mentioning this Moonstone. It must be very special."

"Oh, it is," Raori said, quick to reassure her. "Folk say it fell from the moon and landed in a sea of Éire, and so great was its power that an entire kingdom was destroyed by waves higher than the tallest tree. Our greatest wizards raised it from the ocean floor five generations ago, and they keep it safe in the Alberech Academy south of Giduain. Why, I've even heard that touching it cures you of everything, even of missing limbs!"

"So, it gives you more power and heals your ailments, but does it give you control of these newfound gifts?"

"Well, no," Raori faltered, running his fingers through his hair. "I suppose that only comes with practice." .

"Then, my all means, let us practice together."

"But, you're just a servant! I mean," Raori faltered, "how can you know magic, when you're not being taught? Uh..."

"To the first, you should learn not to judge so quickly. To the second, let me surprise you," Aramina said. "There's just one stipulation, if I help you."

"Which is?"

"You keep it a secret."

She took him away from the temple and the city into the forest fields where a pile of wood awaited them. Raori did not know where she had found the wood or if some woodsman had left it there to be collected later. He asked once, nervous that they were stealing the fruit of someone else's labor. Aramina laughed, delighted by this boy's innocence, and did not answer him. She arranged limbs and sticks for better burning. Raori looked first at the wood, then at her.

"I already know how to light a fire," he complained.

"Ah, but we are here to practice technique." Aramina let her nose rumple with a grin. "This wood won't light by average means. Try it."

With a shrug, Raori snapped his fingers. He clapped. He blinked. Then, with grim determination, he rolled up his sleeves and drew sacred symbols in the air. His arms made majestic sweeps.

The wood mocked him, unlit.

"Told you," Aramina said.

"How–" Raori sputtered.

"Watch," Aramina laughed, ignoring his question. She extended an unshod foot into the air and wriggled her big toe. A spark jumped across the wood. Raori shook his head, disbelieving. "You, yourself, said it's all intent." Aramina coughed, and the spark vanished.

"Yes, but how did you keep the wood–"

"No buts!" Aramina grabbed Raori's hands and laughed again. "Just dance!!"

And together, they danced wildly around a blazing fire.

She was almost finished, and her captors had apparently taken no notice to what she was really doing. Unable to resist a gloating smile at Mohg, she yawned widely and stretched leisurely against the final stone.

Now was her chance. There were many ways to open a ley line, and Aramina knew at least seven. The quickest, and perhaps least known, was a three word chant the pixies used. Touching the stones had been only to ground herself. Now, she was ready. Idly scratching the earth with one foot, she softly began the chant.

A large hand clamped over her mouth and callouses scratched her cheeks. Arms gripped her sides. Finnbhear said, "Where did you think to take us, if the ring worked?" He tightened his grip.

Aramina spat the final word, the sounds muffled. She cursed and attempted to bite Finnbhear's hand. Anything could happen now that the Silver Fox had interfered. Fae magic was the trickiest kind.

Intent! At that moment, she intended to be rid of the Silver Fox somehow. Even if it meant by his death.

"I never even caught it," said Mohg sheepishly. "She's very sneaky."

"Give it up," Finnbhear hissed. "Bodb will cut your fingers off first." The sound of a sword being released from its scabbard sliced the air.

It was a desperate move, but Aramina had to try. She kicked out, twisting her body, and stumbled to run. Bodb's sword cut into her thigh. Biting back her cry, she pulled at the rope around her neck. She could feel blood coursing down her leg, falling to the ground.

Blood and fae magic – here – gods, what a combination...

The stones were humming like angry bees. Finnbhear himself took hold of her rope. Aramina pulled back, and then the air expanded around them.

The four of them stood in the white light of the ley line. Only, it felt different, more alive. Dangerous.

It's the blood. Aramina looked around, knowing it would not be long before they were found. By her. If the ghost got involved, then Aramina's plans would be foiled. She was not the smartest creature, but her instincts were sound. In the past, she often did strange things only to learn that the sensible option meant her death. In that way, she was more elf than canine or even lupine.

Right now, the sensible option was to get away from the ley line, and fast. For once, she agreed.

Finnbhear still had a grip on the ropes that tied her. Bodb, sword still in hand, looked leery as if he expected to be attacked by a hoard. Aramina smiled to herself, despite her nervous fear. His bravery was wasted. Something watched them. Aramina could feel it hiding in the light like a thief in shadow. There was blood here, and the watcher knew hunger.

Finnbhear jerked on the rope. "You got us here," he said, "but you can't force us to go your way."

"Maybe not," Aramina said. She reached out, gathered some light into her hand, and touched the rope around her neck. The strands parted in cinders. "But I will go my way, thank you."

Finnbhear and Mohg both rushed her at the same time. She ducked beneath Bodb's sword swipe and slipped to the side, out of Finnbhear's reach. Laughing, she danced away from them and skipped into the light. Behind her they shouted, but she left the three elves behind quickly. Neither of them were any match for her speed.

She stepped off the ley line at first opportunity, tumbling to the ground at a dead run. She tripped and landed, sprawling, just beyond the ring of stones. The light still gleamed behind her. Fear seized her, and she scrambled in the dirt to get away.

"Don't leave me alone!" someone wailed. Aramina shifted form and streaked across the terrain. Behind her a scream of outrage thundered through the air.

The werewolf never stopped running. For an instant, she regretted that it was her the ghost had followed and not the three elves who surely never knew it was there. Then she was swallowed in the urgency of flight and stopped thinking at all.

***

Raori put the stone away and stared pensively at his boots. The fur was getting thin around the toes. He would have to replace them soon, providing he lived long enough to do so.

"What did you see?" Duinn asked. Everyone clustered around Raori like children eager for their grandfather's horror stories.

"The Priestess got away," Raori said. "She's running right for us." He told his teammates what he had seen, leaving out only the watchful eyes that glimmered in the light of the ley line. There would be time enough to worry about that later, Raori decided privately.

"We'll meet her," Eahn said decisively. "Then we'll wring some answers out of that pelt of hers. Prideful idiot, trying to do it alone!"

"And she should have tried sooner," Duinn complained. "When I think of all those nights that she was nearby and those idiots could have been spelled to sleep, I just want to kick her from here to the mortal realm!"

Following Raori, they rode at their fastest pace. The terrain looked familiar because he had seen it all before, while looking through the stone. Unerringly he turned his horse toward the ley gate where Aramina had reentered the world. It never occurred to Raori that he might be leading his companions in the wrong direction, even after Duinn muttered those doubtful sentiments to his horse's swiveling ears. The Northern Thorn complained bitterly to Picket about Aramina's past and current misdeeds. Raori gritted his teeth in an effort to keep calm.

When the ground started to get spongy and more damp than usual, Raori put his crystal away. "She should be somewhere around here," he said to the others. "But I don't know where she has run or even which way. The crystal lost her a while back. Still, she followed the prince and his company that way before," the mage pointed, "so from here we should be able to pick up a trail to the old ley gate, at least."

Eahn dismounted Picket, who shook his mane gratefully. The pooka was tired of Eahn's ceaseless tirade. When the Northern Thorn changed into his animal form, a boar, the pooka snorted softly. Now his ears could rest while Eahn lead the way. The elf-now-pig snuffled the ground, searching for the werewolf's scent among the other smells found along the forest floor.

Suddenly, the werewolf crashed out of the bush and streaked past them. "Catch her!" Raori shouted, turning his horse about smartly and slapping her rump. The pooka whinnied as he sprang into a gallop, glad to be in action. Even Eahn squealed in excitement, changing into two-legged form and running after the wolf-dog.

A pool loomed up ahead. The werewolf veered at the last minute to go around it, slid at the banks, and plunged into the water. Yelping once, she floundered in the water before finding footing. She dragged herself back onto shore, whimpering. By then the rest of The Five had caught up with her.

Eahn was the first to reach her. He grabbed the scruff of her neck and hauled her further inland. She did not struggle. Her sides heaved with exhaustion as she lay in the mud. Blood pooled at her side.

"Oh no," Raori moaned, dismounting and rushing to her. He cradled her head in his lap, stroking her pelt. "Aramina? Can you hear me? Oh no, Duinn..." Raori's eyes locked with the dwarf's in a pleading look. "Help her."

As a blacksmith, Duinn knew certain secrets to do with healing. Despite his formidable skill with the halberd, his main function with the group had always been to mend things, be it equipment or bodies. When he killed it was always clean and quick, for he hated to see anything suffer. When he healed, he did the best he could for the same reason.

Still, he hesitated. "First I want to know what she told them," he said. "Do they know we live? Do they expect us or not?"

The werewolf made no move as she lay soaking Raori's lap. Eahn crouched next to them, touched Aramina's sodden pelt, and fixed Raori with an unflinching gaze. "How long did she remain a dog?" he asked Raori.

"What does that have to do with anything?" Raori demanded. "She's hurt, Duinn! I think it's deep." He tried to probe her fur, looking for a wound. He found it on her back leg.

"Answer me!" Eahn said, holding up a hand to keep Duinn back. "How long?"

Raori shrugged. "Most of the time," he said. "Duinn, here it is. Just slow the bleeding a little. We can't let her die, not like Leannahn."

Silence fell around them. Raori realized he must be the only one who had remembered their sixth member until now. Cursing himself for a fool, he gritted his teeth and began tearing strips of cloth from his clothing. If necessary, he would bandage Aramina's wound and take care of her himself. The silence around him continued.

Finally, Picket pawed the earth as if to say he had remembered all along. Eahn's eyes were still fixed and intent on Raori. Duinn turned away, obviously uncomfortable.

"She stayed a wolf-dog most of the time," Eahn said. He spat to the side. "She probably doesn't remember us. You hold a fell beast in your lap."

The young mage shook his head vehemently. "Impossible," he said. "She had to stay a wolf-dog as part of her disguise. She turned human when they caught her after the attack on the prince failed. She can't be going mad!" He bowed his head and clutched the werewolf. Aramina whined but otherwise did not move.

"We should kill her now," Duinn said. He pulled out his dagger. The sun reflected off its edge with a bright flash. "We should do it while we can, before she turns on us."

"I won't allow it!" Raori shouted, struggling to stand against the heavy weight of the werewolf. Eahn's rough hand pushed him down and held him.

"Leave it," Eahn said to Duinn. "Heal this wretched beast. We'll tie her and see what's the truth. But," he turned back to Raori, "if she is turning Feral, it'll be you who cuts her throat. And a mercy, too."

Raori told himself Eahn was wrong while Duinn administered the dwarven healing. The werewolf howled and tried to stand when the pain became too much. Dwarf magic did the job but paid little attention to the patient's discomfort.

Inwardly, Raori hoped that Duinn's magic would ultimately make Aramina shift form and become humanoid again, even if it was to stop the dwarf's administrations. Despite Raori's silent urging, she did not lose control of her lupine form. When it was over, a wolf-dog still lay in his lap.

It can't be, he thought. Duinn bound the werewolf's feet and fastened a muzzle for her out of some spare leather. "Aramina," Raori whispered to her. "You have to change back."

She never did. Like a dead thing, she lay where they left her even when enticed with the smell of fresh meat. Duinn called it shock, but they all knew what he really meant. Aramina was turning Feral, half mad, and was liable to do anything. They had to watch her closely.

Raori could not stand the sight of her. When it was his turn to take watch that night, he sat on a rock jutting over the pool and stared into the water. He could hear the water gurgling pleasantly below him.

He picked up a pebble and skipped it across the water. Something squawked in the dark and flapped into the bushes. Probably, he had hit a water fowl of some kind. If he went to look, he would not find it, but Raori was tempted to try. His personal list of favorite meals included duck.

"That wasn't very nice," said a small voice near his feet.

Raori scooted back, drew his sword, and scanned the area. "Who goes there?" he whispered. Belatedly, he thought to call an alarm. He drew breath for a shout.

Bubbly laughter tinkled its way through the night, cutting his cry short. "Won't do any good if I don't want them to wake up. It was I who pulled the wolf-shaped one into the water and made her sleep. The same goes for the others."

A tiny figure pulled herself onto the rock from below. She was no bigger than Raori's hand and looked as delicate as spun glass. Large eyes regarded him with an inner light. For legs she had a fish tail with exaggerated fins, beautiful but unsuitable for swimming.

"Greetings, sprite," Raori said, courteously for lack of anything else he could do. "Is this your pond?"

The sprite giggled. "Of course! And that was one of my children you hit with yon pebble."

"My most profound apologies," Raori said with what he hoped was the right amount of regret. "Had I known you and your children were here, I would have made sure we camped farther away so as not to disturb you."

The sprite huffed. "Well, the poor dear is likely to bruise. And what shall I tell him? That it was an accident?" She slapped her tail against the rock. "They get little enough sleep as it is, my poor dears."

Raori looked at the sleeping bulk of Eahn. Idly, he decided the sprite could spell her children to sleep as she had done his companions. Perhaps Raori could wake them, but to risk it might anger the sprite further. She were amicable enough at the moment.

"What can I do?" he asked dutifully.

"Help us," the sprite said, leaning forward to give Raori an ample view of her tiny bosom. It was attractive enough but failed to capture Raori's attention. Raori wished the wineskins were not empty. Now would have been a good time for a drink.

"There's something trapped within the old ley gate," the sprite said ominously. "Help it out."

Raori stopped wishing for the wineskin. Suddenly he was craving it, urgently. "Oh," he said. He had a feeling he knew what she meant and hoped he would not have to inquire further.

"That way," the sprite said, pointing.

"Right now?"

"Yessss." Her hiss sounded dangerous and spurred Raori off the rock. He paused, looking back at the quiet mounds his companions made in the dark. "I won't release them," the sprite said. "Not until you do what I want! The Feral one especially."

Resolutely, Raori drudged his way through the brush. The sprite's final comment had sent his thoughts into a spiral plunge. Surely she had not meant Aramina when she said "Feral," but who else could she have been talking about. Raori did not want to think about it, but fear kept it alive in his mind. If Aramina were indeed going feral, she would have to die.

Finally, he came within sight of the ancient stones. They were dark silhouettes jutting against the night sky. The mage could feel no life within them, and the overgrowth told him that it had been years since this place had been visited. He looked at the stones for a long moment, unsure of what to do. Finally he went from stone to stone, casting magic to invoke the gate.

Nothing happened. Raori repeated the steps, stood back, and still nothing happened. On impulse, Raori put his forehead to one of the stones and concentrated on the place's atma. He could feel it pulsing through the stones, like a heartbeat. Perhaps if he prodded it just so...

The light came from everywhere. Raori opened his eyes and clung to the rock as if it were a lifeline. Something was coming from within the light: a form which fought to keep its shape. It walked up to the mage and stood before him. For a small eternity, the two beings faced one another.

"I knew it was you," Raori said. The rock was a solid comfort between his arms. He tightened his grip.

"I just saw Aramina," the silhouette said. "Are you tracking her?"

"No," Raori said. "We have her."

The silhouette slid closer and thereby gained better detail. Now he could make out a mouth, eyes, and the delicate curve of a chin. He wanted to close his eyes, to find he was home with a full bottle of ale at his side, to be anything or anywhere else but here, talking with... with... her.

"Is Picket with you?" An inevitable question.

"Yes." His fingers were beginning to cramp, but he dare not release his hold. She watched him with silvery eyes. *Too proud to ask*, Raori thought. *Some things never change.*

"Where are you bound?"

"A mission," Raori said, shifting his grip. Then he took the plunge. It was what she wanted, anyway, and he could think of no other way to distract her. "We could use you."

The ghost hovered nearer still, placing her lips bare inches from Raori's face. "Then take me out of here," she whispered. Was her tremble the spirit remembering its body or the only way she could express her anticipation? Her ghostly breath chilled Raori's cheeks.

"How?" Raori squeaked, telling himself that his friends would never wake unless he did this. Sprite charms were complicated affairs and deadly when tampered with. At least in this, one good might come of it.

With clammy fingers, the ghost pried Raori away from his stone. She pulled him into the light with surprising gentleness. Raori followed her mutely, expecting that these were his last seconds. "Remember." Plucking Raori's dagger from his waist, she whispered again. "Remember."

The dagger was sharp from years of habitual honing. Raori did not feel the cut until after it had begun to bleed. Staring down at his bleeding palm, helpless in the ghost's spell, he could only watch as she cupped his hand to her.

Remember...

Birgha was buried with its master, Fhion, in a place only Vighn knew. The Six were hard put keeping to their animal forms while watching Vighn, who was naturally suspicious of everything and seemed to know something was up. Several times they had encountered wards and curses in Vighn's attempt to keep them away. The last time, Duinn's ankle was sprained and Eahn was burned in the face. Three months had passed, and finally they knew success.

"Ah," Leannahn hissed from her place in the bushes. She and Duinn watched Vighn climb through the rocks in Éire alone. The others ranged around him in their separate forms except for Picket, who had been sold to Vighn a couple of weeks before. The pooka snorted from his tether nearby. Undoubtedly he was bored, which served him right. The rest of them had to suffer with rain and colds while he had been warm in a barn. Leannahn thought it only fair.

Vighn reached the top of the mound and sat a moment to rest. Once he had been a formidable opponent to the people of Fion. Now he was grey, balding, and tired easily. Privately Leannahn sneered at her uncle's fears. This man was no match for her alone, much less against all six of them.

Rested, Vighn stood and began moving rocks to one side. "At last!" Leannahn hissed to Duinn, who nodded silently. The air tensed with the elves' waiting. Vighn rolled the last rock aside and crept into a small hole.

Leannahn left the bushes and crept silently up the hill. She could feel Duinn following her, a shadow. A light flickered from the hole in the hill. Leannahn crept to the edge and paused, listening.

Silence. Peeping around the corner and into the hole's darkness, Leannahn saw the old man. The hole was deep, and he was sitting in the far back atop a heap of gold, picking his teeth. He cackled to himself as he fingered his wealth. The dried corpse of his father lay nearby on a stone slab. The spear Birgha lay in a corner.

"We'll run in and simply grab it," Leannahn whispered. "He's just an old man. What can he do to stop us?"

Duinn said nothing. This was Leannahn's adventure: her chance to prove herself in the eyes of MacKegan. If she made a mistake, they could very well die. But, it was her mistake to make.

Leannahn's animal form was a large ferret. She took the form gladly, wasting no time to rush into the grave and chatter loudly just inches from the old man's feet. The old man shouted, clutching a handful of gold to his breast. "Don't you think I know what you are?" Vighn demanded. "Get out!"

The ferret rushed at Vighn, who tried to kick her. Dodging him, Leannahn turned abruptly and ran for the spear. Dropping the gold in his excitement, Vighn stumbled forward, too late to stop her. Leannahn had the spear between her teeth and bounded out of the cave as if it were lighter than air.

"Thief!" shouted Vighn as he clambered out of the opening. Duinn ran like mad after the ferret, who bounded over the stones easily. Picket whinnied, tore loose from his tether, and intercepted the ferret. With a rehearsed motion, the ferret tossed the spear into Picket's mouth and dove into the bushes.

The old man was weeping openly as he stumbled down the hill recklessly after the pooka. Duinn came speeding after Picket with the ferret loping alongside him. A wolf howled in the distance; Aramina. The dwarf grinned in spite of himself. This was promising to be an easy venture, after all. The old man was soon left behind with only his cries of "Thief! Thief!" keeping pace with the company.

The Six met in a designated spot not far from the tomb. Picket shifted to his human form and held up the spear proudly. The others shed their animal shapes happily and passed the spear from hand to hand so they each could caress it in turn. Leannahn was wild with triumph. She snatched the spear from Picket and shook it wildly.

"Easy!" she cried. "It was too easy! Now we can take this back to my uncle and prove to him once and for all how worthy I am for anything he wishes of me!" She laughed, throwing her head back to let her hair cascade in golden waves down her back.

"Aye, let's take it to him, then," Eahn said. "Come now. We should hurry." And he started up a nearby hill towards the ley gate they had arrived there in.

Something exploded in the forest nearby, setting trees and bushes on fire. Startled, the Six threw themselves flat to the earth. As the explosion's roar died away, the spear started to hum madly. Leannahn's eyes widened as she stared at the object still in her hand.

"The old man found us!" Duinn shouted as another explosion, closer than before, ripped the earth apart. "I knew this wasn't going to be easy!"

"He's throwing fire at us!" Aramina cried.

"Run!" Eahn said. "To the ley line. Hurry!"

"I can rebuff him," Raori said, getting to his feet. He raised his arms to chant a counter spell. A bolt of lightning struck a nearby tree, knocking off limbs to shower on Raori. They were large limbs heavily laden with moss and leaves. He was buried beneath them.

Someone was pushing the branches aside or dragging the larger ones away as if they weighed nothing at all. When Raori managed to clear his eyes of debris and focus, Aramina was just shoving another branch out of the way. She grinned at the mage pulling him up. They staggered against the rising elements around them. Vighn had summoned a wind storm, and it pushed at the Six with all the strength of the old man's rage.

"How did you–" Raori began.

"No time," Eahn shouted over the wind. "Come on!"

They ran. Raori tried to formulate the counter spell as he ran, but there was no time. Not even Picket could change into his animal form as fire, rain, even hail were flung at them. The wind blew against them, against Leannahn the fiercest as she struggled, clutching her prize.

The ley line, nestled in the trees like a hidden shrine, could barely be seen through the sheet of sleet now falling around them. Raori looked behind him, saw Picket helping Leannahn along, then was knocked to the ground by a strong gust of wind. He picked himself up again and plunged onward. There was nothing he could do for anyone else.

The winds were the strongest around the ley gate. The Six managed to get within the circle of stones somehow. The spear hummed loudly enough to be heard over the unnatural storm. Aramina gave Leannahn an uneasy glance as she staggered against the wind from stone to stone, activating the gate. The light blazed forth, promising safe haven. Screaming, the spear began to shake in Leannahn's hands. MacKegan's niece stopped in her tracks, looking first at the spear and then at the forest around them. The storms stopped suddenly around them, but it was only the eye of the storm. All was silent, save for the spear's angry wailing.

"It senses a fight," Leannahn said with awe, looking at the weapon with respect. "It's refusing to come with me. Screaming for blood."

Raori ran his fingers through his hair. "We have to hurry before Vighn gets here. He's coming, I can feel it. That storm was just to slow us down. He's building up for something much worse."

"I'm not leaving it behind," Leannahn said with a proud lift of her chin. "We'll never get another chance." Around them, the light of the ley gate died as it closed. Aramina leaned, panting, against a nearby stone.

"Are you going to fight then?" Duinn asked.

"Yes."

"You'll have to," Eahn snarled. "It would take a god to start this gate again. Aramina is spent, as are we all."

Vighn appeared at the edge of the stones with the clap of thunder. The elves jumped backward in surprise. Behind him, the winds howled madly as the eye began to pass.

This was the doddering old man that Leannahn did not consider a threat? Better they face MacKegan himself, Raori thought madly. Proudly, Leannahn faced her adversary with the spear leveled.

"Give it back," the old man cried, gesturing with his hands. A ball of hot light appeared over his head. It hovered, *apparently orienting, and fixed on Leannahn. The spear's howl took on a desperate tone.*

"Come on," Picket said to Leannahn, tugging her arm. "You can't face him. Into the ley line! With your help, I think we can start it again!"

"No," Leannahn said. "Moirfenn will not be ruled by a coward." She took a step forward.

"I'm giving you one last chance," Vighn said. "Give me back my spear."

"Break the spell, Raori." Leannahn took another step forward. She was inches away from the edge of the ley line where Vighn waited.

"Do what Vighn says," Raori urged. Picket and the others crouched within the ring of stones, able in their exhaustion only to watch Leannahn and the old man face each other off. "I don't have time to break his spell." He had crooked his fingers even before the words finished leaving his lips, for he had expected Leannahn's stormy glance. Vighn saw him, screeched his anger, and let the storm loose.

The wind's blast threw them backward just as his energy light struck. Raori, his face pressed in the earth, dimly made out the figure of Aramina and someone else moving around him. He thought it might be Gredber, but that seemed wrong. Gredber did not have a harp, which banged against the stranger's hips as he swayed with Aramina in a desperate dance: Dancing around the stones.

Insane. They should be running. He tried to move his arms, to pick himself up. The shock of the blast had rendered him immobile. Wildly, he looked around himself.

There was Leannahn's hand, fingers clenched as if still clutching the spear. Elsewhere he could see Leannahn's leg, and part of her thigh. Leannahn's blood was warm against his face. Raori closed his eyes, slipping into darkness...

Raori gasped with the pain of the memory and collapsed. Leannahn's ghost held his hand tightly, slipping into it like water slips into a straw. She disappeared from his sight and awareness, shrinking and becoming solid somewhere within him.

Raori curled up like a fetus, wrapped around the Spear Birgha of Allen, and slept.

Chapter Ten
"Spear of Darkness"

A cold nose shattered the peace of unconsciousness. His head pounding akin to a tavern aftermath, Raori opened his eyes to late morning. Picket leaned down, filling Raori's sight with nostrils and mane, and blew outward. "You should have called me to my watch," Duinn said, "before running into the wild to commit suicide. That's not like you, Raori."

Everyone was there, packed and ready to move on. Aramina pranced in front of Raori, wagging her tail and panting happily. Seemingly for the first time Raori realized she acted more like a dog than a wolf. He shook his head. That was not his thought.

His fingers were still wrapped around the spear.

Duinn was watching guardedly with his sword drawn, the tip pointed ever so slightly at the mage. Eahn walked from stone to stone, musing quietly. Raori groaned, using the spear to get to his feet. Only Picket and Aramina were pleased to see him alive.

"I thought this place looked familiar," Eahn said. He nodded to the spear. "How did you get it out? We thought it was destroyed with Leannahn."

"It was buried in the atma," Raori heard himself say. "It only took a little twist to recover it." Horrified, he bit his lip to keep from saying more.

They can't know the truth yet, Leannahn's voice said inside his mind. Someday, but right now they'd try to destroy me. Besides, that's not completely a lie.

"You're the mage," Eahn was saying while Leannahn spoke. "We can use it against Silver Fox. And at least there is no old man this side of the gates to kill us for it."

"The Silver Fox?" Raori croaked. "Here?"

"Aramina told us," Eahn said. The werewolf snorted. "He guards the prince, although he doesn't seem to remember us."

"Why should he?" Raori asked with a groan. "He thinks us dead." Only now did he realize who the older elf had been all along. He wanted to kick himself. Finnbhear had always remained ambiguous within the wizard's stone. There was something about of his makeup that blurred the reception.

"He never recognized the Priestess," Eahn said with a shrug. "At any rate, Birgha will be an asset. Good work you remembered we had lost it here."

"When did you wake up?" Raori asked as memory seeped into his mind. He hoped the asrai would be happy now that they ley gate would no longer be haunted by MacKegan's murdered niece.

"Late," growled Duinn. "Missed half the morning and without a guard to protect us, too. Our lives are not worth the price of that spear, MacGuinnan!"

"You cut your hand!" Aramina cried, suddenly human and pressing herself against Raori. She pried the spear from his grip and inspected his palm.

"It's not serious," Duinn said at Aramina's imploring look. He sheathed his sword, having decided there would be no harm from Raori nor the spear. "Can't go healing every bruise he gets. Serves him right for leaving us unguarded."

Picket nosed Raori gently, blowing against him. "He says you can ride him today," Aramina translated. "I'll double with you. Picket won't mind." She grinned, wrinkling her nose. It was an expression Raori returned without hesitation. She always had that effect on him. It felt good to be near her again. She nuzzled his palm as if to say she had missed him.

"Make haste," Eahn said, mounting his horse and giving the reins a shake. "We've lost a lot of time. The prince won't have made that mistake. We'll have to ride the ley line." Briefly he recounted Aramina's adventures.

"Take me to the place," Raori said to Aramina. Somewhere in his mind, Leannahn stirred and stretched ethereal fingers outward. He clamped tight fingers on his mind and refused to let up. "I can cast for them from there and see which way they went."

***

Aramina led them to a ley gate just off the main highway to Cnos Fada. From there, Raori's crystal guided the way over the ley line and to another gate further north. They rode in the prince's tracks with Raori, atop Picket, at the lead. Eahn rode slightly behind the young mage and watched with steady eyes. Aramina nestled behind Raori, holding on as if she planned to never let go. The spear was strapped to his back but did not seem to get in her way.

Once ever so often, Raori lifted his hand to touch the spear's shaft. Always, he looked at his hand as if he had never seen it before and lowered it slowly. His other hand absently held a piece of Picket's mane almost fondly.

Eahn exchanged a glance with Duinn. The mage was an odd sight, even for himself, and between the blacksmith and the farmer there was concern.

"Ah, Joalie," Eahn whispered to himself. If only she could see him now; riding with two fell beasts in the making, a refractory dwarf, and a mortal-loving pooka.

He had never understood Picket, but then again he had never tried. Of the group, Picket was the one he could tolerate the most. Picket fell in love with any mortal woman (or mare) that happened to cross his path, but fortunately for his teammates those trysts never lasted long. Eahn always felt that Picket should find another of his own kind and settle down, as he himself had done, but he did not think the pooka was capable of commitment.

Still, he was better company than the werewolf. Eahn's eyes narrowed whenever he glanced Aramina's way. The werewolf pretended not to notice; their rivalry had been going on for centuries. One day, Eahn knew, he would do something about her. He just needed his master's blessing.

Raori signaled for Picket to stop and dismounted. Aramina slid down after him to stand close and silent. "They camped here last night," Raori said, scuffing the ashes of an old fire with his foot. "I cannot read beyond this moment."

"The Silver Fox knows you were watching then," Duinn growled. "He must've counter-spelled us."

Eahn spat. "Doesn't matter," said he. "We know where they're headed. Can't be more than a day's ride. They'll be there by nightfall. We'll be there later than that."

Raori seemed about to say something, but chewed his lip instead. Aramina mistook it.

"I told them nothing!" she said suddenly, drawing away from Raori. She gestured to her leg. "Would the prince have cut an ally?"

"Be still," Eahn commanded, slicing the air with his hand. "You're sometimes more trouble than you're worth, Priestess." He glared at her, wishing he could cut out her tongue.

Cowed, Aramina went to the pooka and leaned against him with her back to them. Raori rushed to her side, trying to reconcile her feelings. Eahn spat in their direction, then turned to the deserted camp.

"How long do you think until they crown the sprat king?" he asked Duinn in a low tone. Aramina refused to look at Raori, who was practically on one knee before her. No doubt he was pleading his love; a redundant and futile gesture on his part. The mage was long on memory but short on common sense when it came to Aramina.

"Three days at the least," Duinn said. "Once they've reached Cnos Fada they might think themselves safe and take longer." Picket sidestepped away from the werewolf abruptly. Aramina, losing her balance, pitched forward. Raori caught her, still talking

"Doubtful." Eahn scratched his chin thoughtfully. "Aramina's mistake will rush them along. We'll be lucky to get within the walls, I'm sure of it, and luckier still to salvage anything from here." He glared at the werewolf, who was still in the embrace of the young sorcerer. From nowhere, as was her talent, Aramina brought out the talisman.

They had not much time left. It was bad enough that Bodb Derg had reached Cnos Fada, despite strict orders not to allow him to do so. Were they in Moirfenn, the Priestess would be suffering greatly for her idiocy. Now it was up to them to see it never came to that, lest they share her fate.

Watching Raori and Aramina, who were now intently studying the talisman, Eahn remembered Gredber. Likely Raori did too, and Aramina would have no choice. Where was the darkling, then, while his chosen possession played games with Raori's heart?

"We'll ride through the night," Eahn said decisively. The dwarf nodded. "We'll ride until our horses drop and Picket is forced to carry us all."

Aramina slumped on Raori's back as evening fell over the riders. They saw no one, not unusual, but it worried them all the same. Patrols could be pacing them in the hills, or stalking them from behind.

A wolf howled in the distance. Aramina sat up with a jerk, looking toward the sound. Raori barely noticed the change in her. His eyes looked inward, and his fists were tight. Eahn, watching the mage, experienced an unfamiliar fear. Fell mages were formidable dangers.

When asked of his health, Raori looked Eahn in the eye and assured him that all was well. Eahn knew that Raori would never lie despite the temptation. His health was fine, then. What else was wrong?

Aramina continued to tug at Raori's clothing. "Let me down," she said for perhaps the fifth time. "Please."

Picket stopped, turning his head to fix Aramina with one eye. Raori came out of his thoughts, shaking his head slightly. "Stay with us," he said. "It's dangerous this close to Cnos Fada. That might not be a true wolf out there."

The Priestess was already sliding off the pooka's back. "You understand don't you, Picket?" she asked. Then she was gone, a flash of fur in the darkness. Raori stared after her, immobile.

Eahn scowled to himself. "We'll camp here," he grumbled. Immediately everyone was dismounting and pulling at the saddlebags. Picket rolled his eyes, tossed his mane, and trotted after the werewolf.

The world was going Feral, Eahn decided after the fire was lit. Elves squandered their atma, chose the form of beast over intelligence, and wasted time serenading the moon. Where was he in all this, but trapped in the middle with the lives of his woman and unborn clinging to fate?

Raori fell asleep holding the spear and snored with his mouth open. Duinn watched him for a while, then stealthily pulled the spear out of the young mage's grip. Raori mumbled to himself and turned over.

"Never thought I would see that black thing again," Eahn said.

"Ha, I'll bet Picket never thought to see Fion again, nor be bent under the double curse of MacKegan's sight stone, too. If that can happen, so can this." Duinn admired the spear by the firelight, turning it round and testing the point with a thumb. Blood stained the tip. Birgha hummed slightly in response.

"Something is wrong with it," Duinn said. "The thing makes me nervous, and that's a fact. We need to get rid of it." Then he grunted in surprise. Somehow the spear had slipped and cut his palm. Blood ran down his arm, splashing on the shaft.

"Give me that," Eahn snapped. He never could stand to see a fool mishandle a weapon. Birgha was handed over reluctantly. Eahn gripped it expertly.

It thrummed but otherwise gave no other signs of life. As a thing of magic, Eahn found it difficult to trust. He wished he could drive it into Raori's sleeping body and leave this entire business.

A whinny shattered the distance. It was answered by a warbling howl.

"They're coming back," Duinn said. "Might want to put the spear back before they get here. There will be more chances to see it later, I'm sure."

"I doubt that somehow," Eahn muttered. He put Birgha back reluctantly. Raori gripped the spear without waking and, smiling, slipped into deeper sleep. For some reason, Eahn was reminded of a corpse.

They rode past the great gates into Cnos Fada by afternoon, next day. Aramina was the only one who gazed admiringly at the ports along the river from which it had grown. She obviously did not remember their last trip there.

People barely gave them a second glance, taking Aramina's admiration as open tourism. Eahn said nothing, afraid of discouraging what might be keeping suspicion away. Any one who remembered them would know why they were in Cnos Fada. That was, providing anyone remembered them.

Two miles down the city's main street, Aramina's looks of wonder gave way to shock and surprise. She gasped, placed a hand to her lips, and stared in horror. The others, alarmed, followed her gaze.

"They must have rebuilt it," Duinn said, admiring the structure before him. "Fairly good replica."

"No," the Priestess moaned, slipping from Picket's back. She took two hesitant steps forward. "Ah," she said after a while. "I remember now."

She turned from the hill, upon which a glittering temple stood, and continued her way down the street. Her face bore a queenly expression, as if just seeing the temple had awakened something inside. Raori barely noticed, staring at the spear the way he was. Eahn spurred his horse after Aramina.

"We need a place to stay," Raori said suddenly.

"How very astute," Eahn sneered. "And where, might I ask?"

Duinn's grin was sly. "We could ask the temple for sanctuary," he suggested.

Even Picket eyed the Priestess while contemplating the suggestion. She did not appear to have heard.

"I'll pay for tonight," Eahn said wearily. Suddenly he was very tired. In the back of his mind he could hear Joalie darning wool. He missed that. "First we need to find out when the coronation will be. And then, we have to make plans. Duinn, you and Raori find the nearest tavern and get the latest gossip. The rest of us will book a room. When you're done, Raori can use his crystal to locate us and meet with us wherever we're lodged."

"I'd rather not," Raori said quietly.

"What?" Duinn asked incredulously. "Did I hear you correctly, or are you turning down a chance to show off your magic?"

"We can stay together," Raori said. "Any gossip can be learned later, while we dine."

The others stared at the mage blankly for a minute before shrugging almost in unison. "Very well," Eahn said. "But, Raori, remember that your place with us is magic. Use it, or get left behind."

As it turned out, it was not difficult to learn the needed information. The news was all over the city and all anyone wanted to talk about. The young prince had arrived yesterday and announced he would assume the throne in seven days. The occasion would be distinguished with an enormous feast for the entire city. Families were coming from all over the country to be there. They were sneaking in under MacKegan's nose, too, but that was one skill most elves were especially good at.

There were also talk of those who were leaving the city before Moirfenn struck against them. Thing were not safe, one old man had muttered into his mead before taking his leave. It was better to watch from a distance and congratulate the winner. Aramina called him a fool and coward, but not until he was gone.

"He'll be using magic to feed the masses no doubt," Raori said knowingly when, later, they sat in their shared room over a bottle of ale. They had found an inn near the temple. It was the only place left with any room, and that was a small space barely able to fit one man comfortably.

"Too bad for the humans among them," Eahn said, feeling a sudden ray of amusement. Enchanted food was usually poison for mortals.

Picket stood at the window, looking out with sad eyes and occasionally scratching his shoulder. "It might improve matters," he said softly. To him the city looked like a massive beehive, spitting out pollution and misery. Even the palace, set aside in massive proportions, teemed with too much life. Only the temple was quiet.

"We'll burn the city again," Aramina said with enthusiasm. "Won't that be a triumph? The same city twice!"

Eahn shook his head. "It won't stop the coronation," he said. "We need to get into the palace and dispose of the prince somehow."

Everyone fell silent. The palace walls were strengthened with metal and spell. Guards, with great dogs of the mountains, were everywhere. Surely there would also be sorcerers stronger than Raori.

Of course, Raori's lack of skill was common knowledge with himself and his companions. Aramina often insisted it was more a lack of self confidence. There was not an elf alive who knew as much as he did, she boasted. Raori had stopped arguing the point ages ago.

"MacKegan is going to have us hung," Duinn said bitterly. "He said for us to kill the prince before he got here, and here he is! Why should we even bother with trying?"

"MacKegan is insane," Eahn said. "The lord may decide to laugh about the whole affair and let the brat live for another year before sending someone else to finish him off. But if we don't prove ourselves by continuing to try, we surely will be hung. I would rather take that chance than to walk to the lord and lower my head submissively for removal. If you want to at least make an attempt at staying alive, I suggest you adopt the same opinion."

"He's right," Picket grumbled. "The best thing to do with a crazy lord is humor him. At least," the pooka grinned, "until something happens to end his reign."

"Don't even joke like that," Eahn said, alarmed. "If MacKegan fell, who would be next? All of his caliber are insane, and some are even worse than him."

"We're not figuring out what to do about the prince this way," Aramina growled suddenly. "Forget MacKegan. How do we get close to that boy and his blasted puppet guard?" The others blinked, chagrined.

"The palace was not burned," Duinn said after a minute. Everyone turned to the dwarf. "The fire came not even close."

"Pity," Eahn grunted.

"Maybe not," Duinn said. Chewing on a fingernail, his eyes bored into Aramina. The werewolf became the center of attention.

She rose to her feet with the very aura of raised hackles. "No," she said. "Never again! I won't!"

"What is he talking about?" Eahn asked.

Raori, who had only been half listening, suddenly smiled. He waved his bottle of ale drunkenly: It was his sixth. "How could've I forgot?" he asked the room. "The passage under the temple! It wouldna burned... and they musta built right on top of it!"

"Of course!" Eahn smacked his forehead. "Still, that doesn't mean the opening is still there. It might just be a dead-end tunnel with the entrance inside the palace walls. We should try to think of another way."

"What other way is there?" Duinn asked. "Picket could get over the walls, that I wouldn't doubt. Aramina might be able to get in, too, but not for very long. Finnbhear knows to watch for her, which means he knows to watch for the rest of us. And, unfortunately, he knows us too well for us to infiltrate the place properly. Besides, it would take too much time. I have no doubt that we could defend ourselves. I also have no doubt the prince would get away in the meantime."

"Not to mention the kinds of wards they must have over the place," Raori said, lost in the conversation somewhere.

Aramina scowled, but said nothing.

"So far it's our only reasonable recourse," Picket said to Aramina. "Besides, Eahn is probably right. There will be no way in, and we'll have to find a more clever way of getting to the prince before MacKegan has our heads." He looked irritated, as if their lord's very name brought pain.

"Even you must suffer for the Master, Priestess. Likely nothing will happen to you." Eahn turned his back to the werewolf.

Shifting into fur and fang, Aramina slunk into the corner and curled into a tight ball. Slight breathing was her only motion.

The Five drew lots for the bed. Raori won, but relinquished it to Picket who had trouble sleeping in human form. Soon they all slept to the lullaby of Duinn's snores, which rattled the room. Eahn awoke in the night, imagining a movement. He lay quietly in his travel blanket, casting his senses about the room. Everyone was asleep, dreaming peaceably beneath the serenade of Duinn's snores. Picket kicked in his dream, whinnying softly.

Crazy. They were crazy to be here, to let Moirfenn control them so. To allow the threat of life and death shadow over them, the brave who chose immortality over an end.

It was insane to choose immortality to start with, knowing the consequences as they did. Too much regret, too much memory, too much forgetfulness could drive anyone mad. Feral.

There are many paths an elf can take on the way to going feral. Deep inside, Eahn wondered if he might have met a fork in the road.

***

Crouching beside the door, Raori breathed a sigh of relief. For a moment it had looked like Eahn was going to get up. The mage berated himself for his clumsiness. A veteran like Eahn would stir if a flea jumped sideways.

Never mind, hissed the encompassing voice of Leannahn. *Get going or I will make you.*

The spear in his hand trembled with excitement. Sighing, Raori crept his way through the halls out the front door. Once outside, he relaxed. This was territory he knew.

Following the spear's guidance, Raori walked down the streets of the mostly deserted city. It was late night, the darkest before dawn, and most citizens were asleep. A couple of harlots still lurked the shadowed streets, calling to Raori in vain. Ruffians slipped into the shadows, discouraged by Raori's trembling weapon. Somewhere, Raori knew the city guard patrolled on their horses.

A dark alley yawned suddenly to his left. Against his will Raori trudged into it, pausing a moment as his eyes adjusted to the light. Something moved in the darkness, trying not to make any sound. Raori walked toward it.

Leannahn twisted in Raori's mind. His hand shot up, flexed, and a burst of atma light flared over him. Two huddling figures crouched under a makeshift tent; a skinny mother and her malnourished child.

Perfect! screamed Leannahn, raising the weapon. Raori tried to lower it, but the ale made him weak. Leannahn laughed at his inward struggle, squelching it with an insubstantial foot.

"Leannahn, don't," he croaked.

The spear stabbed with efficient quickness. Blood splattered onto the ground and across the boy's face. He began to cry, scrambling to get away. Leannahn was swift, cutting off the child's escape before Raori had fully registered that the woman lay dead.

There! Leannahn's voice hissed. Raori's hands, clenching the spear, rose and pointed at the boy. The child whimpered and tried to press against the wall behind him. *The spear cries for blood. That one! Take him!!*

"No," Raori moaned even as his feet stepped toward the child. "Leannahn, please. Don't make me. Please..."

CHAPTER ELEVEN
"INTO THE DARK PATH"

J ust before dawn, an exhausted horse stumbled to the closed gates of Cnos Fada. The rider shouted for attention, argued with the captain of the guard for a few moments, and was finally let in. He urged his horse toward the palace, where it finally fell to the ground and lay still. Ignoring it, the rider begged admittance and won after another heated debate.

He was shown to the council hall, where elf kings of generations had held judicial court years ago. This was the first time in ages it had been occupied, and the smell of dust still hung heavy in the air. Pacing back and forth like a caged tiger, the rider jumped when Bodb Derg entered. Two guards and Finnbhear, who had been pressed into further service by the prince, followed him. Falling to his knees, the rider begged forgiveness for disturbing the prince's rest.

"It must have been important," the prince said graciously. "What is your message?"

"Lord," the rider said, "I come from Hedros, where loyal men have waited for your family's return for years. My leader asks – no, he begs – for help. The southern lord somehow discovered our loyalty, and he has marched against us. What's more, Moirfenn moves against Cnos Fada. The Village of Ramthar lies in ruins, just because two families were loyal to your clan. Troops have been seen following the Nosloraug River. They come this way."

"Indeed," Bodb said with a faint grin. "I'm not surprised." He turned to the Silver Fox. "Are you, my friend? A perfect move I would say from a strategic point of view. Keep me distracted with the threat of assassination and then attack me outright."

"As you say," Finnbhear said.

"I can expect no help from the outside," the prince mused, looking at the floor. "It's just us against MacKegan, even if that black lord crushes the world under his boot. There's too much fear in the land." Cnos Fada was only one city against an entire country. Sympathetic supporters streamed to the city every day, but still they were not enough. MacKegan's move was no small threat, even if his chosen of the Mark had not been involved.

It would not take much for the surplus sons and others who came to Cnos Fada to change their minds and leave. Or to die, for that matter; their numbers were too few.

"Yes, my lord," Finnbhear said, dutifully. Briefly, he wondered what he could do to help his new lord. He had no troops of his own. He did have scant communication with the fairy realm, but they would most likely do harm before giving aide. One did not bargain with the Fair Folk lightly, that much Finnbhear knew too well.

"Thank you," Bodb said to the rider. "Rest tonight, and tomorrow you will be given a fresh horse. Send word that I will do what I can. Your leader and all others can take refuge here in Cnos Fada, if they require it. And if I can send help, I shall."

Bowing quickly, the rider stepped out of the room. Wearily, Bodb motioned for his guards to stand outside. When he and Finnbhear were alone, he turned to the Silver Fox.

"Well, what do I do now?" he asked Finnbhear in a suddenly young voice. "I can deploy all of our small army to face this foe, leaving myself and Cnos Fada naked to attack, or I can weather this out. Our mages may or may not be up to this challenge. Most of them are young, born after the last war."

"I would deploy a third of the men with three mages," Finnbhear said. "One mage can scout ahead and learn the size of our enemy forces. Another mage can send word back to us. The third mage can put up wards and be prepared for any magical attack. If the scout finds that our army is not big enough, we will send more soldiers. Hedros, although under siege, could be a means of bringing the land back under your banner, My Lord."

"And if we run out of soldiers?"

"Where do soldiers come from?" Finnbhear asked with a wry grin. "Recruit them, my lord. Draft them if necessary."

"No drafting," the prince said firmly. "A soldier fighting against his will is no use to me. Besides, MacKegan holds all the lands around us. It isn't wise to press an enemy into service, wouldn't you agree? Let them come on their own honor. If I send help to Hedros, perhaps the others will see that where there is life there is hope. And if they come, MacKegan might be beaten at least off our doorstep..."

***

Duinn volunteered to go with Aramina to the temple. He was surprised that Raori did not want to go, although the young mage should. Raori had served with Aramina in the old temple and knew the way, if it was still open, as well as she. In fact, the mage probably knew more since his memory was the superior between the two.

Dwarf and werewolf arrived separately. Aramina was already inside when Duinn entered through the massive doors. The enormity of the place made Duinn feel smaller than usual. Even the great hall of his mountain was not so wide nor so tall. The place was very different from the original temple, not that it was very fair to expect a group of elves to get it right. Dwarves would have, Duinn reflected. Give a sensible architectural project and a dwarf could do anything.

And what a strange place this was! The walls were bare, but that was hardly noticeable past the flickering candlelight that illuminated the otherwise darkened room. Wax candles were everywhere, lining along the walls or on the various stone altars that were scattered randomly across the floor. Some of the altars were obviously new, but there were a few that looked older and even bore signs of having survived a fire. At least two of the altars were built right from the stone floor and looked weathered.

He stood where the courtyard had once been, then. Duinn grunted to himself, thinking what a waste of space to build a roof where nature once reigned supreme. For the most part, the floor was bare. Duinn's footsteps echoed from the walls as he made his way across, looking for Aramina. The room was empty except for a few elves which knelt before different altars or had left gifts of food and glittery tokens.

Things were simpler back home, where the gods could expect a civilized discussion or nothing at all. Duinn had no use for ceremonial or submissive prayer.

Aramina was found kneeling before the most weathered altar of all. It was in a back corner, mostly hidden by dark shadows and apparently neglected. Three lonely candles sputtered their last minutes nearby and were hardly enough light to see anything properly by.

He remembered that altar... it had been there in the original temple just the same as the others Duinn had found nearer to the front. Duinn had only visited the old temple once or twice, but he remembered this place because Aramina would come here often. She even had met him there once or twice at night, when they were making their plans. Duinn sighed. Sometimes, he suspected that Aramina's memory rivaled Raori's. He knew from watching that she certain had more magic than he.

Whose altar was this? Surely it did not belong to the Morrigan, but Duinn sent a prayer to her for victory anyway. The Morrigan was a warrior, and Duinn's people honored her with every blade and arrowhead they forged. It was said that she rode the wings of battle, screaming, and collected the heads of the fallen. If the Five failed to kill the prince, she would have an opportunity to do that again. Duinn apologized to her silently, hoping for his sake that they would succeed.

Duinn knelt beside the werewolf and coughed to catch her attention. She glanced at him with narrowed eyes and grinned. "It's time," Aramina whispered. Solemnly, she withdrew a knife from her boot and cut a small lock of her hair. It was placed reverently on her chosen altar where it curled, gleaming in the dim light. "Once remembered," she said when Duinn frowned curiously, "how could I forget?"

Ages ago, druids had traveled the land. Elves kept to the forest with their Sidhe cousins. There were no large buildings, just simple stacks of stone littered about the countryside. Then humans came, brought in from sluagh rides one by one. Their ways were exotic, fascinating, and even contagious. The elves changed with their human slaves even as the humans changed for the elves. Gradually, the stones took shape and form until there was very little left of the original druidry. Duinn remembered when the first temple was erected; it was a small thing that barely housed an altar with room for one man. It was even still frequented on occasion.

This temple, great ancestor of human ingenuity, made a business of worship. It was more than a way of life, it was a way to live. Intertwined forever. And Aramina, it seemed, had embraced those new ways with all her heart. She had lived in the original temple, and served longer than most would have. She used to bring gifts of eggs and bread to the high priests, all in the hopes of being raised from her lowly position to something better.

But those days were long gone, Duinn reflected. And so was the young Aramina he knew.

They withdrew from their secret corner and made for the farthest corner of the room. Duinn followed Aramina faithfully, trusting in her knowledge of the place. She paused frequently, searching the corners and cracks of the floor. Skipping new areas, she kept watch on her altar.

"Hurry up," Duinn muttered. Alarm stirred in him; fear that they might be discovered.

"I can't quite remember," Aramina whispered. "I thought it was back here, but they've changed too many things. They might have built over it and blocked it off, for all we know. This is such a stupid idea."

"I wouldn't be surprised if they had sealed it up, especially by accident," Duinn said. "Is it here, or not?"

In a back alcove, they stumbled upon another of the original altars. This one was so worn by time that the engravings were almost smooth. Aramina caressed its surface for a long moment, bowing her head over the offering bowl.

Her lips moved silently, but whether she was praying or remembering Duinn could not tell.

Lifting her head with an almost audible snap, she said, "We have to go back."

"Out there?" Duinn asked incredulously. "You're not suggesting the door is out there, in plain sight?!?"

The werewolf did not listen. She made way across the room, boldly stepping past an old woman who arranged a string of beads on one of the newer altars. A small group of people had arrived while they were snooping in the shadows; Aramina shoved her way right through them. Cries of protest echoed across the temple's ceiling.

Duinn stumped after her, biting back his shout. Aramina threw herself back into prayer position before her chosen altar, caressing the base.

Duinn knelt beside her. The Priestess ignored him. Her eyes were closed in supplication, her lips moved a silent chant, but her fingers explored the altar quickly. Duinn realized she was speaking to him. "Act like you're praying, idiot!"

Duinn obeyed. "How are we going to open it with all these fools around us?" he whispered, looking around. The newcomers were already ignoring Duinn and his friend as they each went to their favorite altars to leave today's tokens.

"We'll have only one chance," the Priestess replied calmly. Her hand caught something, twisted, and there was an almost inaudible click. "If we're quick, no one will be the wiser. Besides, I'm betting they can barely see us. This must be the darkest corner in the entire room."

A soft step behind froze them both. "Forgive me," a gentle voice said. "Perhaps I should not interrupt, but I am just surprised to find worshipers at this particular altar. Truly, it's a wonder you found it at all."

Aramina did not move. Duinn turned slowly and looked up into the eyes of a chubby man. He wore the robes of an acolyte with a blue sash of third rank. Smiling, he bowed toward Duinn.

"Do you know whose altar it is?" the acolyte asked. "It would help the temple out greatly. We tried to restore it as best as we could during the construction of this new place, however no one was left alive who knew what it was for. It's always been a curiosity with us, especially with the more historian types around here. If you could tell us, my masters would thank you a thousand times over."

Duinn had not the faintest idea. He opened his mouth with a proper lie, but lost his breath when Aramina's elbow jabbed him in the side. Tossing her hair, she sat back and surveyed their guest. "It belongs to Ansus, The Trickster," she said with a lift of her chin. "Why is it no one remembers his name, nor his symbol, here?" She touched the worn engraving of a swan adorning the bottom of an offering bowl. "This place was covered with dust when I arrived. And I see nothing else in his honor. It's disgusting."

"You are the first worshiper here in years," the acolyte responded with surprise. "Do not be offended. All your kindred must have gone from the city. All such archaic ways are still practiced outside freely I've always understood." He shuddered. "Dreadful."

"Indeed," Aramina said.

"You're here at any rate," the acolyte said. His eyes glanced over the lock of hair in the bowl. "I must apologize for disturbing your meditation. Truly I am very sorry. It was in the best interest of the temple, I assure you. We have been wondering for so long, and anything you might be able to tell us would be a great boon. Are you very devoted?" He gestured to the lock of hair.

Suddenly Aramina looked old and weary. "I was his once," she said patiently. "It is difficult to turn against one's beginnings."

The acolyte bowed shortly, obviously regretting his decision to disturb these two fine folks. Backing away, he said, "I shouldn't bother you anymore. Possibly I might have angered The Harper by disturbing your prayers, but I was curious. Only curious."

Duinn was behind him in a soft heartbeat. Aramina stood, stepped into the acolyte's face, and gave him a toothy grin. Her canines glittered wickedly in the wavering candlelight. The acolyte looked around in dismay. By some stroke of fate, no one was nearby.

"Too late," Aramina said. A burst of atma flared into her palm. She cupped it to her face, where the shadows played against the imagination. "I suspect you've seen too much. We'll just have to take you with us. The Trickster always appreciates a convert."

"Can't we put a sleep on him and leave him here?" Duinn asked.

"Not really," Aramina said. "Now, open that passageway and let's get out of here. And you, be quiet! If anyone finds us, I'll kill you first."

The acolyte nodded shallowly. From where they stood, no one else in the temple could see them unless they tried. One of the support pillars that held up the roof obstructed the view. Unfortunately for the acolyte, it also hindered anyone who might want to get to them quickly. In order to stay alive, it was apparent that he had to be cooperative.

Duinn leaned against the altar and heaved. Nothing happened at first, then slowly the altar began to slide across the floor. Sweat beaded on the dwarf's brow as he pushed, feeling the stone fighting him. This was dwarf manufacture, no doubt about it. Duinn heaved again, aware of the mechanisms sliding within the altar as they were forced to work after ages. Aramina looked around nervously as the altar made a soft grating sound. The temple seemed completely empty by then. The doorway finally opened. Fetid air escaped, making them cough.

"That's as far as I can push it," Duinn panted. The trio stared down a hole barely large enough to fit the acolyte through.

"Hurry now," Aramina said, slipping into the blackness. Her voice floated up to them. "Send our fat priest next." She lit her atma light, giving glimpses of a stone tunnel.

Without courtesy, Duinn shoved the acolyte into the hole. He fell with a squeal and landed with a dull thump. Aramina stood over his inert body and prodded him with a toe. "Up," she said. Duinn jumped down.

They gagged the acolyte with his sash and bound his hands with strips torn from the bottom of his robe. The acolyte moaned pathetically but did not fight back. His robes hung loosely around his wide girth like an oversized sack.

"Stay close to me," Aramina said, searching along one wall with her fingertips. "My light will not be as bright in here." She pulled something and above them the altar slid back into place.

It was like being buried alive – even to Duinn, who was used to enclosed, dark places.

She threw her light into the air, where it formed into a tiny ball and hovered over her head. Turning to the acolyte, she changed her mind and freed him. They waited while he rubbed his wrists.

"He'll run," Duinn growled.

"No," Aramina said in a tone Duinn remembered from old. "There is no where for him go but with us. I think he'll learn all he would ever like to know about that old altar from here forward." She reached into her shirt and pulled out the medallion. Apparently, Aramina's habit was to produce it when troubled. Reverently, she kissed it, then began to walk.

The tunnel sloped downward. The walls were smooth as glass, the floor flat and slick. The acolyte slipped often and gripped anything for support. Sometimes it was Duinn. Most times it was Aramina's outstretched hands. He apologized often.

Perhaps an hour later, they discovered the carving in the wall. Aramina paused and brightened her light so that Duinn could admire it. The acolyte bowed his head and began murmuring prayers.

"To whom do you pray?" Aramina asked sagely, tracing the image of a swan with an outstretched finger. It was one of many symbols circling a wheel. In the center was the sun which, when Duinn brushed away the dust, encompassed the moon.

"The Mother of the Gods," the acolyte whispered. "That she might hold back the hand of your Oenghus."

The Priestess laughed. It was genuine laughter of the sort Duinn had rarely heard from her. "It was not my Trickster who twisted your arm to disturb us," she said. "Now that you're with us, you should pray for his mercy instead."

No answer. The acolyte resumed his whispered prayer until Duinn took his arm and pulled him along.

Blackness blanketed everything around them like thick fog. The only light was Aramina's atma, which only illuminated a short distance ahead of them. With his underground senses, Duinn guessed they were miles deep in the earth. The tunnel went to go on forever, but it always had seemed that way. Walking last in line, Duinn watched the back of the acolyte's head in distaste. The elf was handling the circumstance martyr-like, as if the gods had chosen him for some divine purpose. When the acolyte stumbled again, Duinn neglected to offer his hand. Aramina did not notice, walking on, and the two had to hurry to catch up.

Finally, the tunnel ended with a plain wooden door. Duinn always expected something more ornate, a fine display of craftsmanship. He admitted he was slightly disappointed. He always was. Still, the door was a well-built piece of work. Duinn could see no signs of rot, except for a bit on the bottom corners. Most likely, it was protected with spells of all kinds. Knowing Aramina, there was probably something else in its making, although Duinn always had trouble guessing what.

"Open it," the she-wolf imperiously commanded. Occasionally, she treated people around her like subjects with her their queen. Duinn usually sneered and refused to obey, just to put her in her place. He almost did this time, but changed his mind. Firmly, he gripped the handle, tugged at the door, then strained when unused hinges refused to budge.

The door opened halfway and no more. The three squeezed through and stood blinking on the other side.

Soft light, full of color and soothing, played around the walls and ceiling of an enormous cavern. Stalactites and stalagmites rose to meet each other from ceiling to floor. They ranged in pastel colors of every description and reflected the light in their underworld splendor. The acolyte gasped in wonder, lifting his hands in an awed gesture. Aramina strode forward as if bored by the display: She had seen it enough to be.

Automatically, Duinn's eyes sought a dark pocket in the cavern. There lay a secret, indeed. Dragon's blood in noxious liquid pools, that is what remained hidden except for the inquisitive eye. Volatile and precious to dwarves, it could be used as a weapon or even an energy source. Nothing was more valuable to his people. Now that he remembered this place, perhaps he could return for it. But now...

Sitting on a natural rock formation a few feet from them was a young elf. He held a harp and played with unusual skill. Aramina knelt before him, gazing upward, and then lay her head by his knee.

"Come forward," the young man said, nodding to the acolyte and Duinn. He never ceased playing.

When the men stood a bare two feet from him, the harp player sighed. He set his instrument to the side and caressed Aramina's hair. "I wish you would stop bringing recruits in this way," he said to her. "Look at this one. Fat and quiet as a mouse. No potential."

"I am not as clever as you, Lord" Aramina said quietly.

The Harper appraised Duinn and the acolyte with arching eyebrows. "I can't take that one," he said with a jaunt of the chin toward Duinn. He looked familiar, but Duinn could not quite place his face yet. "He belongs to The Morrigan." Then under his breath, "Why anyone would want to worship that three-minded feral blood-monger is beyond me."

Duinn puffed his chest in pride. "She is good to my people," he said devoutly. "And I won't have anyone, not even a god, tell me otherwise."

"Don't listen to him," Aramina begged suddenly. "Duinn has been kind to me."

The Harper laughed. He turned to the acolyte, who was knelt with his head bowed. "I thought you worshiped my mother," The Harper said. "Change of heart?"

"Nay, Trickster" the acolyte said. "But I am in the presence of a god and must pay honor." He did not move.

"Rise," The Harper said, standing himself. When the acolyte rose, the harper grabbed his chin and forced him to meet his eyes. "My mother has no use for you, but I do. I claim you by rights. Well, even if I had no right I believe I would claim you. You followed my servant through the tunnel and answered my bidding."

"I know you now," Duinn said suddenly. "You're--"

The Harper released the acolyte and passed a hand before Duinn's eyes before the dwarf could finish his sentence. Blackness crowded in, stealing away thought, smell and sound. The last thing Duinn heard was the acolyte's gasp as The Harper did the same to him.

***

Someone was speaking over him in a soft monotone. The ground was cold against his cheek. There was a crick in his neck.

"He'll come around," said the voice. "Now, pay attention."

Somewhere, someone shuffled their feet. Silence. Then, another gasp.

"Don't be such a weakling," the voice snapped. As Duinn came fully into wakefulness, he realized the speaker was Aramina. "Hurry with the cup." There was a clatter as something fell to the ground. "Idiot!" the Priestess hissed.

A longer silence, punctuated only by soft breathing. Aramina said, "It's done." She giggled.

Opening his eyes, Duinn focused on a confusing picture. Aramina and the acolyte faced each other and were sideways to the world. They held a silver goblet between them. Both looked at him with dilated eyes as if regretting his accidental intrusion. With a groan, Duinn sat up.

"Good morning," the werewolf said with a cheery grin. "Thirsty?"

"No," Duinn muttered. He did not care for what was in the cup. By the look of the acolyte's face, he had not cared for it either. "How long has it been? Blast that Trickster!"

Aramina laughed. "You should have watched your tongue," she said. "He values his privacy. It is late afternoon by now, which is what we wanted anyway. The opening inside the garden is just beyond this cavern."

"I never knew about this place," the acolyte said softly, glancing around himself. He favored his arm, where a long gash marred his pale skin. Blood had stained his robes.

"No wonder," Duinn said, getting to his feet. "With everyone but us dead." He grinned for effect.

To Duinn's disappointment, the acolyte did not seem to notice. He staggered off, gazing at the world as if with newborn eyes. The Priestess gently took his good arm and began to guide him to the other side of the cavern. Duinn could not tell where the cup had gone.

"Coming, Duinn?" she called. Whatever mood had possessed her previously was gone. The look she flashed him was mischievous. Her voice held sunshine.

The tunnel curved upward, narrowing the further they went. Soon they were crawling with Duinn pushing the acolyte from behind. Aramina crept ahead of them in a sudden fit of claustrophobia. Duinn could hear her grunting ahead.

"It's stuck," she hissed. "Feels like something is blocking it."

Her atma light flared brightly in response to her frustration. Duinn could see her shoving against a stone door. Judging by her quick and excited breathing, she was getting nervous. He had never known the Priestess to get nervous with enclosed spaces.

"Let me," the dwarf said.

"No," the acolyte said suddenly. His kidnappers eyed him with mistrust. He smiled timidly. "I can do it."

With obvious misgivings, Aramina shifted into a lupine so that the acolyte had room enough to pass by her. She did not shift back but instead crouched by Duinn and watched silently. There were times she gave herself away by acting tame and friendly. This was not one of those times. Her silence and watchful posture were entirely primeval.

The acolyte knelt by the door, caressing it with his hands. He began to whisper. Duinn, despite his acute dwarven hearing, had trouble catching the words. Stone grated against stone. Beside him Aramina prepared to run. The acolyte shoved the door.

Weak illumination streamed into the tunnel, lighting crevices that had not seen the sun for years. Aramina scrabbled past Duinn and the acolyte, shooting through the foliage that overhung the opening. Slowly the acolyte crept out after her, followed by Duinn.

"They planted bushes right over it," Duinn commented with satisfaction. The aforementioned bushes lay broken against the ground and probably never would recover.

Behind them the door shut with a slamming sound. The acolyte peered into the bushes like an old woman.

"It's sealed," he said. "I don't think it was meant for anyone to enter this way."

"You're right," Duinn said. "Now, where is that blasted wolf?" Aramina had disappeared, undoubtedly scouting the area. He dare not call her.

"What if we get caught inside the palace?" the acolyte asked with faint alarm.

"Depends," Duinn said, scanning the ground for tracks. "If Aramina makes the mistake of changing form and is recognized, she's dead. Same for me. Now, you could always betray us." The dwarf shrugged. "After which I would have to kill you."

"Even after being executed yourself?" The acolyte snorted his disbelief. "Sure of yourself, are you?" He stepped into the concealment of some bushes and peaked out like a wild dryad. Duinn continued to scan the ground.

"I have my ways," Duinn said. "I'm sure The Trickster could arrange it for me, as it would entail taking revenge for his only surviving priestess."

"You mean Aramina."

"Yes," the dwarf said with a smile. "Couldn't you tell?"

"She told me," was the noncommittal answer.

Duinn finally found the faint trace of Aramina's tracks running toward the palace. He cursed the Priestess for leaving him with the acolyte.

"Maybe you should hide," the acolyte suggested in a low tone of voice.

"Maybe," Duinn answered. "But I have a priestess to catch. She's went on her own." Again, he added to himself. Eahn would not be happy.

"You won't get very far." The acolyte's voice was a mere whisper. He tried to sink further into the bushes. His belly protruded like a large hen's egg.

"Why?" Duinn asked, looking up.

Two guards had just patrolled their way into the garden. Their heads were turned in the opposite direction, so they had not noticed Duinn as of yet. The dwarf cursed. He stumbled backward, seeking concealment in the leaves as the acolyte had done. The tallest of the guards looked his way and shouted.

Duinn did not bring any large weapons with him because the temple would not have allowed it. All worshipers were required to leave their weapons at the door. All he had was his knife. He pulled it out and waited.

The tall one reached him first. With only his dagger, Duinn barely deflected his opponent's sword and dodged sideways. Dwarves looked clumsy and slow, but when pressed they could move faster than crocodiles. Before long, the guard was on the ground clutching his belly. Duinn's knife hilt protruded from between his fingers.

"Elven chain mail couldn't stop a bee sting," Duinn spat at the dying man.

The second guard had watched this with his sword drawn. Duinn casually picked up the first guard's fallen sword. Their eyes met. The guard grinned at Duinn's unspoken challenge.

"I won't have to fight," he said as the sound of running feet reached their ears. "All I have to do is keep you here."

"Blast!" Duinn lunged forward and was parried easily. Duinn moved deftly, but the guard could not be budged. He got a lucky nick on Duinn's cheek. The dwarf fell back, panting from the exertion.

"Wha–" the guard said just as the acolyte stepped out of the bushes and struck him over the head with half a brick. With a sappy expression, the guard slumped to the ground. The acolyte threw the brick to the side, made a face of terror, and put his fingers to his lips.

"I never thought he would do that," the acolyte stammered.

"Worry about it later," Duinn said. "Let's go before the rest arrive."

They were too late. A small unit of guards rushed into the garden. Within seconds the wall cornered the odd couple. In vain Duinn looked for signs of Aramina. It was obvious they were on their own.

Behind him, the acolyte threw himself on the ground. "Help me," he cried. "This crazy dwarf kidnapped me. Look what he did!" He gestured to the cut on his arm and the blood. "He was going to sacrifice me! Use me as hostage! I am a servant of the temple!"

The guards drew their swords, looking to their captain for guidance. Their captain cocked his head in curiosity. The plume in his helmet made him look like a confused rooster.

"That so?" he asked. Duinn spread his feet apart, holding the sword in front of him. "What say you, dwarf? By the look of him, the sacrifice has been made. Or maybe he's sacrificing you, eh?"

The acolyte groveled, bemoaning the whims of the gods who had put him there. He gestured repeatedly to his arm wound and the crusted blood that stained his clothes. Duinn glowered at him and the guards, swung his sword for effect.

Finally, Duinn turned and booted the acolyte's fat stomach. "Cowardly bastard!" he said. Coughing, the acolyte tried to reply. The wound on his arm was bleeding again. "I should have killed you rather than show mercy when you found us!"

"That settles it," the captain said. He signaled for his men to move forward. The acolyte scrambled behind them and huddled there. "Now, would you be so kind as to reveal who 'us' means before you die?"

Duinn attacked the nearest elf. The startled soldier fell back, but two replaced him. Duinn tried to duck and run around them to freedom, but three more soldiers cut him off. They soon had him backed to the wall. The dwarf knew he could put up a better fight, but it seemed to him there were better days to die. He relinquished his freedom after only a small struggle.

"You should have told me what I want to know," the captain said with a grim face. One of the soldiers kicked the dwarf in the groin. Two others kicked him from behind, while another slammed his fist into Duinn's head.

Rope was sent for. The acolyte stood behind the captain, staring at his feet. Blood dripped from his fingers. "Of course," said the captain as if speaking from a distance, "we have to take you into custody, acolyte. Just until we know if you're telling the truth." Duinn felt lightheaded from the beating he had just received. The state of euphoria grew stronger when someone grabbed his hands and tied them.

A startled glance at the captain, then the acolyte's eyes returned to his toes. "I understand. Go to the Blue High Priest and ask after Midna. He will know me."

When they escorted Duinn away, who could barely stagger let alone walk, they took the acolyte elsewhere. *Which is just as well*, Duinn told himself. He could possibly plead self defense concerning the dead soldiers, but outright murder on a temple servant was a hanging offense.

***

Once inside the palace and lost in the countless smells left by the inhabitants, Aramina could no longer resist the temptation. She had dashed wildly through the gardens, quickly found by guards and chased until she ran across a tile floor.

From her place in the thickest bushes of the garden, her golden-brown eyes gleamed with semi-plotted mischief. The dwarf put up a good fight, as she could only expect, before finally giving in to guards' superior numbers.. The wolf-dog remained hidden while they took her companions away. She watched while they tracked her paw prints into the castle.

They knew to look for a wolf. If the Silver Fox was still nearby, he would know to search for a woman also.

Chapter Twelve
"Rats in the Cellar"

icket snorted to himself, stamped a foreleg, and chewed boredly. He was uncomfortable. His mane and tail were matted, his hide was dusty, and flies were attracted to his sweat.

"Be still," Eahn whispered into an ear. "Leastwise you're safe unless we're recognized. And you're probably safe after that, if Finnbhear still holds a soft spot for your folk" He patted the pooka's flanks companionably before walking off to barter with the blacksmith.

Picket flicked his offended ear. Raori, sitting in Picket's new saddle, fingered his spear almost sadly. He barely noticed the occasional pebble bouncing from the street. Picket was getting annoyed when he knew it was supposed to be the other way around. The least the mage could do was pretend to be bothered.

He should be nervous, Picket decided. His beloved and the dwarf were infiltrating the palace at great risk. If they were caught, the outcome was unpredictable. Duinn would die rather than betray his friends, but Aramina was something else. She seemed odder than in the old days.

So did everyone else, for that matter. Eahn was understandably on edge. Duinn made it no secret that he was forced into this mission. Raori had always been strange, but lately he was introverted. The spear was a fascination to him.

Picket hoped it was not a Feral creature he had on his back, although the pooka did not believe the mage was becoming that way. He did not have that smell about him; Not like Aramina, who stank of it.

They should rid themselves of her. Picket chewed on the idea for an instant before spitting it out. Should of, could of. Won't. He could never do that to her, and Raori would not allow it.

However, she was a danger to the group, to the mission, and to herself. The Fell were known to turn in half an instant, then turn again to the dismay of their new allies. Most times they simply ran wild, packing with others and leading nasty lives.

Pookas were almost exempt from the situation. Picket nodded his head in instant satisfaction. His kind was half mad to begin with.

Raori stirred, shifting his spear point down. The shaft was warm against Picket's neck. Then it was gone as Raori jumped to the ground, using atma to float on the way. The mage stroked Picket's muzzle fondly. Picket brought his head back sharply, uncomfortable with such familiarity.

"Be careful," Raori said sharply, his eyes going inward. "He doesn't know." He cocked his head as he listened to something beyond the pooka's hearing. "You wouldn't let me explain before. And I am sober now. You can't control me."

The mage turned, walked down the street and was soon lost in the crowd. Picket perked his ears forward, swished his tail, and looked at the smithy. Eahn leaned casually against a beam, watching an apprentice sharpen their weapons. They did not need sharpening, but Eahn wanted them reinforced with dwarven spell. It would be a long time before he was ready to go.

Shrugging casually, Picket trotted after Raori.

At first, he feared Raori was already lost. Picket sniffed the air in an attempt to find him, but the scents of so many people drowned it out.

Swinging his head ponderously, Picket searched from side to side as he plodded along the street. Finally, he saw a likely clue. People near one end of the street were giving something a wide berth, letting it by, then closing again like waves of the ocean. Picket pointed his head in that direction.

There is something to be said about a horse, especially of the magical persuasion, when it decides to go somewhere. Two men, mistaking him for a runaway, tried to grab his halter and found themselves pulled along several feet before they let go. Those not intelligent enough to get out of the way were trod upon, and heavily. Howls of pain chorused behind Picket, who swiveled his ears in appreciation.

Everyone, it turned out, was avoiding an elf girl who was barely in the beginnings of womanhood. Gingerly, she held a bull by the reins of a halter and slowly coaxed it down the street. Apparently, it had never been to town before. Nervously it lowed and watched the world with red eyes. It froze when it saw Picket.

Picket got along with most creatures. Sheep were too stupid to care what he was. Horses sometimes shied from him but overall listened to what he had to say. Chickens and geese loved talking to him for fresh gossip. Goats were always good for a bit of mischief, usually involving the barn.

Bovines were, in a word, uncontrollable.

The bull hesitated half a moment before roaring his charge. He strained against the slight strength of the girl and her reins. She pulled back and her feet dug into the earth as the bull dragged her a good foot.

"Run!" she yelled to the world in general. "The spell won't hold it!"

The reins burst and sprayed magical motes that shimmered in the girl's hand like a soap bubble. They had been nothing more then spider silk, and the bull's rage had been too strong for them to hold it. The girl watched in horror as two tons of bull pounded toward Picket. Calmly, Picket stood very still until the bull got within feet of him. At the last second, he leaped.

It was an impossible leap for a horse. Picket, being no ordinary horse, cleared the bull's back with no effect. He landed behind the bull, turned and waited. The bull, realizing his target had moved, bawled and skidded to a stop. He turned, snorting, and reoriented.

"Move it," the girl shouted. She ran forward, throwing the silk toward the bull. Atma leapt through the air and snapped at the bull's harness. Lights shimmered across the bull's face as a new set of reins began to form. The bull charged, not noticing the girl, and the fragile tendrils of the new spell were broken.

Again Picket waited until the bull was almost upon him. He leaped, dancing a quick tattoo on the bull's cranium on his way over, and landed neatly on the ground. The girl's angry shouts turned to shock and dismay. She placed her fingers against her lips in a pretty gesture.

The bull staggered, tried to turn for another attack, then fell heavily to the ground. With a cry, the girl ran forward. Picket snorted at her. Blood trickled out of the bull's nose.

"Buffoon!" A small hand smacked Picket's muzzle from nowhere. "Imbecile! Fool!" Each epithet was punctuated by a smart smack. "Oaf!"

To the girl's surprise, her wrist was caught in the strong grip of a man's freckled hand. The hand's owner, a red-haired man with dark eyes, stood in the horse's place. A grin played around the corners of his mouth as if it was always there. Anger played on the rest of his face.

It was a bemusing combination.

"What call have you for that, now?" Picket demanded. The girl jerked her hand away and rubbed her wrist. She was no more shocked that Picket was now a man than if her laundry were dry after a summer's day.

"You killed him," she declared.

"He attacked me," the pooka said. He prodded the inert body of the bull with his foot. "Should I have let him run me over, just to please your pretty face?"

"Have you no sense around bulls??" the girl cried. "They can't stand your kind, and suddenly I don't think I can either!"

"My kind, is it?" Picket asked in fascination. "Well, will wonders never cease! And you knew me, just like that?" He snapped his fingers.

"Of course, I did!" the girl cried. "Anyone with half a bit of the Sight could see what you really were!" Suddenly she groaned, placing her hand over her eyes. "Where am I to get another gift for the coronation? Mother is going to be furious!"

Somewhere within Picket's mind, an idea stretched its limbs and felt its way around. "I can get you a new one," he said. He shook his head and sighed mournfully. "I'm sorry about your bull. I should have thought."

"Yes, you should have!" The girl's eyes flashed, looking him over. They lingered too long in certain areas. Picket realized she was blushing. "Your clothes..."

"This world," Picket complained as he let his form waver, "is overrun with the ideas of humans. Clothes are for mortals, who have a right to shame." Hooves landed firmly in the road. He shook his mane.

The girl's eyes were flashing again. "You've more to be ashamed of than I," she cried. "Treacherous beast!" She twitched her skirt and strode away, shouldering her way through the crowd of onlookers. Amazed and intrigued, Picket followed her. Those who had stopped to watch the bull fight Picket had already lost interest and were returning to their personal business. The girl took long strides past them, ignoring the pooka who trailed after her like a beloved dog. The chorus of pain-filled voices followed them as fresh feet were trodden upon.

The back gates to the city were within sight when the girl suddenly whirled around. Her flashing eyes targeted Picket. "Go away," she said. "I have to find a new bull, much thanks to you, and I don't need your help!"

Picket, deprived of human lips, shook his head and snorted.

"Go away."

Picket shook his head again.

"What do you want?" Throwing her hands into the air, the girl sighed. "What am I asking him for?" she asked the world in general. "He's a pooka. It's obvious what he wants."

Picket took two steps back to express his confusion. Shaking his mane, he bobbed his head and stepped forward again. Pressing his muzzle against her arm, he blew out gently.

"Forget it," the girl said flatly.

Picket knelt before her. The girl stood and stared at him for a long second.

"Oh," she said at last. "That." Her skirts rustled as she stepped around him. The fabric brushed against his leg as her weight settled gingerly on Picket's back. She gripped his mane tightly. "I'm warning you, pooka," she said tightly as he carefully stood back up. "One trick and it will be a harness for you!"

Prancing like a gentleman, Picket gently carried the girl past the gates. People who lived outside the city walls stopped whatever they were doing to watch the girl ride her bespeckled horse down the dirty road and to the fields beyond. Horseback riding was nothing knew to the people, but it was always of interest to see who came in and out of the city. Children shouted and laughed together as they played in the dirt or dodged pebbles that flew at them mysteriously from nowhere.

After a while, the pair came to a fork in the road, and the girl had to choose which way to go. She was confused, at first, which signals were which to tell Picket where to go. It was obvious by the way she sat that she had not ridden very much. Fortunately, the girl caught on quickly, and they were on their way with very little fuss. Picket bobbed his head, content.

The girl fetched him a sharp slap on the neck. "You're bouncing too hard," she snapped.

Picket slowed, carefully placing his hooves as he walked. The countryside yawned by as they rode in silence. They passed a small homestead, where another girl was washing clothes outside. Picket's rider signaled a halt and called merrily to the washer.

"Where did you get that horse?" the second girl asked, amazed.

"He's a pooka," the rider said proudly. "He's giving me a ride home. He killed the bull, and now I have to find another one." Irritably, the girl kicked Picket's side. The pooka grunted, but did not move. He flicked his ears at the second girl, who giggled.

"Well, he certainly has a personality on him!"

"I know. But, wouldn't Da have been impressed if he were to see me now!"

"Oh, you better be careful with him," the second girl cooed. "I can see it in his eyes. He'll play a prank on ya before the sun goes down, mind you!" She laughed.

"Oh, speaking of the sun... Let me get home, now, Dearnha. I'll see you when I come to help with the shearing!" Picket's rider kicked, and the pooka leaped away. Behind him, the washing girl squealed as dirt landed in her wash water.

The girl's fingers idly began to trace the hourglass pattern high on Picket's shoulder as she rode. She hummed to herself; a tune of contentment.

"Here," she said, suggesting with a squeeze of the knees that he should turn down a small path. Already the sounds of civilization were reaching his ears. Hens clucked while they scratched in the dirt. A pig squealed nearby. The grassy roof of a farmstead came into view just as Picket, intent on studying his surroundings, stepped into a hole and stumbled. The girl swung down and slapped his neck again.

"Oaf!" she angrily said. "You could have broken your leg! Or my neck! Watch where you're going!"

"Brighde!"

In midslap the girl's gesture turned into the casual raking of hair from her face. A middle-aged human woman came hurrying out of the house, carrying a toddler in one arm. Picket snorted, trying not to let it sound like laughter. "The pooka was nice enough to give me a ride, Mother," Brighde said meekly. "After he killed the bull." She glared at him.

Pooka stared at the girl as glimmers of understanding began to illuminate his usually dense mind. Inwardly, he winced as his earlier words came to mind. It was no wonder she had been insulted when he spoke about mortals the way he had done. He would have to mind his language around such as her, especially concerning the mortal race. Not that he should care what she thought or felt, being a complete stranger, but the pooka found himself caring all the same.

The woman curtseyed slightly, holding her child close.

"Please forgive my daughter," the woman said. "She thinks that just because her father was friends with your folk, she can take liberties." To her daughter, she said, "He was also nice enough not to dump you in a river during the ride. Get inside."

"But, Mother--"

"Get! And take Liram with you!" The toddler burbled as he was handed from mother to sister.

With a last disappointed look toward Picket, Brighde trudged into the house. Her mother measured Picket up. She sighed. Picket regarded her in the same fashion, wondering what he had gotten into.

"Daughters," she said. "Barely into womanhood and thinks she's a million years old. The bull broke the spider silk tether, didn't he?"

Picket nodded.

"I told her to use leather. And a stronger spell. She's too much like her father and doesn't listen." Another noisy sigh, one that sent a stray hair dancing across her rosy cheeks. "Well, come inside. I'll lend you some of my husband's old clothes. He won't be using them anymore. You will be staying for dinner? Certainly, you will allow us to share our humble home with you in return for the favor you did for my daughter."

Picket nodded again, feeling he could not decline if he tried. The woman's sparkling black eyes lingered on his face for a bare instant before she turned toward the house..

"You must forgive Brighde," the woman chattered as she lead the way. Picket stood outside, waiting, until she brought out a bundle of worn clothing. "Her father was a chieftain," the woman continued when she was within earshot. "He also used to play sticks and bones with one of the local Brownies. Now, for me that's no different than the day I was stolen to come live here, in Fion, but other folks thought that was something special. She's proud, is my daughter. I'm afraid it shows."

When Picket changed into his usual human form, the woman was not embarrassment by his nudity. She handed him his clothes calmly and never ceased her chatter. Picket dressed with only half an ear in the conversation.

"He brought me here when I was barely her age," the woman was saying. "Had a fancy for mortals, no doubt. He died in a local skirmish with another chieftain. (Here, let me help you with that.) Brighde was the apple of his eye. She took it hard, poor thing."

"How long ago?" Picket asked, squeezing his question into her chatter quickly. The woman shrugged fetchingly.

"Four or six seasons, perhaps. Time is hard to keep track of here in Fion."

Picket stamped in his borrowed boots, enjoying their comfort. Their former owner had been just his size. Brighde's mother fussed with his shirt, mumbling something about mending it. Inside the house, Liram started to cry. His wails were lusty and ear-splitting.

"Oh, now what did that girl do to him?" the woman demanded. "Come inside, pooka. I'll have something ready to eat soon. It's the least we can do after your help."

Picket, in a daze of almost love, followed the bustling woman into the house. It was a modest dwelling she shared with her children. There was a short flight of stairs leading to a loft which smelled of fresh hay. The hearth took up most of the bottom floor. Brighde sat on a bed of rushes in the corner, trying to soothe Liram.

"Hand him to me," the woman said in a businesslike manner. The child was soon in a corner, playing with a set of crude, wooden blocks. Brighde sulked on the bed, arms crossed."All we have to eat is some old cheese and stale bread," Brighde said with a pointed look at Picket. "The prince would not have missed the bull. I could have sold him, but now he's dead."

"Hush," her mother admonished. "You might have carved him up, also, but instead you rode this pooka for pleasure."

Brighde stood up with a shout of indignation. "He insisted! I was walking home, and he followed me!"

"I said hush!" The toddler listened intently with wide eyes as he watched his elders with one hand poised over his toys. His mother patted his head. "You know as well as I that his kind are creatures of honor. He would have helped you. It is his way."

Picket's guffaw silenced them both. "You remind me of my own mother," he said to the woman. "I am honor bound, true, but she did not hurt me. Her slaps were mere flea bites, Aihn."

"How did you know my name?" the woman asked. "Ach, I shouldn't be so foolish as to ask. You probably know more about us than we can guess." Brighde settled back onto the bed, still sulking. She had a charming way of wrinkling her chin any father would love.

"I didn't. Twas my mother's name, and it seemed the right one."

The woman nodded, accepting it.

***

Night fell in a shroud of twilight. Picket was faintly aware that he should have returned to the others a long time ago, but he was enjoying himself. Aihn fussed over him like a mother hen while Liram slept and Brighde floated around nearby, alternately pouting and staring at him in fascination. Somehow the meager meal of cheese and bread had expanded into stew loaded with chunks of meat. Everyone was full and happy.

While Picket sat by the comfort of a fire, Eahn waited in their shared room at the inn. Picket was recounting colthood tales to Aihn when Raori stumbled into the inn room, bleeding from a gash in his forehead. The Spear Birgha was clenched tightly in both fists.

"Feral beasts!" Eahn fairly shouted at the dazed mage. "All of you, mad!"

He tried to grab the spear from Raori. With sudden life, the mage jerked away and shocked Eahn with a burst of atma. The farmer fell back, out of breath, against the bed. Raori stood with the door against his back defensively. His breath came in short gasps, and he was trembling. Eahn, blowing on his fingers, noticed the blood for the first time.

"What happened?" he demanded. "Where is Picket?"

"Don't know," the mage murmured as he leaned on the spear for support. "Where is Aramina?"

"I don't know," Eahn spat nastily, daring to step close to Raori again. "Where did you go? Blast it, that dwarf and your dog were supposed to be meet us at the garden wall, and you two run off like children at the fair. Idiots!"

"Did you go?" Raori asked faintly. He slumped down the wall, melting into a flesh puddle on the floor. Eahn kicked him.

"Aye!" He spat to the side, giving Raori a break from his hateful glare. "They weren't there, and guards were everywhere. Captured, no doubt about it. It's the pit in Moirfenn for us both if we don't do something."

Raori nodded. It seemed the only thing he was capable of.

Eahn's anger disappeared suddenly. He turned from the pitiful mage and began to pace the room. "What can we do?" he asked. "The Priestess will tell them about the gate, I'm sure of it. I know of no other way in, not with the Silver Fox's guard up. This entire business is bad, I keep saying.

MacKegan was crazy to send us. He might as well have killed us outright!"

Blast that wolf! This mess was her fault, and typically it was up to him to straighten things out. When he finally got his hands on her, he would rip her throat out. It was a merciful punishment compared to what Moirfenn was prepared to deal out.

Eahn whirled suddenly, facing Raori who had managed to stand, albeit white-faced and grim. Raori blinked and lost his balance. He crashed to the floor. The spear landed across his lap.

"Find Picket," Eahn ordered. "You're the mage, do some magic. Where's that stone of yours?"

At the mention of magic, Raori's face lost what was left of its color. "I can't," he said. "It's hard enough keeping control without--" He cut himself off, lowering his eyes to the spear.

"What are you talking about?" Dread washed over Eahn. A Fell mage with possession of the Spear of Birgha was a chilling thought. Was Eahn the only sane one in the entire group?

Poor Joalie, who would never see her husband again. The babe would grow up fatherless. They would starve without him to provide. If, that is, they were not killed by Handfast and his lackeys.

He was sure no harm had come to her so far. He would have known it, as sure as he knew his own mind.

Raori struggled to stand again. With a sudden rush of pity, Eahn helped him to the bed. The mage lay there, still as death, and never released the spear.

"Are you all right?" Eahn asked. Raori's brow furrowed and his lips twitched, as if he were fighting himself. When he did not answer right away, Eahn asked again.

"I'm fine," Raori said faintly. "It's the blood. I've lost too much."

"What happened?!? Gods, heal yourself." Eahn shrugged. "With all your training, you should be able to do that much."

"No." Raori's voice held a final ring to it, as if responding to something more forcefully put than Eahn's demand. "No."

Eahn turned to the window, wondering what to do.

***

A different window, just above ground. It was a dungeon, where very little sunlight traveled. Someone stood in the dark, too short to see more than sky, also wondering what to do. Perfect hindsight replayed events, changed circumstances, made different choices.

Perfect hindsight is rarely good for anything.

Memory replayed minute details: Raori, clutching the spear like a lifeline and shunning Aramina. Eahn spitting to the side and glaring about himself with glassy eyes. Picket brooding over Aramina as if she were a mare. The acolyte blubbering on the ground, his belly shaking in a fleshy earthquake.

Behind him, a wavering light made its way to the cell door. Duinn ceased his contemplation and turned. He grunted.

"I remember you now," the Silver Fox said from the other side of the bars. He held his torch higher for a better look. "Although I thought you dead with the others. But no." His face flickered with memory and realization. Or maybe it was the firelight from his torch. "She was one of you, too. Wasn't she? How many of you are still alive? Certainly not just you two."

Duinn glared at his captor and said nothing. It did not seem to bother the tall elf, who held his torch like a warrior's trophy. *I could kill him*, Duinn thought. It was only a small matter of reaching through the bars and twisting.

"Now now," the Silver Fox said, stepping just out Duinn's reach. The dwarf growled and pulled his hands back inside the cell.

"You always were one to gloat," Duinn said.

"Not gloating," the Silver Fox replied. He set the torch in its place on the wall. "I'm trying to understand you. Your wife, daughters, the village you lived in were all destroyed by

MacKegan and yet here you are, serving him loyally. I confess I cannot make sense of it."

Duinn looked back toward the window and the imagery of freedom. There were things the Fox pried at; things Duinn had buried deep in his mind to be permanently forgotten. Fighting memory with every ounce of his being, Duinn closed his eyes and pictured his forge.

"Well," the Silver Fox said after a long silence. "I have you at last. Where you go, the others are bound to follow." He turned and walked away. Duinn was left with the torch to tame the darkness.

He sat in the darkest shadow he could find and wallowed in self pity. The day, what he could see, faded outside. Duinn knew Eahn, Picket and Raori were waiting at the wall, but they would be disappointed. Soon the last rays of sunset weakly cut across the cell.

Something whined a few feet from him. It padded to the bars of the cell, nails clicking on the hard surface of the floor. A long nose poke between the bars.

"So you weren't caught after all," Duinn whispered.

The owner of the nose sneezed.

"Get me out of here," Duinn said. "You might want to hurry about it, too. Silver Fox is ready for us. He remembers, Aramina, although I'm not sure how much. It's more than enough to get us killed, at any rate. He knows we're not dead, not that we could help that being alive and breathing before him. Get me out of here. And hurry."

The black wolf paced before the bars, then stalked away. There would be no trace of her visit, not with the entire palace on alert for her. Duinn's only hope lay with her concealment.

Despite that, he could not bring himself to pray for her safety.

Through the darkening halls of the palace, a black wolf crept from shadow to shadow. She reached the gardens and, with a sudden bound, began to run. Whether she ran from imagined enemies or real danger, she did not stop until her breath came in painful gasps. She collapsed in the darkest corner she could find.

There was joy at being free from the shackles of her humanoid body. An exhilaration at the danger around her. Interest for the first time in ages with the events of her life.

In her own way, Aramina was wondering about Raori's and the others' strange behavior, but not in a human fashion. In her primeval mind she was aware that things were strange. Raori had been so eager to see her, and suddenly he had withdrawn from everyone and everything. *Even the bottle*, the sapient part of her said.

Finnbhear, flanked by two guards, rounded a corner and walked down the hall. Aramina's ears pricked forward. The trio passed her hiding place without noticing her, much to her relief, and stopped just out of sight.

"Double the guard around the prince's chambers," the Silver Fox ordered them. "Extra patrol around the grounds, especially the gardens. Scout the area, look for tracks. Wolf tracks, mind you. Put someone near the dwarf, unobserved, and have them listen. If the bat is with them, he'll go to the window. If that happens, kill the dwarf first. We can't take any chances. Under no circumstances are you to use atma of any kind, unless in an attempt at capture. It will only excite them. Understand? Dismissed."

The guards nodded, turned smartly and went in different directions. Finnbhear did not relax until they turned the corner. Then he sagged and exhaled. Turning away from her, he reached for a nearby door, opened it and went into the room beyond. He flicked his wrist, lit the room with atma, and closed the door. Aramina slowly crept forward.

The wolf-dog paused. She knew she had to rescue Duinn before it was too late, but here was something else. This elf held a fascination for her, always had, and now she had him alone and vulnerable.

Suddenly a naked woman stood at the threshold of the room. Aramina's newly aware mind remembered what he had said. *If the bat is with them...* Gredber had not come and, oddly, had not followed her. He would not have let her go unless ordered to. Were it up to him, she would spend her entire life as his brood mate whelping his pups. Freedom would be a fantasy. He owned her, so he often said.

There was the slim possibility that he had finally grown bored with her, but somehow Aramina doubted it. She remembered the way he had looked that night when she left him. Her cheek still burned from his parting kiss.

He had used her sometimes, when she was too tired to fight him off. In the past, she had used him in turn, before she had understood completely what that meant. All rights wed them. Gredber always took their relationship much more seriously than she had.

Aramina took a tiny step forward, aware of the sounds within the room. Her acute hearing provided images of Finnbhear undressing, washing his face, preparing to sleep. Alone.

Wolves mate for life.

But I'm not a wolf! Aramina cried inside. Oh, she could take the form and hunt like one. She knew their language and all the nuances of their society. When it came down to it, however, she never felt like a wolf. All she did was assume their form, not their soul. She was a wolf-dog, plain and simple.

Leannahn used to say that Aramina was nothing more than a big dog. That she had the honor of one and the scruples besides. Leannahn had never understood what it meant to be truly free.

For half an instant, Aramina turned to leave. Then, like a diver plunging into an icy river, she opened and stepped through the door.

An arrow thunked into the wall inches from her face. Instinctively, Aramina rolled to the floor, shifting, and bounded at her adversary. Finnbhear dropped his crossbow, shifted, and grappled her fang to fang.

It was a brief encounter. Aramina flipped him neatly and pinned him. Her growl was a warning when he started to struggle. The Silver Fox immediately sagged and showed submission in the only language she would understand: He bared his throat.

Her eyes were the last to change. Naked, towering over him, she pressed him down with her body and laughed. Finnbhear shifted, too, and held her in his arms. She did not resist him.

"You're getting too old for this," she said.

"I should raise an alarm," Finnbhear said.

"Then do it."

Slowly and gently pushing her away, Finnbhear said, "Be careful. You'll get your wish."

"You wouldn't do that to such an old friend as I." Aramina grinned at him, all confidence and flash. "You want to hear what I have to say too much."

"Usually," Finnbhear said, "you greet me this way after you've gotten what you came for."

Aramina shrugged.

"Say something," Finnbhear growled.

A ripple of laughter floated through her. "It's good to see you again, Finnbhear." She leaned forward. "My comrade. You have my dwarf locked in your dungeon."

"And the acolyte? He isn't yours?"

"Oh, him." A flick of the wrist, an expression of unimportance. "Do what you will with that one."

Finnbhear rolled out of reach. His expression was thunderous, but not frightening to Aramina. She had him in her glamour; it was a trick he always fell for the moment he looked into her eyes. Indeed, he never knew he was under the spell half the time, or even how she managed to cast it so well. She liked it that way. It was her secret, and although he may not be utterly at her command, he wouldn't hurt her, either.

"I wish you and I could be on the same side," he said. "Just once."

"It doesn't matter," Aramina said softly. "It wasn't I you wanted. Where are the keys to his cell?"

"What makes you think I will tell you?"

"Because you love me."

"Enough of this. I think it's time to do something about you," Finnbhear declared, shifting into a fox again. Aramina shifted, too, but only out of the way. Silently, she released her strongest burst of atma into the Silver Fox's body. Finnbhear slumped forward, unconscious. Aramina huddled into herself, waiting for the atma to rebuild. Sparks of it, residue from what she had done, flickered across his back.

Aramina picked up the fox's small, still form and carried him to his bed. She tucked the blankets around him and stopped to watch the fabric rise and fall with his breath. Tenderly she stroked one ear and smiled to herself. He would be out until late morning.

She grabbed Finnbhear's set of keys from its hiding place in an urn and thanked The Harper for the habits of long life. Then she slipped out without a backward glance.

The survivors camped high in the hills near Nebhirrlos. The ley gate stood behind them, keeping their memory fresh with Leannahn's demise. Morale had plummeted and refused to rise as their situation looked bleaker.

Finnbhear the Silver Fox had been waiting for them with twenty soldiers at Nebhirrlos.

They, trapped between the ley line and Finnbhear's men, huddled around a small fire. Raori sat apart from them and concentrated on their wards, the only thing keeping the Silver Fox out. His face looked pinched with horror and exhaustion. Heartbroken, Picket took solace in his equine form and suffered no one's touch. Aramina stared at the ley gate in silence, as if all the answers were there. Only Duinn and Eahn remained alert.

"This is ludicrous," Eahn complained to Duinn over the fire. "Our escape waits, but we can't go because our horse and wolf won't step through. In the meantime, Raori is killing himself fighting off the Silver Fox while you and I sit here and do nothing."

The dwarf shrugged. "We called for help. Moirfenn will not let us die here. We have known nothing but success under his service. He values us."

"True," Eahn agreed with a dark scowl, "if the spells got through. But this first time we have failed him, and lost his niece and heir besides. I think it would be better to die at the Silver Fox's hands than face MacKegan now."

Somehow, they had to convince Aramina and Picket to cross back into the ley line. The closest working gate opened near enough to Jurbhean that the companions could return and face MacKegan. If they were allowed to live... A flicker of light near the stones caught Duinn's attention. The gate was opening. He turned in time to see six elves and a dwarf arrive, bathed in the light of the gate. He cursed under his breath. The Silver Fox would not miss this new arrival.

Raori groaned, confirming the dwarf's fears. "They're doubling their effort," the young mage gasped. "I can't hold them out. One of them is a mage..." He sagged to the ground, trembling with effort.

Eahn stood to welcome their rescuers as they approached. The leader, an aged elf a foot shorter than he, looked him in the eye. "I always knew your elite little band was worthless," he said with conviction. "Where is Lord MacKegan's niece? I am under orders to get her out first."

Guilty glances were exchanged among the little band. Picket stepped toward the short elf. His ears were back, and white ringed his eyes. Aramina spared only a glance at the men, then ran to help Raori. Momentarily she looked as dazed by the magical attack as he, until her atma linked with Raori's and new strength was born of the union.

The short elf noted the magic battle with a disapproving eye. "Foolish as well as worthless," he said. "You build wards and fight them off when all you have to do is step through the ley line. Then you send for help, and I have to risk my men to save your hides." He looked around, ignoring Picket's warlike stance and Eahn's calculating surveyance. "She is not here.

What has happened? MacKegan will have your heads if she is injured."

"She's dead," Aramina said with a wild laugh. Raori leaned against her, his strength spent. The wards had finally fallen. "And we will be, too."

Picket danced in place, obviously fighting his fear of the ley gate. The soldiers from Moirfenn drew their swords. Their leader barked at them to remain where they were.

"We were ordered not to engage in combat," the leader said to Eahn. "Leannahn is not here, and we are leaving. Come with us and die standing before MacKegan, or die here. The choice is yours." He turned toward his men, giving orders to return to the gate.

"You're right," Eahn said in a quiet tone that stopped the arrogant elf in his tracks. "We are what MacKegan made us: a wolf that thinks like a dog, a pooka from Éire, a dwarf with no love for metal, a drunk mage, and an elf who despises atma."

"Worthless as worn out boots," Duinn said conversationally. Picket trotted toward the ley line and stopped ahead of the elf and his men. Aramina, with Raori leaning against her, closed in on the other side.

"He's coming," Raori gasped. "He has not far to go. I had to shrink the ward borders to conserve strength."

"Now you," Eahn continued, "I think are worth a lot. Your men are efficient, yes? Each of them handpicked by MacKegan himself, too. Only the best to save the life of his niece."

The ley line flickered.

Finnbhear and his men spread out, surrounding the area in quiet stealth. The bright light of an activated gate had pushed him into pressing his advantage. He worried why, after the gate had been opened, the young mage still held the wards. It was no small feat, to be sure, that the mage had held such a large space with so little magic. But that was Raori, when sober, and sometimes when drunk. Of all the Six, Raori could be the most formidable.

It confused Finnbhear, as well, that the Six had not escaped back into the gate from the beginning. He was sure they had their reasons; a lot of their actions did not make a whole lot of sense, but most of them did. If they refused to go back into the ley gate, the question to ask was why.

If he could capture, or at least destroy, these Moirfenn spies, there would be one less weapon for MacKegan to use. Whatever their reason for avoiding the ley gate, it worked to his benefit. If only the gods would see fit to delay them until his men topped the rise of the last hill.

Finally they made it. Finnbhear raised his hand to make the signal but never dropped it. His sharp eyes studied detail, noticing each person's position. They were all dead.

His men searched the carnage for clues. Finnbhear himself searched what was left of the body of the dwarf. Six soldiers were put to digging graves.

A seventh soldier was sent to fetch a necromancer, in order to bind the werewolf's body to the earth. Werewolves, once killed, came back as vampires, so the old women said. Finnbhear decided not to take any chances.

"Looks like Moirfenn stopped them, sir," said a young soldier as he stooped to grab what was once the Northern Thorn's shoulders. "They must have done something wrong."

"Typical southern butchery," the soldier's partner agreed, grabbing the body's ankles. "Make one mistake and you're useless."

Finnbhear watched them haul the body to its hurried grave. There was no feeling of relief like he thought he would have at seeing this carnage. Moirfenn justice always turned his stomach, veteran that he was, and this more so. To turn so readily on the most loyal of your servants, who brought you whole cities without the use of an army, was madness.

There was one thing Finnbhear had learned. To keep your place as leader, and your followers in the bargain, you did not kill your best servants. It was said thousands were murdered under MacKegan's hand, but somehow these tales never came from the lips of Moirfenn's citizens themselves.

Elves, dwarves, even humans flocked to MacKegan's banner in droves. The elven lord gained ground with each day, battle or no. He had the grudging respect of the northern chieftains, even the king.

The soldiers unceremoniously threw dirt over five of the bodies. Finnbhear turned away, letting his gaze fall on the sixth. The mutilated face was turned from him, but the locks of ebony hair were sadly familiar. A fine-boned hand, though more calloused than he remembered, lay curled at her side.

Yes, by all appearances the gods had granted his wish and delayed the Six. Permanently. Against all common sense, nothing looked out place. Now he would have to tell his wife that her sister was dead. He dreaded the moment.

Across the river from The Temple of Jurbhean, five figures stumbled out of the light and clutched their ears. The very gate was screaming, the light wavered and crashed around them. Suddenly, it was gone with a crack.

Raori doubled over, began to puke on the ground. Aramina buried her face into Picket's shoulder and, wrapped in his freckled arms, wept.

"Did you see," she sobbed, "what Leannahn did to the one we took with us?" She shuddered.

"It was no worse than what we did to the others," Duinn said in a faint tone. "Wise of MacKegan to pick soldiers who resembled us."

"It was horrible," the Priestess said with a muffled cry. "Horrible. Did you see? Did you??" A hysterical note touched her voice.

"We saw," Eahn said, surprised his voice sounded neutral.

They all had seen.

CHAPTER THIRTEEN
"OUT OF THE BAG"

Darkness was comforting, like being wrapped in a womb of solitude and peace. It helped to heighten senses such as smell and sound. For a dwarf it was more a natural state of being than an inconvenience.

Duinn knew a guard was stationed near his cell out of sight. He could hear the elf shuffling, clumsily attempting to be quiet. Most humans thought elves were silent as sunshine. They would have been sorely disappointed in this fellow.

Duinn's extraordinary senses told him that somewhere in the cell with him was a colony of rats. Right outside his cell window, another elf waited with average stealth. Feet from the elf outside his cell, something on four legs crept forward.

Hearing a large predator leap on an unsuspecting man and rip him to shreds lends a lot to the imagination. Duinn grinned to himself and stood by his door. The Priestess, two-legged and grinning, fairly trotted out of the shadows, holding the keys in one hand.

"Hurry," Duinn whispered to her, looking over his shoulder to the window. The keys clinked together as the werewolf looked for the one that would fit the cell door lock. She discovered it with a triumphant "aha!" and fit it in the keyhole.

Aramina cracked the door and ushered him out. Then she shut it and tossed the keys into the cell. Duinn took a peek at the body of the unfortunate guard.

"You were right. The Silver Fox is ready for us," Aramina said, stooping to steal the dead guard's cloak. Mindless of the blood, she draped it around her naked body. "Bodb is under heavy guard. We can't possibly get to him."

"We have to try," Duinn said. "By the gods, I started this blasted mission, and I will see it through! The others have probably gone back to the inn and think us dead. They almost were right. I hate to hear Eahn's lecture, this time."

From nowhere, the medallion appeared in Aramina's hand. She kissed it and held it close. By all appearances she was praying, but Duinn did not believe it. She might have been an acolyte once, but now she was just as forsaken as he.

"I say we kill the prince while we can. There are ways to reach him," Duinn continued, faltering as he ran out of things to say.

"Yes," Aramina said, turning glittering eyes to the dwarf. "Not tonight, though. We would not make it." Her eyes narrowed.

He had seen that look before, years ago, when she suggested they burn the temple. He dreaded what she was going to say next.

"At the coronation. It will be perfect."

Duinn groaned. His anticipation had been correct.

***

Raori slept the sleep of near death. His hand never released the spear, even when his other hand flailed in the abandon of dream. Occasionally bursts of atma exploded over his bed. They were small, reflecting his battle with some imaginary enemy. Sometimes they shaped into miniature dragons that roared silently as they faded, or arrows flaming as they sank to nonexistence on the floor.

Eahn watched by the window and worried about Joalie. She was helpless at the hands of Moirfenn, and he was miles away. If any harm came to her and the babe, he would go berserk with grief. And there was nothing he could do.

The sun began to rise, casting an amber light over the world. Eahn was not a spiritual man, but he took the moment to pray to BileEll. He would sacrifice anything to know Joalie was all right and the baby provided for.

Raori stirred, moaning softly. He opened his eyes and looked at Eahn. A clearness Eahn had not seen in them for a long time reflected his image, but then it faded to the customary inhibition of the past few days. Eahn wondered if the mage had finally learned to lie; was everything as fine as Raori claimed them to be?

"Has Aramina come back yet?" Raori asked, sitting and holding his head in his free hand. "Gods, I have a headache Duinn's anvil would envy."

"No," Eahn said, spitting out the window. "Nor yet Picket."

"We'll have to find out where they are," Raori said with dread.

"There's your crystal."

"No," Raori said quickly. "No." Sliding out of bed, he lay the spear down. The action surprised Eahn, who had begun to believe Raori would never let it go. "I would not be able to see past the wards over the palace, regardless. There are other ways to find them."

"We just have to figure out where they are," Eahn spat before pointing suddenly toward the bed. "What is that spear doing to you, mage?" Walking forward, reaching for the spear, he was not surprised when Raori scooped it up and brandished it.

"Leave it alone!" the mage commanded. His hands were trembling, or it could have been the spear. Eahn blinked at what he thought was a trick of the light.

"Easy," Eahn said when Raori did not lower the weapon. By the look in the mage's eye, Eahn was dead if he made the wrong move. He swallowed hard. "Let's go downstairs and have a drink. Picket will be back soon, to be sure. Then we can find Aramina and Duinn."

"Nothing to drink," Raori said, suddenly weary. He lowered Birgha. His expression said he could not believe what he had just done. There was fear in his eyes.

Eahn wondered how to get the spear from Raori. Looking back toward the window, his eyes scanned the waking world below. Few people were about; just the usual early risers, most walking and some on horseback.

Suddenly, Eahn forgot the mage. "Picket!" he yelled out the window, leaning his muscular frame forward. Several faces turned toward his voice, but not the face of the spotted stallion making its way down the street. "Cursed creature. Picket!"

Storming out of the room, Eahn ran down the stairs of the inn and out the front door fast as he could go. He stumbled onto the street just in time to confront Picket, who stood still with an amused expression. An adolescent girl giggled from his back. She held a bundle of clothes in her hands.

Eahn grabbed one of Picket's ears and wrenched it. "Fool!" he cried. Then in a lower voice, "You leave me to meet Aramina and Duinn alone, and only now do you come back? Who is this riding your back then? Another fancy?" The pooka regarded Eahn with serious eyes. "The dwarf and the Priestess were not there, Picket. Doesn't that mean anything to you?"

Slowly, Picket nodded his head. Eahn kicked at the ground and spat. "Get over there and change to a decent form so we can talk about this," he commanded, pointing toward the inn.

Somewhere deep in his throat, the pooka made a rumbling sound. The girl sighed and slid to the ground. "You never said you had friends," she said accusingly. "Is this going to keep us from finding a new gift for the coronation?" Picket resolutely walked toward the tavern. The girl followed the pooka with an endless flow of chatter. "Who are they? Is this why you wanted to leave last night? What about Mother and my brother?"

"I think Picket's found himself a family," Raori said as he walked slowly up to Eahn. He used the spear as a walking staff, making it the most natural action in the world.

"Won't be the first time," Eahn growled.

"Hai. I swear, he takes up with them faster than water to a lake. And they fall for it, every time. It's a glamour, I tell you. Has to be." Raori ran fingers through his hair, contemplating the sky. "I remember that one girl south of MacKegan's keep. What was her name?"

"Violet, or some such," Eahn growled. "This will cause trouble, mage. Especially if he decides he has to stay with them. If we're lucky, he'll grow bored with this one as quickly as he did that one."

"Now that's not fair to the girl," Raori chuckled.

"Aye," Eahn agreed, narrowed eyes on the tavern.

"Here now, you can't be coming in here like that!" a voice inside the inn cried. "There are stables for your type! Out you go, pooka, and don't come back in until you're decent!"

"I think he's found the innkeeper, too," Raori mused.

"You leave him alone!" the girl cried shrilly. "He's mine!"

Thump! Hooves hit one wall forcefully within, and someone howled in pain. The commotion turned into curses, then more commands to get out. Picket, wearing only a pair of pants and clutching his shirt, laughingly ran outside. The girl followed, pausing only to shake her fist toward the door.

"Now we will have no place to sleep tonight," Eahn cried to the giggling pooka. "You're worse trouble than the Priestess! What have you done in there?"

"It wasn't me," Picket protested. He hugged the girl to him with pride. "It was Brighde. Kicked the poor man 'tween the legs, the little imp!"

"Get your shirt on," Raori commanded. His eyes flashed. "Just who is this girl, anyway? Take her back where you found her. We have to find the rest of our company and finish the mission besides."

"Mission?" the girl echoed.

"Never you mind," Eahn said with a murderous glance Raori's way. "Go play."

The girl lifted her chin. "I'll have you know I'm the daughter of a chief," she said haughtily.

"All the more reason for you to leave."

"She can help us," Picket said from somewhere within his shirt. He had put it on backwards and was turning it around. "She can get us into the palace, to the coronation if necessary. She knows people here."

"Can you get us inside?" Raori asked, smirking. "That would be convenient."

The girl squirmed under the sudden scrutiny. "Mayhaps," she said. "But what for? Why can't you just go yourselves?"

"Lass," Picket said, his head finally popping out from the fabric, "it's because we're not exactly welcome. We're expected, but not welcome." The pooka chuckled.

"I don't understand." The girl looked from face to face, searching for clues. "Why should you have problems if you're expected? They say the prince is real friendly..."

"Never mind," Eahn said suddenly, glaring at Picket and his blathering mouth. "Can you get us inside, or not? On second thought, forget it. We don't need a child following us around. Your sex is more trouble than its worth, and bad enough we have Aramina to worry with. She never came back last night," to Picket, "and Duinn, as well. We're dead before this adventure has begun, my friend."

"I won't be treated like I'm not here!" the girl cried, hands on her slight hips. "Picket said I could stay with him! He owes me a favor for killing that bull yesterday!"

"What bull? No. Wait. If I know Picket," Raori said somberly, turning the spear to and fro in his hands to watch the light play off the handle, "that debt was repaid before the sun rose this morning. Even if this bull was as big as a mountain."

Picket shrugged after his fashion.

"What bull?" Eahn asked, echoing the mage.

"Just get rid of the girl," Raori said, overriding Picket's answer. "We'll have to get rid of her. She'll get us into trouble. Things are bad enough without us knowing where Duinn and the Priestess are. Although I suspect they're already dead."

"I'll not have it," Picket said, protectively thrusting Brighde behind him. "You'll leave her alone."

"I can take care of myself!" the girl cried. Raori and Picket grabbed each other murderously. Birgha fell to the ground, rolling towards Eahn's feet.

"Stop! Shut up! Peace!" Eahn shouted, waving his arms madly. People passing by paused to stare. Raori and Picket stopped, their knuckles white as they clutched each other's arms. Slowly they disentangled, brushing themselves off. Catlike, Raori retrieved his spear and tried to act like nothing had happened.

"For now, we need to get off the street." Eahn sighed noisily, shaking his head. "Raori, you are going to have to use that crystal and try to see where the others are. Picket, you can very well decide what to do with your pet."

"I'm not a pet!" Brighde protested shrilly.

"Argue about it later," Picket said, pulling her along. "We can go to my place for it, although Aramina and Duinn may have trouble finding us there."

"Your place?"

***

Finnbhear opened his eyes and instantly berated himself. Aramina had fooled him again. He knew better than to trust her for an instant, knew not to even let her touch him. His shoulders were on fire, burned by her magic. The blankets were tangled around him and rubbed against raw parts of his skin.

If Bodb Derg found out about this, he would be sent home in disgrace. Being sent home would not be such a bad thing, it was the disgrace. None would respect him after that, least of all his son. The lad would probably disown him. Not that Finnbhear would mind, so much as he really did loathe the widening of an already growing rift between himself and his only child.

He wondered sometimes why he bothered at all; he had done everything he could by his boy and more. He knew he was lucky to even have a child; he was sure it was the result of some mixed breeding on one side of the family. He was not sure which. And a blessing it was, too, with so many families dying with no one to carry on names and traditions.

But, sometimes being a parent was quite frustrating. Yes, he had loved Aramina once. And once, Aramina had been more loving and kinder than the creature she was now. And she was his son's aunt...

The boy wanted his aunt's head on a pole, and after last night Finnbhear was not sure he disagreed with the lad.

Mohg had already left for home, the lucky beast. Prince Bodb had insisted the Fox stay. Finnbhear was sorely tempted to take his punishment if only to leave.

Too old for this, he berated himself as he stepped out his door with only the blankets to cover him. Shouting for the guards, he wandered the hall until he found the captain of the guard on the battlements. People scurried out of his way... No one wanted to face the frustrated Fox.

"Has anyone thought to check the prisoner?" he demanded of the plumed captain, who merely raised an eyebrow at Finnbhear's blanket arrangement.

"Nay," the captain said with a smart salute. "The lads changed shifts with no trouble."

"Where are they now?"

"Bidden and Mairk would have gone off duty, having stayed awake through the night and all the day. Their relief would be there now, listening as you ordered."

Blaming every god he could think of, Finnbhear ran for the dungeon. His blankets flapped around him like woolen wings as he bounded down stairs, shocking several ladies and a small child, and through the hall. He skidded to a halt at the dungeon door and fumbled for the handle. The thud of booted feet echoed their way to him as the captain and three of his men arrived, red-faced and panting..

Why did he run? Judging by the scene beyond the door, the crime had been committed hours ago. The guard's blood was dry and brown; his eyes stared ghoulishly at the ceiling in a last expression of dismay. The keys, winking in the morning light from where they lay in the now empty cell, teased Finnbhear with failure.

Somewhere there would be the body of the guard who was listening outside the window. It was as sure as the sun had risen.

"All of you," Finnbhear said dully, "go check the prince. Move him to a new room with twice the guards. Do what you must, but do not let anyone or anything near him."

Left alone, Finnbhear leaned against the bars of the prison cell. He felt like crying.

Triple the guard, draft everyone in Cnos Fada, and it would not be enough, he thought as later he rode his horse down the city streets. Searching faces for anyone who might resemble The Six of Moirfenn was all he could do at the moment. It was a futile act, but it kept him from going insane doing nothing indoors.

The prince was put under heavy guard in his apartments. Finnbhear had expected some kind of protest, but the young elf smiled knowingly and submitted like a guilty prisoner. A temper tantrum, threats to his life, even a scowl would have been welcome. Not this condescending compliance, as if the end would be the same no matter the act.

Things were bad enough trying to keep the prince from assassination. Threat of MacKegan's approach made it far worse. Soon Finnbhear would be called to war himself. He knew that. He was experienced, and they would need that expertise.

Guards lined the walls, patrolled the entire palace, paid special attention to the ground for signs of infiltration. The wards around the area were strengthened and maintained by seven of the strongest mages in Bodb's service. Yet the Silver Fox had a nagging feeling he was forgetting something.

Finnbhear reined his horse to a halt and looked long at the city's back gates. Traffic was slowed almost to a halt as a small detachment of soldiers searched the travelers. Surely the folk who had traveled to see the coronation, and thereby risking MacKegan's wrath, were frustrated to no end. And it all seemed so futile to Finnbhear. As if nothing mattered.

The Six would not be in the city after this. No, Finnbhear decided as he urged his horse toward the gate, they were elsewhere deciding on a final plan. Aramina had only been playing with him last night, else he would be dead for his stupidity. She was up to something, whether her companions knew it or not.

After the coronation, Bodb Derg planned to lead a sluagh ride through the human realm. Finnbhear was not sure it was a good idea. The prince's life would be in danger so long as MacKegan wanted him out of the way.

Things were simpler in Éire. Finnbhear had spent a few years on the edge of the veil and remembered them with longing. The humans lived simpler lives, with each chief priding in his hamlets and homesteads. High kings, rulers of vast lands, were foreign, baffling concepts to the mortals. A man to rule all of Éire seemed impossible, unless the tyrant-to-be wanted to face fifty bristling chieftains and their large families.

Most importantly, they had plenty of beautiful babies to be envied by the mostly barren elven women. No wonder humans were brought over the veil, where lessons might be taken by their simplicity and the bloodlines could be enriched.

Such simple, happy lives humans lived. When Finnbhear left, the tribes were just beginning to unite under one ruler with no so much a central government as a counsel of peers. Skirmishes were common between battling clans and even brothers, but it still seemed that they had everything going for them.

CHAPTER FOURTEEN
"POWER OF PRAYER"

Raori listened to Picket and Aihn argue softly in the loft. Understandably, the mortal was upset when she learned who Picket's friends were. Why she bothered to allow them to stay was beyond the mage, who sat near the single fireplace and fought the desire to curl up somewhere and sleep. Fairy glamour played heavily in Picket's situation, although Raori was unsure if it was intentional, or even if the pooka knew what it was he had done.

Eahn was outside somewhere, presumably tending to the various livestock in return for lodging. In the distance, Aihn's single cow lowed mournfully as she undoubtedly missed the bull. Faint curses floated through the modest homestead from outside; Eahn was closer to the house than expected. Raori wondered what had happened.

Brighde had been severely berated by her mother and sent to the fields with their small flock of sheep. Raori was none too sure just why the child had received a tongue lashing when it was Picket's influence that had caused the trouble, but he was not one to meddle in family affairs.

The Spear of Birgha leaned against the front door, propped against the frame. However, it did not matter where it was. Leannahn was in Raori's mind now, despite being tied to the magic of the weapon. He could feel her fluttering around in the back where he had banished her the night before. Once in a while she muttered something. He had beaten her only temporarily, and she knew it. Satisfaction oozed like fish oil from her.

It felt good to put that spear down for a while anyway. Raori flexed his fingers appreciatively, practicing a few hand positions. Nimble fingers were essential to a mage and his craft; most of the more powerful spells involved intricate finger positions and movements. Raori winced as his pinky gave him a twinge; it was sore from some unremembered abuse. He rubbed it ruefully.

The voices coming from the loft rose, then fell back to an angry murmur. Someone fumbled with the door. Guiltily, Raori fished his crystal out of his pocket and made himself look busy just as the door opened.

"Have you found them?" Eahn asked as he shut the door behind himself.

"No," Raori said. He hoped it was not too obvious that he had not been trying. To relax enough to use the crystal meant letting go of his mind. Leannahn was waiting for just such an opportunity.

Say that the wards are too strong, Leannahn suggested smugly.

No, he answered silently. *That would be a lie.*

What does one more matter? She laughed in a silvery tone. *You've been doing nothing but lie these few days. And they believe you, too. Because you don't lie!*

I haven't been lying, Raori retorted. *It's been you. You're afraid they'll figure us out and rid me of you. You're the one, telling lies through my lips.*

Are you sure?

No, he was not. Pushing his doubt down where Leannahn could not see (Could she? Why the smugness, the calculating way she watched his every move?), Raori rolled his crystal in his palm.

"The wards are too strong," Leannahn said. In Raori's mind, she laughed again. Fighting to push her back, surprised that he did not have to, Raori tried to think of some truth to soften the lie. He could not.

"Picket can find them," Eahn said. "He can go tonight."

Picket's face appeared from the loft. "Maybe I can," he said. "Why doesn't the mage use the crystal instead of playing with his fingers?"

Raori hunched his shoulders, sinking into himself like a tortoise in its shell.

Eahn looked not at Raori, but the spear. Deliberately he reached for it, slowly as if gauging everyone's reaction. Leannahn nearly screamed inside him, but Raori bit his lip and said nothing. The grizzled farmer gripped the spear tightly without sparing a glance at the mage. Leannahn hissed, subsiding to her dark corner in Raori's mind. Drumming his fingers on the spear's shaft, Eahn turned to Raori.

Leannahn had retreated as far as she could go in Raori's mind. If he wanted, he could tell the truth. She would not stop him, although he could not say why. Freedom was but a breath away.

"I'll go with Picket," Raori offered, standing. "Aramina might be hurt." It was the truth, but it was colored with feigned concern. Lately, for no reason at all, he could not have cared less. He blamed it on Leannahn.

"I never agreed to any of this," said Aihn as she appeared behind Picket. "You never told me you were MacKegan's servant, Picket. I would not have let you into my home, dead bull or no. There are still *some* who care nothing for MacKegan and his black handed ways."

"Still your tongue," Picket ordered with a flash of teeth. "Neither you nor your children will suffer, and when it is done you'll have me to stay. Is that not what you want?"

Leannahn surged upward, twisting Raori's fair countenance into an angry snarl. She stepped forward, dimly aware of how strange Raori's muscled thews felt. Helplessly, Raori was flooded with her emotions and thoughts while his body acted without him. "You can't stay with that creature!" Leannahn shouted with Raori's voice, pointing. "You should put her back in her own realm and make her forget us! Disgusting!"

Leaping from his perch, Picket landed neatly in front of Raori. His eyes showed too much white around them as he said, "You have no call telling me who to stay with. 'Tis my own life."

"You didn't always feel that way," Leannahn said miserably. She retreated to her place in Raori's mind and left him facing Picket's challenge. Averting his eyes was the only answer as he clenched and unclenched his fists. Behind him, he could hear Birgha thrumming softly in Eahn's hands. Dizziness threatened him with humiliations; it was all he could do to remain standing.

You can't let yourself be jealous, Raori told Leannahn. You're dead, and he does not know you are with me.

Her only answer was a silent wail.

The door opened without preamble, startling everyone within. Brighde paused outside, sensing the tense atmosphere, then stepped forward as if treading thin ice. "Someone comes," she said quietly.

With one last glare at Raori, Picket looked through the window outside. "A single rider," he said. "His horse is lathered, poor thing."

"Hide," Aihn said, crawling down from the loft as fast as she could go. "Hurry now. It might be a soldier, Picket, to take you away." She motioned for everyone but Brighde to get into the loft.

Raori did not like the watchful way Leannahn noted Brighde's place at her mother's side. Brighde nervously glanced his way, sweeping a stray hair from her face. Her tiny smile was for Picket, who winked at her from his hiding place. His entire way of looking at her was a father's stance, the age-old way of saying, "See her? That's my daughter. How beautiful she is."

Leannahn liked that even less than how Picket had taken up with the girl's mother overnight.

Raori never pretended to understand the ways of pookas. Perhaps Picket took this woman like a stallion steals mares from the pasture. Maybe it was instinct; he had seen Picket take a wife quicker than this more times than not. Aihn might have to share space with a herd or be content with her pooka's duplicity on the fields at night before all was said and done. There was the slim chance he might fall in love and swear loyalty so long as she lived. It was known to happen, although Picket was more the sort to wander away when he grew bored.

Leannahn snorted. Faithless, she said. She'll never know more than the grief he has given me. Or, perhaps she will know at that.

You're being silly. You're dead, Raori protested.

He promised forever, was the disdainful reply. But what is the promise of a man, of a pooka? If I were alive, things might be different. I died protecting him, you, all of you!

You died out of greed, Raori said, knowing the effort was wasted. You wanted to be strong to succeed your uncle, and in your eagerness you forgot that even you are not expendable to him.

Nothing was important enough to keep when it came to what MacKegan wanted. Even his niece, his only heir, was sacrificed in the name of a paltry weapon. The rest of them, loyal as they were, ended not only dismissed in disgust but punished.

But it was not for Leannahn's death, despite what the old lord had said. But, Raori did not like to think about that.

Outside, a horse grunted from exhaustion. Someone scratched at the house's single window.

"Who is there?" Aihn called, her voice tiny and soft compared to that of the strong and angry woman of earlier.

"Finnbhear on the prince's business," was the commanding reply. "Open up."

"How do I know you're telling the truth?" Aihn said, slowly cracking open the door and peering suspiciously outside. "The last ones came here stole three sheep and knocked down part of the fences besides. Took me and my daughter all day to put it back up!"

"As you can see, I have come here alone," Finnbhear said.

"So?" Aihn chirruped. "What defense have I against a lout like yourself? You've probably got those others hiding somewhere out there. Were my sheep tasty?" she shouted into the yard. "Have you come back for more?"

"These people that came," Finnbhear asked thoughtfully. "Were they man, elf, or dwarf?" From his hiding place, Raori could see the Silver Fox's shadow as the elf leaned against the doorframe, apparently unconcerned with Aihn's troubles. Raori knew that girth and size; he would know it in his sleep. He had never much liked the Silver Fox, he recalled absentmindedly, for all they had even shared mead a few times.

"Two elves and one pooka," Aihn said. "Devilish creatures! Stole my sheep--"

"Yes," Finnbhear said. "Is that all they did, steal a couple of sheep and knock down a fence?"

"No," Aihn said. "They tried to take my daughter, but she's got a bit of magic and managed to threatened them off. Bastards! How will we eat this winter with three less sheep than before? If this new king were noble at all he would replace them, he would! My husband was a chieftain in these parts and supported him. He died for that support, and what has that left my family? Nothing!"

"My father would have those men poked on poles!" cried Brighde from behind her mother. "He wouldn't have let a widow and her children starve. Not he!"

"Brighde," Aihn said, turning on her child with real concern. "Hush, child."

"No," said Brighde. "It's about time someone said something. If Father had not been forced to stand against Magguire in the king's name, he would be alive!"

"It's all right," Finnbhear said from outside. "I understand the child's anger. Can you tell me which way they went?"

"That way," Aihn said, thrusting one of her pudgy arms out the door.

"Thank you," Finnbhear said grudgingly. His shadow moved away from the frame, and his horse snorted when the Silver Fox regained the saddle. Soon, Raori could hear the Silver Fox's horse cantering away. Aihn withdrew with a heavy sigh and leaned against the wall in relief.

"I hope," she said to Picket, who proudly bounded to her, "that this will not become a habit in my life."

"Nay," he said, tenderly touching her face. "When I am through, we'll move to a better place. Back to Éire, even. Wherever you want."

"I want only to keep what I've fought to have," Aihn said.

"He'll hardly believe your slip of girl frightened us off with a bit of magic," Eahn muttered. "We'll have to leave as soon as possible."

Picket shook his head. "I'll leave when I'm ready and not before," the pooka said.

"He won't have gone far at any rate," Raori said, sighing. "He's not through here."

***

True to Raori's prediction, Finnbhear did not go far from Aihn's house. He cantered his horse over a low hill, dismounted, and slapped its rump to send it home. Then he shifted form and used his superior nose to snuffle the ground until he found a familiar scent.

Even had he not been able to trace Aramina by scent alone, he could tell the woman was lying merely by checking her fences. They were old and badly in need of repair. And they had been in the ground for years, with no intended replacements to be seen anywhere laying about. And of sheep; Finnbhear had no doubt the woman at least told the truth about that. Mutton was a favorite of dwarves and wolves alike.

He also did indeed doubt that her daughter could threaten away any member of those assassins by herself, even if she possessed the lost magic of Cnos Fada's first temple.

He followed the scent to the back of Aihn's house. Many voices traded arguments inside, but he ignored them. The scent told him everything. He crawled behind an empty barrel and lay down to wait

***

Picket, with Raori on his back and disguised as a woman in hopes of being mistaken for either Aihn or Brighde, cantered out of Aihn's yard just after noon. Clever, his disguise was, even if the mage said so himself. Glamour enhanced what was actually there; sheep's wool tucked in his shirt to give him a rounder appearance with his head wrapped in a long cloth. The pooka even agreed to act docile, if such a thing were possible.

Eahn had wanted the two to leave later in the day to be sure the Silver Fox was gone, but Picket impatiently insisted on leaving immediately. The farmer agreed to it, but grudgingly.

Raori sat like a resigned lump on Picket's back and barely held on when Picket chose to walk at a jolting pace. When the mage began to slide off and made no move to stop it, Picket snorted to himself and walked more sedately. Unknown to the pooka, Raori smiled to himself. There was more than one way to get Picket to behave. And he needed that from the pooka, at least, in order to maintain their fragile illusion.

He had left the spear with Eahn. A sense of freedom he had always taken for granted soared inside him. Leannahn could only hold him within a certain range of the spear. The closer they got to the city, the farther away she became. By the time the pair reached the settlements crowded outside of the city walls, Leannahn was barely a presence in the mage's mind.

Ancient, chipped and gray with age, the city's northern gates towered over elf and rider. For an instant, Raori suffered a brief memory: Watching the city burn to the ground as he stood just beyond those very gates. Someone had thought to repaint them after the fire, but that paint was cracked and peeling. Beneath it, scars of damage defined the earlier time.

Without hesitation, Raori guided Picket in. He ignored the guards flanking the entrance. They were there mostly for show. The real guards, Raori knew, were hidden nearby. He prayed to Ansus that his disguise was complete enough to fool them. It was not until they were well out of sight and moving slowly through the busy streets, that he relaxed.

Immediately, Raori got rid of the wool and unwrapped his head. They went to the inn first, hoping there was some small sign of Aramina or Duinn. The innkeeper said he had not seen anyone and suggested that Raori find better things to do than annoy an innkeeper with trivial matters. Raori thanked the fat elf coldly.

Resolutely, he pulled his crystal from his pouch and fingered it. He was sure Leannahn could not do anything as far as he was from the spear. In the back of his mind she was a distant presence and preoccupied by something else. Carefully he plunged his mind into the crystal and began to search.

Immediately, Leannahn's spirit rose screaming to the surface. Too late, Raori tried to push her down. Laughing, she batted him away and seized his body. They were one for a split second filled with the tingling of life. Drunk with the sweetness of breath, Leannahn kicked Picket's flank and sent him hurtling down the street.

Raori, aware of the indignant shouts and Picket's willing confusion, swam in a sea of murky darkness.

Was this where he had banished her? Flecks of red flashed before his ghostly eyes. It was a sterile place and oddly, he felt nothing; no anger, nor joy, not even heat and cold. There was only a vibration around him. Eternity dwelt here.

Clarity suffused him for the first time in his life. He remembered his family, faces he loved that had chosen to grow old and die. Aramina was giggling as he bungled a simple spell and sent flower petals swirling everywhere. Leannahn laying her head on Picket's shoulder, lying dead in pieces.

Leannahn's spirit ripping the soldier's entrails out while he screamed, still alive.

When asked, Raori denied being a believer in any sort of god or higher power. He always viewed the various spirits and gods as stronger beings to be treated as royalty. Sometimes he wondered if they ever heard the occasional prayer he sent whispering to the sky, especially since he had never received an answer. There were times he suspected the gods did not exist, at least not for him.

Perhaps in this in-between place, the gods could hear him. He certainly needed some divine intervention. Raori began to pray fervently. Oenghus had to hear him and grant him freedom. Leannahn had spent her chance and now was stealing his own. She had to be stopped, and he was not strong enough to do it alone. Did not the god owe him, Raori, some sort of favor after all the mischief the mage had caused in his honor? Are not the gods ever powerful and capable of putting Leannahn back into her place, wherever it might be?

I hear you, my son, a quiet voice said.

Ansus, I have no choice but to put myself into your hands. Please do something.

I am not Ansus, but I will help you, was the reply. Golden motes of light danced with each syllable spoken.

Not Ansus? Who was it, could he trust it? God or no, Raori could not bring himself to trust one like Carmen, goddess of ignorance and destruction. Despite the deeds of his past, Raori had a fondness for sentimental things like puppies and children. The Bard had always catered to that by enhancing Raori's love for laughter.

Raori wondered if one of the smaller gods, worshiped mainly by isolated clans, had answered his prayer. There were dozens of gods, some called by different names by various clans and most known only to a few. It could be anyone, anything. How could he trust it?

You have always known me. Through your family.

BileEll? Disbelieving, muted by his slight inability to feel, Raori remembered how long he had spurned his family's tradition. BileEll was one of the more well-known deities in Fion, this was true, but Raori had only devoted what little time he thought to spare from a sense of obligation. He had never cared for this... apparently glowing... deity. And yet, another emotion washed away his doubt.

Hope surged in Raori's breast. And it was strong.

Soft hands, golden in Raori's mental sight, cupped him in their giant palms and lifted him up. The thumbs were calloused, but the glittering skin was not rough to the touch. The murkiness thinned, dropped below him. He could see the sky, reached his fingers out to touch the clouds and found them as intangible as he.

The world jolted, bounced, jogged him around like a sack of potatoes. Clinging to Picket's mane, he shouted for the pooka to stop. Picket did, skidding and stopping neatly at the end of an alley.

Raori tumbled to the ground, coughing. His lungs were on fire. The pooka danced away from him, snorting and looking alarmed. Gasping, Raori tried to reassure Picket but the words could not come.

Freckled arms picked him up and patted his back until he could breathe again. Dimly Raori noticed that he was covered in tomato juice. A stray chicken feather clung to his lip. He tried to blow it off. Somewhere along the way, he had also lost most of his disguise.

"It's been too long since I enjoyed such a wild ride," Picket said as he delicately plucked the feather from Raori's lip. "You ride like Leannahn, I do believe."

"Whatever," Raori said, searching himself. "Where is my crystal?"

"You were holding it when you went crazy and must have dropped it," Picket said with a wry grin. He patted Raori's back. "I could take you with me to Éire without regret, for sure."

Raori groaned. Without the crystal, he had no hope of finding Aramina and Duinn. Inwardly he cringed for Leannahn's automatic laughter. It did not come. Missing! She was missing from his mind.

"What's gone is gone," Raori said with satisfaction, getting to his feet. Picket looked dubious. A mage's attachment to his bit of crystal was legendary. But Raori was not talking about his crystal.

He looked at the pooka for what seemed like the first time in years. "Picket, you have got to start wearing clothes."

***

Civilization usually begins when one person gets tired of civilized life and moves away from that institution. They find the most lonely and unpopulated spot they can and settle down there usually because they like the privacy, the country, or for freedom. Then, to their surprise, they discover just how difficult the simple life can be, and they either move to a place that has at least one other settler, or they invite their relatives to share the house. As more people arrive, the area naturally becomes more inhabited. More people, usually relatives of the relatives of the first settler, follow and also settle nearby. Gradually a village is born.

Towns are built from villages. From towns cities are born, recreating what the original settler moved to escape from. Spreading out, the city cringes away from its beginnings. The wealthy move outward. Places that were once populated by the rich fall to ruin, becoming slums and harboring forgotten stories and imprints left by former residents.

Cnos Fada had its poor inhabitants, too. They lived mostly on the city outskirts in small houses, or mounds, although Cnos Fada also had its slums closer to the center. Most of the poor were humans or descendants of humans. Many lived along the city walls in the alleys or just outside the city wall in places built alongside.

Cnos Fada's origin had begun near a small circle of stones. When asked, natives to the area speculated the stones were the foundation to Cnos Fada's first settlement. Like bleached bones in the grass, lay these stones, worn by the elements. No one built near them. Lovers wandered there in the afternoons, but few stayed long.

Aramina stood there now.

She had left Duinn in the city, near the inn, in case the others should come looking for them. He was to meet her at the western gate when the sun set. Until then she had an errand to take care of.

The stones lay lifeless, withholding their histories.

She could remember when they were larger and carved by the people who had placed them there. No, they were not humans, these monument makers, nor elf. They had been something older and wilder, with a love for justice and truth. Like ghosts were they, riding the wind with invisible ease and kissing the cheeks of those who listened for them.

How long? So long ago, things have changed. Especially I. Aramina pushed those thoughts down, knowing that to become aware of time would be to approach her age.

Reverently she stepped forward into the ring and onward to the center. A wind picked up, whipped at the cloak she wore. The blood crusting it made it heavy. Its movements around her were slow and ponderous.

She knelt, opening her mind in prayer. Somewhere behind it all, a flickering memory of days when this step was unnecessary nagged at her. Once upon a time, it was a mere matter of finding a secluded spot to speak her mind for everything to listen. The ravages of civilization had effected even her, as everything must be with time. Pushing the thought down, Aramina focused her attention on her knees and the grass that surrounded them. The presence of a myriad personalities enveloped her, wrapped her in their existence.

Master, help me. I have tried to obey your orders, but I am failing. My tricks are turning them against me. I fear they will not listen. And Eahn–

You worry needlessly, was the dark reply, interrupting what might otherwise have become a stream of babble. *Continue as you are.*

Please. So simple a plea, but she cringed inside. Her memory told her she had been punished in the past for less.

Continue, was the stern command. The aura of the voice had darkened, but no sentence was levied. Suddenly her god was gone, but the others – the little ones – remained. The wind caressed her, pulled her cloak away gently. She was reminded of Gredber's last kiss.

Won't you run with us? asked the youthful voices.

"I'm sorry, little ones," Aramina whispered as she stood. "I have so much to do."

Always too much to do, complained one of the spirits. You never play with us anymore.

You brought this on yourself, you know, said another one. You could have stayed with us, but you went into the city.

The trouble began when she went south, said a wise voice to another. Always the lover of justice, our Aramina.

"We all were lovers of justice," Aramina said in weak defense.

Yes, came a chorus of agreement. No lies, hate lies. They hurt. All life is precious and deserves respect. Remember. Aramina. You remember, always remember, when you were better than this.

"I remember." She retrieved her cloak, feeling the stiff fabric in her hands. It should have been washed, but somehow that did not matter.

Between two sides, she had chosen to play the more exciting role. Perhaps it was considered evil by those who did not understand the laws of balance. At the time, she had reveled in the feel of adrenaline, an unfamiliar heartbeat, and pumping emotions. Naiveté kept her from understanding that darkness grows, just as does good. Too much of either throws the balance askew. Had she been wiser, she would not have chosen sides at all.

Please play with us, said the first voice with a plaintive whine. All its companions soon joined it. *Please please please please please please...*

"How can I resist?" she said with a giggle. The cloak fell back to the ground, forgotten.

CHAPTER FIFTEEN
"FREED BY FIRE"

Eahn despised being left behind, alone, with the human woman and her brats. For lack of anything to do, he sat by the homestead's single window and stared blankly into the yard. The girl played with Raori's spear. Raori had decreed it not to be touched. Eahn supposed if Raori wanted it left alone, he should have hidden it rather than setting it by the door.

The woman was feeding the baby in the loft. She refused to come down. Eahn felt her disapproving looks through the ceiling. He wished he could put her eyes out.

He saw the dust clouds before the riders reached the house. He had been waiting, knowing to expect this. He opened the door before the newcomers dismounted. His sword was casually propped against the door frame.

"Dias duit," Eahn said formally, nodding to each sorcerer in turn.

"Where are the rest of your team?" the apparent leader demanded. He was a handsome figure in his black finery. Eahn hated him for it.

"Couldn't tell you to be sure," Eahn drawled. "In the city I expect, working for MacKegan's pleasure. Do my wife and child still live?"

The old sorcerer nudged the youngest with his elbow. "As if Handfast would kill such easy sport!" His cackle cut the air unpleasantly.

"They will be dead by nightfall unless you have something favorable to report. Not that it matters. MacKegan is only playing with you, and we all know it. You should spare yourselves some pain and go back to him to die. It's what he wants," said the one in black. He twisted his fingers. A blinding bolt of atma hit the house with a loud crack. "We will know when your companions return!"

Most efficient, these sorcerers, who remounted and spurred their horses back the way they came. Their policy was to never spare time for idle chatter. Say your piece and leave. Eahn went back inside and lay his sword on the table. The baby was crying.

Eahn happened to look up at Brighde. She had dropped the spear and was staring fixedly at her palm. Blood dripped to the floor in a steady rhythm.

***

Duinn, bored and unhappy, chased a few flies from his face and blew outward in a noisy explosion. If anyone dared to tell him how much he resembled Picket right then, he would have cold-cocked them on the jaw. Not that anyone who knew him would have dared to make the comparison.

An army of ants, collecting food from somewhere within the inn, marched back and forth across the dusty soil. Boredly, Duinn watched them a while, drawing lines across their path with one stumpy finger to occasionally confuse them. He chanced to look up and only just caught sight of Raori mounting Picket as he left the inn. Forgetting the ants, Duinn sauntered in their direction. There was no hurry, or so he thought.

Just as he drew near enough to shout, Raori sent Picket thundering down the street.

He stood where Raori and Pooka had been, open-mouthed, until he saw something glittering on the ground. Just as an urchin was reaching to pick it up, he placed his boot over it.

The child looked into his wicked grin and fled. Duinn claimed his prize.

Raori's crystal. It was still warm from use. He held it up to the sun and squinted, trying to see if any fading images were trapped within. The light cleared a bright path through it and, cut by the prism of the crystal's center, made a rainbow across the dwarf's face.

Smiling at his first luck for days, Duinn cupped the crystal in his callused palms and whispered, "Find your master."

Jumping, then sliding across his palm, the crystal almost got away. The dwarf held it tightly, almost losing it as it jerked against his fingers, and followed its direction. It pulled him through busy streets and alleyways, through the market and almost over a woman with squashed tomatoes and a dozen loose chickens, all excitedly clucking as they eluded the woman's efforts to capture them.

For a few moments, the crystal stopped moving. Duinn did not let this dishearten him, for the disaster of the pooka's passage was easy to follow. Pigs milled about, knocking over stalls in the market while their owners desperately tried to catch them. More chickens squawked as they made their bid for freedom, running from trampled cages. Feathers were everywhere. Angry merchants shouted after Picket, then at each other.

When finally the crystal came back to life, Duinn was getting worried. The trail had started to get cold, having led out of the market and down another alley. Eagerly Duinn picked up his pace, pushing anyone aside who got in the way.

He caught up with the duo just as Raori was mounting Picket to leave again. Shouting their names, he ran at his fastest speed. Raori had just lifted his head to the shout when Duinn slid, panting, up to them.

"Feral madness!" the dwarf cursed. "Had you waited before taking your wild ride through the city you might have noticed me. I was right there at the inn, waiting for you."

Raori laughed. It was the first laughter Duinn had heard from him in days. "It wasn't my fault," he said merrily. "At any rate, you've found us. Right? Come to think of it, why didn't you meet with Eahn as planned? What happened to you?"

"What happened? What do you think?!" Waving his arms in the air, Duinn went into a full rant. "We were captured, of course! Blast that Priestess! She took off just as we got inside, leaving me with a hostage she had taken fancy to, and the guards had me in no time! Now she's gone outside the city for some reason she won't name and left me to wait for you at the inn!" His voice echoed off the alley walls, reiterating his statements with force.

Picket tossed his mane. "A hostage? Do you still have them?" Raori translated more from habit than necessity. Duinn could understand Picket easily, if he chose to do so.

"Of course not!" Duinn shouted. "Didn't I just tell you we got captured? We were lucky to escape, sure enough, but now the Silver Fox knows we're here. Worse, he knows we're alive!"

"We can't have expected that old ploy to work forever," Raori said in a reasonable tone. "So, we faked our deaths... and then we continued to run around, very much alive and causing further trouble in Fion. The Silver Fox was bound to recognize us sooner or later. I'm surprised it waited this long. No, make that astounded. At any rate, the Priestess has her reasons for what she does," Picket grunted, neither agreeing nor disagreeing, "and they're always good ones, Duinn, and to our benefit. You should know that at least."

"Well," Duinn said, letting his anger deflate, "lucky for me, you dropped your crystal. Or lucky for you, depending on how you want to look at it." He handed the crystal to Raori, noting Raori's look of satisfaction as he lifted it to the sun, inspecting it.

"Is Aramina to meet us at the inn?" Raori asked after tucking his crystal safely away. "Waiting outside the walls? Tell me, what is going on?"

Raori pulled Duinn onto Picket's back behind him. The dwarf settled uncomfortably, remembering earlier mishaps riding the pooka, and began to recount his adventure in the palace. Picket was unusually docile as they listened. Soon, they reached the gate where Aramina was supposed to meet them. No one was there except an old drunk and two street urchins who ran at the sight of them.

"Blasted, motherlorn, feral, stinking, cowardly," Duinn muttered when he reached the end of his tale. He slid off of Picket's back and began to pace. "Simple-minded, wasted, idiotic, twisted--"

Raori's laughter cut him off. "Enough!" he cried, throwing his hands up in surrender. "I understand, you're furious with Aramina. All right!"

"She at least could have the courtesy to come back a little early," Duinn growled, kicking a nearby pebble across the street. "I hate waiting. I think I hate waiting more than Leannahn ever did. That wolf-woman should be here."

"Since we both know she won't be for a while," Raori said, taking note of the sun's position, "I could do with a drink."

The black wolf did not approach the city gate until the cover of darkness was deep. She sniffed, swiveling her ears as she listened, and followed the sound of breathing. The trio huddled by the wall never knew of her until she was in their midst. The shortest of the trio yelled, groping for his missing weaponry, and fell to cursing.

"Don't do that!" Duinn whispered fiercely. "You nearly cost me the rest of my life."

Raori chuckled, reaching down to ruffle Aramina's fur. "My, but we're feeling secretive tonight," he slurred. He smelled strongly of ale and leaned against Picket's barrel body for support.

The pooka looked at the wolf and snorted as if to say the mage had been like this all afternoon. He sounded tired, but satisfied.

"Now we can leave," Duinn said. "Picket, you lead the way. Carry Raori, or we'll be all night."

The wolf paced away a few steps, stopped, then trotted back. She gently took Raori's hand between her teeth and tugged.

"I think our Priestess has more on her mind than goin' home," Raori said. Too drunk to resist, he staggered with Aramina's pull.

"No," Duinn said. "I'm tired, I've been in the sun all day waiting for you to come back, and I want to get some sleep." He crossed his arms and glowered at the werewolf, daring her with his eyes. "Don't forget, we've got important matters to tend to. Or have you forgotten?"

Raori staggered further away from them, still following the general direction Aramina had indicated.

"No," Duinn said again.

Picket snorted curiously and plodded forward a few steps after Raori. The wolf silently padded ahead of the drunk mage, pausing only to allow them to catch up. Duinn soon found himself standing alone.

"Hammer fells," he muttered, using an ancient dwarven curse in his frustration.

The Five minus one made their way down the darkened streets. Raori, weaving as he went, provided the perfect cover for them although he did not realize it. Somewhere along the way, he broke out into song, waving his arms dramatically as his voice rose and fell. Night guards took them for drunken revelers and ignored them. Aramina's fanged presence deterred other types of trouble.

It soon became apparent that the Priestess was leading them back into the city. There were times she disappeared in the shadows, presumably to scout ahead, then reappeared with barely a gleam in her eye to warn them. Duinn followed at a distance, then alongside Raori to help him walk. The mage barely knew it as he sang about the harvest, elven girls with blond hair, whatever came to mind.

Aramina did not stop until they faced the temple. It was not as dark here as other parts of the city. Giant oil lanterns lined the steps and were carefully tended by young acolytes.

The four watched as a pair of young boys refilled the lanterns carefully.

"Be-yootiful," Raori said softly. "We never had that when I was here." Lanterns filled, the boys solemnly walked inside and closed the massive front doors behind them. The four comrades were soon the only souls to be seen.

"And why are we here?" Duinn demanded of Aramina. "You can't expect us to take the tunnel again. The mere thought is ludicrous, as well as useless! No doubt the Silver Fox has a guard stationed outside the door, if he knows about it that is. If is memory his any good, he might. After all, Raori did tell him about it."

"Hey," the mage protested, "I was drunk." He hiccupped.

"When are you not?" the dwarf growled. "And you were drinking with the enemy, besides. You're lucky MacKegan never found out."

"He wasn't so bad back then," the mage murmured, weaving slightly as he manfully stood without support. "The Silver Fox, I mean. MacKegan's always bad."

Aramina snorted. Picket's form wavered and the man said, "No. She says there is something inside the temple we have to fetch."

"Why can't she tell us that herself," the dwarf muttered. He had a faint suspicion about what the wolf wanted, and he did not like it.

Ignoring the recalcitrant dwarf, Aramina padded up the steps. Her nails made soft clicking sounds in the night. Raori, suddenly walking steadily and clear-eyed, followed her without hesitation. Picket shrugged to Duinn and followed. Only Duinn waited before following the wolf's path.

Aramina sniffed a moment at the threshold before changing into her two-legged form. Raori, standing beside her, touched the massive doors reverently before shaking away his awe.

The doors to the temple were never barred, not even during war. Or so it was said. Aramina and Raori knew the truth of the matter and exchanged a glance as they linked hands. The lock on the great doors was simple; it burned away quickly beneath the concentrated atma of the elves. Swinging open silently, the entrance revealed an empty and darkened space beyond. Once they were inside, Aramina returned to wolf-dog form.

She put her nose to the floor and, with quiet snuffling, began to hunt. With a small yip, she caught her trail and followed it. It led them out of the main chamber and into the interior of the temple where the priests lived. This Duinn expected and followed cautiously, glancing around suspiciously.

Subdued and growing more and more sober, Raori paused frequently to study various tapestries or count doors to the left. "They saved that from the fire?" he suddenly asked, incredulously pointing to a tapestry. "Why that one? Why not the one of BileEll or the one describing Fion's history? Gads, what horrible taste!" He made a face in the dark, shaking his head as he continued walking along. The Priestess had not stopped following the trail, ignoring the trio behind her.

"The nerve of them. That one you described with the nubile sprites by the water would have been a better pick," Picket said.

"You're right," Raori agreed. "Yick, what a horrible tapestry! Any one would have been better than this one... Someone had terrible taste."

"I'm pretty sure they were in too much of a hurry to pick and choose," Picket chuckled. "Wasn't the temple burning down around their ears? Ha, I'll bet they were glad to get what they could!"

"Why don't you just find the High Priest and ask him what happened?" Duinn asked sarcastically. Any minute he was sure they would be caught and recognized. Then it would be all over. "As deep inside as we are, he's sure to be nearby. We can just wake him, I'm sure he won't mind--"

"Hush," Picket said with uneasy caution. The Priestess had stopped before a door and scratched at it. She whined and looked at them, beseeching them to hurry with her eyes. The mage grabbed the little handle.

"Hey," Raori said in a surprised tone, "this door is bolted shut."

"What poor creature has to be locked up by the temple?" Picket asked. Even humanoid, he threw his head back and his nostrils flared at the thought.

Aramina was watching Duinn, he marked to his dissatisfaction.

"Of course," he grumbled. "Get the dwarf to do it. They're excellent locksmiths, those dwarves. Got an iron nail you want straightened? Go get a dwarf. Your sword not looking so shiny anymore? Go get Duinn, he'll do it."

"Just do it," Raori hissed.

"Elves," Duinn muttered, reaching for the lock. It was a simple bolt mechanism set high above everyone's heads. To reach it, he needed twice the help an elf would. Sitting on Picket's shoulders, the dwarf fiddled with the lock as quietly as he could. Aramina paced the hall while Raori kept nervous lookout.

"Stop wiggling," Duinn hissed to Picket. All he had was a dagger, and it made a poor tool. It was also hard to see under the dim torchlight that served for illumination in the hallway. So far, the lock had resisted his efforts. He mumbled counter spells continuously under his breath.

"If you wouldn't keep putting your elbow in my face," Picket said, "I might not have to wiggle. My eyes would be safe from harm."

"Just hurry," Raori said. "Someone will come any time."

The wolf sat her haunches and whined.

The lock fell with a sudden scraping. Duinn grunted in satisfaction. "Now, let me down, you four-legged hay-muncher!"

By mutual consent, they sent Raori through first although he did not have the Spear of Birgha. Indeed, the only weapon Raori had was his magic. He paused just beyond the threshold, then stepped quickly inside. "Who are you?" his voice inquired while the others filed in after. The door shut softly behind them.

"Midna," said a plump acolyte sitting on a plain pallet. Other than a small tallow lamp, the room held no other furnishings. "I am sorry I do not know you... Are you robbers? Take what you want, just don't hurt me. How did you get in here?"

"We have ways," Raori said softly, turning to the wolf beside him. "You certainly can't mean that this is our sixth member? Are you mad?"

"Aye," Duinn scowled, apparently answering both questions. For the first time, the acolyte noticed the dwarf standing just inside the door. His face went deathly pale when the dwarf said, "I should kill him now and reduce our number back to five."

The wolf grunted, shaking her head vigorously. Picket said, "She says he was doing what he was told to do. What that is I haven't the faintest." Aramina growled softly. "I don't see why it has to be such a secret," the pooka argued back. "We're in the middle of the temple--"

"Shush," Duinn said. "Time for that later."

"How did you get past the guard?" Midna asked, rising from his blankets. "On the other hand, how did you escape, Duinn? Certainly not by these fellows. What do you want with me?"

Aramina bared her teeth silently.

"Oh," the acolyte said softly.

"Come on," Raori said, grabbing the acolyte's arm and pulling him forward. The acolyte winced and hissed in pain, jerking his arm back. "We can discuss this when we're safely out of here." Midna said nothing as he favored his arm. The cut was still there, and it looked slightly infected. Perhaps the orders of magic had forgotten so simple a spell as minor healing, Duinn speculated.

Perhaps not. It was hard to imagine anything good coming from the temple, especially lately. A little cruelty could only be expected when some certain gods were involved like the

Morrigan or another, unfriendly deity. For some reason, the more loving deities seemed to be represented by a growing mass of hateful priests in later years. The Morrigan's followers had nothing on some of the other priests Duinn had recently met. One had even tried to steal a dagger from his arsenal immediately after telling Duinn all about BileEll and how he loved the world. It was enough to keep a wicked dwarf awake at night.

"Where are the guards?" the acolyte stammered. "Are they dead? They threw me in here right away. They won't even let me have a poultice for my arm."

"There are no guards," Picket snorted. "Crazy priests."

"I used to resemble that remark," Raori said as he opened the door. Aramina hung back and whined.

"Somehow I'm not surprised," a familiar voice said from the hallway. "An unsuspected new member would be a wonderful addition to your little clan. Besides, he would be useful. Although, really... Aren't you carrying your little grudge against the temple too far?"

The wolf-dog crouched and growled while the rest of the band expressed their dismay in separate ways. Raori hissed and summoned a ball of atma fire to hover just over his head. Duinn reached for his halberd, which was not there, and cursed ineffectively. Picket shifted form and pranced in place, snorting nervously. The acolyte, with a yell of fear and a glance at Duinn, dashed to the farthest corner in the room to huddle there.

It was Finnbhear that had them cornered, of course, with four, young and belligerent soldiers to back him up. The soldiers spread out behind their leader in the hall. Finnbhear grinned, the bags under his eyes enhancing his gruesome appearance in the dim light, and slowly drew his sword. The metal rang in the air. "I know you well enough not to expect a simple surrender," he said, "but I'll ask for one anyway. Just like old times."

With a shout, Raori released his ball of fire. Flaring brightly, it sailed toward the open door and then extinguished in a puff of smoke. Reminiscent of bygone days, the Silver Fox chuckled at his adversaries' confusion. The air smelled of burned sulfur.

"The room is counter spelled!" Duinn shouted. "We'll have to fight our way out!"

Apparently, that was the werewolf's cue. She dashed through Raori's legs and leapt at Finnbhear with a wild howl. Four paws hit the elf with her full force, knocking them to the ground. The Silver Fox tossed his sword aside and grabbed her throat. The pair rolled until Aramina had Finnbhear pinned. Her teeth gleamed as she snapped at him, drool flying.

Concern for their commander bred carelessness, and the soldiers surrounded the fighting pair, fumbling with crossbows and daggers. Duinn and Picket edged into the hallway. "Forget me," Finnbhear cried, holding the werewolf from his throat with both hands. "She won't hurt me! The others are escaping!"

Midna tried to be ignored, but Raori dashed back into the room and grabbed a plump arm. In seconds the young priest was running down the dark corridors, gasping for breath and whimpering. Four-legged, the pooka galloped far ahead, followed closely by the dwarf. Midna and Raori , last in line, were losing ground. The wolf-dog's snarling echoed down the hall, following them. Somewhere in the excitement, Finnbhear's soldiers were left behind.

"Run faster, you fat idiot," Raori gasped through clenched teeth and yanked Midna's arm. Midna did not have enough breath to answer back. If he had, it probably would have been a plea for his life.

Stumbling outside the temple, the men blundered into another detachment of soldiers. Surprise saved them, for the enemy merely gaped as the runaway villains swept passed. Slowly, Picket turned and remained to distract them. There were only five soldiers, making it easy for Picket to hold them, and he was positive the other four had turned around to save their commander. Picket kicked two soldiers square in the chest and reared while the other three kept their distance. Raori, Duinn and the acolyte ran on.

When they were blocks away, Raori finally released Midna's arm. Wheezing with exhaustion, the companions plus abductee leaned against a convenient wall to rest. Eventually, Midna slumped to the ground and closed his eyes. His legs had never hurt so much.

"We'll... wait here," Raori managed to say between heaving breaths. "Picket at least... will be sure to catch up to us."

"Why didn't we fight them?" Duinn choked. "We're no better than cowards!"

"She wanted us to get Midna," Raori said, eyeing the gasping acolyte, "although I'm not sure why. So we have him." The mage shrugged. "You know what happens if we get in her way with these things."

"Aye," said the dwarf. "Still got a scar on my arm, after all these years. Those teeth of hers can be quite sharp." He poked the huddling priest, delighting in Midna's startled jump. "He's probably just another fancy of hers," the dwarf growled. "I'll lay bets he's no more worth anything to us than a rock to the eye."

"No better than Picket's current fancy," Raori said.

"Well, we at least can go back to Picket's – or that woman's – house," Duinn said. "The pooka knows the way and can find us there. If there's one thing I know for sure, its that Picket can get out of anything. He'll find his way back to us."

"And the wolf?" Midna asked feebly. "Is she lost, then?"

Neither elf nor dwarf answered. They were not sure.

***

It was deep night. The trio were well on their way to Aihn's homestead when the soft fall of hooves caught up with them. They huddled alongside the road and hoped they would not be found. Midna found himself huddling alone, as his white temple robe was visible even in the moonless dark.

A cold nose touched his thigh. He yelled and scooted away. Somewhere on the road, a horse snorted in equine mirth.

"Fat fool!" Duinn exploded from his hiding place with Raori just behind. The acolyte squealed in fear and scooted away from two just as they stopped short of him. The nose's owner, the black wolf, butted her head against the Raori's leg.

"Aramina, you made it out," the mage exclaimed in pleasure, forgetting the acolyte. He knelt and scratched her neck. The wolf-dog groaned in pleasure, leaning against Raori's administrations with eyes closed. Ghostlike, the pooka appeared from the dark and stood just behind the acolyte. His sides heaved, and his coat was dark with sweat.

"Nice to see you, too," Duinn said. Absently he patted Picket's flank and felt along the pooka's long legs for damage. The pooka showed his appreciation by lipping the dwarf's hair.

"You knew it was a trap," Raori said accusingly to Midna, the thought apparently having been mulled over since their escape. Glaring at the acolyte, he continued to fondle the wolf's pelt. "I might kill you, but for Aramina."

The wolf growled. Picket shook his head, snorting. The beasts eyed each other for a long moment. Elf and dwarf alike could feel the mounting tension between them. Duinn wondered what it was they were arguing about.

Had he been born of fey stock, he could have understood the language of enchanted beasts. In the past, Aramina did not mind speaking for herself as much as she used to these days. It seemed that she depended more and more on others to make translations for her. Duinn reflected on Finnbhear's accusations of Feral tendencies. It worried him.

This time, Aramina gave in to Picket's fierce obstinacy. She lowered her eyes, hunched up, and shifted. The naked woman frowned at the pooka before turning to Raori.

"He's doing well," she said with a nod in Midna's direction. "It was a good trick. The temple thinks he is kidnapped, and you think he is a spy."

"I never said he was a spy," Raori protested. "He could have warned us about the trap."

"How?" She shrugged, sending a ripple through her hair.

"Forget it," Duinn said, brushing his hands off on his legs. "Can we just get to Picket's before Eahn thinks we've run amok?"

"The acolyte can walk," Raori said heatedly as he strode down the road. Aramina watched him go only a moment before shifting back into a lupine. Once a wolf, she bounded after him a few paces, then paused to eye Midna.

"Might as well get going," Duinn said to the acolyte. "Your priestess has a short temper when her pupils do not obey."

Resignedly, Midna trudged after the wolf.

"Sometimes, she gets mad when they do obey," the dwarf continued, following Midna with the pooka clip-clopping close behind. "Then again, she might just ignore you for the rest of your life. She's practically a fey in that regard. Don't get too attached."

When they finally reached Aihn's homestead, it was to find things quiet and withdrawn. Aihn sat in a corner, darning wool and frowning to herself. She barely looked up when the group opened the door. Brighde was a slight form on the bed with the baby cuddled into her side. Eahn was the only one who showed any life when the group opened the door.

"There you are!" he hissed angrily. "You could have sent me a message somehow, you know, or at least a sign! I thought I had another blasted family to feed plus the one I already have and you," he pointed a finger at Raori, "have some explaining to do!"

"What has happened here?" Picket asked, caressing Aihn's hair and kissing the top of her head. She paused long enough to allow him to do it, then returned to her work. Just then, Raori asked, "I? What have I done?"

Two stories began at once. Aihn, with a slight tremor in her voice, told Picket that Brighde had been playing with the spear and cut her wrist. It was a deep cut and would not stop bleeding. Eahn had finally worked a spell to close the wound, but Brighde fell into a swoon. She could not be awakened, no matter what they tried.

Meanwhile, Eahn told his version of the story that started with a complaint about wasting precious atma to close a half-human's minor scratch then moving on to the arrival of Leahr, Skagg and Aes.

"It was horrible," Aihn interjected, meaning both the sorcerers and her daughter.

"They bespelled the house," Eahn said darkly, "so they would know when you returned. And they were not happy."

"It's because we've failed Moirfenn twice," Raori said gloomily. Memories flared to life within him and refused to be quiet. Although he was looking at Brighde, he barely saw her.

Picket stamped one foot furiously. "I'll not have them destroying my home," he fairly shouted. "Chulain can kill the prince himself if he's so adamant about it."

"That's Feral talk," Raori said, coming back to the present and glancing around himself. "Picket, show better sense."

"No," the pooka said. "Would it matter? He has already sent his hounds after us."

"Stop it," the Priestess hissed, shifting to two legs just to utter the words. Everyone looked at her in surprise. When they entered, she had curled under the table as a wolf and gone to sleep. Now she stood as a woman between Raori and Picket with arms stretched as if to hold them off and glared at them both.

"What we need to do," she said, "is make new plans. Let the prince rot underneath his crown! Finnbhear will surely have followed us here. What are we going to do? Do as Moirfenn wishes or make something of ourselves?"

The men exchanged glances over her head. "We're bound to him," Raori said slowly. "In case you've forgotten. One does not break an oath lightly. Especially his kind."

"Lightly?" Aramina cried, whirling on him. "Do you call what he did to Duinn's family a frivolous matter? Or how he holds Eahn's wife and unborn captive? And you, Raori, what he did to you? Don't tell me you've forgotten because I can't, I won't, believe that!"

Everyone but Aihn and Aramina looked at their toes. Finally Raori said, "Don't you remember, Priestess? We tried to get away once." His voice was quiet and fell into the room like raindrops into a deep barrel. Wanting her to remember, he refused to drop her gaze.

Her eyes dilated for a moment before she said, "Yes. I do. We should never have went back."

"When he found us that time, I knew we were done for," the dwarf said. "I think we were lucky to have gotten off as lightly as we did."

"Lightly?!" the Priestess exclaimed. "He beat us within an inch of our lives and separated us indefinitely! You call that lightly?? We haven't seen each other for years, until now with this stupid mission to kill some child, and for what? Because we ran away to the north! We weren't even on a mission back then! We just wanted to get away for a while!"

"Worse will happen to us at MacKegan's hands than the Silver Fox can do," Duinn said. He shivered once in dread.

"I won't turn," Eahn proclaimed. "I have my wife and child to think about."

The werewolf's shoulders slumped in defeat. Cradling the medallion in her hands, she said softly, "We can't go on like this. He'll have us like those in the woods and fields before long. I don't want that."

Not even Aihn needed to ask what she meant.

"What we really need to do right now," Eahn said after an eternity of discomfort, "is get out of here. On that, the Priestess is correct."

"So now you're leaving?" Aihn asked Picket, grabbing his hands. "Like a whirlwind, you come through my house and then leave me bereft?"

It was obvious the pooka was having trouble choosing between duties. Snorting to himself horse fashion, he bobbed his head. "You're not safe with me here," he said at last. "I will be back soon enough. Before the next moon."

For the first time, Raori noticed there was something different in the room. "Where is Birgha?" he asked. The spear no longer leaned against the door frame.

"I burned it," Eahn spat. "Good riddance."

"Burned it?!" Raori demanded in a sudden roar. "Without my permission and no cause? How dare you?!"

"I dare as I please," Eahn said calmly. "It's obvious what it has done to you, and the girl as well. I deemed it the best alternative before more harm was done."

There was no warning. Raori leapt, catlike, at the farmer. They grappled, almost spitting, and rolled on the floor. Chairs were knocked over. The men rolled up against a wall. Aihn shouted in dismay while everyone else got out of the way.

On top, Raori pounded Eahn's face with one fist. The farmer grabbed Raori's hand and forced it back slowly, then shifted his weight to the side, hoping to roll and gain the upper hand. Prepared for such a move, Raori slipped off and rolled to his feet. The two elves crouched, weighing their advantages.

"Enough," Aramina was shouting. "Stop it!"

They ignored her as they rushed each other, clashing like raging bulls and groping for strong handholds. Raori was driven against the wall, the breath leaving him on impact. Weakened, his hold on Eahn slipped. Eahn punched Raori in the stomach, kicked him in the groin, then stood back in triumph as the mage sagged to the floor.

It was that moment the door opened.

"Tut tut," Leahr said as he entered in a swirl of black cloaking. "Fighting amongst ourselves?"

Fists clenched, Eahn turned to face the newcomers. Aramina shifted into a lupine and crawled under the table. Coughing, Raori tried to stand but could not. Duinn and Picket took protective positions in front of Aihn, who had grabbed Liram from the bed in alarm. Midna merely stood as he was, face slack from incomprehension.

Skagg laughed, pointing at Raori with his staff. "At least he's getting a bit more backbone," he said to Aes. "I doubt he'll live long for it, though."

Aes ducked, looking at the wolf under the table. The two stared at each other, gazes never flinching. Aramina began to growl.

"What is it you want?" Eahn demanded, striding forward. "Can't be anything good." In the background, Aramina still growled at Aes.

"Depends on your point of view," Skagg cackled.

Aes straightened to regard Eahn steadily. Leahr said, "Chulain is a little concerned, Northern Thorn. By now your band should have had the prince on a pole, but instead we find you here hiding behind a human woman's skirts."

Raori, still clutching his stomach, lurched to the table and stood in front of Aramina. The silence was thick around them. It was the acolyte who broke the mounting tension.

"My lords," he said a little timidly, "perhaps it is my fault. I seem to have gotten in the way twice so far."

Raori thought his eyeballs would pop as he went agog at Midna's quiet offer of blame. The acolyte did not know what he was doing, surely, but even an idiot would not want to confront three of Moirfenn's most powerful mages.

"And who are you?" Leahr asked, turning his attention to Midna. From nowhere, Aramina the woman stood in front of the acolyte. Raori was sure he had never seen her move so fast. She wore black robes similar to Midna's, but embroidered on the bottom with silver runes. Raori wondered where she got the clothing from.

"He is mine," she said with a lift of her chin.

"A new member?" Skagg asked with glee.

Around Skagg's cackling, Aramina and Leahr's wills clashed. The house trembled at yet another confrontation within its walls. It was Leahr who looked away first.

"So now you are six again," he said. "No matter. You can take him with you to Moirfenn. If Chulain has any use for him, he will live."

"And the rest of us?" Raori asked with dread.

"That I cannot say." Leahr twitched back the hem of his cloak. "I was only sent to collect you. Bring you dead if necessary."

"No," Aramina said quietly. "I won't go."

"What?" Raori asked incredulously. The Priestess looked incredibly tiny, standing before the massive bulk of the acolyte in her black robes. She gave him a courageous look before turning her eyes back to Leahr.

"I won't," she said again. "Not until I have finished my mission."

The old wizard cackled again, nudging Aes in the ribs. "That's loyalty for you, eh?" he said. "Determined to do what MacKegan tells her, despite the odds."

Aramina said nothing from behind her steady eyes.

"The prince is not crowned yet," Eahn said. "When he is, then we will have failed."

Leahr opened his mouth to speak. "True," Skagg said, preempting Leahr's unformed sentence. "But you were supposed to keep him from gaining Cnos Fada, which he has. If we have much more of this nonsense of you five flitting about and playing when you're supposed to be taking care of the problem at hand, MacKegan will have to destroy the city and everyone in it."

"It's not like it hasn't happened before," Aramina said shortly.

Skagg cackled again, nudging Leahr in the ribs with a boney elbow. "You hear that? It's almost like old times, I tell you. If they can't have the city, they'll burn it! Twice! I think we should let them have their time, Leahr. What's a few more days to MacKegan?"

When Leahr said, "Very well," without further argument, Raori wondered what they really were sent to do. Raori could not begin to guess what it might be for; MacKegan's logic defied all reason.

The three left the house with a singular backward glance from Aes. Raori followed them as far as the door.

"Mind you," Leahr said while his partners prepared a spell for departure. "When the time comes you will return with us. I suggest you stay here, where we can find you."

They were gone in a sudden gushing whirlwind. Sand flew into Raori's eyes, and he was forced to shield them with his arm. It was a while before he could see clearly again.

***

Finnbhear ordered his troops to surround the house and wait. Behind him, a soldier waited with an lit torch. To the east, the horizon was just beginning to pale. His prey probably thought themselves safe from discovery by now and were asleep.

He had scouted the area ahead in his fox shape that evening and found dozens of tracks leading in, but no tracks leading away. The small flock of sheep the human owned had bleated in alarm, but they calmed when he fled the area. His chosen second, an untried youth named Harren, was relieved when Finnbhear returned. Stories of The Six's fierceness had been exaggerated much through the years.

Well, Finnbhear thought with an inward sigh, it's now or never. Followed by six of his men and the torchbearer, he approached the front door and beat unceremoniously on it. He had to do so twice before his sharp hearing heard signs of life from within; hurried rustles then urgent whispering betrayed the occupants. He pounded the door again.

"Who is it, this time of the night?" the woman's voice demanded from inside. "Leave a poor widow in peace!"

"Eahn the Northern Thorn," Finnbhear shouted. "Give it up, Moirfenn spies! We followed your trail here. Come out!"

Voices rose and fell in whispered debate behind the door. Finally, a man's voice said, "We have claimed this woman's protection, Finnbhear. Even a chieftain's widow has the power to stop you."

"Mayhaps," Finnbhear said, "but she can face the king for her guilt as well as anyone. If she is involved with your plot to kill Bodb Derg, then it is on her own head."

"You'll not touch her, Silver Fox," another voice said in a dangerous tone. "She has no part in this, save for feeding us and providing a roof over our heads. T'would be inhospitable for her to do otherwise."

"Aye," Finnbhear agreed. "Then you should respect the courtesy your hostess has done by you and come out."

No answer from the house. Finnbhear reluctantly took the torch from the young soldier. The wood hissed by his ear and something popped as the fire devoured it.

"Must I burn you out?" Finnbhear said, waving his torch in demonstration.

"You wouldn't dare!" Aramina's voice cried. "There is a baby in this house, Finnbhear, and the dead chief's only daughter! They would perish!"

"Just as Bodb Derg will if I let you go," Finnbhear said. He walked to a nearby haystack and made as if to cast the torch on it, hoping someone was watching. "Come out!"

"You break the law!" the widow's voice carried out more clearly than Finnbhear had heard her speak before. "Foreign I may be, but I know that when protection is claimed it must be honored!"

Lowering his torch, Finnbhear stared at the closed door almost hard enough to splinter it. The universal law of the land gave the woman the right to harbor these criminals, but only so long as they stayed on her land.

His bluff called, Finnbhear had no choice but to retreat.

"I will allow that," he said to the house. "But the minute you step beyond this woman's borders, I will have you." He threw the torch to a patch of bare earth where it would burn out without causing any damage. His men looked slightly disappointed. Finnbhear scowled at them.

He and his men withdrew to a low hill just beyond the human's land markers. After sending someone to bring more troops in order to surround the land, he hunkered down by a small fire to chew a bit of jerky and wait.

There was a time when Duinn's village had prospered in the foothills. MacKegan had ordered its demise, the enslavement of its denizens, and the public slaughter of Duinn's family. Spies had told Finnbhear it was because of Duinn's failure in his mission: the mission he was thought not to have walked away from.

If the dwarf's teammates were punished in like fashion, it had not reached the ears of the Silver Fox. However, there was no doubt in the old elf's mind that something had been done. Horrible things, knowing Chulain MacKegan.

Why, then, did they still serve their master? Aramina (a pang of regret, the image of his dead wife's face) once said that she served no one but herself. That was ages ago, when even he was young. Before MacKegan.

"What holds them?" Finnbhear asked the fire.

The prospect of understanding came to him from beyond the pop of curling wood. Raori, their mage, would tell him. Finnbhear had met the lad once through Aramina when they both had served the temple. He was a likeable fellow, loved his drink. Willing to tell you just about anything, for the right price.

All mages carried a crystal to cast by.

CHAPTER SIXTEEN
"TELLTALE"

Outside, Aihn's scrawny rooster flapped his wings and crowed. Raori turned away from watching through the window and moved to awaken Eahn. Aramina stirred in her corner, shifting to human form, and stopped him with a steady hand. Raori blinked, unsure of how she had gotten so close in such a quick time.

"Let them sleep," the werewolf whispered. They were the only two awake in the house at present. "There's not much to do at this point, anyway. The Silver Fox is still out there. I can smell him."

"We're trapped," Raori whispered back in frustration. Liram stirred in his infant dreams, but came no closer to wakefulness.

"I told you we should leave," the Priestess whispered back. "But the Northern Thorn does not like me enough to listen. Idiot." She frowned for a second, then assumed a neutral expression. "You have to use your crystal, see where the Silver Fox is hiding."

"I plan to," Raori said. "But I don't think it will work. He blocked me before on the road, remember? He will do it again."

Aramina shook her head. Her hair played around her youthful face with the gesture, settling in alluring waves on her shoulders. Raori felt the sudden urge to touch it, but refrained.

"I don't think he will," Aramina said. "Besides, I can help you through the barrier. You and I together are strong enough to break any hold over us."

"Let me wake Eahn first," Raori said with a nod of consent.

"No," Aramina said urgently. "He will distract us, or he may not let us do it at all."

Locked in Aramina's unfathomable eyes, Raori reached into his belt pouch and withdrew his crystal. Feeling its warmth gave him a small comfort. He took her hand, and together they walked outside. The early morning chill bit Raori's face.

The barn provided the most privacy. Sitting inside an empty stall (they had sold the horses days ago) knee to knee, Raori placed the crystal between them. Breathing on it, he closed his eyes and let himself slip out of his body. Immediately he felt Aramina's presence buoying him up, giving him strength, and merging with him.

They had done this frequently when they served together in the temple; happy, youthful times. Later, when they served together under Moirfenn, the act lost its innocence. Once he had cracked his eyelids to look at his beautiful partner, but she had not been there. Despite his other senses telling him that her spirit flowed with him, her hands still held his, all he had seen was a tiny ball of light. It was disconcerting, and he had never looked again. He imagined it would be the same for her, should she look.

So Raori flowed with Aramina's strength, looking outward past Aihn's homestead to the hills around them. Mentally, he counted the soldiers stationed at various points as he spanned further out. The camp's little circle drew him like a moth to flame.

A rider cantered into camp, dismounted to speak with a ranking soldier, and strode toward the fire. Aramina's invisible presence pulled Raori toward the fire, downward, until the Silver Fox's face all but filled his vision.

Finnbhear, who stood by the fire and watched the rider approach, turned to look straight at Raori. He smiled. Raori knew he could not be seen and was simply seeing events with an ethereal eye, but he was troubled anyway. Instinctively he looked for a place to hide.

The Silver Fox sat by the fire, still looking at Raori, and withdrew a crystal of his own.

Strong arms held Raori in place, even though he struggled to get away. Finnbhear cupped his crystal in his hands and took a breath. Silently grunting, Raori kicked backward.

Finnbhear blew on the crystal.

There was an explosion of sound and mind. The arms released Raori, taking one hand in a tender motion and squeezed. The Silver Fox floated upward, out of his body, and walked toward Raori. The terrain around them dimmed. Partly it was because Raori stopped concentrating on it. Aramina was somewhere, but he could not see her. She was a ghost in the corner of his eye.

Even here I will not breach the widow's hospitality, Finnbhear's soul said. Can I expect the same from you?

Yes, Raori said, reluctantly. Only Aramina's hand in his held him in place. He wanted to escape, felt foolish at this folly and strangely curious. *What do you want?*

Information, Finnbhear said as if he and Raori were the best of friends.

No, Raori said. I will not betray the Six.

Chewing his lower lip, Finnbhear looked away for a moment. He seemed to be listening to something. Turning his eyes back to Raori, he said, *Well. The rider informs me that I am needed at the palace. Perhaps later, you will consider telling me.*

As I did before? Raori snorted. You won't fool me twice, Silver Fox. I was drunk then, besides.

Finnbhear shrugged, stepping away.

That was when Aramina manifested herself between the two of them. She looked more light than flesh as she reached a shimmering hand to grab Finnbhear's shoulder. He stopped when she touched him but did not look surprised. Something passed between them, above Raori's level and out of hearing.

In unison, they turned to the mage.

The survivors stood before Chulain MacKegan in his great hall and were stared down by his unflinching scrutiny. Picket's eyes rolled in their sockets, horse fashion, but he held his man form under duress. Raori shuffled his feet in fear, discomfort and impatience. Chulain leaned forward in his chair, placing his chin on a fist.

"Failure," Chulain drawled. "I am disappointed."

The Six minus one did not respond.

"It was such a simple errand," Chulain continued. "Fetch me the Spear of Birgha. An old, tottering human was all that stood between it and me. But you fail."

Someone coughed nervously. It was the only sound.

"Now I must think of what to do with you." Musing, he stroked his beard softly. His servants remained standing, glancing at each other from the corner of their eyes. The moment crawled on. Finally, Picket stepped forward.

"My lord," he said humbly. "We do not deserve to be treated as common drudges over this... We have been loyal, and we have brought you many victories. This is only our first

failure." Dipping his head, he mumbled, "It is punishment enough on what we have lost."

"Leannahn only received what she deserved," MacKegan said in a bored tone. "Moirfenn does not need a fool leader."

Even Picket, with the wound of losing her, dared not argue with MacKegan. He stepped back as Chulain snapped his fingers in feigned inspiration.

"Not mere drudges, but examples to show that even my pride must know the humiliation of defeat," he said. Warily, the team mates eyes their leader. "Eahn the Northern Thorn, approach me."

Haltingly, Eahn obeyed. His footfalls, usually heavy and loud even without boots, were muted as he carefully made his way to Chulain's chair. Chulain beckoned with one finger until the elf stood a mere two feet from his lord. The others had trouble seeing what their master was doing, but soon Eahn gasped and sagged. A bright light was born from his chest, cupped in Chulain's palms.

"I take part of your essence," Chulain said. "And I bind you to my service forever. Rise, my Northern Thorn. I will send you to the veil to watch and wait. Until I need you again."

Grey-faced, Eahn stumbled back to his place among his partners. Aramina, in a rare show of concern, touched his shoulder. He ignored her.

"Picket, approach me."

Snorting, Picket delayed only a moment before tracing Eahn's path forward. Chulain repeated his gestures, and soon he again cupped a glowing essence in his palm. "I take part of your essence," the lord said. "And I bind you to your promise to serve me forever."

Stronger than Eahn, Picket only swayed. He said, "So long as I remain in Fion. Aye." He staggered back to his place on the floor.

Duinn was next. He stumped forward sullenly. His scowl met Chulain's neutral expression.

"I cannot take your essence without killing you," Chulain said with a disappointed sigh. "You dwarves are so very human in that respect."

Obviously Duinn did not like that statement, but wisely held his tongue.

"You are useful to me yet," Chulain said, casting a look over all of the company. "And so, Duinn, I take away something almost as precious." Signaling to a captain who had been waiting in the shadows, Chulain instructed, "This dwarf's village: destroy it. Every man, woman and child must die. His wife and daughters first."

"No," Duinn cried, falling to his knees. "My lord, have mercy! Punish me, not them! If you must have my essence then take it, but please not my family!"

"Very well," Chulain said, staying his captain. In a sudden rare show of his magical prowess, he began to chant a spell. Glowing traces of atma trailed his fingers, weaving around each other, snaking toward the dwarf. When they settled on Duinn's shoulders, the dwarf fell thrashing to the ground.

The hall echoed with Duinn's tortured screams. Eahn, staring at his toes, took no notice. It was the same for Picket, who would feel his loss of being more acutely than the others. Trying not to wince, Raori found himself wishing the dwarf dead if only to provide mercy. Aramina's breath caught, released, caught again as she suffered with her friends.

Finally the cruel display was over. Gasping on the floor, the dwarf was immediately forgotten as Chulain beckoned to Aramina. She stepped forward hesitantly, wringing her fingers in distraction.

The essence Chulain took from her was brighter than the rest. She crumpled at the release of it, falling with the grace of a discarded leaf. Raori fought the temptation to rush to her side.

"Gredber," MacKegan called. The bat creature detached himself from a deep shadow and fluttered to Aramina's side. He changed, elongating into his handsome man shape, and

crouched. Trembling with excitement, he narrowed his eyes in triumph.

"She is yours," Chulain said. "See that she remains with you until I need her again."

"No," Raori cried despite himself. "My lord, please."

Raori's eyes looked straight into his master's. "There is no greater punishment I can deal," Chulain said, "than what you are already cursed with, mage. So you are to watch Duinn's family die. In fact, it will be you that guides my soldiers to the dwarf's village. You will watch Gredber claim Aramina this night when the moon rises. Watch Picket and Eahn grow weaker until finally they must kill in order to replace the essence I have taken. And know," he said with a lifted finger, "that had you not failed it would be different. I will trust your memory to teach you this lesson. Approach me."

It felt like his entire body was being ripped into tiny shreds when Chulain took his essence. Not as brave as his companions, he screamed an anguished cry to rival Duinn's. He found no merciful faint rising to greet him. There was only the knowledge that the sorrow would continue forever, in small ways.

"I'll kill you," Duinn's voice said through the haze of disorientation. As if through a memory, he watched Duinn rise to his feet and leap for Chulain in one fluid motion. A bored flick of Chulain's wrist and Duinn was screaming again, writhing at his lord's feet, caught in the hold of the spell.

MacKegan kept the dwarf like that until the moon rose high in the night. Duinn's screams and whimpers haunted Raori just as Aramina's cry of outrage when, tied to a stake in the courtyard, she was forced to consummate her union with Gredber. The haunted looks of Eahn and Picket, seeing nothing but their new internal emptiness, stole Raori's sleep as they were revisited behind his closed eyelids.

Watching Duinn's village burn to cinders while the bodies of his family swayed on hastily tied ropes increased Raori's depression, seared the memories deep within where they would never let go. Guilt formed with the awareness that despite the blue face of Duinn's youngest daughter, he could only think of Aramina as she was carried away to Gredber's forest.

And fear, that he would never touch her again.

"No more, Aramina," Raori said, breaking out of the memory, away from the crystal. Tears, unwanted and strong-willed, gathered in his eyes. He turned his face to hide them. "Why are you betraying us, telling him?" he croaked.

"I have a plan to get us out this mess," Aramina whispered, solid and sweet-smelling. Her arms were around him, her face before him no matter how he tried not to look.

Gently her lips embraced his throat, his chin, his mouth. Her hands caressed his neck and sent chills up his spine. Raori could not help but to respond and forget about anything else.

***

"Traitor!" Eahn cried, slamming the table with his fist. "I should have known as soon as the noose tightens, you would be off to save your necks!"

Hand in hand, Aramina and Raori chose to face their leader when the group was breaking the morning fast. They had expected his explosion, the looks of dark anger from Picket and Duinn. Foreknowledge did not make it any easier, coupled as it was with the dangers the situation held. If Eahn decided the pair were to be punished as traitors, then they would be put to death.

"The Priestess has a plan," Raori said quickly. "Listen to her before you judge us. Have any of her tricks let us down before?"

"She's been making mistakes a plenty lately," Eahn growled, spitting to the side. In the loft, Aihn grumbled. Liram was with her, cooing to himself. Brighde still slept on the bed.

"Well, we could listen at least," Duinn said. Raori wanted to kiss him. "It's an easy 'no' if we don't like it, before we kill them."

The affectionate urge died, squelched by the boot of reality.

Aramina did not give Eahn a chance to voice more objections. "Now that the Silver Fox knows some of why we still serve MacKegan," she said, "he will want to listen when I ride out to him--"

"So you can get away," Eahn interrupted. "Likely to hang the rest of us!"

"No," Aramina said calmly. "He will be curious, worse than a cat!" She had faced Eahn's ire before, and it always amazed Raori how she held her temper each time. Were it Raori's move, Eahn would be cinders against the wall. It had taken great restraint for the mage to refrain from magic when he and Eahn exchanged blows earlier.

Reminded, Raori touched tender spots on his face. He had not found the motivation for a healing spell yet.

"I will tell Finnbhear we want to bargain," Aramina said.

"He'll believe us," Raori enjoined fervently. "He'll have to. You know that killing Aramina is the last thing he wants to do. This way, we'll get close enough to finish the prince besides removing the soldiers from around Aihn's land."

Eahn bowed his head and gave the matter some thought. "I can't believe," he said, "that the Silver Fox would fall for such a simple trick. It's too easy. How can you be sure he'll believe you in the first place, or even will allow you to live long enough to say anything?"

"He will not hurt me," Aramina said. "Were it another one of us it would fail, but he knows me. I don't lie about things like this, Eahn. I won't have to lie when talking to my brother by marriage."

"Oh, so you are defecting!" Eahn roared.

"No," Aramina said calmly. "Eahn, you of us all know the art of diplomacy. Were you not born to a nobleman's house? There are ways to present things. If I want out, I will tell the Silver Fox so... so long as I don't tell him that I am getting out... and he trusts me, even though he would like to deny it."

No one could doubt the bond Aramina and Finnbhear shared. She was his wife's sister, once his lover, and had defended him as a friend on more than one occasion. Opposite sides, she often told her companions, could not change such bonds.

Which was why Raori was terribly afraid Eahn would not go for the plan. It was a poor one and hinged solely on Aramina's ability to win over Finnbhear. If the Silver Fox believed them, he still would never trust them, no matter what Aramina said to the contrary. Getting out of Aihn's homestead would be easy. Keeping out of the palace prison was the difficult part. Convincing Eahn to trust Aramina would be even more difficult than that.

"I like it," Picket said. "It's not Aramina's best plan ever, but it just might work." To Raori, the quick look the pooka exchanged with Aihn spoke of more than tricking a northern general.

Irrevocably, Raori's eyes were drawn to Brighde.

"You like anything to do with mischief," Eahn, who had missed the silent exchange between Picket and Aihn, mumbled. "Even if the plan is guaranteed to fail."

Picket merely shrugged.

"I won't stop you," Eahn said. Raori bit back a grin. Aramina nodded, apparently restraining her jubilation. "We have nothing to lose either way."

"Then we decide on our stories now," Aramina said efficiently. Releasing Raori's hand, her stance changed. Suddenly, she was the Priestess, their thinker and spy. She demanded Eahn's knife, and with it in hand, she scratched a rough map onto Aihn's table top. In the loft, Aihn sighed angrily and withdrew from sight.

"The Silver Fox has us surrounded," Aramina said, gesturing with the knife. "But he camps here." She dug a small hole into the wood where the Silver Fox's lair was.

"Anvil marks," Duinn swore. "The bastard left himself wide open. Even Midna could walk in and take him... there's a clear path from here to his very doorstep."

"Which means it's a trap," Eahn said. The others nodded.

"Finnbhear is a great statesman, but he never was very clever," Aramina said with a smile. "Besides, that wouldn't be

Finnbhear's style. I'm willing to bet its an invitation. And I mean to take it. The Silver Fox wants to talk. He's always wanting to talk. So, we'll talk."

That afternoon, Aramina embarked on her appointed mission. Astride Picket, who plodded slowly and hung his head as if in utter defeat, she rode solemnly toward the hill where Finnbhear waited by his fire. Although they passed the line where Finnbhear's men ringed Aihn's land, there was no sign of them. Aramina knew the soldiers were there, hiding with their elven skills. Neither she nor the pooka would be killed unless Finnbhear gave the command. There was no doubt in her mind they were safe for the moment.

Just as Aramina expected, they were allowed to ride directly into camp where Finnbhear sat alone by his little fire. Empty tents surrounded him like a barren forest. Aramina dismounted, discarded the urge to tether Picket to a tent stake, and approached cautiously.

She stood silently across from the fire until her feet began to hurt. Finnbhear continued to stare into the flames, lost in a silent thought process. Suddenly, as if it had finally dawned on him that she was near, he began to think aloud.

"I should have you pinned by arrows," he said with a tone one would use to discuss the weather. "Better not to trust you, but I have to admit I'm curious."

"What more can I tell you?" Aramina asked softly. "You know why we're bound to Moirfenn."

"Yes, through your mage's perfect memory," Finnbhear mumbled so the pooka might not hear. Deigning to look up, he saw only a lithe girl standing shyly nearby. There was no hint of the glowing being he had seen through the crystal. "You want something. What is it?"

"That's funny," the girl answered slyly. "I'm here because I thought it was you that wanted something."

"What is it you want?" Finnbhear insisted.

"Freedom," was the simple answer.

"I will not withdraw my men until the prince is king and safe from your hands. I'm defying all common sense by allowing you to live right now."

"Blast the prince and his army besides!" Aramina said with sudden impatience. "Do you honestly think I care if that child becomes king or not? I could have killed him the other night, but I refrained in honor of my colleague. In fact, I've had plenty of chances. The first was when he left your party to flirt with that asrai downstream! Doesn't that tell you anything?"

"Maybe," Finnbhear said. He brushed his hands off, standing, and turned to eye the pooka. "But the others may have different pursuits in mind. You always were on a different mission than the others, Mina, even if the ends were the same."

"Will you withdraw or no?" Aramina said. "We are prepared to bargain."

"Bargain for the life of my king?"

"No." Dramatically, she paused to take a breath. "For our freedom from Moirfenn."

She had planned for the statement to drop suddenly. Even though Finnbhear knew that, he was stunned all the same. Hope rose in his breast. Before the moment was lost, he reached across the fire and grabbed her hand.

"I want to believe you," he said past a rising lump in his throat. "But how can I? Well I remember the one time I trusted your mage and released him. The city was ashes before a fortnight."

"Believe me," Aramina said weakly. Tears filled her eyes, threatening to spill over. Clumsily, Finnbhear brushed them away. "Even should we succeed with the prince now, a punishment awaits us anyway. I don't want to go on living as Gredber's toy hidden in the woods. The others have things to fight for as well." Here, she sighed and gestured to her body. "Look at me, Finn. Have I aged a day since my sister became your bride? For all our youth and vigor, we are worn thin as old cloth. I convinced them this morning to let me talk to you."

"Suppose I refuse to bargain and kill the pooka while I can."

The pooka lowered his head and pretended to graze.

"Then I, too, am dead. The mage waits for me. If I don't return by sundown, his atma will find me. After that, they will stop at nothing to get the prince."

Indecision made Finnbhear pace around the fire, alternately glancing at Aramina and the pooka. Slowly, as if by some silent signal, his men reappeared from the hills. They settled themselves around the camp, weapons ready, and watched their commander. Neither of their guests seemed to notice the infiltration.

"You," the Silver Fox said suddenly, pointing at the spotted horse. "What say you to this?"

He thought the pooka would merely stamp one hoof and snort. Instead, he watched as the horse reared on its hind legs and melted into a freckled man. The pooka shook the hair from his eyes, as if the change were disconcerting.

"I have no loyalty to MacKegan beyond a promise," the pooka said. "He made me swear to serve him so long as I stood on the soil of Fion."

"And you intend to break that promise."

Picket snorted a horsy laugh. "Aye, for the bond was broken ages ago. I'd kill you to be free, Silver Fox, if I thought Moirfenn would honor his word. But," he held up one finger just as Finnbhear reached for his sword, "I have been shown that he will not. Also, I need not remain in Fion. Éire is my home, and happier I am there. I would take the widow yonder as my bride and lead a settled life. Moirfenn kidnapped me from Fion and breaks his promise yet. I have no bond with him." The pooka shook his head, apparently having said all that was needed.

"Fair enough," Finnbhear said.

"The mage wants only to forget what has happened and go home, if such a thing is possible for him. The Northern Thorn has a wife and unborn child held hostage by MacKegan's lackeys. The dwarf misses his forge and the peace he had found in his mountain." Aramina paced away, ignoring the bristling weapons around her.

"What of Chulain's niece?"

Genuine shock rounded not only Aramina's eyes, but the pooka's. "Finnbhear," Aramina said in a delicate tone. "She is dead. Did you not know?"

"As dead as the rest of you? If that is the case, I am talking to a well-preserved corpse."

"Nay," the pooka said sadly. "She is truly dead. Killed by the Spear of Birgha in Éire."

It took Finnbhear a moment to comprehend the truth of the statement. The Six reduced to five. "And the temple servant?"

"Midna is mine," the werewolf said with sudden possessiveness. "He came to me and found himself a new master. MacKegan may or may not know of him. It is hard to tell."

The fire was beginning to die. Absently, Finnbhear fed it a small log. Although it was warm with early summer, Finnbhear liked the security of a constant fire. When the flame rose to his satisfaction, he sat back down. Aramina and Picket shifted uncomfortably where they were.

"I will have to put you into my men's care," Finnbhear said. "I will ride to the palace and speak with the prince. I can make no promises beyond that."

Aramina nodded.

"If he says to kill you, then I will obey orders."

Over all, Aramina took the statement calmly and allowed two soldiers to lead her away. Picket balked once, watched Aramina's compliance, and followed her example. Finnbhear was relieved: The pooka could be more trouble than the rest of them put together.

If it came to their murder, Finnbhear convinced himself as he urged his horse to Cnos Fada, then it must be done. It was one thing to let the mage go one intoxicated evening before they had done anything worse than secret meetings beneath the moon. Also personally forgiven was how he had allowed Aramina near the prince before he remembered who she was. To allow her to put him into a stupor was a move guided by the heart. Now that he had her, and the pooka besides, there was no room but for duty.

Clattering past the palace gates, Finnbhear noticed two soldiers loitering outside. They looked like they had just come in from the field. One wore blood-soaked bandages around his head. The Silver Fox nodded cordially as he passed them.

Bodb Derg was holding court in the long hall. Finnbhear could hear shouting as he strode past the immobile guards and swung open the doors. Two harried generals, the shouters, paused to stare at him.

"Who is this?" one of them demanded. "My lord, must our interview be interrupted?"

Bodb Derg chuckled. "This is Finnbhear the Silver Fox," he said, gesturing for his commander to take place at his side. "And I am glad to see him."

"My lord," Finnbhear said, bowing to the prince. He also bowed to the generals, who were mollified by the introduction.

"These good soldiers have come fresh from battle," Bodb said. "It seems Moirfenn's army has crossed the Nosloraug and are moving inland. They met my forces just south of Hedros."

"It was a disaster," the outspoken general said. "Their mages are highly skilled while our three could barely keep pace. They have undead at the fore." He turned to the prince, sank to one knee and bowed his head. "We need more soldiers, my lord."

"The Silver Fox seems to think we need what few troops are left here." Bodb smiled grimly. "To keep my life safe from The Six of Moirfenn."

"The Six?" said the second general incredulously. "MacKegan has sent The Six against you? But they are dead!" The outspoken general got to his feet in surprise.

"No," Finnbhear said. "I have just spoken with two of them myself. Although they claim one of their number, MacKegan's niece, really is dead." Finnbhear scratched his chin, realizing he needed to shave. Beards, the common style between men and elves alike, were an annoyance to him.

"The acolyte makes them six regardless," Bodb said quietly.

Distrust held Finnbhear's tongue as he looked at the two generals. Both began to argue at once. More guards should be put around palace, where would more troops come from, an assault should be planned on Moirfenn to throw some of the heat from Cnos Fada. Bodb Derg listened to their suggestions, arguments and pleas in silence.

When the river of words finally dried, Bodb shook his head in negation. "I won't place more guards around me," he said. "There are too many as it is. Even Chonnall, brother to me in all but blood, has a difficult time speaking with me from across the dinner table, so surrounded am I with bodyguards, weapons and spells."

"But, my lord," the first general began.

"That is my final word," Bodb said. "You need the men more than I, and you shall have them. If we do not have enough, then recruit. And I suggest you start now." He pointed majestically toward the doors.

This prince had a gift for drama, Finnbhear noted to himself as the two generals, bowing, backed out of the room. Neither of them looked happy, but at least they would have more men to fight with. When the doors were shut, Bodb turned casually to Finnbhear.

"Well?" he asked, a different person from when he pointed the generals out. The eyes he turned Finnbhear were tired and youthful. "Your reports say that you had The Six penned. What has happened?"

"The werewolf came forward to parlay," Finnbhear said. "They want our help, or so they claim to escape from Moirfenn's clutches."

"She has a funny way of asking for help," Bodb snorted, rising out of his chair to pace the room. He touched his arm where the werewolf had bitten him.

"It may be a trick," Finnbhear cautioned. Watching the prince pace to and fro, keeping his face carefully neutral, he mentally swallowed that fact. It went down painfully and settled like mud inside.

"True," Bodb said thoughtfully. "And it also may be a chance to get close to them." He stopped pacing, stared at his furred boots, and froze. Without moving he said, "Bring them here."

"My lord?" Surprise broke Finnbhear's resolve. His voice cracked on the words.

A small smile touched Bodb's lips. "I said to bring them here. Can't you obey one simple command?"

Finnbhear knew a warning, and a dismissal, when he heard one. Without preamble he turned heel and was out of the palace as fast as he could go. Sundown was not far away, Aramina was waiting for him, and he had good news to deliver.

CHAPTER SEVENTEEN
"TO CATCH A KING"

When Finnbhear cantered into camp, his horse was dripping lather. Dusk was deep; The sun had sunk below the horizon hours ago. Fearfully, he landed on the ground and strode toward the tent where Aramina and her pooka were being kept.

"It's been very quiet in there," the young soldier guarding it said with a jerk of the thumb. "Looked in just before you came and they were still there."

Relief washed over him. Ducking inside, he found himself standing in the dark. Someone shifted their weight, aware of his presence, but otherwise nothing happened. Resorting to atma, Finnbhear placed a globe of light over his head.

Aramina winced in the light, shading her eyes with one hand. She was curled next to the pooka, who held her in one arm and also winced.

"The prince wants to see you," Finnbhear said. Jealousy of the pooka made his tone of voice harsher than he had intended.

"Blessings to you!" Aramina said, scrambling to her feet. "I knew I could count on you, Finn!"

"It wasn't I," Finnbhear said. "Bodb made this decision for reasons of his own."

"All the same, thank you," Picket said. Finnbhear searched his face but could find nothing but gratefulness.

"You are free to go to the others," Finnbhear said. "Come to me at dawn, and we will escort you to him."And they came, walking wearily with the pooka prancing ahead. None of them would meet Finnbhear's eye as they ranked alongside each other by his fire, as if preparing for some dire punishment. Swallowing one's pride was always a difficult act. For them it appeared almost as painful as the memory Finnbhear had witnessed through his crystal.

For their protection, his soldiers flanked them on all sides. Permitting them to have horses might have been a kind gesture, but Finnbhear had none to spare. The journey to the city was a slow one.

Word had somehow gotten to the civilians. Crowds both angry and curious waited alongside the road. An occasional rock made way through the air, sometimes missing their targets. Aramina bared her canines at the hecklers, but restrained the pooka from leaping at one elf who threatened them with a shovel. When The Six were finally escorted into the palace walls, Finnbhear's men wore hunted expressions.

Unceremoniously, The Six were marched into the long hall and told to wait. Everyone else except Finnbhear withdrew to take discreet positions throughout the castle. Aramina's eye caught Finnbhear's.

"Are we refugees or prisoners?" she asked.

"I might have asked the same thing myself," the Northern Thorn rejoined. "But I'm afraid of what the prince does to prisoners who ask too many questions."

"Silence," Finnbhear growled. The Six obeyed with sullen expressions. The men of the group exchanged unfathomable glances. "I cannot decide how the prince will deal with you," Finnbhear continued. "Best you wait patiently and find out."

Fortunately they did not have to wait long. Bodb Derg entered, flanked by two guards, and strode masterfully to his chair. His hair looked ruffled from sleep, and he clearly stifled a yawn. Seated, he rubbed his eyes with one knuckle before facing his guests.

"Merry met," he said to Aramina. "Again."

"Lord," she said, falling to one knee and bowing her head.

"Greetings to the rest of you in turn," Bodb said, letting his eyes linger on Eahn the longest. "I should say welcome, but I am not sure as to our positions in this matter yet."

"You can help us," Aramina said with uplifted eyes. "I know what we ask is not an easy matter, but--"

"How can I trust you? Even the acolyte?"

"We could kill you where you sit," the mage said nonchalantly. With the true arrogance of a practicing wizard, he examined a table laden with bottles of wine and a bowl of fruit. Choosing a decorative goblet, he poured himself a full glass. It almost emptied the bottle.

Were it not for the staying gesture by Bodb Derg, Finnbhear would have dealt with the mage's insolence immediately. He felt his lip curling as, like a dog to its master, he took position beside Bodb Derg's chair.

"Why don't you?" Bodb challenged the mage. "I won't stop you."

Five glittering pairs of eyes targeted the reclining prince with mounting hostility. Only one looked down; Midna's. Yawning, Bodb turned his face from them and waited. Finnbhear reached for his sword.

"We did not come here for this," the sultry voice of Aramina cut through the atmosphere. "I doubt you would be fool enough to allow us this close if you thought we did."

The tension did not abate, but did seem momentarily tamed. Bodb turned back to his guests with a sigh.

"Very well," he said, sounding as if the weight of the entire universe had settled on his head. "What is it you want? Your message begged for asylum."

"Yes," Eahn said, kneeling beside Aramina. The others took the cue and followed suit. It was odd to Finnbhear, seeing The Six of Moirfenn humbled in such a way. It was almost, no very, unbelievable.

"Even if we did kill you now," the Northern Thorn went on, "we cannot be sure Moirfenn would forgive our earlier failures. Life beneath his hand is harsh enough already."

"We want only to lead our lives as before," the mage said from somewhere behind his bowed head. The goblet was placed nearby, but so far untouched.

"The widow beyond the hill waits for my return. Moirfenn would not allow it."

"My pregnant wife is held hostage by Handfast under MacKegan's orders."

"My family is dead, my village destroyed. Now my forge grows cold while I am away on this fool's errand." If ever a dwarf sounded miserable, Duinn was it.

"What of you, Priestess?" Bodb asked, leaning forward. Aramina met his eyes steadily.

"I want freedom," was all she said.

The prince leaned back. "What can I do?" he asked with just a trace of insecurity. "Not even Tech Danaan has the atma to block the geis Moirfenn holds over you."

"Spells were made to be broken," Eahn said evenly.

"Twas our essence MacKegan took," Raori said. He paused at Bodb's widened eyes and waited for the prince to regain his composure. "If MacKegan were to return some of his, we would be completely free. An impossible task. Instead we must find another way."

"I am not half the mage you are," Bodb said to Raori. "But even I know what you suggest could kill you. Are you willing to risk your lives for this?"

"Better than what MacKegan offers," Eahn said, working his mouth in the effort not to spit. "There are more Feral spawn now than ever. More will join them tomorrow."

Tapping his chin with a finger, Bodb looked to be in heavy thought. His foot swung in time with his finger. Midna shifted his weight uncomfortably from his place in the back of the room. Aramina stood, paced a minute, then faced the silent prince.

"Why the charade?" she asked cuttingly. The prince looked up, finger poised in the air. If his face registered anything, it was expectancy. Finnbhear gripped his sword, hoping Aramina would not say anything too foolish.

"You made your decision when you told Finnbhear to bring us," Aramina continued. "Had you wanted us dead, you would have ordered a trap laid. And he would have obeyed you, even unto me." The smile she gave Finnbhear was small and sad.

"True." Bodb Derg stood, walked to the table and picked up the bottle of wine. He downed the remaining liquid in one gulp. Tension kept The Six silent, waiting for his final word.

"I know of a way," the prince said, wiping his lips and placing the bottle back on the table. "The Moonstone in Tech Danaan."

It helped Finnbhear's personal fears when the original members looked at one another with wonderment in their eyes. For the first time in years, he felt a small amount of hope for Aramina. *If only she would keep to her word this time*, he prayed to any listening deity.

"I thought the Moonstone destroyed," Duinn said haltingly. "In the war, when it used to be kept here. At least its out of reach, yes?"

"Naturally we would not allow Moirfenn to know we had saved that, one of our greatest treasures. Not even your acolyte knows, for all he used to serve the temple." Bodb Derg's tone went dry, as if explaining such rudimentary facts were annoying.

"Could it really," Aramina stepped forward with tears in her eyes, "could it possibly be a chance?"

Bodb Derg need not have answered.

***

"You knew he would have placed us under guard," the Priestess reasoned with Eahn. The six of them had been put into a spacious apartment with every comfort, but the door was locked by spell and iron with two guards outside. The only window was too small for even Raori in his animal form, a cat, to escape through. Even if he could get past the wards, which was difficult with two arms much less four legs.

Picket and Raori took turns looking out, studying the gardens below them. Eahn bristled at Aramina, ignoring the protective stances of Duinn and the acolyte. The werewolf took it calmly, lounging on the large bed like a hairless pet.

Indeed, she sometimes seemed more cat than lupine.

"Have a grape," she said to Midna, who took the proffered fruit without hesitation. He was the only other one comfortable with the situation.

"He'll keep us here until after the coronation," Eahn complained bitterly. "Then what will be left to us? Trial by MacKegan, expected worship by Bodb and my wife and child dead!"

"You worry too much," the Priestess said. "The sun has not even reached its zenith yet."

"Two days," Eahn moaned, pacing back and forth, treading Duinn's toes heedlessly. The dwarf bellowed with pain and retreated.

"I wonder if Brighde is any better," Picket said as he looked beyond the gardens, toward his new home.

"I'm sure she is fine," Raori said quickly, patting the pooka's shoulder. "When you come home, she'll be running out the door to greet you."

"Aye," Eahn muttered. "Except he'll never get home, thanks to this faithless woman here."

Aramina bounded off the bed, snarling and biting a reply. It was then the door to their prison opened. The Six stopped in their activities to assume neutral positions, like errant children caught by their father.

"Come along," Finnbhear said calmly. "The prince has need of your presence in the long hall."

Bodb was not alone. A long table was laden with a meal fit for six kings. The prince sat at the far end. Aes, Leahr and Skagg sat at the other. All stood when The Six filed in after Finnbhear.

"Sit," Bodb bade them impatiently, regaining chair and goblet in one motion. Slowly the three sorcerers sank back down, carefully ignoring the newcomers. Finnbhear took his place at Bodb's side and watched his charges take chairs on the far side from the sorcerers.

The Six waited uncomfortably, some staring at the mages openly, some staring at the floor, while Bodb and his guests finished their meal. Servants gave them plates laden with meat and gravy, but no one expressed an appetite. Raori downed three goblets of wine, spilling some on the table as his hands shook. He was working on his fourth, and a new bottle, when Bodb finally pushed away from the table.

"These gentleman here," he said without preamble, gesturing to the three mages opposite him, "have come to carry you to Moirfenn."

"They are criminals to our lord," Leahr said with an uplifted chin. "By rights they should be brought to stand before Chulain MacKegan. Give them to us, and we will let you live in peace."

Raori felt it when Eahn turned his head to glare at Aramina and himself. She wriggled in her seat, feeling it too. Her hand sought his and held tightly.

"They have begged my protection," Bodb said as he sipped his own wine.

"You would protect the ones who burned this city and ransacked a temple?" Leahr asked incredulously. "Who recently made at least one attempt on your life? You would trust traitors, first to your father and now to MacKegan?"

"If they deserve it."

"Then I say they don't," Skagg proclaimed with a snort. "Especially from you, Bodb Derg. Give them to us."

The prince turned to Eahn. "What say you, Northern Thorn? I leave this choice in your hands."

Every eye in the room turned to the elven farmer, whose face went slack. Aramina's hold on Raori's hand tightened. She whimpered almost inaudibly. Finnbhear did not miss the complete look of fear she wore.

Neither did Eahn, who seemed to relish it with a gleam in his eye. Dragging the moment on, he leaned back in his chair and looked upward. Even the dwarf looked on edge, waiting for his leader's decision.

Despite his outward appearance of calculation, Eahn's mind was in turmoil. *Maybe we should go with the sorcerers, he thought, for the last thing The Six needed was to be considered traitors by MacKegan.* If they did, though, the mission was forfeit and the lives of his family with it.

If he declared sanctuary under Bodb Derg, the sorcerers were sure to tell MacKegan. It was certain Joalie and the baby would be killed immediately. Then, should he ever fall into MacKegan's hands...

But, MacKegan was already angered....

Aramina's large eyes bored into him, begging him to follow the plan. Spitefully, he pursed his mouth to accept the sorcerer's demands. The werewolf read his intent, and her eyes widened.

"We accept the prince's protection," he said. Aramina and Raori visibly relaxed.

"You'll pay for it!" Aes cried, standing with a flourish. The Mark on his cheek stood lividly against his flushed anger. "Your families first, then your lives!"

"I have no family left!" Duinn shouted.

"Enough!" Bodb shouted in turn, slamming the table with his goblet. He pointed to the sorcerers. "Your master will be the one who pays this time, for invading my land and threatening my life. As of this moment, The Six of Moirfenn and their families are under my hand. Get out! Tell MacKegan Cnos Fada stands against him, with The Six at its side!"

Angrily the three sorcerers stalked out of the room. Aes twitched his cloak when passing Aramina, but otherwise did not acknowledge her. When the door shut behind them, Bodb turned to The Six.

"I pray that I can trust you," he said, standing. "You are free to do as you will." With Finnbhear in tow, the prince walked out of the room. Finnbhear paused at the door: He was not comfortable leaving The Six to their own devices.

Relief washed over every member of The Six when servants closed the doors after Finnbhear. Midna wiped sweat from his brow with one sleeve. Eahn turned to Aramina with fire in his eyes.

"Was this part of your plan?" he whispered fiercely, grabbing the shoulder of her dress in one fist. "I suppose it did not occur to you the wizards would know we came here willingly."

"It had occurred to me," Aramina said, firmly clamping a hand onto Eahn's fist. She squeezed, tight, until he withdrew it. "I hoped they would not."

"What happens now?" Raori asked, feeling more vulnerable than ever before. Visions of Chulain's steely eyes reflecting the bright light of elven souls danced in his mind.

"I will handle them," Aramina whispered. "Meanwhile, the rest of you go about your business. Picket, go home and see to your new family. And, don't mess this one up, dear brother. Aihn is a good woman." She smiled. "The rest of you, get to know this place. Must I tell you how to do this, after we've come so far?"

Hooves sparking against the floor as he galloped, Picket was first out the door and away from the palace. Duinn clung to his back like a burr. His muttered curses floated back to the rest of their companions.

"Slow down, ninny! You almost ran over that woman! (Sorry, we're coming through, sorry) Pooka! Don't jump over... blast it, pooka!"

Shamefully Midna went back to wait at the temple until the Priestess sent for him. He had a lot of explaining to do, he complained, and possibly would be locked in his cell again. Aramina reassured him that The Harper would not let him rot there when he was more useful elsewhere. The acolyte did not look comforted.

Irritably, Eahn went to their shared room for a nap.

Arm in arm, Aramina and Raori strolled through the gardens. They embraced occasionally, always when in sight of someone, and held hands. Judging by Raori's expression, he was in paradise. Bravely he kissed her lips dozens of times.

"Peace," Aramina said laughingly, pushing her lover away. "You'll wear me away to nothing!"

"I can't help myself," Raori protested. He plucked a nearby flower, changing it as he brought it away from the plant. Placing the new-made garland in Aramina's hair, he put another kiss on her brow. "I would stay here with you like this forever," he declared imperiously, "even as a traitor to Moirfenn!"

"Would you?" A serious expression wiped the smile from her face.

"I am not saying I will turn against MacKegan," Raori said quickly. "I meant only that I am happy with you."

The smile returned, touching her eyes with a glint. "I know what you meant." She kissed his hand. Flower petals shed themselves into her hair.

"You look like a goddess," someone said from nearby. Tensing, Raori reached for his knife. Aramina patted his hand to calm him. The smile did not leave her face.

"Oenghus, I am pleased to see you," she declared, turning around. The harper stood a little to the side, partly concealed by bushes. He bowed, first to Aramina and belatedly to Raori.

"I wanted to see you before going to Tech Danaan," the young elf said. "Did you get the medallion I sent by your friend here?"

"Yes," Aramina said happily, almost mechanically. Displacement pushed Raori's senses out of focus. He felt as if he were watching a badly rehearsed play. His world lurched when Aramina kissed the bard on the lips. "I keep it with me always."

"I saw the pooka on my way here," Oenghus said. "He's terribly cruel to the dwarf, I'm afraid."

"That's just his way," Raori said faintly.

"Duinn doesn't mind as much as he lets on," Aramina added.

"I'm not surprised," Oenghus said with a grin. "Well, I can see you're taken at the moment. I'm off to the inn. One has to earn a living in what ways they can. Even bards as talented as I."

Raori entertained strong doubts to Oenghus' ability to make a living by his music. Any elf, lovers of music that they were, would entertain strong doubts. The memory alone of Oenghus' playing made Raori cringe.

"Might I see you later?" the bard asked Aramina in a low tone. Raori gritted his teeth, thinking of places to put Oenghus' harp.

"Of course," Aramina said happily. "This evening."

"You know where I'll be."

After the bard had left, Raori turned to Aramina. Before he could utter the first protest, she was kissing him. "Don't be so possessive," she said in his ear. "I have to leave the palace tonight anyway. What excuse could be better?"

She was his loving companion for the rest of the day. They explored the palace in an idle stroll. Dining alone in the garden then returning arm in arm, they found the room delightfully empty. Raori and Aramina spent the hours of dusk curled in the bed together. Not once did the mage allow his agitation and jealousy surface for the werewolf to see.

***

Some think that fire can solve almost any riddle. It warms away the cold, rids the world of trash and frightens away savage beasts in the wild. Even nature calls upon fire when a forest needs renewing. Fire seems to be the answer to almost anything.

Behind Picket's new home, the ashes of a fire were stirred slightly by the wind. They swirled, dancing and dissipating. A charred spear head was soon uncovered. It reflected the sunlight sharply, although it was made of dull stone.

Eahn had thought to solve Raori's problem by burning the Spear of Birgha.

It was the wrong answer.

While the wind outside whispered through the roof, Aihn mended an old shirt. The shirt needed only a small patch where a moth had gotten into the cedar chest. It had belonged to her first husband, and now it would belong to her second.

She felt slightly uncomfortable with the arrangement she had made with the pooka. They barely knew one another a day, and already they planned a life together. It would not be so bad, she reasoned to herself, if he had cast a fairy charm on her. He had not, she was sure, but still she could not resist him.

In every tale she had heard, indeed in all she had witnessed while living in elven lands, the fair creatures were always faithful to their vows. She knew the Picket would never leave her once they were officially wed. It was the humans who left their lovers, when longing for home became too great or their hearts could no longer take an elf's frivolity.

She sat by her eldest child who still lay sleeping in the house's only bed. Liram rolled about on the floor, pausing occasionally to chew a wooden toy. Brighde moaned, turning her head and sighing. The wound on her wrist was angry red and throbbed with infection. Aihn had tried every poultice she knew, but her limited stores of knowledge were exhausted.

She adjusted the shirt in her lap and wished Picket would come home.

In her warm nest on the bed, Brighde cried softly in her sleep. Sweat mingled with her tears.

That was how Picket found them.

Later, Aihn sat beside her pooka, watching Brighde, and waited for Duinn, who had left to gather herbs. Only faint hints of daylight were left in the sky. The girl had not opened her eyes once through the day. Her fever was so high the heat could be felt radiating through the blankets.

When Picket thought he would go mad from waiting, Duinn shouldered his way into the house. He held a cloth full of herbs. Their smell perfumed the air. Picket's fears eased as visions of the hills in Fion awoke in his mind.

"I couldn't find everything," the dwarf was saying apologetically as he lay the bundle onto the scarred table. "But I got enough I think. Aihn, I need a pot of water. Picket, feed the fire."

While Brighde's wrist lay soaked in a cloth dripping with of herb-steeped water, Duinn made a poultice with strips of cloth. Aihn's adept hands were convenient for crushing leaves, straining the mixture or holding the mixing bowl while Duinn whispered incantations. When the poultice was in place, Duinn summoned Picket. The pooka lay hands on Duinn's shoulders, closed his eyes and released his mortal shape.

What Aihn saw was hard to describe, but she continued to try even in her last years. Picket's form melted into a soft light reminiscent one moment of a man, the next of a horse and finally settling on a mixture of the two. Duinn was a dark blotch in the perfection of Picket's true self, reaching for something invisible. His arms worked quickly, catching things in the glow and pulling them down. Then the dwarf pushed and held.

Unsure if the light had merely faded or popped out of existence, Aihn soon blinked her eyes to two tired men. Duinn heaved a sigh, leaning against the bed and mopping his brow. Picket slumped into a nearby chair.

On the bed, Brighde stirred and slowly opened her eyes. She saw her mother and smiled. Overjoyed, Aihn hugged her daughter to her breast.

"You've been sick since yesterday," Aihn said tearfully, stroking her daughter's hair. "That horrible weapon must have poisoned you when you touched it."

"I'm sorry," Brighde said. "I won't do it again. Did I miss the coronation?"

CHAPTER EIGHTEEN
"THE HILLS"

Utter darkness. A dark shape slunk through the shadows around the palace. Guards on patrol were not aware of its passing, for all they had been told to pay careful attention to the dark places. There was no moon that night. The slinking form had no trouble finding its way.

A paw set down on the city street. The shape broke into a run, loping easily through alleys, leaping fences, pausing to chase an unfortunate cat and finally trotting beyond the eastern gate. A fresh scent tantalized its senses and made an easy trail to follow.

Moirfenn's three sorcerers had chosen to wait before reporting to their twisted master. Formidable as they were, they dreaded encountering their lord as much as the Six did. The sorcerers camped by the ley gate near Cnos Fada. Wards triple-ringed them, making the area safe enough for all to sleep without standing watch.

Their snores could be heard thrumming through the earth. The shape followed them to the source.

Fur and fangs appeared from the gloom, rising over the twitching Skagg ominously. Swinging her head ponderously, she examined the sleeping elves. For mercy's sake they were not dead yet, but she could kill them easily. The wolf nosed Skagg's eye.

The old one awoke with a screech, grabbing his staff and bursting atma over his head. The power was absorbed by the wards until it was a mere flicker, but it was enough to wake the other two. They were on their feet, holding their staffs, even as Skagg scrambled away from the wolf. Aes released the wards while Leahr began to chant a chilling litany. Skagg regained composure enough to relight the fire with a nod and peer at their guest.

"Stop," he commanded his companions. "It's the werewolf."

Leahr withheld his spell but did not disperse it. Aes grinned, boldly stepping forward.

"How did you get past the wards?" he asked the wolf-dog in a tone that was meant to charm. Grinning as only a lupine can, Aramina let her tongue loll.

"As if she'd tell us," Skagg sniffed. "What does she want? Can't be anything good, traitor that she is."

A breeze picked up around them and swirled the earth at their feet into tiny dust devils. Aes soon realized that if he strained his ears, he could just barely hear the slightest hints of laughter floating with it. Before them, the wolf's shape melted and rose.

The Priestess wore her hair in a flower garland that littered petals around her face. Somehow, she had carried a woman's dress into her transformation. It fit her lithe figure in graceful folds and melted into shadow where the cloth touched the ground to cover her feet. She left her teeth sharp, her ears pointed and her eyes golden. Her smile would have chilled other mages, but these were wizards of Moirfenn. They had seen worse in their day.

"You cannot go to MacKegan," the werewolf said quietly.

Her statement was met with derisive laughter. "We shall," Aes said while trying to regain a straight face. "Your traitorous act will be heard for him to decide what to do with you. At least you bought yourself some time, Aramina. Be glad of that!"

"I say kill her now," Skagg cackled. "I don't trust this one. Never did." He lit the end of his staff and aimed it toward Aramina.

"Nay," Leahr pronounced. "MacKegan would be angry if we stole his sport."

"You won't go," Aramina said, stepping forward. The wind rose higher, pulling at her hair and skirts. The wizards' bed rolls and cloaks flapped where they lay on the ground. The giggling grew louder. Even Skagg looked around briefly, trying to place the sound.

Unusual weather did not frighten Aes. Not much else scared him, either. Even facing a fell beast had lost its chill through the years he had spent under MacKegan's wing. He ignored the look of death in her eyes. Many times he had faced the same look in other faces. While he had walked away, their bodies rotted in the earth. "Stop us, if you dare," he said.

The wind began to grow cold. Despite the warm summer night, the wizards shivered.

"You won't stop my mission," Aramina was growling. "I will finish this. I will complete it!"

The voices in the wind began to howl.

***

The inn was packed. More people were expected on the morrow, the day before the coronation, and already no room was left despite the threat of MacKegan and his army. Locals whispered·it was because of MacKegan, in fact. There was no end of complaints these days about the dark lord and his strange ways. Travelers were tired, thirsty and hungry. All local establishments expected to fatten their purses for three days, at least, after the king was crowned.

What strange people these days, Oenghus thought as he tuned his instrument in a corner. In years past coronations were private affairs, not a city-sized festival with the prince as host. If his memory served him correctly (and it did, with a farther reach than Raori's) there should have been the obligatory battle between chieftains over the neck ornament. Nowadays, it was a crown.

It seemed times would be changing again, for the worse if MacKegan advanced any closer to the city. Battle was on the horizon, the bard could see that much. The prince could not spare much of a force to meet the dark lord, but he had sent some anyway. Two groups had left outside the city gates that morning. One was sent to help their allies in Ramthar, and the other marched to meet MacKegan in the field. Privately, Oenghus grieved over those young men who would be lost to bloodshed.

That had always been The Morrigu's favorite part. Oenghus had trouble understanding why. He had stopped trying to ages ago.

"You," a gruff voice said from a nearby table. "Give us a story, hai? Something to while away this lonesome night!"

Oenghus raised his eyebrows. "A story on such a warm night? Well," and he placed a thoughtful hand on his chin, "this is a special occasion, what with the prince being crowned among other things. But what tale would suit such a night, eh? Perhaps that one about The Spear of Birgha…"

"Nay, give us a song, man!" someone shouted from the back. "Aye!" someone else shouted, standing to be heard. Owners of other voices thumped their tables and boisterously agreed. Even the man at the nearby table thumped his mug, shouting.

Sighing, Oenghus stood and bowed to the company. "Glad to," he said. "Any requests?"

"A song about the Battle at Boruan!" "Fai, give us something about Fion!" "Sing the Ballad of Cliodna Fairhair!" "The Sluagh Ride over Dark River!" "Baile in Scail!"

Oenghus raised his hands prophetically. "I will sing them all if you like," he said. "As you asked for them."

He began to play. The expectant looks of his listeners fell as they realized what Oenghus was actually doing. The bard ignored their disappointed, even irritated looks, as he lifted his voice to sing.

His voice was worse than his playing.

When in the company of elves, it is not a good idea to sing or play badly. Elves are extremely sensitive to vibration, and they are especially sensitive to music. A note off key or the twang of a breaking harp string crawls a fae's spine like cats with their claws extended. It causes them a degree of pain, depending on how badly the music is played. People have died because of a minstrel's lack of talent. Usually it was the minstrel.

Oenghus' playing could have sent a pure-blooded elf into fits of hysteria. Oddly it did not. His audience listened painfully, but they made no move to stop him.

Someone stepped through the door and slipped quickly into the shadows. All turned to see who it was, then slowly returned to the bard. His song had reached its end. Clumsily he fingered the final chords, bowing with a flourish.

No one applauded. Oenghus did not seem to mind. Just before he struck the chords of his second song, Aramina approached from the shadows.

"I thought you might not make it for a moment there," Oenghus said, smiling They kissed like longtime lovers.

"So did I," she said truthfully. Her clothes were ripped in places, but it was nothing she could not mend. The garland was gone. A stray flower petal clung to her hair. Oenghus picked it out tenderly, rolling it thoughtfully between his fingers.

"You and the mage are becoming very close," the bard said with a trace of regret. "Would it be wrong for me to ask what you plan to do?"

"Yes," Aramina said. "But I shall tell you anyway. I plan to sit here and listen to your wonderful playing. I will drink as much as this place can give me, eat what your listeners feel obliged to pay for and be your adoring audience."

"Fair enough," the bard said, strumming a chord. The rest of the inn had fallen back to their conversations, but that chord brought utter silence. Dread hung over the room.

Oenghus began to play.

This time his audience sat enthralled. When skilled elf musicians play, their songs create rainbows of sound. Oenghus' music left that far behind.

Aramina smiled happily through every request. Only once did her brow furrow with worry, but she quickly pushed the thought away.

***

Finnbhear was dreaming.

He was in his garden. Two roses were before him; one yellow and one red. He reached for the red rose, but came away with the yellow. Shaking his head, he reached for the red rose again. Only it was gone.

The yellow rose withered in his hand. The red one tantalized him by reappearing, only to be gone again when he reached out his hand. Throwing away the yellow rose, now brown and crisp, he lunged for the red rose with both hands. Miraculously, he caught it even though it wriggled as it tried to escape.

As he took the blossom away from the bush, he noticed his hands were bleeding. His skin turned brown and cracked. Soon, he could no longer hold the struggling rose. It fell to the ground as Finnbhear withered and died...

Finnbhear was awakened by his own cry of terror.

As he dressed, he resisted the urge to look into the hall. No one had heard him, he was sure, or they would have burst through the door. Embarrassed, he took dark, unpopulated hallways in order to avoid traffic when he finally went out. When he reached the battlements, the first rays of dawn touched his face, feeling good in their clean, summer glory.

Bodb Derg's messenger found him there. Would the Silver Fox please attend the young prince at breakfast? Finnbhear accepted, of course, but chewed his lip at the unusual chore. Bodb Derg liked to break his fast alone. The messenger beckoned for Finnbhear to follow.

The prince looked as if he had been dressed before dawn. A small table, set for two, was placed near his bed. He was laboriously chewing a piece of bread when Finnbhear entered. Without ceremony, he indicated Finnbhear should eat.

For Finnbhear, it was an uncomfortable event. Although the prince took obvious pains to be friendly, Finnbhear could not escape the suspicion the prince wanted something. He concentrated on his plate in order to avoid the prince's face.

Finally, the prince cleared his throat. "Finnbhear," he said hesitantly. Obediently, the Silver Fox looked up. "I have invited you here to discuss The Six."

Here it comes. He should have expected it. No one trusted The Six, not even their master. Now it would be up to him to dispose of them. Even Aramina.

It would have to be done quickly, before they suspected anything. In their sleep perhaps. Poison might work, except for the pooka. Well he could cook something special up for that one, never fear, but he dreaded the task all the same.

"I think they would be of great help to us. They know Moirfenn's secrets, some at least."

Finnbhear closed his mouth, which had dropped open all of its own. With much clearing of his throat, he finally managed to say, "They cannot do anything against MacKegan until their bond to him is broken."

"I know," Bodb said. "Well, tonight I go into my vigil. I will not be released until dawn." Thoughtful silence hung in the air, expecting Finnbhear's response.

"I dare not leave you until after the coronation," Finnbhear said. "Surely we have more time in which to free The Six. After the coronation we could ride the ley lines to Tech Danaan. How far away is Moirfenn's army?"

"Eight days at the least," Bodb said. "Their forces are too vast to ride the lines, or they would already have taken them." He smiled. "Silver Fox, my friend, you can leave any time you wish with our guests. I have others to protect me here. True, none are as shrewd as yourself. Often I find myself saying how very little slips by you."

Guilt made Finnbhear swallow reflexively.

"I trust I would be safe until you return," the prince finished.

"As you wish," Finnbhear said, staring straight ahead.

"It is your decision. You shall succeed, whatever you choose. Trust me on this one, old fox. I do what I do because I know it's the best choice, even if it does not seem so. I'm asking you to take Moirfenn's fugitives with you and cure them. That's the best thing for them as well as us."

"You have my word," Finnbhear said fervently. Their eyes met and locked. "I will get them to the Moonstone immediately. When we return, you will have five faithful allies."

"Take the acolyte with you."

***

"Ow," Aramina moaned, falling out of bed and clutching her head simultaneously. Her blankets fell with her, heaping on her head. They provided a merciful darkness that way. She lay still.

Raori, sitting by the window, snickered.

No, it was too much effort to do anything right now. She could kill him later, when her head did not hurt so much. And her guts did not feel like a kraken writhing inside her body. And her mouth was not so swollen and dry...

"Oh, get up," Raori said jovially. "You shouldn't have drunk the entire tavern's stores, plus whatever could be provided from next door."

Aramina's answer was a soft grunt.

"Your brother came to see you this morning," Raori said. "He wanted to talk to you, but he settled for me. Business."

Her brother? Which one, and how did Raori– Oh.

Speech came with difficulty. "Where is Eahn? He's our leader."

"Don't know," was the nonchalant reply.

Eahn had been gone for too long. Aramina hoped he was with Picket, but she sincerely doubted it. They were going to have to look for him even though Aramina preferred he stay lost.

"Finnbhear says we have to leave with him this evening," Raori said brightly. "We're going to Tech Danaan to see the Moonstone. After that, he hopes to win us into Bodb Derg's services."

Despite her misery, Aramina sat quickly in alarm. Then she winced as the light stabbed her eyes. Her stomach lurched. "We can't do that," she said thickly. "We have to be here for the coronation. That's the plan. Wherever Eahn is, we have to find him."

The two of them searched the palace top to bottom, but no sign of Eahn could be found. Aramina could not nose out a scent trail, partly because everything was being scrubbed spotless for the coronation. Mostly because her senses were dull from last night.

Raori tried to find him with the crystal, but all he saw was darkness. Either Eahn was somewhere dark, which seemed unlikely at midday, or he was blocking Raori. Neither answer looked good.

Without asking, they borrowed two horses from the palace stables and rode for Aihn's homestead. Brighde burst out the door just as they galloped into the yard. Picket, followed by Duinn, were not far behind.

"Where is Eahn?" Aramina demanded, swinging down from her beast. She only winced a little when her feet met the ground. Renewed, her headache pounded mercilessly against her temples.

"I thought he was with you," Picket and Duinn said together. They exchanged a glare between themselves. "We have to find him," the Priestess said, absently patting Bridge's head. The girl ducked and scowled with the gesture. Inside the house, Aihn stepped to the door and remained just within the shadows. Liram was on one hip and pulled at her hair.

Quickly, Aramina told the men of Finnbhear's plans. Duinn stomped a foot and cursed. Picket nodded his head.

"Things never are simple," the pooka said. "Well, come inside and have some bread. We can decide what to do about Eahn, and this."

Helped by Brighde, Aihn briskly served her guests with meat, hard cheese, and watered wine. Less help than hinderance, Brighde was always getting in the way. Apparently, the girl did not know where anything was kept; cups, plates, or spoons. When the girl-child dropped a plate of bread, Aihn finally sent Brighde outside to feed the chickens. She sighed loudly when her daughter was gone.

"That girl," Aihn said, "would be lost in the front yard."

Everyone chuckled. "I shall never become a mother," Aramina said crisply. "Aihn, I don't know how you do it."

The human smiled with pleasure, taking the remark as a hearty compliment.

"Unless Eahn returns this afternoon," Picket said, airing everyone's concerns, "we will have to carry on without him. What are we to do? Kill the prince at his vigil? We certainly won't be there for the coronation as planned. Aramina, its time you came up with some fresh ideas."

"His location is secret," Raori said. "I heard two guards discussing it this morning."

"We can find him," Aramina said with faith. "You and I, Raori, will use the crystal together. If that doesn't work, there are other ways." She glanced meaningfully out the window.

"So we assassinate him while he is meditating," the pooka said with a shrug. "Easy enough."

"Sacrilegious, too," Raori said.

"Yes," Aramina sighed. "The hard part will be getting away. For sure, someone will know what we're doing and give chase. Ah, well... Raori, let's get started. Where's that crystal of yours?"

After Raori had fished his little crystal from his belt pouch, he and Aramina crowded over it with fingertips touching both sides. First, they tried once again to locate their lost teammate. The little instrument still showed nothing but blackness, despite Raori's cleverest incantations. After a while, they gave up and turned their attention to the prince and where he was going to be for his vigil. Immediately, the crystal turned milky white.

It was shielded, no doubt about it. Neither Raori nor Aramina were surprised. They would have been disappointed if such an important location were not shielded; where would the challenge be in that? The werewolf sighed, sending a spark of atma into Raori's hand by accident as her will met with the shield and was halted. The mage winced, but said nothing.

"Fells," Raori muttered, brow furrowing as he concentrated. Aramina closed her eyes and pushed with all her might, but the atma shield protecting the knowledge held firm. Finally, Picket placed a pinky finger over the crystal and helped them to push. The wards broke with an inaudible crack.

"Why couldn't you have helped us before?" Aramina muttered, glancing at the pooka. Picket shrugged, withdrawing his hand and looking away.

Inside the crystal, the whiteness faded away as an finally image came into view. At first, it was only a senseless jumble of images; fire, metal and sunlight. Then the scene cleared, darkening with color. Suddenly, the image of Bodb Derg kneeling in a cave as he prayed came into clear focus.

"But where?" Raori muttered, pushing harder.

The image jumped back as if the crystal's eye were stumbling backwards. Bodb faded from view. In short order, the crystal oriented on a cave mouth. Several guards hid near the entrance, but otherwise the cave was unprotected. Raori grunted, and the crystal's picture jumped again. When it reorientated, the assassins were given a clear picture of an old ley gate.

"I know that place," Raori said with a slight bob of his head. "Hai, he's not far from here at all!"

"Well, where does he have to go?" Raori said, letting the spell go in relief. He wiped a bit of sweat from his temple and took a deep breath. "I think he's lucky to be that far out without MacKegan finding him."

Aramina laughed. "Well, we just found him. So much for that."

Equipped for the journey to Tech Danaan, the four spies returned to Cnos Fada and the palace. First they sought out the

Silver Fox, to divert suspicion, and listened to the old elf talk to them about the Moonstone. Finnbhear had nothing new to tell them that they did not already know, but they pretended to listen anyway while privately glorifying in the prince's future demise. When asked, Finnbhear said only that he had not seen Eahn all day. When finally released, the comrades went to their room to wait for Eahn. The sun sank in the sky, but the Northern Thorn did not return.

When Finnbhear arrived to collect them, Midna was with him. The acolyte carried a backpack filled with, judging by the smell, food. His pudgy face was solemn.

"Eahn is not here," Aramina said angrily. "He has not been here since yesterday."

The Silver Fox digested this, looking down as was his habit when receiving bad news. "Much as I hate to suggest it," he said after a minute, "but perhaps he went to Moirfenn with those sorcerers."

"Impossible," Aramina said shortly.

"If he thought his wife would die–"

"Impossible!" Aramina fairly shouted. The Silver Fox blinked in surprise and shut his mouth. "No, he's somewhere," Aramina continued in agitation. "He could be waylaid for all we know. Your people hold no love for us." She paced the room in quick steps, pausing once to angrily give her pack a swift kick. The others stood in a small huddle and frowned.

Suspicious thoughts flickered in the Silver Fox's mind. It had been apparent that Eahn did not agree with The Six's defection each time the Northern Thorn had scowled at Aramina's backside. He could have taken opportunity to hide somewhere in the palace. He also could be trying to delay The Six from leaving. Finnbhear knew Aramina, and he knew her defection could be nothing short of a ruse. For all that he loved Aramina greatly, he privately thought Bodb a fool for allowing her and her companions into the palace. He thought himself the greater fool for suggesting it in the first place.

Then again, Aramina was probably correct that Eahn had been harmed in some way. If that were true, there would be difficulties. The Six would not take it kindly that one of their number, the leader at that, was harmed.

"I will have mages and soldiers search for him," Finnbhear offered. "Between the two, he will be found shortly. When he is found he can be brought to us. Meantime, the prince says we must go."

The Six did not like it, not one iota. Uneasily they shifted their eyes, avoiding one another's faces. It was Aramina, stepping into leadership as easily as one would a comfortable pair of boots, who broke the mood.

She snorted.

"We'll go," she said. "If Eahn is dead there is nothing we can do. If he is hurt, we'll find him and then find out why. If he has run, then it was his own decision." Slinging her pack over her shoulder, she stepped into the hall. She did not even look to see if she was followed.

"Wait," Finnbhear called. Aramina turned, eyebrows arched. The Silver Fox opened the acolyte's pack, reached inside a moment, and withdrew a short rune stick. It was stained black and the runes, carved and painted white, glared balefully. Waving it at the werewolf he said, "We have something to do first."

Each member of The Six took sharp breaths when Finnbhear drew his dagger and pricked the end of his finger. Smearing the blood along the stick, he muttered words, incantations, which hung thickly in the air. When he was done, he held offered the stick to the dwarf.

"You expect us to bind ourselves to you when we are already bound to another?" Duinn exclaimed. "Are you mad? It could kill us! What would be the point in our betraying MacKegan then?"

"I've no choice," Finnbhear said, still offering the stick. "This is by the prince's command. And it isn't for everyone, Duinn. This is for you. You are not under a bond-geis like the others; merely a painful curse. What's one more curse when it means your freedom from MacKegan, eh? So. Swear to me, Duinn of the mountains, that should this be a trick, should you raise a hand toward Bodb Derg, try to escape me before reaching the Moonstone, do anything which goes against what I have been told, or should your companions do the same, you will be subject to the power I have placed within.

"If your intentions are honest ones, Blacksmith, you've nothing to fear from this black stick. But, if any harm comes to me through you in any way, even if its only a good intention of your companions, it will invoke itself. I know your companions will go along with you so long as you are bound. They will have to, or you will die.

"Of course, if you refuse to take this oath, you will die," Finnbhear said flippantly. "Is it so hard, to strengthen what you have already promised?"

Aramina and Duinn exchanged a look as if to say, *He trusts us so much?* With a shrug, Aramina made a negligent gesture with one wrist. Duinn hesitated a moment more before accepting the rune stick from Finnbhear. The dwarf tore a hole in his thumb with his front teeth and smeared his black blood into the grooves. The acolyte blanched a little before turning his eyes away.

"I swear," Duinn muttered, "that no harm shall come to the prince by me or mine, or my life will be forfeit." He tossed the stick back at Finnbhear, who caught it midair. The elf grinned as he placed the stick back into the pack

That left only one, no, two doubts for Finnbhear to chew on while they walked down the main road and outside the city. Where had Eahn gone and why? Would the dwarf's company stay with him, or would they take the first chance to track Bodb Derg down? MacKegan may have earned the loyalty of men and elf alike - gods only knew how - but he was also a cruel master. Sometimes, Finnbhear thought he knew just how cruel at times when Aramina paused to look at the horizon with sad, haunted eyes.

At first, Finnbhear considered taking a small company of soldiers with them as a precaution, but then he decided against it. It would be nigh impossible to keep The Six under his control alone, and a military escort might change their minds completely even with Duinn under a geis of blood. He would not blame them, either. With Duinn bound as a motion of distrust, a hostile escort would only be rubbing salt in the wound. Eahn's disappearance would only raise further complaint. This was a tricky situation and could not be handled by conventional means.

For his personal comfort, Finnbhear had left the rune stick in his room, hidden in a place Aramina would never discover. At least, he hoped she would never discover it. Sometimes that nose of hers was too canine for Finnbhear's comfort.

They did not take horses with them because of Midna. The acolyte was terrified of them, it turned out, and refused to ride Picket. The others grumbled as they walked, but the acolyte refused to look guilty. Finnbhear had to admire the doughy elf's mettle.

The sun was gone when they finally reached the nearest ley gate. The Six sat, grateful for a rest, and refused to budge.

"You can't expect us to barge into the temple exhausted like this," Midna whined. "The sun has set, their doors will be closed and they probably won't let us in anyway!" His companions agreed with him in silent unison.

"We should camp and rest," Aramina said. "One more night won't hurt anything, and Eahn will have time to catch up to us."

Their reluctance was touching in its own way. Possibly they dreaded the finale of their journey. They also might still be stalling, but Finnbhear refused to worry. Bodb Derg was safe, hidden from all but a select few. The Silver Fox was not one that knew.

Finnbhear finally agreed to camp and hoped he was not wrong by trusting these renegades. Just in case, he elected to take first watch after they had cooked a pot of soup and shared a flask of wine. Duinn stared at him with black, angry eyes before rolling over to sleep. Finnbhear suspected the dwarf would still be glaring, if he had eyes in the back of his head.

His ancestry came in handy during times like these. Finnbhear could stay awake for days, drawing on reserves deep within like a tree does in times of drought. Long after the breath of his companions changed from that of mock sleep into the truth, Finnbhear was awake and quietly sharpening his sword. Occasionally he looked nervously at the dwarf to wonder if he had gone too far with him.

Stealthily, Aramina crawled to him and crouched at his side. He was not surprised, although he paused his mindless stroking to indicate such. Laying his sword down with the flint on top, he picked up his water skin and drank. Aramina did not move.

"Why aren't you asleep?" he asked finally. "You'll need the rest tomorrow."

"I'm not very good at sleeping at night," Aramina said. "You know that."

"Too well," Finnbhear muttered. He tried to ignore how she wriggled close to him, the way she breathed, how her delicate hand lay on his arm. This trick was one he knew too well. As gently as he could, he withdrew from her.

"So you hate me now that we're on the same side?" she asked slyly. "Isn't that ironic."

"Why?" Finnbhear asked.

"As if you didn't know," was her reply. "All these years following me, and now that I'm here you pull away."

"It isn't that," Finnbhear protested. Then the full impact of her comment hit him. "I never followed you!"

"No? You didn't track us to the ley gate where you found the bodies? Or when you conveniently happened to be near the fountain every day I was sent to wash it? Perhaps the time you happened to be looking for a horse (which didn't exist) where I gathered herbs was just coincidence. An accident by the gods?"

"I meant after you turned, before you swore to that vile waste of carrion in the south!" Finnbhear flustered.

"I see," Aramina said sagely and turned slightly to face the campfire. "Then it was my sister you trailed after." Her smile, illuminated by the waning firelight, was thin.

"Will you always hold that against me?" Finnbhear almost wailed in misery. "You haven't the right, you know. Not after you swore to MacKegan because of Gredber and while you keep grips on the heart of your mage."

"Gredber tricked me," Aramina growled. "I thought what we were doing held no importance. I had no idea that I was betraying my god for his." Her face flickered with memory, painful and sad. "I was too new at this."

"Do you know why they call me 'Priestess?'" she asked suddenly, wearing a passion of honesty across her face. "Not because I served in the temple. No, they call me 'Priestess' for what I could have become, were it not for Gredber. The title is a mockery."

She played with her hair and looked at the ground. Finnbhear wanted to hug her, to tell her he was sorry. Years ago he might have, but now he sat beside the enemy. The sad part was, that enemy was not supposed to be on his side.

"Tomorrow you will be free," he offered.

Snaking out, her hand caught his and tugged. Caught in her glamour, knowing it without caring, Finnbhear stood with her. When they reached the edge of the camp, Finnbhear pulled back. Her grip on his hand was strong.

"I swear," Aramina said fervently. "Bodb Derg will not die tonight. But I may die tomorrow. Where is the harm in enjoying my last days in this body?"

She had tricked him in the past, but Finnbhear knew this time she spoke the truth. He followed her into the darkness.

***

Aramina touched the shoulders of each of her companions right over the Mark. The electricity of her atma woke them instantly. Quietly, they cast off furs and grabbed cloaks.

The werewolf contemplated Midna, almost touched him, then left him snoring. He would not be needed, indeed would only get in the way. Her mission depended on perfect timing now.

The ley gate deposited them into a rocky region. Duinn grunted.

"Foothills," he said. "Place looks familiar."

Each shifted to their various animal forms: a spotted horse, a black wolf, a wild boar and a grey cat. The strange group raced together through the trees. When the cat grew tired of falling behind, he leapt onto the back of the horse and clung with his claws. The pooka did not seem to mind as he galloped on, ears flat.

It was a wild ride as, heedless of pitfalls and other dangerous terrain, Picket bounded through the night. Raori growled directions when his mage's sense told him they were going the wrong way. The boar grunted, squealing, when the wolf playfully nipped a heel. The cat's ears pricked forward.

A sharp outcropping lunged out of the darkness as if invisible until then. Picket reared, dumping Raori to the grass, and wheeled around. As any cat would, Raori landed on all fours and immediately started licking his back as if to say nothing had happened. Aramina and Duinn were already snuffling around it, seeking entrance.

After a minute without success, Raori regained his two-legged shape and stepped forward. He pushed the animals away and felt along the rocks. Just beyond the tips of his questing fingers, something moved out of place. The rocks shuddered, then slowly slid aside.

Two burly elves rose from the rocks, weapons poised to kill. Aramina was immediately on one of them, bearing him to the ground in a silent rush of fur. Duinn grunted, rushing the second guard with intent to gore. Raori, again a cat, streaked past them and into the hole. Picket ghosted after him. Behind them, one of the guards screamed shortly. Then, the silence returned.

Two more guards waited in the tunnel, unaware of what was happening outside. Picket was on them without warning, pawing the air and gnashing his teeth. Unnoticed, Raori ran between their feet and kept going. Faint light called him ahead.

An elf might have stumbled into the yawning space. As a cat, Raori merely paused at the edge and examined the area with a questing nose and searching eyes. Lit candles littered the entire area, creating a beatific display of melting wonder. In the center of them was a young elf, bowing over a bronze sword and whispering to himself.

Shifting back to a two-leg, Raori pulled his dagger from its sheath and crept forward.

***

Bodb Derg had excellent hearing. He could hear the fight with the pooka near the cavern's entrance. The Six were coming for him, just as he knew they would.

As a child, his father had once told him that his vigil was an all-important part in becoming king. "Let nothing distract you," his father had said. "Not even an earthquake! You will be well protected, even if your guards are all killed outside. Trust in the spirits, my son. Not even MacKegan could break your vigil once the spells were set and the sword lay in its place."

So Bodb Derg remained as he was, staring at the family sword and concentrating on the task at hand.

The mage has just stepped into the cave, someone said near Bodb's right ear. *You must defend yourself.*

"No," Bodb whispered hoarsely. He had been speaking with these beings for hours now, and his voice was tired. "You must stop him. I cannot leave this vigil. Father, are you still there?"

Of course my son, a deeper voice said from somewhere behind him. Other voices chattered excitedly in the background. Bodb strove to ignore them. Each and every speaker where ghosts summoned by his mages for this one night. The hardest part had been getting used to the disembodied voice of his father whispering in his ear. Now that he finally had the hang of it, he dare not let his connection go.

"What advice can you give me as king?" he asked.

The people are your children, the deep voice resonated softly. *Treat them fairly, just as I treated you. Protect them just* as I protected you. And never forget that your life is theirs and not your own.

Prince, another voice said, he stalks you. We cannot stop this one.

No, other voices chorused. She wouldn't like it.

It would make her angry.

Turn around! He's almost on you!

Use the sword!

Do what you think is right, his father said. Trust your feelings, my son. Even if they appear to be steering you wrong.

The cold edge of a dagger touched his throat. Bodb had not even known when the mage came up behind him. It was easy to get lost when taking your vigil with spirits.

"Greetings, my lord," a breathless voice said behind him. The spirits fled at the sound, leaving Bodb alone and slightly confused. The dagger began to cut into his flesh.

"No," a woman's voice echoed across the cavern. "Raori, think of Duinn!"

The mage grabbed the back of Bodb's hair and pulled his head back. It was the only movement Bodb made, even when the dagger disappeared from his neck. He could see the darkness of the ceiling and the mage's perspiring face. Bodb knew if he moved now, he was dead.

"I can break that spell," the mage said haughtily.

"Before Duinn dies?" the woman asked. "I could smell the type of geis it was before even Duinn blooded it. Finnbhear did not lie when he said it will invoke itself."

"We'll tie him then," the mage said with finality. "We could even take him to MacKegan alive."

"When the rune stick is broken," the woman promised.

"We'd better hurry." Bodb was released, tossed to the earth with contempt. He started to get up, but a boot placed firmly on his back. "If the Silver Fox thinks we've escaped, Duinn's life is forfeit."

"No more than if you had cut his throat."

The boot was removed after some hesitation. Dignity was the first thing to reclaim by rolling to his knees, then Bodb grabbed his sword. Bodb stood, but the mage was already weaving his atma, creating shimmering ropes of light and throwing them over the prince. The woman, Aramina, stood before him with her hands clasped before her.

He opened his mouth to protest, knowing it was futile, and the words died in his throat. His fingers let his sword fall to the ground, which it hit with a dull thump. The spirits, whispering excitedly, were returning. Vibrations of their passing made the candle flames flicker. Some even extinguished.

The Priestess had her head cocked, listening to them.

Chills ran races down Bodb's spine as he watched Aramina. The voices faded. The Priestess gestured to the mage with her head and lead the way out of the cave. Bodb cast one last look on his sword, laying forlorn on the ground, before he was forced to ply his attention to the tunnel.

He wondered how his father felt about this. Possibly he was cursing his son for a fool, or whatever the dead did when angry. If they got angry. The prince was given the impression that spirits did not experience emotion the way mortals did. If nothing else, his friend, Chonnall, would be having some serious fits. He always did lecture Bodb about failing to defend himself. And, the mage wanted blood, badly. No doubt the others did, too.

Except for the Priestess, who looked at him with the interest of a merchant buying horses. There was no emotion to her, just calculation. Somehow that was more chilling than the rest.

They walked him at a cruel pace. The pooka was gone on an unknown errand, or they might have ridden. However, the prince had spent his entire life training for battle and hardship. When they reached the ley gate, he was barely winded.

The Priestess had charge of him while the mage cast the incantation. The dwarf stood nervously nearby, worrying about some kind of rune stick. Aramina laughed, assuring him that since Duinn himself had not harmed the prince it would not be invoked yet. So matters stood, until Finnbhear discovered what they had done.

The dwarf got a wild look in his eye and threatened the pooka's life.

Just as the ley gate lit, the Priestess leaned toward Bodb's ear. "You will not die tonight," she whispered. "I swore."

Not for the first time, Bodb strained against his bonds. The mage had done a thorough job. He had even blocked Bodb's powers to break the spell. The prince cursed himself for a fool, placing his vigil before his life. His instincts had never failed him, until now.

Finnbhear was awake, sitting by a fire and waiting for them. Picket was there also, sitting across from the fire and nursing his hand. Midna, the acolyte, was tied with a rope nearby. The Silver Fox twirled a rune stick thoughtfully. He and Bodb Derg exchanged casual nods. Relief lifted Bodb's spirits a fraction. He knew the Silver Fox was to be counted on.

"He's alive yet," the Silver Fox said smugly. "It's nice to know you care for your teammate, if nothing else."

"The cur took it," Picket said as if he could not believe the fact. "He didn't even need a sword."

Ignoring the elf by the fire, Duinn took charge of Picket's hand. The pair blocked the rest of the world out as they concentrating on the healing.

"What now?" the Silver Fox asked, turning to the Priestess. "We seem to be at an impasse. You keep the prince, I kill the dwarf."

"We let the prince go, the dwarf is dead anyway," Aramina returned.

"You had a chance with the Moonstone."

"Bah," Raori snarled, roughly shoving the prince behind him. "What's one master or another? It's all the same." Duinn and the pooka watched the mage silently. Even Aramina shrank from Raori's sudden fury.

Finnbhear positioned his fingers over the rune stick and began to invoke it.

"Stop," Aramina said. The Silver Fox shook his head and continued with the spell.

Everyone rushed at Finnbhear, except for Bodb who stood where he was, a spectator. Duinn got within two feet of the Silver Fox and froze, veins popped out and muscles bulging. The others kept coming, just behind him.

Duinn's first scream erupted in a shriek, echoing across the fields. Bodb winced at the sheer pain in it. For a second Finnbhear was distracted, his fingers faltering in their movements. In that instant, Picket and the mage were on top of him. The stick rolled on the ground to be scooped up by Aramina.

The dwarf continued to scream, crying for death and mercy as he crouched on the ground. The mage grabbed Finnbhear's hair while the pooka held him pinned by his arms. The Silver Fox's Adams's apple bobbed uncertainly.

"Release it," Raori said. "You're killing him!"

"I'm not doing it," Finnbhear choked. "I never got to finish the incantation."

"Oh no," the Priestess said, falling to her pain-wracked companion's side. "MacKegan's doing this!" Duinn stilled at her touch, sighing with relief as she concentrated. Her atma flared around them, creating a bubble of light.

"Your sorcerers must have finally told him," Finnbhear said with a grim smile. With a curse, Raori released Finnbhear to rush to Duinn's side.

It was all very interesting how Finnbhear was momentarily forgotten in concern for their friend. Bodb watched while Picket nodded to Midna and the rope untied itself, then slithered like a snake to wind around the Silver Fox's legs. The Silver Fox put up a valiant fight, but it was a rare elf that could match a pooka's strength.

With the Silver Fox safely bound, the pooka rushed to his companions. They linked hands, concentrating over the dwarf who still moaned in pain. It was soon apparent the force of the spell was too much for them, even bound together. The mage sagged to his knees, followed by Picket. Never did they break their concentration.

Bodb had not noticed the acolyte until the chubby elf touched his shoulder and spoke his name.

"Will you help them?" Midna asked in a soft whisper, eyeing The Five warily. "I know you can, my lord."

Even the acolyte had found a measure of loyalty with The Six. Bodb wondered what they did to command such emotion, even from a fat acolyte who had every reason to hate them.

"You would have to release me," the prince whispered back. "And I can only help them if they will allow it."

"I will not let the Silver Fox go," the acolyte said. "He would kill them this time."

Before Bodb could say anything, the acolyte touched the bonds and broke them one by one. Standing free, the prince flexed his sore muscles only once before dashing to the dwarf's aid. The others did not take notice. Their entire wills were bent on holding back MacKegan.

It was like holding a mountain of glass shards with bare hands. Bodb Derg concentrated, pushing back the force to its source. Someone touched him with a glowing hand. Suddenly he was filled with strength, a feeling he never knew he had lacked until then.

Bodb wrenched, pulling at a key place. The mountain of shards began to slide, scattering into harmless flickers of atma. Before long the prince was the only one standing by three exhausted elves, who shielded the dwarf with their bodies.

"Midna," Raori gasped. "Kill the prince. We'll carry his head to MacKegan if he have to, to show him the sorcerers are wrong."

"But he helped you," the acolyte protested meekly.

"Do it!" Raori managed to shout, half rising from the ground.

Bodb backed away, fighting to keep standing and looking for a place to go. Without a weapon and weakened from the extensive use of atma, he had little defense. If he could free Finnbhear–

"No," a low voice said from beneath. "You fat ninny, you leave the prince alone. I won't have it."

Weakly, Duinn got to his feet and stood swaying before the prince. Judging by Raori's expression, he could not decide if Duinn was serious or preparing to attack.

"You saved me from that torture," Duinn said. He knelt, humbling himself further by lowering his face to his knee. "I am forever your servant, my lord. Command me."

Numbly Bodb reached out and touched the dwarf's shoulder to accept his fealty. It was the only thing to do. He wondered what his father would have done. Chonnall, he was sure, would have kicked the dwarf and run while he could.

"Feral madness!" Raori swore, painfully standing and searching for his lost dagger. He found it near Finnbhear's feet. In vain, the Silver Fox tried to kick the mage. "I'll do it, then!"

"Through me!" Duinn said, standing before the prince.

"I'm with Duinn," Picket said clearly. He stood beside the dwarf and appeared fresh, for all his ordeal before.

Midna took position by the pooka. He was visibly trembling, but his quiet stance was unmistakable.

"Blast you all," Raori said before stumbling into the darkness. Everyone watched him go in a mixture of shock and relief. Aramina started to follow then paused at the edge of camp.

"I have to go with him," she said without facing them. "The mission... I'm sorry." Then she bounded into the darkness on all fours, howling as she went, furry tail the last of her they saw.

Chapter Nineteen
"Choice over Promise"

Weeping, Raori stumbled blindly through the night, heedless of how the dagger blade cut into his hand. Behind him, Aramina's howl flowed through the air. He knew she followed at a distance, but he did not care. The sting of betrayal kept his feet pounding the turf noiselessly. His breath came in ragged gasps.

When he was too blind with exhaustion to see, he tripped and sprawled on the ground. Futilely he grabbed grass, roots, whatever was in reach and pulled himself forward. Soon he could not even do that. His tears fell to the ground unheeded. Soil made his mouth gritty, his eyes burn.

Aramina's lupine presence wrapped around him, tickling his nose with fur. They remained entwined on the ground until Raori fell asleep. The sun rose, and they were still together.

Enveloped in Aramina's soft fur, Raori felt warm and oddly comforted. When he should be getting up he continued to nestle beside her, feeling her tail wrapped around his neck. Her breathing was a gentle rhythm in his soul. His fingers flexed, caressing her pelt.

Voices surrounded them. He thought he heard Aramina's voice answering them, but that was impossible. She was right by him. Yet her voice was over his shoulder, to the distance.

Raori opened his eyes and lifted his head. The voices stopped immediately. He looked for their owners, but the only thing nearby was a grove of stunted trees. Aramina rolled away from him, grunting as she did.

"I'm sorry," Raori said. "I thought I heard someone."

She did not change, although he wanted her to. Forced to take comfort in her lupine shape, Raori sat next to her. Aramina did not mind, indeed closed her eyes in pleasure when he scratched behind her ears.

"What do we do?" he asked the wolf sadly. "The others will have reached the Moonstone by now. MacKegan will be furious. There will be only you, me and Eahn if he can be found."

Three would be left under Moirfenn's control. Poignant sadness at the revelation filled the mage. He thought of how close the team had been, and Leannahn. Of Duinn's senseless yelling, Picket's pranks, the rush of adrenaline before a mission.

Would Aramina miss it, also?

No one was quite like Aramina. Burning the city of Cnos Fada centuries before had been her idea. Everyone else had not believed it could be done by the five of them alone. With a simple combustion spell and ten barrels of foul-smelling liquid obtained from the dwarves, she had not only achieved her goal but won them favor with MacKegan.

Like Picket. If it was trouble, causing it came in second only after running from it. Preferably with the angry victims close behind, plenty of pebbles on the road and a few tall fences in the way.

As a dwarf, Duinn never took sides in fae creatures' battles. But he took sides when caring for his teammates. Never had Raori known a softer-touched healer. Or someone who fought so hard not to show how he cared.

And although Eahn scowled and spat with each order, there always came a sheen of delight in his eyes while carrying them out. There was no denying he loved his work.

Raori supposed the only thing to do was return to Moirfenn and take what may come. MacKegan might not be outrageously insane with anger, if he could be made to understand that Raori had returned of his own.

The wolf looked up, ears forward and half-barked. She crept forward, stood, looked back at Raori. Her eyes gleamed with mischief. She wanted to play and forget their troubles.

Raori could not be bothered by that now. Plans had to be made. His first order of business was to find a way to contact Eahn. If that failed, MacKegan was the only thing left.

Aramina tugged his clothes, let go to pad forward, returned to tug his clothing again. Raori shooed her off. Dancing, she dashed in and grabbed his belt pouch.

Raori felt a sharp pull, then the strings parted. Aramina came away with the pouch firmly between her teeth. She ran a few feet, then dropped the pouch. Her entire stance said, *Come and get it if you can.*

"Give that back!" Raori shouted, getting to his feet to retrieve the pouch. Aramina grabbed it up and ran further away.

"Aramina," Raori begged, walked forward slowly. The wolf backed away, toward the trees. "Please. We have things to do. We can't play right now."

The wolf just stood there, watching him with lupine eyes.

Raori ran his fingers through his hair and sighed. There was no sign in her of the woman he loved. Eahn had called her feral more than once. Perhaps she had decided to embrace the sickness, now that there seemed to be no other choice.

He wondered if it was so bad, to allow yourself to become lost in the freedom of a simpler life. As if in response to his unvoiced question, the wolf came forward and lay his pouch within reach. Raori looked at the pouch, the wolf, the pouch and the wolf again.

Shrugging, Raori released his mortal shape and landed softly on paws of silver-grey. The wolf yipped and bounded at him, initiating their favorite game. She streaked after the cat toward the grove.

The pouch was soon forgotten, even by memory. Laying nearby, the swan medallion shared its fate.

***

Tech Danaan.

It was an island north from Cnos Fada, set in the middle of a placid lake. No one remembered how old it was, but people journeyed even from Moirfenn to reach it.

The temple was a wonder of architecture, especially at night when the stars shone overhead and all the lamps were lit. The entire building was of pale stone and carved to resemble trees covered in vines, flowers and butterflies. It covered most of the island and seemed to be floating on a lake of flickering light.

Duinn had to remember to breathe when he first saw it.

"Took me that way, too," Finnbhear said casually. "For different reasons, I imagine." His thoughts were on his youth. If he knew dwarves, Duinn's thoughts were on a set of chisels and a hammer.

"Are you sure they will let us in now?" the pooka asked nervously. He scratched his shoulder in agitation.

Morning was still a couple of hours away, but Bodb Derg wanted them in Tech Danaan immediately. Finnbhear was more than eager to reach the Moonstone. It was only a matter of time before the geis turned the pooka against them. MacKegan seemed to have given up on the dwarf for now, but there was no telling for sure. With MacKegan, anything was possible.

"Let's find out," he said jovially. A little bridge was the only way to cross the water. Stepping onto it, he paused only to motion for them to hurry.

Midna groaned when they were halfway across. Duinn was right behind him and feeling nervous with the water so close to the soles of his feet. Dwarves sank like stone in water and breathed with less skill.

"Move along, you ninny," Duinn fairly shouted. He shoved the acolyte and watched with satisfaction when the elf stumbled forward.

"Oh, they'll rush to let us in now," Picket said with a snort. "Who wouldn't welcome a band of spies, crossing the water like an angry mob?"

"Peace," cautioned Finnbhear. Taking Midna's arm, he helped the acolyte the rest of the way. Once on dry land, Midna sank to his knees and did not move.

"Feeling sick?" Duinn asked. He could not help but goad the lad. Of course, it might have been more satisfying if he had received more than a soft grunt as an answer.

Finnbhear lifted one of the massive knockers on the brass doors and pushed with all his might. The resulting sound was surprisingly dull.

The doors swung ponderously open almost before the last vibration faded from the air. Two acolytes, belted with red sashes, bowed deeply while barring the entrance. Another elf, a priest of low rank, stood behind them.

"Why do you disturb the temple before dawn?" he asked.

"We have business here," Finnbhear said. "Surely the messenger from Cnos Fada has already come and gone."

"You are the ones the new king sent to us?" The elf looked around with beady eyes. "I see only four of you. Were there not three more?"

"They found better things to do," Duinn snapped, pushing through the acolytes' legs. Being short had its advantages. "Where is the Moonstone?"

"Patience," Finnbhear said with amusement. He and the pooka stepped forward, making it pointless for the acolytes to remain in the way. They allowed them through with no argument. "Take us to the High Priest. He knows to see us."

The priest acted as if no chore could be worse, but he did as bade. They were led to an alcove and instructed to wait while the High Priest was summoned. Picket settled down comfortably in a corner. Midna touched every wall with a look of amazement fixed permanently on his face. Finnbhear and Duinn busied themselves counting cracks in the floor. The game became more fun when both discovered that counting aloud confused the other's train of thought.

The High Priest must have been standing in the alcove for a long time before Duinn noticed him. His voice faded to a murmur, shushing Finnbhear's in turn. The High Priest, an old elf of medium stature, smiled coldly.

"So, I stand before members of The Six of Moirfenn," he said. "Should I be honored, or afraid?" He kept both hands clasped, tucked in his sleeves, as he bowed.

"Are you willing to be helpful?" Finnbhear asked, struggling to keep the irritation from his voice. "They have come to visit the Moonstone."

"So I understand." The priest examined them from where he stood. "Where are the other two, the mage and Aramina?" His voice dripped with suspicion.

"You might ask, where are the other three," Finnbhear said coldly. "Who do you take me for, one of them?"

"I had assumed," the High Priest said. "Are you not?"

"No." Finnbhear introduced himself, then the others. "The Northern Thorn has disappeared. We fear treachery. The mage and Aramina parted ways from us not long ago."

With the introduction, the High Priest was mollified. "A pity," he said. "Not every hare can change its winter pelt, but the girl I had hoped to see. I knew her, you see, when she first came to the temple in Cnos Fada. Indeed, I saved her life."

"Funny she never mentioned you," Finnbhear said, feeling a pang of jealousy. He had first come to know her while she was serving the temple.

She had been bitter, he remembered, about being there for so long and not even ranking acolyte. He used to help her with her chores around the temple, listening to her gripe and telling jokes to cheer her up.

"She may not remember," the High Priest said. "I found her unconscious in the hills outside Cnos Fada, gored by an animal and burning with fever. But that cannot change things now. Follow me and I will take you to the Moonstone."

Midna eagerly bounded after the High Priest, but Picket and Duinn hung behind. They stood close together, almost back to back, as if surrounded by enemies. Finnbhear blamed the High Priest', who had not made him feel welcome either.

The Moonstone, it turned out, was a giant white rock polished to a gleam and shaped like a teardrop. Placed in the middle of a bare room, waves of power oozed from it and set the skin tingling. Finnbhear began to feel slightly giddy.

With pale faces, Picket and Duinn paused outside the room. A sense of comradery caused Finnbhear to stop with them. All eyes were fixed on the glowing white rock.

"You will get used to it," the High Priest said reassuringly. "Still, I suggest you visit it only one at a time."

"I don't think I can," the pooka whispered. The dwarf merely looked, mouth agape.

"May I?" Midna asked, braving a step forward. Compared to the majesty of the Moonstone in his ripped robes, he looked like a beggar.

With the High Priest's nod, Midna approached the Moonstone. Picket and Duinn actually looked like they might be sick. The pooka scratched his shoulder. His fingers came away bloody.

"Priest," Finnbhear breathed. "If they can't go near it, how is it supposed to free them?" Blood was staining the back of Picket's shirt, spreading slowly out across the white fabric.

"My name is Mornnacht," the High Priest said with a haughty sniff. "Don't worry. There are ways. First you will eat with me. Nothing will happen until they visit the stone. MacKegan's power cannot touch these two in the temple."

In the room, Midna touched the stone and cried out in ecstasy.

Disgusting, Finnbhear thought. Throughout a simple meal of bread, wine and cheese the cry of Midna rang in his mind. The acolyte had been removed to a room by himself, where he slept deeply.

If that was what the stone did, Finnbhear would be happy never to touch it.

"There will be volunteers to help you," Mornnacht was saying to Duinn. "I knew you might not be able to approach the Moonstone alone, but with five to shield you and keep you on your feet it can be done."

The dwarf mumbled something into his glass.

"What will you do, once the Marks are removed?" the priest asked almost wistfully. "Have you thought beyond this moment?"

"Aye." Picket nodded with the word. "I have a family to care for. They will be content in Éire, to be sure."

Duinn flicked his eyes toward something beyond the walls. "The river is clean here," he said. "I might build a forge nearby. I could grow old here."

"Yes," Mornnacht said. "I had been told your little band chose immortality. A gift our people have forgotten, pity. It's not a popular choice these days, considering the price."

"Well paid," Duinn said.

Finnbhear yawned. All eyes turned to him, accusing him for interrupting. "I'm sorry," the Silver Fox said. "But it has been a long time since I slept properly."

"Then you must rest." Mornnacht waved a hand, and the priests from the door rushed forward from the shadows. "You each shall have a room and whatever you need. I will have you sent for at noon."

Finnbhear's room was small and apparently furnished in a rushed last minute. He would have been grateful for a blanket on the hard floor. The worn couch provided was more than enough. He was asleep in seconds.

A soft click, Finnbhear's eyes were open before he knew he was awake. Sunlight coming through a small window near the ceiling streamed in, hitting the foot of his bed and warming his toes. The door was closed. He was alone.

And something was wrong.

Finnbhear shut his eyes and softened his breathing. There was another click, then the soft creak of a door being stealthily opened. The Silver Fox was careful only to move, as a restless sleeper, to turn his face toward the door. There was no other sound.

Life as a soldier had taught him when to move, and he did. Someone stabbed the couch were he used to lay, cursed at Finnbhear who was on the floor and rolling to his feet. When the Silver Fox rose, he came equipped with his sword.

The assassin was dressed in black robes lined with silver. His sleeves were thrown back, leaving the Mark of Moirfenn visible on his forearm. No doubt his dagger was dipped with poison as well. The glint of it was purple-red.

At first the assassin lunged wildly at the Silver Fox, who deftly dodged to the left. He swung his sword, but missed. The assassin crouched, grinning with blackened teeth.

His grin never faltered as the assassin turned the dagger on himself and buried it deep in his groin. He sagged to the floor with a small gasp, sprawling at Finnbhear's feet.

The sunlight moved an inch. Finnbhear did not move during this time. The shock turned him tree-like, unmoving while his mind digested recent events. Then, slowly, he crouched on the floor.

Finnbhear turned the body over. Already the corpse was turning blue. The Mark on his arm was fading, spreading across the skin like dye on wet cloth. His dagger had lost its angry glint in lieu of a more normal silver color.

So this was a black assassin. Finnbhear had heard of them, but never thought to face one. They were said to be insane, beyond feral and mad for blood.

Still, an insane creature should have the sense to attack rather than commit suicide.

Finnbhear hid the body as well as he could, then locked the door behind him. He hoped no one would come along before he found out more of what was going on.

Picket was not in his room, but Finnbhear found him in Duinn's. The two ceased talking immediately, looking at Finnbhear with suspicious eyes. Between them lay a familiar-looking dagger.

"It's not midday yet," Duinn said into the silence.

"Nay." Finnbhear leaned against the door frame, crossing his arms. "Where did you get that?"

"Found it," the pooka said shortly.

Finnbhear lost his patience. "Enough of this. You placed yourselves into my hands, now you have to trust me a little."

Pooka and dwarf looked at each other and held a silent debate. Finnbhear was tempted to knock them both on the heads.

"All right," Duinn said. "We were attacked this morning. By a black assassin."

"Funny that," Finnbhear said. "Did your attacker kill himself, or did one of you do it?"

"It was self defense," Duinn argued.

"Understandably." Grimly, Finnbhear related his own experience with Moirfenn's assassin. "Apparently if MacKegan can't get you one way he'll try another."

The two exchanged another look. "He hasn't had time to send his assassins," Duinn said. "Not those. They're kept... elsewhere."

Elsewhere could be anything with Chulain MacKegan. Finnbhear elected not to ask just which elsewhere Duinn meant.

"I want to see the Moonstone now," Picket said, with a stamp of one foot. "Priest or no priest."

Getting lost in a structure as huge as the temple, they found, was easy. No one was about to ask directions of although the morning was quickly approaching noon. It was assumed everyone else was still asleep or outside working.

They stumbled across the High Priest's chambers accidentally but fortuitously. After a quick argument, it was decided they would see if he was in. Picket motioned for Duinn to open the door.

"Let the Silver Fox do it," Duinn snapped.

"I can't pick a lock," Finnbhear protested.

"It's time you learned," Duinn replied gruffly.

"I'll do it," Picket said, touching the lock almost nonchalantly. The door swung open with the touch.

"Why didn't you do that when we kidnapped the fat acolyte?" Duinn demanded loudly.

"Maybe he wanted you to look foolish," Finnbhear said. "You did look funny, perched on top of his shoulders like a stumpy weather vane."

"A weather vane, am I?" Duinn rounded on Finnbhear. It was like being threatened by a fat rat. "Stumpy, am I?"

"Hush," the pooka reprimanded. "You'll have the temple thinking we're here to kill the priest."

"Looks like somebody beat us to it," Finnbhear said with dread.

The room was destroyed. What furnishings Mornnacht had owned were shattered. The couch looked like his killers had vented their frustrations on it, and then the floor. The High Priest was no where to be seen.

Picket carefully closed the door. He walked down the hall as if he knew where he was going. Duinn was not far behind. It took Finnbhear a moment to catch up.

Picket started to whistle.

"Let's not have that," Duinn said. "That's a dead giveaway if ever I heard one."

"We haven't done anything wrong," Finnbhear mused.

"Want to lay bets the killers want them to think we did?" Duinn asked.

"Just what I was thinking." They stopped at an intersection. Finnbhear felt something new in the air; It made his hair stand on end. Without thinking he turned down the new corridor, toward the strange element.

"I hate being lost," Picket said.

"We're not lost," Finnbhear said. They stepped out of the corridor and into the room that held the Moonstone. "We're right where we wanted to be."

Belatedly he realized he had entered the room alone.

Picket and Duinn were both sagging to the floor and staring at the stone like zombies. Shakily, the pooka scratched his shoulder. As before, his fingers came away wet with blood. Finnbhear knew without looking that Duinn's shoulder was also bleeding.

Then it dawned on him that he was not as affected with the stone as before. Whatever the Moonstone was doing, it only seemed to affect Picket and Duinn.

Finnbhear hauled the pooka to his feet. Picket was heavy as three horses and made no effort to help. His blood coated his back and smeared Finnbhear's chest. Some had gotten onto the floor. The Silver Fox slipped in it, almost losing his balance.

"You wanted to see this blasted stone," Finnbhear grunted. "Now walk to it, you great idiot." He staggered forward.

The closer he got to the Moonstone, the heavier Picket seemed to become. It was all Finnbhear could do to prop the pooka against it when he finally reached it. Picket shivered where he was, moaning softly, then fell to the floor unconscious.

Duinn was more difficult because he was short and had to be carried like a small child. Twice Finnbhear sagged to his knees, slipping in the dwarf's blood. The Moonstone was beginning to affect him, sapping his strength as it did the others. When Finnbhear finally lay Duinn beside it, he felt as if he had died five times over.

Weakly, Duinn touched the Moonstone and passed out.

It was a long time before Finnbhear had the energy to open his eyes. He did not want to, but someone was talking to him.

"Surprised at you. You've more mettle than I thought," the High Priest was saying from where he stood just at the edge of the room. "I am curious to see if you have the strength to make it out."

Behind him, the lesser priest and two acolytes in red stood with their arms crossed. Finnbhear thought they might want to step in and give him a hand. He did not have time to express this opinion before he blacked out.

***

Duinn opened his eyes. Yes, there was the ceiling. He remembered the crack shaped like a lightening bolt. His couch was a comforting lump beneath him. His fingers clenched on fur.

He sat, trying to ignore the pounding ache between his eyes. Someone had placed a small bowl of fruit just inside the doorway. Greedily he bit into a pear and drank the juices. When the bowl was filled with empty husks, he tried to open the door.

It was locked.

Now that was funny. Perhaps the High Priest wanted him to stay immured for some reason. Possibly it something to do with the ceremonies before touching the Moonstone. Mornnacht had said he would send someone. Duinn waited.

In another cubicle that was furnished only with a bail of hay, Picket stood with his nose hanging between his forelegs. He was only just waking up, but preferred to remain inert. His tail flicked once, as if brushing off a dream fly.

His ears swiveled, trying to detect sounds that were not there.

A hoof lifted, lowered slowly, was lifted again.

Picket raised his head.

Pookas are wild creatures by their very nature. Their supernatural strength, spirit, their very outward appearance reflects this personality. Beneath a mild-mannered face lurks the mind of a beast; One with the soul of the wind and the sureness of the hurricane.

Picket was a storm locked in a tiny room with a bit of straw.

First he squealed, then trumpeted his warning. He bucked, smashing the door with his hind legs. They did not give away at first, but after the fourth impact they splintered into the hall. Picket changed to two legs just long enough to step into the hall. After that he was pounding the polished floor with his hooves as he thundered away.

No one rushed to stop him, nor opened doors to investigate what the commotion was. Picket surged toward Duinn's room, a new urgency in his flight.

He crashed through Duinn's door and stood among the shambles, nose quivering, tail swishing, forelocks out of place and ears flat. Duinn looked down from his perch halfway up the wall, mouth agape.

"You ninny!" Duinn shouted, climbing down gingerly. "Now look what you've done!" Mournfully he crouched over the remnants of the door and fingered the splinters. "It must have taken the craftsman weeks to carve this door alone, and you destroyed it." He looked like he might weep.

Picket was forced to shift back to two legs to explain. "There's more wrong here than we thought," he said. "There are no priests about. Where is Finnbhear? How did we get to our rooms after the Moonstone? Where did the black assassins come from? What--"

"Wait," Duinn said, raising a gnarled hand for silence. "You're telling me last night was no dream."

"Of course, but--"

"Hammer Rings and Broken Shards!" Duinn threw down the splinters. "Picket, we have to get out of here."

As if the move were rehearsed, Duinn jumped onto Picket's back just as the pooka shifted form. While Picket galloped down the hallway, Duinn leaned as far forward as he could and explained in the pooka's ear.

The dwarf had begun to suspect something was wrong the minute they were allowed in the temple. It was not the High Priest's chilly greeting, expected considering the Five's past. It was the emptiness of a place that should be filled with hundreds. There was also the way Mornnacht would not, almost could not, approach the Moonstone himself. More than that, it was an aura about him; something only a blacksmith learned to feel.

The scent of weaponry. More specifically, black-dawned, blood thirsty weaponry as such could only be found in Moirfenn. There was no telling how long ago the real priests of Tech Danaan had perished under MacKegan's blade, but it was done.

Picket's reaction to Duinn's tale was to lay his ears flat against his head. His stride became choppy with fear and anger. It bothered him that none of The Six knew about this. Duinn was forced to dismount and run alongside the pooka, who shifted alternately between forms as he ran.

It was best to get out while they could, Duinn advised, without wasting time to search for Finnbhear or the acolyte. If they happened upon them they would do what they could to help, of course. More than likely, Bodb's favorite servant was dead.

They slid to a halt when they came upon the Moonstone for the fourth time.

"Blast it!" Duinn shouted. The only direction they had not tried was on the other side of the Moonstone. He had no desire to attempt approaching the spectral object again.

Picket's momentum had carried him a few feet farther than Duinn. He froze in man form, facing the stone, before automatically scratching his shoulder. Sweat trickled down his back, glistening his buttocks.

A small part of Duinn's mind decided that later there must be time to teach the pooka how to shift with his clothing on. Even his freckles were shivering in fear of the rock ahead. Somehow being able to see them—all of them—was too lewd for the dwarf to say.

"That's the way out," Duinn said, averting his eyes from Picket's back. "I would lay my mother's life on it."

"But would your mother?" Picket asked half-heartedly.

Both fae beings looked longingly at the opening. The Moonstone might have been a mountain for all their power to cross the room.

"Well," Picket said hesitantly, "did the Moonstone work for you?"

"I wasn't the one bound by my soul," Duinn said. "What about you?"

The pooka shrugged.

"We'll have to try," Duinn said heavily.

Together they began to cross. The force from the Moonstone made their heads light. Picket nickered to himself. Duinn punched his ribs to bring him back to sobriety.

Seven steps and they were past the Moonstone. By that time, they felt like Raori on a good day with seven wine bottles. They linked arms and staggered out the last few steps. The far doorway welcomed them.

Mornnacht and his lackeys were just inside the next room.

"You were supposed to stay where you were," the High Priest whined. "Can't you obey one simple command?"

"We're leaving," Duinn announced. "You're not our keeper, and you'll not hold us here." The effects of the

Moonstone were beginning to wear off. Proudly he noted that the steps he took toward Mornnacht were steady.

"But I am indeed your keeper," Mornnacht said smoothly. "MacKegan asked me to keep you here, until he has decided what to do with you."

Duinn froze. Beside him, Picket panicked and lost control of his shape again. He settled on the spotted horse, the easier form to manage, and pawed the air menacingly.

Mornnacht raised his arm to signal. His sleeves fell away. Moirfenn's Mark was revealed. The acolytes who had greeted them at the door appeared as if from nowhere, dressed in the black attire of Moirfenn's deadliest killers. With wicked grins, they advanced as if going to a picnic.

Somewhere, Duinn decided as he dodged the first attack and extended a leg to trip an adversary, the gods were having a good laugh at Duinn the dwarf. Only a sadistic deity would throw him from one situation to another with only a half-crazed fairy for a companion.

The half-crazed fairy companion performed one of his impossible leaps, clearing the heads of all three assassins and landing in front of Mornnacht. The High Priest screamed thinly, scrambling away.

Then Duinn found himself cornered by two assassins and lost track of what the pooka was doing. Which was just as well. Worrying about someone else, even a friend of over two centuries, while in the middle of a fight could be fatal. Duinn could always mourn over Picket's body later, but if he lost his own he would be too dead to care.

To make matters worse, he was caught without a weapon again! This was becoming a habit and needed to be stopped. Duinn remedied the situation by punching one assassin in the groin, then tossing him at another.

The second assassin dodged his flying comrade and drew his needle-thin sword. Duinn merely shrugged.

Elves had their divine atma, the source of their incantations and prophetic doings. Fairies were something else, a conglomeration of atma perhaps and allowed their beings to reflect that state. Dwarves had their wits, their strength and knowledge.

The assassin faced a blacksmith dwarf who had lived long enough to learn more than he ought and was very determined to keep doing so. When Duinn sidestepped to give himself room and buy a little time, the assassin should have made his move.

He also might have rushed to stop Duinn's artfully placed fingers and whistled tune. Or performed a fancy kick, flipping over the dwarf and slicing Duinn's cranium in one fluid motion. Instead, he stood still and watched what he thought was a useless action.

After all, what could the dwarf do against a Black Assassin of Moirfenn? The assassin always had found it amusing to allow his prey time to think. It gave them a false sense of hope. Nothing was more satisfying than seeing the light die from his victim's eyes.

When nothing happened, the assassin chuckled to himself and swiped at the dwarf. It was not a fancy move, just a practical one. He aimed to cut the little one in half, but the dwarf was no longer where he was supposed to be. The sword hit the wall, making a tiny chink sound, then shattered.

Duinn smiled into the assassin's face just before punching his nose, pushing the cartilage into the brain and ending that aspect of the battle. He looked for Picket.

Picket was backed against a wall. The other two assassins were pressing him from both sides. The pooka's eyes were almost white with terror. His legs were stiff and dark with sweat.

Only one of the assassins held a weapon, his sword. The other had his fist raised, extended toward the pooka. They laughed together, taking delight in Picket's discomfort. Picket rolled his eyes.

Enough was enough. Duinn scrambled forward as fast as he could go, bowling into the assassins before they had a chance to turn their heads. The sword clattered to the floor, sliding away in its inertia.

Duinn was on the nearest assassin, groping for his neck. Someone grabbed him from behind, lifting him up. Suddenly he was landing on the ground, the breath knocked out of him and his senses dazed.

His side exploded. The last air left his lungs. Duinn gasped, feebly trying to get up. Something squealed, crashing beside him, thundering the floor with its weight. Instinct kicked in. Duinn scurried out of harm's way, and did not stop until he was beyond the door to the Moonstone. Only then did he look back.

Picket was bracing an assassin's body on the floor with his forefeet and pulling its hair with his teeth. The other assassin was clutching his groin, doubled over and helpless.

Duinn had felt the power of a normal horse's hoof and could only imagine the pain the assassin was feeling. The dwarf grimaced in sympathy.

Then he ran and used his momentum to deliver a punch to the assassin's face and laughed as the assassin flew backwards. Picket abandoned the corpse to face this new sport. The assassin, crumpled against the wall, did not move.

Picket pranced in place, snorting rapidly and tossing his mane. Absently, Duinn stroked his neck.

"What did that assassin have?" he asked. "I've never seen you so terrified."

The neck pulled away, dissolving as it went. Picket coughed almost delicately into his fist. "A hollow stone," he said. He shrugged his shoulders to indicate a direction.

Discarded, forlorn, where it had fallen was a small stone with a hole through the center. Its grayish hue, the polished sheen from constant handling indicated other uses. It might have been a sight-stone but for its lack of runic carving.

Then Duinn noticed how the grains of color in the stone blended, forming the pattern of a sun with the hole as its eye. The dwarf whistled softly to himself, pocketing the stone quickly.

"A natural sight-stone," the dwarf said wondrously. "Never thought I'd see the like." Hooves clipping the floor,

Picket the horse stepped forward and pushed Duinn's shoulder with his nose. "They would have seen your true self."

Comprehension of a fairy's true self. It was an impossible deed, but mortals and wizards attempted it repeatedly. Threat of the act made the gentle folk shy of encounter and terrified of those holding the hollow stones.

The pooka flicked his tail, pointing his nose toward the deepest parts of the temple and walked forward. Going to find the Silver Fox and that blasted acolyte, Duinn figured. What else could he do but follow?

Just as he passed the Moonstone, his eye caught a separate spark on the floor. Nestled in the larger stone's shadow was a piece of rock long as his forearm. It was no natural break, Duinn determined as he inspected the groove it came from. Someone had broken it away with a chisel. With a shrug, he picked it up.

Picket was long gone. The dwarf had to run to catch up.

It was a beautiful day, even compared to some nights. The sun shone like an enormous bonfire over the young land of Fion. Its heat warmed Duinn's leather to uncomfortable temperatures, forcing him to discard it as he traveled. He would collect it on his way back to camp.

Violet petals caught his eye, drew his hand down to pluck it from the earth. It went into a small satchel full of like blossoms, a rare display of botanic blues. They would be dried later and stored for medicinal purposes.

Something moved in the grass on a hill. Ever curious, Duinn forgot his harvest and trudged toward it. He expected whatever it was to take flight, but it took no notice. The sun flashed in his eyes. Dwarves were creatures of dark tunnels, and the sun taxed his sight mercilessly.

Even standing a few feet away, Duinn could not quite make out a form. It might be a colt or a young man laying in the grass. Duinn blinked. The shape before him finally settled for two legs and a long face covered in freckles.

"I hae' nothing for you to take," said the stranger in an antique accent. "So forget about robbery." He was naked but

did not seem to mind. Disconsolately he chewed one of the purple blossoms.

Duinn squatted in the grass and studied this apparition. "Why don't you run?" he asked. "I never thought to see one of your kind in broad daylight, naked and waiting for capture."

"Tis too late for that," the man said with a nod of his head and neck.

"Why?" Duinn asked, carefully settling into the grass so as not to frighten away the faerie. They were elusive at best, and this was a rare opportunity. If he played his cards right, he might be gifted with a fortune.

"On account of your lord yonder." The man flicked a wrist away, toward the direction of Duinn's camp. There Duinn's employer, Chulain MacKegan, waited with a sore throat and aching joints for the bounty of Duinn's harvest.

Duinn had met Chulain MacKegan years ago when he and his uncle visited MacKegan's keep during a merchant's expedition. It had been a perfect chance to display his skills. Perhaps he had overplayed his hand by gifting the somber lord with a dagger carved to resemble bones. He and his uncle had left the next morning feeling strangely unsafe, for all of MacKegan's lavish hospitality.

Then the messengers had arrived, for Duinn alone, with offers of employment. He had been tempted by the new lord's offer of large pay in return for making arms for his troops. Dwarves took neither side when it came to the wars of elves, so he accepted the position in Chulain's court.

And if his new lord required other services such as a swift raid with Eahn or collecting plants for MacKegan's ills, then Duinn found no discomfort. It broke the monotony of seeing his forge every day and brought an extra sack of gold besides.

MacKegan had been requiring odd errands ever more of late, but Duinn put it down to a lack of trusted servants. And no more than Duinn could trust this lord. He wondered if the feeling were mutual.

"He looked at me with the sight-stone," the man said. His posture was of a horse whipped and tied to a firm stake. "While I was bathing yonder."

Well there went any chance for gold. It had been a nice delusion, though.

Poor creature. Shifting as many of the fae folk were, their true essence was said to be the most beautiful sight in the realm. Legend said to look through a hollow stone let the viewer witness a faerie's actual self and gain the power to command them. The fairy would be bound until the moon's cycle had run a complete course.

Duinn knew no tales that spoke of a faerie's fate in this circumstance, but his imagination gave him room to run. Knowing MacKegan as he did, he felt a great amount of pity for the creature before him.

"'Tis only a temporary thing, you know that," Duinn said, offering the only comfort he could to this stranger. Against all reasoning, he felt the urge to stroke the man's nose. He fought it off with a shrug.

"Long enough to hurt me," the fae said. "Or make me hurt someone else. Either way, I'm dead to the others until I'm free."

Duinn knew next to nothing about faerie society. He had heard of the faerie's situation and of others being rescued in a vengeful display of power. Wisely he said nothing.

"I would ask my parents for help, but what can they do? I am a mere horse, not even important. The kings care nothing for the likes of me."

"You are a pooka then," Duinn said.

"Aye."

Duinn grunted. "Come with me," he said. "I'll speak to Chulain. Perhaps you would like to be my partner a while? I promise you'll fare better with me than at what whim suits the master."

The pooka's long face turned to the dwarf. A glint in his eye said he would like that very much, probably had even planned it. "Thankee," the pooka said. "You are very kind."

CHAPTER TWENTY
"BODB DERG"

Candles in tall holders carved like saplings and vines lined the walkway to the chair in the hall. The gentry were crowded behind them, whispering to each other in excitement. The High Priest, a frail elf with a tick in his right eye, waited patiently by the chair.

It was a very crowded and awe-inspiring scene. Leaning against the wall outside the chamber, Bodb wished he had siblings to pass his inheritance to. Right now.

Even a little sister to complain about would be nice. Unfortunately his mother had died giving birth to him, and his father had never loved another. Bodb was sure his father would have told him if he had a half-sibling somewhere.

"I wonder if they're looking forward to seeing you or dining on the feast afterward." The comment was from Chonnall, who leaned nonchalantly against the doorframe. He peeked through the door with his hands nonchalantly behind his back, as if eavesdropping were a natural matter.

"They're probably waiting to dine on me at the feast," Bodb muttered, fretting with his cloak and pacing a little.

"Especially that one," Chonnall observed. "Gods, she licks her lips as if she's tasted you already!"

"Let me see." Bodb rudely shoved Chonnall aside and fixed his eye in the crack. "I can't see her. Which one?"

"The one wearing the green mantle," Chonnall said, taking Bodb's former place by the wall. "See her yet?"

"No I, wait, yes I do." Bodb stood back in disgust. "Chonnall, she's a little girl!"

"When you're through convincing her father to let you have her, she'll be grown," Chonnall said nonchalantly. "Might take that long just to get into their yard, judging by the sight of you." He indicated Bodb's fancy clothes and wrinkled his nose.

Bodb punched Chonnall's upper arm. The two grinned and began wrestling in earnest. Their laughter echoed down the hall.

"My lord, please stop," a lesser priest hissed at them as he slipped in through the door. "You have the people in there looking around in alarm. They think MacKegan has come to slaughter them!"

Guiltily, both young elves banished their play and looked at their feet.

"I suppose it's time to begin," Bodb said with a sigh. He had wanted to give the Silver Fox more time to return with his new allies. Brave assurances or not, he would feel better when he had the wizened elf around again.

"Get going," Chonnall said, giving Bodb a friendly shove in the small of his back. "Do I have to go out there for you?"

Bodb found himself shoved ungracefully beyond the door with the priest whispering instructions behind him. The assembly turned in one silent motion to witness the newcomer.

Bodb grinned and made a small wave. Someone near the back clapped. The lonely sound faltered to an unsure halt.

The High Priest impatiently motioned for the prince to approach. Straightening his shoulders, Bodb walked down the aisle like a prince should. Every pore in his body breathed self-assurance.

His father once told him that no matter how insecure you felt inside, let others only see confidence. It made leading them easier, for most were eager to follow someone who knew where they were going. Even unto their deaths, as if knowing the end was coming made it a softer fact to accept.

That was what his people were doing at that very moment; dying in battle against a foe with numbers that swelled with every man killed. Reports from the field grew worse every day. Soldiers found themselves pitted against comrades slain in the battles before. Morale was sinking to bottom depths, yet still Cnos Fada stood against Moirfenn.

Because of Bodb. So long as they had a leader who confidently reassured them they would win, they picked up their lances, swung their swords and hoped. It made Bodb squirm with guilt at night, when no one was around to see him.

Something had to be done to stop MacKegan, before his armies reached Cnos Fada. Bodb was hopelessly frustrated for wanting to know what it could be.

"Kneel," the High Priest commanded. The prince had reached the old elf without realizing it. A part of Bodb obeyed the command while the rest dwelt on the problem at hand. Dimly he was aware of the High Priest's recitations.

He supposed he could challenge the southern lord to a contest, with the winner forfeiting his claim to the land. It was the traditional method of settling disputes but not one MacKegan could be trusted to honor. No, there had to be another way.

"Rise, my king, and face your people!" the High Priest said with a flourish.

Bodb blinked back to the present. Had he missed the entire thing? This was worse than his vigil. At least he had known some of what was going on in the cave.

Bodb worried for his sanity. Were the rumors true about the Feral disease being contagious? Perhaps he had taken too big a risk, allowing The Six so close to him...

Bodb had let his thoughts take him away again. Shouts of jubilation and loyalty echoed across the room. The High Priest was offering Bodb a silver scepter adorned with mistletoe and holly. Bodb accepted it and turned.

Some of the shouts turned to startled cries of outrage. An elf, filthy from head to toe and splattered with blood, pushed forward and stumbled down the aisle toward Bodb. Bodb scanned the corners of the hall where his best guards were supposed to be, but the stations were empty.

Blood dripped to the floor in a silent tale of woe. The elf must have slaughtered each guard in silence while the ceremony was taking place. He stopped just feet from the new king and stood panting in barely contained bloodlust. Froth bubbled at his mouth. With a jolt, Bodb perceived it was Eahn.

"It's a Fell Beast!" someone shouted. The cry caused instant pandemonium as fear of the dread sickness hit the room like a lightening bolt. Everyone ran screaming for the entrance, trampling anything and anyone in the way. Guards, alerted by the commotion, tried to fight their way in but were soon overcome.

Bodb fought to block the distractions out. He stood facing a Fell Beast with only a gilded scepter for a weapon. Guiltily he realized that he should have at least sent someone to collect his father's sword from the cave.

From somewhere in Eahn's throat a groan issued forth. It sounded almost like a word, "Joaleee," but Bodb could not be sure. The king took a cautious step back, seeking an avenue of escape. The Fell Beast rushed forward.

Bodb Derg sidestepped just in time, stumbling over a candlestick. He fell to his knees, the breath knocked out of him, still scrambling forward. A clatter issued as the candlestick struck another, causing a chain reaction against them all. Candles and their former holders rolled everywhere, tripping stragglers still looking for the way out.

Eahn lunged across the floor after Bodb. Bodb crab walked back, slamming hard on his bottom when he slipped on a candle. His hand grasped something cold and hard. Without thinking, he swung it out and knocked Eahn across the face.

It was a clumsy blow and would have been utterly futile if Bodb had grabbed a candle rather than a holder. Eahn howled in pain and staggered back. Bodb took the opportunity to get to his feet.

Eahn grunted, flexing his shoulders and clenching his fists. Shape-shifting, Bodb discerned with dread. If the crazed elf succeeded, it would be near impossible to stop him.

Bodb swung hard as he could, slamming the candlestick onto the back of Eahn's head. It connected with a loud bong and vibrated, jarring Bodb's elbows. The Northern Thorn slumped to the ground, stunned. Bodb hit him again and again, striking venomously. He did not stop until the candle holder was slick with Eahn's blood.

"All hail the new king," he said breathlessly, tossing the candlestick aside.

Kneeling, Bodb placed a hand in front of Eahn's nose. He felt no breath, but the elf's chest rose and fell slightly. Satisfied the Northern Thorn was still alive, Bodb stood and brushed off his shirt.

"See what happens when you trust the scum of Moirfenn?!" the captain of the guards demanded behind Bodb. Three guards, standing nearby, nodded silently. How long they had been there was a mystery, but Bodb was too tired to ask.

Also, it was pointless to berate his captain on the fine points of defending one's king. Either Bodb could defend himself and deserved the respect of his people, or he was a craven coward not fit to lick their boots. Sometimes Bodb wished he was the latter, but his pride got in the way of that goal.

The captain booted Eahn's inert form. "The rest of them will do you worse before they succumb to Moirfenn's madness, I swear to that!" One of the guards picked Eahn up and slung him over a shoulder.

Wearily, Bodb sighed and wiped his face with one hand. "Put him in the tightest cell you can find. And be careful."

At the guard's strange look, Bodb understood what a strange request that must be. He had just beat the creature senseless after all.

"Be careful," Bodb repeated in case the guard misunderstood him. "We have him now. No sense in killing him when he might still be of use."

Bodb went to the banquet hall more out of a sense of duty than appetite. It was almost deserted, which suited him just fine. Without waiting for service, Bodb grabbed a plate of meat and took his chair. An attendant gave him cheese and a goblet of wine. He asked for the entire bottle.

"About time you showed up," Chonnall said, taking a place beside Bodb.

"I might have come sooner if someone had helped," Bodb said darkly. His plate was hardly touched, but his goblet had to be refilled.

Chonnall took the bottle away. "This is no time to get drunk," he chided. "You've a sluagh ride to attend and a crowd to greet. Besides, I couldn't get in to help you. People were running like mad and guards were everywhere. I tried."

Bodb grabbed a piece of meat and chewed angrily. Chonnall snickered into his sleeve. Finally he burst into open laughter.

"You look like a mad bull."

Bodb snorted for answer. Chonnall was sent into new peals of laughter. Bodb tried to hold onto his sulk, but he had no defense against his friend's merriment. His lips drew into a smile, a chuckle tickled his chest. Before long he was laughing with his friend, snorting involuntarily, breaking into new laughter with each intake.

The meal was forgotten, shoved across the table and cold. Bodb stood, manfully containing his laughter and straightening his cloak. He noticed a small rip near the corner. His laughter died with the reminder of his recent struggle.

"What am I going to do with them?" he asked himself.

"You mean The Six?" Chonnall asked, suddenly as serious as his friend. "Well, supposing they return you might consider killing them. If their leader was that taken with the sickness, there is no telling what the rest of them will do."

"No," Bodb said with a sigh. "I have a feeling they trust me." There had been something odd about Eahn when The Six made their petition. The others seemed like normal Moirfenn slaves, but Bodb's very atma had vibrated uncomfortably.

It was the sickness. Bodb wished he had known it sooner, before things had gotten so out of hand. Even if The Six returned with cleansed souls, there would ever be madness and strife around them. His vassals would never allow them near without a fight. Attempts might even be made on their lives.

"Come on," Chonnall said impatiently. "You can brood later. The company is ready for the sluagh, waiting for you."

"Aye," Bodb said, following his friend out of the chamber. He was no longer in the mood to ride between the veil, but there was more than himself concerned. Some of his guests had never attended a sluagh ride and eagerly had accepted his invitation. Each looked forward to the music, companionship and experience.

Twelve lords and their coveted ladies awaited at the edge of the city. Minstrels and charmers increased the number to twenty, but technically they were not in the ride so much as part of it. Instruments were tuned discretely. Delicate horses stamped, jingling silver bells and chomping their bits. Bodb expected the company to be larger, but he was not surprised. Most of them had been frightened away by the coronation's activity.

Bodb rode his charger to the fore, pausing only to signal with one fist he was ready to ride. Horses snorted. Bells set the time for the minstrels' tunes. The charmers spread their hands, casting their glamour, and the company began to glow.

They sang as they made their slow way across the land. It was not the music found in taverns, but the soul-wrenching music wrought by magic. All the elves present felt their spirits buoyed on the song, making their heads giddy. Occasionally laughter broke into the music, harmonizing for stronger magic.

It was rapture.

Already the charmers were weaving new atma, throwing it out in rainbow displays of power. The atma danced, curling around each other, solidifying into a wall of light. Through the door of atma the veil was opened. Bodb guided his horse into it.

Like swimming through color, the minstrel's music melting around them and creating impossible hues, the ride made its way forth. Éire was before them, solid and waiting. Bodb's horse touched earth and the colors followed, flowing into the ground, seeking hidden niches.

"Mortals," a maiden said, pointing.

Bodb had never seen a sluagh ride from the outside, but he knew the stupefied looks mortals wore as they passed. It was unspoken policy to carry away those whose eyes glimmered intelligently, which were none too awed by the elves' presence. Even questioning it.

Humans like that, many believed, held traces of the old blood in them. Nothing less could produce an intelligent mortal. It made those rare people from Éire worthy to be part of the elves' dwindling race.

There were two of them, male and female, holding hands and looking around in awe. "Lords and ladies!" the girl said excitedly, tugging her companion's hand. The boy's eyes reflected only dazzling lights and nothing of the beings who watched them.

One rider leaned down and scooped the girl up into his saddle. She cried out and tried to slip out of his grasp. Behind them, the lad shouted the girl's name as, to him, she suddenly disappeared. The fae host ignored him, passing by and down the hills. The boy cried wildly in despair.

The girl sobbed into her kidnapper's shoulder. She might end up a slave or even abandoned in the foreign countryside. Kinder elves would offer a choice between her home and Fion if she persisted in her grief.

Nearly all mortals taken in sluagh rides chose to stay. Occasionally an angered mate desperately broke the veil to win back their loves. Those encounters always ended in sorrow, with either the mortal forced to return or the mate slain.

The human's sorrow brought a sour note to the music. Her captor touched her brow, whispering, sending her into unnatural sleep. The music regained its flavor.

Too soon, the sluagh ride ended. The charmers held the veil open long enough for each guest to ride for their separate homes. Bodb, last to leave, nodded cordially to the charmers and minstrels as he rode out of the light. Cnos Fada lay before him, dark but for the occasional light in a window. The stars overhead were dazzling in their clarity after riding through the murkiness of magic.

Yawning, he rode into the city.

CHAPTER TWENTY-ONE
"RESCUE"

Leannahn adjusted her mantle and stepped deeper into what scant shadow the corner could afford. The human woman called her daughter's name, searching, wanting to go home. The halfling babe wriggled in her arms, fussing. Leannahn stay very still.

Somewhere below them Eahn lay in a filthy cell, wounded and needing help. If the cursed human would give up and go home, Leannahn could make her way to him. The only other souls to be seen were guardsman, making their rounds with extra care. Leannahn wanted to scream from frustration.

A heavy step just beyond her line of sight betrayed another guard. Leannahn held her breath, drawing into herself, fighting the temptation to waste atma on an invisibility spell. The human woman spoke to him, asking if he had seen her daughter.

"Nay, my lady," the guard said in a deep, heavy drawl. "P'raps we might ask some of t'others. There be plenty of us in the palace not to have missed her."

The couple moved away. The human described her daughter as they went. Leannahn's eyes narrowed on her retreating back. Were it not for the baby, she would have killed the woman.

The corridor was vacant. Leannahn dashed away as fast as she could, almost shifting to capture Eahn's scent. Someone stepped around a corner without warning. She bumped into his chest.

"Easy there," said the friendly youth, steadying her by the shoulders. "Where are you going in such a hurry?"

"I'm lost," Leannahn stuttered, pulling away from his rough hands.

"And panicked," said the youth. "Well, be easy. I'll help you find your way."

"I'm sure I can find my own way," Leannahn said quickly.

"Nonsense," said the youth. He placed a friendly arm around her shoulders and proceeded to guide her down the corridor. "'Tis my duty to help a lady in distress. Especially one as pretty as yourself."

Leannahn turned her grimace into a shy smile of pleasure. She felt strange with the elf lad's arm around her shoulders. Feelings stirred within her that had nothing to do with love or lust. Trying to place these odd sensations, she sighed.

"You sound disappointed," said the youth, mistaking her expression.

"I so wanted to explore the palace," Leannahn said softly.

"Well then," said the youth, taking the hint brilliantly. "I will have to show you around! What would you like to see first?"

Leannahn clapped her hands childishly. "Everything," she said. "Even the dungeon!"

"The dungeon, too?" The youth withdrew his arm to scratch his chin. He was unsuccessfully trying to grow a beard. It made him resemble a shorn sheep.

"I've never seen a real dungeon before," Leannahn said as innocently as she could. "Besides," she continued in a conspiratorial whisper, "I heard they put that Feral creature down there."

"That's one reason not to go down there," the youth said. Leannahn silently fretted the lad would not take her while giving him her most puppy-wide eyes. The halfling's body was built perfectly for it, down to the dimple in her chin which trembled when held just so.

"Couldn't hurt anything," the lad said at last. "He's behind bars and chained down, I'll expect."

Leannahn made no attempt to hide her joy. Excitedly, she grabbed his hand and pulled. "Come on," she said. "Hurry hurry!"

The lad chuckled as he went with her. Replacing his arm around her shoulders, he walked in a new direction. Leannahn could barely contain her impatience when they stopped to look at murals or tapestries. Twice they met guards on patrol, who nodded cordially to her guide and ignored herself. When they reached the dark stairway leading down, she breathed a sigh of relief. There would be nothing to see down there except the prisoner.

The air was chilly as they descended. Leannahn drew her mantle closer around her and stepped quickly. Her companion was hard put to keep up.

"Good eve to you, Lord Chonnall," a guard said, stepping from the shadows as if borne from them. His ash black hair and silver eyes glinted in the dim torch light. He bowed to Leannahn. "And you, lady."

Leannahn knew this one's clan: The dark ones, elves who reflected the moon and its softness. Not all were malicious, as humans believed. However, they had funny ideas about honor and could easily be turned. One way or the other, it mattered not to them. This one might have been serving her uncle a season ago, and might again. Their minds were flighty as Picket's, being mostly fae themselves.

The new king was a fool, Leannahn decided. She would never trust this elf. Bodb would do well to feel the same.

"We've come to see the king's assassin," Chonnall said lightly. "A gruesome sight, so we're told."

"I'd be careful," the guard said in a warning tone. "He's awake in there, make no mistake. Glares like a cockatrice but thrice as ugly."

"Might be a sight worth paying for," Chonnall rejoined laughingly.

Leannahn left the two talking and stepped into the gloom. The bottom of the stairs rose sharply. She slowed her steps cautiously. A dim torch glowed on the wall to her right, barely illuminating the area.

She could hear something rustling nearby, smell the stink of fear and blood. In the third cell to her right, she found Eahn huddling in a bit of straw and watching the world with baleful eyes. He growled when he saw her, his teeth flashing brightly against the caked filth on his face.

"Eahn," Leannahn breathed, sinking to her knees and gripping the bars of his cell. The Northern Thorn snapped, barking, and showed no signs of intelligence at all.

"I'm sorry if this has upset you, lass," Chonnall said, stepping behind her and laying a gentle hand on the crown of her head. "I should never have brought you here."

"Nay," Leannahn said, standing and smiling. "What a brute he is! And I hear tell the king invited him here on top of it all!" She shook her head as if in wonderment.

"Perhaps he was not as far gone then."

"I imagine not," Leannahn said. The subject of their conversation crept into a corner of his cell, curled up and closed his eyes. He might have been seeking sleep, but Leannahn felt he wanted to hide. The Northern Thorn was not so far gone he could not understand his captors.

"Does he have a family I wonder?" the girl said, placing a fingertip to her chin while glancing sidelong at Chonnall. "A wife, perhaps even a child (who knows?) who think about him, where did he go, will he return, will the same fate happen to them? Perhaps they're starving without him to feed them. Or surviving but lonely without the other half of their marriage oath."

"What an imagination you have," Chonnall declared.

"So I have been told. What will your lord do about him? Build a gallows?"

"I cannot say," Chonnall replied as he fell into his own musings. "He might try to help, although I cannot see how. Death might be a mercy."

Leannahn hid her troubled expression. She clenched one of her fists, feeling atma flow around her fingers. Chonnall leaned against the bars of the cell.

"Have you had a good enough look?" he asked. "There's plenty of other things to see about the palace." He proffered a hand to escort her away.

Leannahn accepted his hand, squeezed and released. Her atma burst forth, flaring momentarily, brightening the dungeon. Chonnall jerked once and fell, landing heavily.

Leannahn knelt by his body and found, to her disappointment, that he lived still. The strange stirring awoke again, taking control of her hand. Her fingers crept around his throat, feeling his larynx and slowly tightening.

Leannahn bent down and caressed the youth's lips with her own. She sucked, tasting all of him. Strength returned to her depleted spirit. When she leaned back, she knew her form almost shone for the power contained within.

She looked up. The dark elf had just stepped from the stairway. His flashing eyes might have been watching her or a crack in the floor. He started to walk toward her, but paused to assess his situation. Leannahn felt no fear. He could not harm her now, so full of power was she. His only option was to raise the alarm.

Let him. Turning a smile to the dark elf, she extended a hand. "Keys," her lips said. The elf thought he might argue, changed his mind, tossed a ring of keys to her. Mounting the stairs, he was soon gone from the room.

Leannahn forgot him. She unlocked Eahn's door, swung it open dramatically, and stepped inside. Eahn lifted his head, barring his teeth, and unfolded his limbs. He started to rush her, but her invisible wall of atma held him back.

"Sense, Eahn!" Leannahn commanded. "You know I am here to help you. Down, Fell Beast! As MacKegan's niece, you obey my order!"

"Brighde-brat," Eahn snarled. But he subsided, watching her with his too-bright eyes.

Leannahn was sure she had enough atma to escape, but she hesitated. How strong would she be later? If Eahn saw she could not defend herself, he might hurt her. She could not believe the madness had taken him so much that he would kill a comrade, but he might do some damage.

Still.... Leannahn pointed her finger, released a bolt of atma, and Eahn slumped to the ground.

His body was too heavy to carry. Leannahn had to grab him by the armpits and drag him a foot at a time. When she finally got him out of the cell, she was forced to waste time and catch her breath.

She was a little surprised hoards of guards and angry lords had not rushed down the steps to stop her. The dark elf had plenty of time to raise the alarm. The thought gave her a sense of terror, lending her strength when she should have none. Trembling nervously, she hugged Eahn and began to chant. Memories of her life at the temple, studying to become strong enough to overthrow her uncle, gave her the knowledge she needed. There was a deafening boom as air found an empty space and rushed to fill it.

Leannahn lifted her head into the wind, studying her surroundings. She was further from the ley gate than she had planned, but it was better than nothing. Any pursuit would be here after she had made it home. Panting, she grabbed Eahn's heavy body and pulled him through the dirt.

***

Picket and Duinn found Finnbhear hogtied in the cellar. He had worked the edges of his mouth raw biting at his gag. Rats had found him: His fingers were bloody from their administrations.

The acolyte had been more uncomfortably accommodated in his room, tied to his cot with feet in the air. Left that way for too long, he would slowly have suffocated. Duinn administered small healing magic on the suffering acolyte to bring him to his senses. When Midna's eyes opened, he uttered epithets which made Picket's eyebrows rise. They never thought the chubby elf possessed such a temper.

A complete tour through the temple ended with Midna forced to find a private spot to be sick. The priests were murdered in their sleep, and their bodies rot where they lay. There were too many to bury decently. It plainly grieved Midna to leave his brethren as found while they journeyed south for Cnos Fada.

"There is nothing that can be done," Finnbhear said when Midna turned for a last look over the water. "Right now you have your comrades to worry about. Duty. Aramina would tell you so."

It made sense, too, the taking of Tech Danaan. Now only Cnos Fada was left to stand against Moirfenn, and without the support of their temple things looked bleak.

The four trudged through the mist, occasionally looking upwards to the heavy sky. Rain sleeted down suddenly, drizzling through their hair and Duinn's beard. Picket found some escape in his equine form, where the rain did not bother him so much. Duinn walked slightly bent under Picket's belly, paced himself with the horse, escaping some of the falling water; another advantage to his height.

They camped without a fire. All curled miserably in their cloaks, hiding their faces from the pouring onslaught. Halfway through the night, Picket could no longer ignore the feel of water coursing his barrel sides. He sent droplets spraying through the air with a fluid ripple of his hide, snorted angrily to himself, sneezed when he inhaled more water.

That was the final straw. Picket took off running.

It was a pleasure, galloping through the pouring rain. Lightening lit the terrain in flashes, reflecting his features grimly. He reared and screamed his challenge to the sky. His voice echoed off the clouds, the hills, reverberated around him. The horse ran, eating the miles under his hooves, for a blissful while neither Cuiddal, Picket nor faerie.

Near dawn, the rain finally ceased its attack. Snores drifted through the air from the campsite. Duinn snorted, rolled, resumed his sawing. Picket kicked him with his bare foot.

"Get up, ye worthless half-wits!" he caroled merrily. Somewhere he had found an old cooking pot. He waved it in one hand, sloshing its contents to the ground. Some splashed into Duinn's beard.

"That's hot, you demented wight!" the dwarf roared, getting to his feet and pawing at his face. Midna and Finnbhear fuzzily raised their heads to the commotion.

"'Tis only the dirt making the complaint," Picket said, setting the pot in the fire with a shrug of his speckled shoulders. He wore a ragged kilt, that was all; the gods only knew where he had found it.

Picket knew, but he was in no humor to answer questions. Gesturing toward the simmering stew, he mentioned curtly that they should rinse in a nearby puddle and eat. Duinn gave him strange looks as he slowly washed. The pooka assumed it was his manner of dress: The dwarf should be used to having his beard singed of a morning.

"Mutton," Picket said when Midna sniffed the stew in question. Satisfied with that answer (and never stopping to wonder where the mutton came from), Midna ladled himself a bowl.

"You took off last night," Duinn said by way of accusation.

"Aye, what of it?" Picket was not very hungry, having grazed all night, but he took a cup of stew for appearances. "It got your breakfast."

"And left our backsides unguarded," Duinn growled into his cup.

"You never told me to play sentry," Picket pointed out. "Neither did any of you wake up to take a turn. Who left your backsides unguarded in truth, I wonder?"

"Who's kilt?" Finnbhear asked a shade too carelessly.

"Mine," Picket said.

"Before you had it?"

"Always was mine," Picket said, turning his back to the elf and eating his stew. He could feel the others exchanging glances behind him. Choosing not to acknowledge it, he finished his meal.

"The day goes fast," Finnbhear said, shading his eyes with one hand and looking around. "Will you carry us today, Cuiddal Cernach?"

Picket had been expecting such a question. Hunching his shoulders, he shook his head.

"Why not?" Duinn demanded. "The sun does not stand still for us, and the new king is waiting. We might be needed at this very instant!"

"Peace, dwarf," Finnbhear said. Turning to Picket, he said, "I know a little of the Unseen Ways. Why else would the unshod pony suddenly, willingly, take the shoe. And in his family colors, no less. You are free from MacKegan now. Did you gain by your visit to the people?"

Picket tied the pot, suddenly clean, with a bit of rope and slung it over his shoulder. "Some," he murmured. He walked toward the ley gate. From the corner of his eye, he saw Finnbhear shake his head negatively to Duinn.

What should have been a joyous reunion with his long estranged parents was a cold reception beyond the willows that marked the faerie border. Wear the family kilt again, aye, but that was more to please mortals than the Sidhe. Balance, an uncle had reminded his speckled nephew. There were many things Picket need answer for. He had caused much suffering. How was he going to pay for it?

So he would return to his bride, fight for the new king and watch Liram grow to be a man. Such a short time, but all the time his folk were willing to give. When Liram knew his twenty-first year, Picket must come forward again to reckon his deeds. Three sets of seven years in which to atone for his imprisonment. Magic numbers, coupled for the invoking.

They had not camped far from the ley gate. Midna was the first to see it. He shouted happily and trotted forward. The other three fell behind.

Picket hung farther back while Finnbhear touched the stones. Duinn turned to his friend. "Hurry up," he said. "The sooner we're gone from here, the sooner we have warm beds to sleep in again."

Picket shook his head, snorting. "Go," he said. "I will be there before the day wanes."

Again, the Silver Fox stopped the dwarf with a warning glance. Picket shifted as he turned, reared and churned earth with his hind legs. He streaked across the terrain away from Finnbhear's understanding, from the fat nuisance that was Midna, from the forbidden banter with his friend. Light burst upward behind him as the ley gate swallowed his companions.

Run like hate bit your heels, keep to the brambles. These little things put balance to the times he had chosen the soft road, ridden rather than walked on his own legs. Thorns ripped his flesh as they would to a mortal horse. Pain lanced his foreleg when a sharp stick lodged beneath his hoof. It was a small price to pay: Picket paid it in full.

He was not to be held accountable for the things MacKegan had forced him to do. Picket surged forward with a grunt at the thought. No, there was something else he had done. For a lark, and not a tiny thing. The tiny things were paid for every day, when Picket let a companion sit his back, or cooked a meal without being asked. There was one thing, a crime to his kind, that he knew he should not have done.

Should not have done, but what harm? None it seemed at the time, in his naiveté, but pay he would now. If he failed to balance himself, he would have to wait another three sets of seven for another chance. If another chance could be provided.

Picket galloped on, heat steaming from his fae body, hooves sparking stones, racing the sun and trying to beat it. Teeth barred, eyes near white from anger and frustration, mane flying in fiery splendor, the earth a scarred victim behind his wake.

Aramina met them every night when the priests thought her safely abed. She loved to ride Picket's back. His pooka tricks never frightened her: Indeed how could they? She knew death more intimately than they, knew no fear for it, only a respect for pain.

It looked innocent enough to her. Picket made sure of that. When she rode, he darted toward passing bodies of water as if to dump her but never actually did so. Always she squealed in delight, like a small child, and clung tighter. Water soaked her skirts, darkened Picket's hide, and she never complained but laughed out loud.

This night, he turned a little too fast just as he released the magic that held her to his back. She fell backward with a cry and landed in the mud. Daintily he pranced back, waggling his ears comically and snorting in her face. Aramina sputtered, looked up (and thereby into his nostrils) and burst out laughing.

"That was a trick worthy of my lord Mac Ind Og himself!" she cried, throwing her arms around Picket's neck. He returned the embrace with a caress of his nose.

Picket loved her like the sister he had never known. His real sisters were dark things who preferred to swim in their pools and comb their hair. Many times he had wished for a brother to run with, but that was a wish not to be granted. However, Aramina was just as fun. He would do anything to keep her.

It could not possibly do harm, this thing he had planned. Surely the elders frowned on it for the same reasons adults frowned on many of the things children played at. It was not proper, but not dangerous. Nothing ill would come of it. Surely.

"Lass," Duinn said as he approached them. The shadows were deep: There was no moon. He rose out of the dark like a stump does to the unwary traveler. "Let me help you up. Your skirt will be ruined. How will you explain that to your master?"

"He never notices," the girl said, standing and vainly trying to brush off the offending mud. "Just the floors and how well they've been scrubbed." She stopped brushing to fix Picket with a passionate glance. "I haven't lived since coming there. Can you understand, Picket? Why bother breathing, when there is nothing to breathe for?"

It was a complaint she expressed often. Picket tossed his mane, eager to get on with it. Eahn would be waiting nearby with the cup and bowl. The knife gleamed dully from its place at Duinn's hip.

"Come, Mina," Duinn said, taking the girl's hand and leading her away. "Eahn is waiting."

Aramina groaned with the mention of the other elf. He made it no secret, his dislike for her. Although she tried to be friendly (Picket felt she should try being a little meaner, but it was her own path), he ignored her favors and snarled his hellos.

Eahn waited, standing, with the cup and bowl on a tree stump. Gredber stood next to him, a still shape in the darkness. Aramina met with him once or twice, even had dallied with him when the mood suited her. Her eyes favored him as they walked forward.

With Aramina's approach, Eahn picked up the bowl and held it to the night sky. "We welcome our sister," he said. "Step forward, Aramina, and accept this bowl of life blood."

Aramina hesitated, fidgeting with her fingers. "You never said what this was for," she whispered to Picket. "Do I have to do this?"

Fortunately for Picket, who remained an equine, Duinn had exceptional hearing. "We each went through something to join this unit," the dwarf said somberly. "This we deemed appropriate for you. You have to prove your loyalty to us, even above the temple."

Eahn held the bowl forward and watched. He did not expect her to go through with it. Picket dearly hoped she would. They would be leaving soon to complete an errand for MacKegan. It would seem a dull chore without Aramina. Besides, if not allowed to return to Cnos Fada, he might never see her again.

"You're not serious," Aramina said, hesitantly stepping forward.

"Things are only as serious as you make them," Duinn replied.

Mollified by Duinn's evasive answer, Aramina accepted the bowl from Eahn. "Drink," he bade her. The elf girl obeyed, screwing her eyes shut in dread, opening them in pleasant shock at the taste of fresh milk. Eahn reclaimed the bowl, turned it over to allow the last drops an escape.

"Who do you serve?" Eahn asked then, setting the bowl down and picking up the cup.

"Mac Ind Og," Aramina said with a small smile. She hoped to become the High Priestess to her god, also called the Young Fool, The Harper, The Young Trickster and many other names. Always it had been this way, from the instant she awoke inside the temple and first spoke to her rescuers. She held no memory of a life before being found in the countryside, gored by wild animals and burning with fever. Her sister Joalie often came to visit, but of her parents and brothers no one knew. Aramina did not mind, unaware as she was of what she missed.

Picket sometimes liked to pretend she was a lost relative, found and waiting for the memories to retake root and recall him. Often she played that game with him. It made her feel complete, she said, and it drew them closer together.

"The knife," Eahn said. The chill in his voice broke Picket's thoughts, brought him to the present. Duinn placed the knife hilt first in Eahn's hand and stepped back. "Your hand," Eahn said to Aramina.

"What are you going to do?" she asked naively as she extended the required member. Eahn did not answer. Duinn grabbed her wrist and held while the knife was brought down. Aramina cried out, trying to jerk away, but she was no match for Duinn's stocky solidness.

Picket's throat rumbled in concern as he stepped forward and nudged her back with his nose. Gredber rustled as the scent of blood tingled his senses, but otherwise did nothing.

The cup was spilling her blood before Eahn indicated Duinn could heal Aramina. The magic warmed the air slightly. Eahn held the cup to the sky, offering it to the stars and emptiness.

"This night our sister turns from her ways to follow us, making us four in the sight of our lord, Chulain MacKegan. She hereby vows to spurn the temple and the gods it represents. A new identity is now her claim." Eahn lowered the cup, pouring some of its contents on the ground. *"We offer now this heart blood as part of the pact and summon the gods to choose. Morrigu, Sheidrikan, BileEll, Mac Ind Og, Carmen ..."*

The recitations of all the gods they knew went on, joined by Aramina as she realized what Eahn recited was heard in the temple every solstice. Her throaty voice continued where Eahn's memory faltered, rising with confidence. She knew this part for what it was: A calling to all the sacred entities to decide who she belonged to.

There had been no doubt in her mind, she told Picket later, that the Harper would come. She claimed he had chosen her seasons upon seasons ago. That explained her look of horror after the recitation ended, the cup passed around for each to drink, and the fire lit. For the flames burst not natural orange, but pale blue, flecked with purple and dark black.

"You said it wasn't serious," Aramina wailed to Duinn as the flames took shape, rising, forming arms and a face. She stepped back but wisely did not run. There was no place for her to go, for she had committed the deed and knew the consequence.

Gredber fell to his knees, lifting his hands together and crying in joy. He had helped Picket plan the ceremony, explained what each motion represented. That had given him the right to attend. Picket had not understood what it meant until that moment.

"My master," Gredber breathed.

Aramina wept as the flaming hand brushed her brow, touching her atma and claiming her existence. Even Eahn looked shaken by the answer to their half-hearted summons. To be touched by the Dark One meant damnation of a kind. Even she, he once said later, did not deserve it.

How to atone for the guilt of that night? The crime became evident in Aramina's new demeanor; sarcastic, quiet and occasionally hateful. She laughed less, and her nightly rides with Picket changed.

Although he missed the innocence of before, now she delighted in danger more than ever. Picket found himself liking this new sister he had helped to create. But when she brought Raori to the fold, initiating a rite of cruel sacrifice as his deed, Picket felt a strange sinking in his breast ...

CHAPTER TWENTY-TWO
"GODS AND BEASTS"

A soft knock on the door roused Bodb from much needed slumber. Padding barefoot to the door, he cracked it and asked his waker's business.

"The fell beast has been rescued," Phadraig whispered.

"I expected as much," Bodb said heavily. "When?"

"Now. I just left the chamber. His rescuer looked nothing like MacKegan's niece, but she might have changed herself. They say she had that power."

"What else did you see?" Bodb beckoned the silver elf inside, closed the door silently. "You have someone tracking them, I trust."

"Nay, lord," Phadraig said. "They did not walk out."

"Transportation," Bodb said with dread. "But that skill was lost when the temple burned."

"MacKegan's niece studied there, lord."

"True." Bodb paced a moment while the other elf stood at attention, watching his lord with eyes of mountain water. "Can you trace them?" the king asked at last.

"I did, lord," Phadraig said. "They stepped into the ley gate, and there the trail ends."

"Moirfenn," Bodb said. "Although I cannot imagine what help Leannahn expects to find there. As his niece and heir she must have some influence, though." One thing was sure. The Six had lied about her death.

He had known not to trust them, to keep them away, kill them at first chance. But a small voice inside, the voice of precognition, said to let them come. Bodb confessed to himself that he was surprised. His visions were seldom wrong.

"You did well," Bodb congratulated his servant. "I commend the fact you chose to obey orders. It must have been difficult, allowing the spy to take the Northern Thorn."

The dark elf held no love for Moirfenn. His sister had been bought by MacKegan, then tortured for his pleasure. Phadraig wore a silver lock of her hair close to his breast, to remind him of his purpose.

"Something else, my lord."

"Aye, what?"

"Lord Chonnall has been terribly hurt. The healers are with him now."

Dread made Bodb stop in his tracks. Orders, meant to be obeyed, were sometimes obeyed too well.

***

Finnbhear led the way into the palace, shoving anyone aside who thought to stop him. Most let him pass without argument. They knew who he was and bowed to his authority. Duinn and Midna followed like ducklings behind their mother.

One servant who thought to scuttle away was not so lucky. Finnbhear grabbed his arm, jerking him backward. The tray he held clattered to the floor, spilling wine and bread.

"Where is the king?" Finnbhear asked. His voice was mild, but his knuckles whitened as his grip hardened.

Making various faces of pain, the servant squeaked, "The infirmary, lord. Lord Chonnall is seriously ill." He whimpered.

The Silver Fox let go without apology. Taking long strides, he continued down the hall. Duinn and Midna stumbled to follow, ignoring the servant who clutched his arm and complained of bruises.

The infirmary was located in a long room that had been the center of the palace years go, but as the elves' society grew the palace grew. Now it was a room used for various things; storage, feasts, parties or the ill. It was not full now, but Finnbhear knew as the battles got closer the wounded would swell. At the moment two soldiers slept in the corner.

Bodb Derg sat on the far side of the door beside a pallet. A young man lay there. Finnbhear was surprised at how sound he looked, aside from the pallor of his skin.

Finnbhear stood silently behind the king with his charges and waited for acknowledgment. Time passed.

"I should be happy you are alive, and I am. Believe me I am. When you did not come back from the sluagh, I wondered if you had died." Bodb sadly gestured toward the sleeping man on the cot. "My lifetime companion. The healers have done all they could, but there is no hope for him. Look, his breathing slows even now."

Duinn crouched and looked at Chonnall as if he studied a new rock formation. "What causes this?" he asked at length.

"No one knows," Bodb said. "Do not touch him."

Duinn pulled back his hand with measured ease. Something in Bodb's voice put Finnbhear on edge. He reached for his sword, ruing Bodb's next order.

"Perhaps I can help,' the dwarf offered.

"Help?" Bodb laughed, cut his mirth short with a scowl, stood to face his guests. "'Twas one of your number that did this to him. And you said she was dead."

Duinn looked perplexed. "The Priestess?" Stroking his beard thoughtfully, he continued with, "My lord, she stood before you alive and well. Who claims her dead?"

"Not your Priestess, as you well know," Bodb snapped. His eyes were bloodshot, bright with unshed tears. "She came, freed your Feral companion, taking Chonnall's life in return. Now his body wastes away. He'll be dead before an hour is gone, and you stand here pretending you do not know!"

Finnbhear bowed. "Lord," he said before Duinn could argue further, "please tell us what happened."

"No." The king turned his back on them, resumed his position beside Chonnall, buried his face in his hands. "Take them away, Silver Fox. I refuse to discuss the matter anymore."

Finnbhear backed away. After some hesitation, Duinn and Midna followed. By the looks on their faces it was plain to see they expected to be locked away. The Silver Fox was unsure if Bodb wanted that or just for them to leave his sight. They stopped for a whispered consultation just beyond the door.

"I expect you'll tell me how Leannahn hasn't been dead all this while," Finnbhear hissed.

Duinn shook his head in vehement denial. "Leannahn is dead," he said. "We saw her die. She was torn limb from limb, I swear on my family's graves."

"Then who is he talking about?" the Silver Fox demanded. "Tell me, dwarf, or I will be forced to put you away. I promise you."

"Who is Leannahn?" Midna quietly ventured.

Duinn was silent at first. Then he told the acolyte, ending with the tale of Leannahn's death. All three men stared at the floor when the tale was done. Finnbhear broke the silence with, "Does MacKegan possess the spear?"

"Nay," the dwarf said. "Raori recovered it from the ley gate..." His eyes snapped up. "Hammer Fells," he swore. "Of course! Raori was acting so strange after getting that spear, and when it was burned everything was fine. But it wasn't before the fact"

What was the crazy dwarf talking about? Finnbhear tapped his foot impatiently.

"Raori will know," the dwarf explained. "I can't safely say more than that."

"He's gone, remember?" Finnbhear blew out, wiping his face in frustration. The king had mentioned a Feral companion, locked away. He knew who that was through the process of elimination. And it made sense; Eahn's disappearance, the inability to locate him.

But he could not see how Raori knew about this, unless he had helped the Northern Thorn in some way. The Six had planned to dupe the prince with their "defection." When that ploy turned real, Raori stumbled blind into the dark like a Feral thing himself. Could he have circled back and met with Eahn? Maybe the Feral companion was not Eahn, but Raori. If so, where was Aramina?

"We have to find the mage," Duinn said. "If Aramina is with him, t'will be easy."

"How?" Midna asked, mystified.

"We wait for the pooka." Finnbhear strode away, shouting for servants to attend him. He ordered a bath readied, grabbed the first servant wench he saw and took her to his room.

Giggling, she helped him undress and washed his back briskly. Closing his eyes to this half forgotten pleasure, Finnbhear leisurely asked after the latest gossip. The wench gladly told him everything she knew.

So it was that Finnbhear learned of Bodb's coronation and how the fell beast was downed by the courageous king. Out of mercy and kindness (according to the maid), Eahn was not slain when the guards finally arrived but put away in the dungeon.

"My sister and the guard tha' watched it are friendly," she confided while scrubbing Finnbhear's shoulders. "She says he described tha girl maun be half human at least. Dressed like a lord's daughter and how could she nae, commanding that much power! The beast called her something, I'm nae sure I can recall." Her motions slowed as she paused to think.

"Go on," Finnbhear entreated, now fully awake, bath forgotten.

"Briann?" the servant girl guessed to the air. "Breindh? Brighde. Anyway, he was hidin' just beyond sight and mightn't hae heard properly."

Finnbhear wondered, with a sense of foreboding, where Picket might be. The pooka had spoken of his new family with love and pride. How was the sprite going to take this turn of events?

***

Picket reached Cnos Fada when the sun was low. Finnbhear was in conference with the king, but Duinn and Midna waited near the front gate. The pooka greeted them aloofly.

Duinn's eyes spoke questions he kept to himself. Picket wanted to answer them, but found he could not. He sipped his cup of mead in silence, eyes lowered to the liquid. The dwarf shifted in his seat, disturbed by the scratches crisscrossing Picket's arms. Midna excused himself to walk the gardens.

Finnbhear appeared and made a beeline for the couple. He was speaking before covering the last few feet. "The king wishes to speak with you, Duinn," he said. "It's a good sign, but be careful. He grieves for his friend."

Chonnall had died while they discussed matters just outside the door.

The long room was dark, lit by the bare essentials. Bodb Derg sat his chair with a bottle by his feet, a goblet in one hand, his shirt unlaced and his feet bare. He was a sorry sight. Duinn bowed deeply and remained bent.

"Rise," the king said. He waved one hand to a nearby chair. "Sit, blacksmith."

Duinn obeyed with misgivings.

"Finnbhear tells me Black Assassins were in Tech Danaan. All my people there are dead. Can you explain this? Tell me, should I have you killed?"

"I owe you my life," Duinn said past the lump in his throat. "I must trust you to do with it as you see fit."

Bodb took a drink from his goblet.

"Give me leave to find the mage," Duinn said into the silence. "He knows how Leannahn came to be here. I'm sure of it. I do not know how else to prove my loyalty to you."

"I confess you and yours bewilder me," Bodb said. "And it seems I must trust you, for I feel to my very bones that we must find the mage. Soon, before he suffers the fate of the Northern Thorn."

It was Eahn who had gone Feral then. Duinn shuddered deep inside. There had been no signs, unless the little things were examined. Chiefly, his sudden disappearance spoke of his fate. And his temper, shorter than normal and laced with paranoia of the Feral disease. Long term silences that could have been taken for deep thought.

Panic and concern for his family possibly had pushed it farther than it need go. But it was done, and Eahn was lost to them.

"Have faith in me," Duinn said. "Were it not for you, I would still be under MacKegan's boot and headed for the same destiny."

"I cannot let the Silver Fox go with you," Bodb said. "He is needed. Our forces tire, MacKegan presses the attack. His experience will be a boon."

The statement came as no surprise. Duinn nodded his acceptance and stood. "Then I have no one to hold me back," said he. "I will leave immediately and fly if I must. If nothing else, I will return with news of them."

"You will return with them, dead or alive," Bodb said. "I cannot afford to be lenient anymore."

"Lord," Duinn said, bowing low. The ragged edges of his loose britches swept the floor, exposed his worn boots, emphasized his need to serve. He hated what Bodb asked of him and would do everything in his power to win Aramina and Raori back. But if they refused, then he would do as ordered.

Finnbhear came to mind. For the first time, he understood how much the Silver Fox went through on behalf of his kingdom. Resentment for the elf was replaced with empathy.

Dismissed. Duinn hunted Picket down first thing and entreated the pooka to join his quest. Picket shook his head, casting his eyes down.

"For all I love Aramina and want to help," Picket said, "I cannot. I have already promised my help to the Silver Fox."

Finnbhear waited just out of hearing by a rose bush. He talked to it lovingly, caressing its only blossom. The petals changed color with each touch until they settled on a soft gold.

Satisfied, Finnbhear placed his hands behind his back and looked for another distraction.

"I'd swear he was born of the Sidhe," Duinn said when Finnbhear found another flower to experiment with. "But he is too civilized to be anything but elf."

Picket looked long at Finnbhear before saying, "Aye." Duinn was not sure what he was agreeing to.

"Be careful," Duinn bade his friend. "How dull it will be, without you to fight with."

Picket smiled fleetingly. They clasped hands, then Duinn left them. He had a long journey, on foot not to miss any sign of his quarry.

The acolyte met him at the city gates.

"Get yourself back," Duinn told him impatiently.

"I want to help," the acolyte said.

"What can you do, save slow me? Now get yourself back there. There's plenty to do for the wounded when they come." Duinn started to stomp past the plump elf. Midna grabbed the dwarf by the shoulder. His grip was strong.

"Listen to me," Midna half hissed. "For better or worse, Aramina and Raori are my companions, too. Or have you forgotten how I was brought into The Six?"

Actually Duinn had forgotten, but he was not about to admit such to the elf. Straightening his shoulders, thereby shrugging off Midna's hand, he looked the acolyte square in the eye. "Fine," he said evenly. "By my anvil, you'll regret it."

Midna merely nodded, shrugged on his pack, and let Duinn lead the way.

***

The bard pressed through the thickets, cursing as he went. Loudly he lamented his precious instrument being scratched by merciless thorns. Said instrument was snug in its case, but the elf took no stock in that fact. Occasionally he stopped, placed his hands around his mouth, and called out.

"Priestess! Mage! Hai, fiends! Must I come all the way to you?"

Showing no surprise at the answering silence, the bard continued making his tedious way into the thicket. Something ahead leapt further into the brush. Oenghus did not give chase. It was merely a rabbit. He would chase it later. It would make supper, when he had finished this annoying business.

"Hai!" The bard paused to capture his second wind and look around. He was getting close, but the few feet left seemed a long way to go. Cursing mortality, he pushed forward again.

The silver cat had watched for hours. Oenghus pretended not to notice as he fought valiantly ahead. The cat did not move in all that time. Annoyance battled with prudence. Suddenly the bard stopped, placed hands on his hips, and turned toward the feline.

"You're no faerie, Raori MacGuinnan, to be sitting around in smug invisibility. Now hie to your lady, and tell her I'm here."

The cat hissed.

"What now, Leannahn has taught you well," Oenghus said with an uplifted eyebrow. "You know well she sits yonder, laughing under her breath at the fine joke she plays on me. Go now!"

Raori washed himself thoroughly before disappearing into the brambles. Oenghus allowed him that. Cats needed such pretenses for pride and self respect. Mages, too, for that matter. In the meantime it allowed him to rest.

"And ye might show a bit more respect toward myself," Oenghus called when the cat was gone. "You certainly were grateful enough at the tavern, not long ago!"

It was hot. Oenghus always took summer weather for granted until recently, when he was forced to endure it. He unlaced his shirt and flapped it in an attempt to cool down. When he finished with this adventure, he planned to stay comfortable for six months at least.

Then the bard remembered it would be six months every year from now on, and he scowled. Where was that blasted woman?

Gleaming eyes appeared, shining, within the thicket just when Oenghus drew breath for another shout. He let the breath go in a single huff and pointed his finger. "Aramina, 'tis not funny. Get out here and talk to me, werewolf. I paid a high price to help your eminence, and the least you can do is be civil!"

She emerged from the thicket as if born from her mother's womb. Her coat was snarled with sticks and leaves. Mud was spattered on her legs and underbelly.

"Look at you," Oenghus said, kneeling and taking her fur under his fingers. "Letting yourself go like that. Tsk."

The wolf closed her eyes in pleasure and leaned toward him. Debris fell to the ground as Oenghus worked her coat clean. When that was done, he scratched behind her ears lovingly. Aramina sighed and lay her head into his lap.

From nowhere, the silver cat flew into Oenghus' face. Yelling in surprise, Oenghus batted him off and stumbled back. The wolf, deprived of his attentions, turned on the feline who had fallen into the thickets.

She growled, half barking, with her tail lowered and ears back. The cat hissed, then yowled. She barked again, snapped toward him, turned her back. Raori looked shocked for as long as a cat dared, then slunk into the shadows.

"Did you have to be so blunt?" Oenghus asked the wolf. "Such a lesson can be taught with less force."

The wolf shook herself as if to say he'll get over it. Oenghus sighed and reclaimed her coat.

"My love," the bard said. "'Tis time you thought of finding the others. They'll be looking for you. What are you going to do about them?"

The wolf did not move.

"Don't you ignore me," Oenghus said sternly, withdrawing his fingers. "You don't belong to him anymore, make no mistake, and I can make you."

Whining, Aramina lowered her eyes to the ground.

"Up, Priestess," Oenghus ordered. He did not replace his hands on her pelt. "Just consider it part of the plan."

Sighing, the wolf sat and shifted. Aramina, bare but for her hair cascading over her shoulders, frowned up at the bard. Delicately she held up one hand. Oenghus helped her to her feet.

"Shall we find the mage before we go?" the bard asked gallantly.

"He'll follow," the Priestess said. Without preamble, she started to walk. Oenghus adjusted the shoulder strap to his harp case and followed. The thorns that had fought his entry now fought his departure. Aramina passed through without harm. Oenghus frowned at her bare back, fighting the temptation for small revenge.

Aramina paused at the edge of the thicket as if struck. "How long has it been?" she asked, paying no attention to the bard's protest.

Oenghus knew she had been asking herself that question a lot lately. No surprise she should ask it of him.

"Centuries," he evaded. "And a pretty lass you were. Make no mistake, you're beautiful now but 'tis not your own beauty. 'Tis Aramina's."

The Priestess' response was a thoughtful grunt.

"Are we going to stand in the thorns all day?" Oenghus demanded. "For all they're sacred, I don't enjoy the pricks against my skin."

"Why," Aramina said with affected charm, "they shouldn't bother you at all, my lord."

Oenghus sighed inwardly. She had no notion of the price he had paid to win her back. Now was not the time to tell her. "Please let me out of here," he forced himself to say. The humble request made his guts twist.

Aramina obeyed, but slowly. Oenghus felt impatience nipping at his temper. Grinning mischievously, she thought to ask, "So you prefer my real face? You might have told me before I gained another."

The bard grabbed her by the shoulder and turned her to face him. He cradled her face with one hand, kissed her nose and said, "I love you no matter what shape you wear. Now hush. The mage eavesdrops and has too many questions already."

Confident that Raori would follow, they stepped from the thicket and onto smoother territory. Oenghus led the way, worrying with his harp case, tripping over roots and swearing. Aramina giggled behind him. The bard ignored her and tried to pick a smoother trail. Something streaked under his feet. He tripped again and fell flat on his face.

"Alas," Aramina laughed, "but you'll not make a huntsman."

"Blasted cat!" Oenghus said, looking for the silver nuisance. "Jealous wretch, ungrateful besides!"

Aramina laughed harder and crouched beside the trail. A clump of bushes growled at Oenghus. "Come on," she beckoned to the bushes. "Silly elf, I told you he's no threat to you. Now please do as I say and behave yourself."

Raori, man-shaped and furious, erupted from the bushes. "No threat?" he demanded. "So he takes you away to an unknown fate? Duinn and Picket have betrayed us, Eahn is who knows where and now this? Suppose you're taken, Mina? I cannot save you alone!"

"Well Oenghus is right," Aramina said with a lift of her chin. The bard had always found the motion endearing. "We can't hide in the wild forever. Can't you feel it, Raori? We're going mad. Feral! Hiding as animals will only work so long. When MacKegan claims our minds, we'll be animals forever. I do not want that."

Raori growled, barring his teeth. Oenghus could see the madness, ready to erupt, just behind his eyes. He had seen that look before, when he shared Eahn's camp in the rain. Perhaps it was not too late for the mage, but that was a decision for Raori to make. Even gods could not choose the paths of most men and elves.

"Raori," Aramina said, grabbing the mage's arms and shaking him slightly. The act brought Raori back. He blinked, focusing on her face. She kissed him.

Their lips parted. Raori had the decency to look ashamed. "I'll come," he said. "Although I do not see what we can do alone."

They walked ceaselessly for the rest of the day, reaching the grasslands by nightfall. Camping in the open, they risked a small fire. Supper was rabbit, as Oenghus has known, topped with early berries. No one spoke, except when Oenghus offered to play a tune on his harp. Raori violently vetoed the offer with a threat to use the harp for kindling.

Shaking the dew from their bodies next morning, they devoured dinner scraps for breakfast and resumed walking. The sun beat them down with a vengeance. By noon, Aramina had to shift into wolf form to preserve herself from sunburn. Oenghus' eyes scanned the grasslands, looking for traces of life. The grass, like an ocean, went on forever.

***

Raori was dreaming.

He stood on the hillside by the one he loved and watched her look down. The object of her scrutiny was a dying elf maiden. Blood coated most of her body, and her entrails trailed the grass. It was a miracle she had not been preyed upon by scavengers. Fever had set in long ago. Now she was too weak even to moan.

"I've always wondered why they fight so hard to live," his beloved said. Her speech was not words, but a mixture of color and emotion. "Look at this one. It's been days and no one has come looking."

"Instinct," Raori said with the same speech his beloved used. He lay a hand on her glowing translucent shoulder. She turned to him with a face that might have held human features or might have been pure light. "They are good creatures, deep down. Don't judge them too harshly."

His beloved gave forth the equivalent of a sigh, sending hues of blue and green through her shapely form. "I suppose I should not. For I do not understand them."

"Impossible to do so."

"I think it is possible." Her radiance became thoughtful. Then her attention focused. "Ah, her spirit finally leaves."

With a dreamer's omniscience, Raori knew what he saw was not something the average mortal could. The elf maiden's body glowed, lost its form within that light, reappeared as the light lifted upward. Confused, the light hovered for an instant. Features flashed on its surface; a baby's face, a child's, the woman on the ground.

"Welcome," said his beloved. Tendrils of her essence reached out and touched the newcomer.

"Am I dead?" The new one sounded frightened: Her essence became flecked with ultraviolet hues.

"Reborn," said his beloved. She enveloped the newcomer in a soft hug, by which communicating necessary knowledge in one quick instant. When the two parted, the newcomer was relieved and even happy.

"Thank you," she said, floating away a pace. Then she was gone, fading out to her next chosen step. It might be another chance to live, to sleep or haunt the hillside. Raori's dreaming mind felt all the choices were irrelevant, but he said nothing.

His beloved hovered over the body still, curiosity in every molecule.

"There is nothing for you here now," he said.

"Not here," his beloved replied faintly. "But there..." She reached out to touch the abandoned husk.

"Don't," Raori protested in alarm.

Before the word was completely uttered, she was sinking into the body, filling its members with her light, pouring into cavities. Suffused with her energy, the physical shell took a deep breath, gasping like the drowned emerging for air. The eyes opened, widened with shock and pain. She screamed.

Raori bit back a scream of his own, throwing his furs from him. The dream clung to his mind like molasses. He looked around, fighting to regain reality, breathing quickly and wiping away sweat.

Night still held a tight grip over the land. The campfire was reduced to tiny flames. Aramina was a ball of fur curled at his feet, breathing softly in and out. Her ear twitched as she dreamed, but otherwise she was still. She knew no nightmares as Raori had.

The bard sat near the fire, facing Raori. He played his harp, but silently so the notes carried but a little way. It was not badly played, yet played absentmindedly. Oenghus never blinked as he stared, stared ceaselessly at Raori. He grinned as if they held a secret, just between themselves.

"Who are you?" Raori whispered. In that moment, the mysteries of the universe were held in the bard's unblinking eyes. A bard's business was knowing unusual facts. Oenghus seemed to know more than even that; things the gods kept secret.

Oenghus did not answer. The tune changed, but his eyes never dropped from Raori's face. Raori closed his eyes against the bard's disturbing gaze. Immediately the dream came back, trying to get a new foothold. The mage battled it away, thinking of happy times with his siblings. Dawn had come when next he opened his eyes.

For an instant he thought he was dreaming again. The elf maiden faced him from over a merry fire. She smiled, eyes lighting with mischief, and said, "About time you came back to the living, lazy elf!"

Raori shook his head violently and blinked. The maiden was still there, still smiling. She offered a bit of meat to him. The bard laughed from nearby.

"Give him a chance to wake completely, Aramina," the bard said, stressing the maiden's name as if giving an introduction. Raori tested the name in his mouth, looked at the maiden and knew it fit.

He had forgotten! At an inconvenient time, but it had happened. Marveling at the new experience, Raori examined his surroundings. There may be something else he had forgotten.

There was not. Or maybe if there were, he just could not remember. He wondered if the average elf had this problem.

No matter. To taste others took for granted was enough. He accepted the meat and chewed happily. Aramina shifted to her lupine shape and curled next to him, laying her head in his lap.

"It will be hotter today," the bard said with dread. He was oiling his harp case, paying careful attention to the embossed swan design it sported. "Lucky for me the dwarf is nearby. He'll be here very soon. He's been searching for you for weeks."

"Surely we haven't been gone that long?" Raori asked in disbelief.

"Aye, surely." The bard scratched his nose, leaving a smudge of oil on his face. Unaware of it, he bent back to the case. "The king sent him. If he cannot turn you, he must kill you."

"Duinn would not."

"Surely," the bard repeated himself. "Although he regrets the necessity."

There was no reason to think the bard lied. Raori patted the wolf's head thoughtfully. The bard finished his chore, put away his tools and stood.

"Take my advice," the bard said. "Go with him when he comes. Let him help you. I've done all I can for now." He walked away, back the way they had come.

"Where are you going?" Raori called after him.

"Away," was the short answer. Raori tried to stand and stop Oenghus, but the wolf leaned her weight against him.

"I cannot say I want him to stay," Raori said to the wolf, "but you might at least object to it. You and he seem to share something special."

The wolf bit at a flea. She took great delight in the task, smacking as she worked.

"He could have said where Duinn was." Raori leaned back, laced his fingers behind his head and gazed up at the sky. Clouds were scarce, promising a perfect summer's day. Small birds flew overhead in their hunt of insects for their young. Honking, a white swan glided by with a sweep of its massive wings.

Aramina pricked her ears forward and lifted her head. Her nostrils contracted as she sniffed the air. Her eyes followed the bird as it winged out of sight.

"You can't possibly want to go hunting right now," Raori complained. "We just ate, and it will be hot soon."

Aramina sighed wearily and lay back down again.

The fire was dead before Raori found motivation to move. He buried the ashes lightly, using his feet. A hot coal touched his foot where the boot had worn through. He yelled, hopping on his sound foot. The wolf snorted with laughter.

"You take care of it," Raori snapped. Anger tightened the muscles in his neck. Walking away a pace, he folded his arms and turned his back to her.

Someone, a stumpy silhouette against the sky, was coming toward them. They spotted Raori, waved madly and started to run. Raori reached for his sword, swore when he realized it was lost and gestured to Aramina. The wolf stepped forward to investigate, barked under her breath, then howled joyously.

Raori soon recognized his rushing visitor; Duinn. The dwarf was coming to them fast as he could. Another time Raori would have greeted his companion with open arms (despite the danger of being trampled by Duinn's momentum), but the bard's words stayed foremost in his mind. He was not sure if what he waited for was friend or executioner.

Duinn slid to a stop several feet from them. Aramina bounded to him, licked his face and yipped. Behind them Midna's slower bulk cut across the grass.

"I've been hunting you for weeks," Duinn panted, doubled over with hands on his knees.

"We know," Raori said warily. "You might not have found us today, either."

"Well no more hiding," Duinn said. "I've come to bring you back with me."

"To Moirfenn?" Raori asked for spite.

"You know better," the dwarf said.

"Where is Picket?"

"With the Silver Fox," Duinn said. "Gone to battle I hear." He worked his mouth a bit before adding, "Eahn went feral."

Shocked silence. "How can you be sure?" Raori asked quietly.

"He attacked the prince at his coronation. They say he was foaming at the mouth..." Duinn swallowed, apparently uncomfortable. "We need you, Raori. MacKegan is ruthless, as you may remember, and the king is a kinder master. I've been to the Moonstone and it works. Imagine!"

"Freedom," Raori said numbly.

"Aye." Another silence while Duinn studied the ground. Midna was closer now. With a practiced eye, Raori noted how much weight the acolyte had lost. Duinn would have harried him mercilessly without Picket to fight with.

Raori paced, pretending to think the matter over. Duinn moved a hand closer to his dagger, but casually as if there were no weapon to grab. Raori continued to pace until the acolyte finally reached them.

Panting, he flopped on the ground beside Aramina. She let him scratch her ears before padding to Raori. Butting his leg, she whined.

"I leave it to you," Raori said to the wolf. "I don't want anything to do with this anymore, but we're trapped until the end. Shall I kill Duinn before he stabs me with his knife, or shall we go with him to die by another's?"

Embarrassed, Duinn dropped his hand with a flustered motion. "I wouldn't have done it," he muttered.

"Yes, you would," Raori said.

Aramina danced in place before traded her pelt for smooth flesh. Shaking the hair from her eyes, she stretched. Raori tried not to ogle, but as always she appeared a beautiful creature.

"Let's go with him," she entreated with a wrinkled grin. "What a grand adventure, Raori, to best our enslaver for glory!"

Trust Aramina to take fun from the worst tragedy. Raori gestured his submissiveness. His memory retreated to a room where Aramina had stood against a sorcerer defiantly, swearing to see her mission to the bitter end. Her change of heart seemed a cruel lie.

"We can start now," Duinn suggested. "You've rested, and I am not yet tired."

Midna groaned, but got to his feet. No one noticed Aramina had shifted back again until she was a four-pawed motion in the grass. Privately Raori was disappointed. Their reunion might have been a bit more nostalgic.

CHAPTER TWENTY-THREE
"THORN FOR THRONE"

The cadavers were tireless as they made way across the land toward Cros Fada. Were it not for the living that lead them, Fion's forces would never have found rest. MacKegan's generals halted the armies when they needed to sleep, but those periods of repose were never enough. Bodb Derg's troops, most rebels from small homesteads, were exhausted. Their neglected needs weighed heavily on morale.

Finnbhear did not lead one unit but joined forces as he met each. The pooka took him swiftly from camp to camp, where he would spend a day and night conferring with the captains. Then he would away again to the next company.

Bodb had provided a silver mirror to help him in completing his task. It flashed brightly when Finnbhear went the right way; dark when he did not. With it, he had found all of Bodb's armies but one.

Riding through the thickest part of the forest, Finnbhear chewed slowly on a green apple. He held the mirror in one hand, turning it at random. Picket's steps were patient and steady as any normal horse. Twice Bodb's armies had tried to confiscate the well-toned wight. Finnbhear had let them, knowing Picket would escape later to find him.

"There must be something more useful for you to do," Finnbhear said around a large mouthful, "than carry me around like a common work horse."

Picket snorted in agreement. Finnbhear might have expected more conversation from the pooka, who had been in a surly mood since their departure. Indeed, he had not turned into a man for most of the journey.

No blame however. Picket's intended, first grieving the disappearance of her daughter then faced with her groom called to war, was distraught. The Silver Fox held his tongue concerning Brighde. His suspicions were not confirmed about Leannahn, and Picket needed not the extra worry.

The apple core bounced onto the ground. Picket did not cease his rhythmic pace. Turning the mirror in his hand, Finnbhear again resigned himself to a semi-solitary trip.

The mirror stayed dark. The Silver Fox was concerned but paid it no heed. The army went this way. Signs of their passing were still evident: slashed vines, trampled trails with faded boot prints, old cook fires. Before long Finnbhear would get near enough for the mirror to respond affirmatively.

Find them all, Bodb had instructed the Silver Fox in the privacy of his chambers. I won't ask you to general, Silver Fox, but you must find them. The sight of you should give them hope, and there are the medicines I send with you. Above all, be my spy. I must know what is going on beyond the city walls, and you are the best man for it. I know you will do whatever else comes as part of your duty.

Finnbhear imitated the missionary's path, bringing rare medicines, hope and news. It was better than leading the soldiers to their death in some ways. Some nights, when he curled in the solitude of a borrowed tent, he wished he were at the fore. Bodb's strange orders were utterly useless, for all the relief and renewed vigor the troops knew when they saw the war hero's arrival. The trail turned sharply uphill. Picket slid on the loose earth, grunted in effort, gained the top.

Automatically Finnbhear pulled the reins to halt his steed; an unnecessary action. Picket's legs were stiff, his neck thrown back, his breath held. Finnbhear let the reins drop.

It was carnage before them, hanging from tree limbs and spewed on the ground. The troops might have fought bravely or despaired in the slaughter of ambush. There were few whole bodies wearing Moirfenn's colors and only a dozen undead.

They had been young, inexperienced, most of them surplus sons who volunteered for honor. Now their eyes, those uneaten by scavengers or cut out from spite, stared into the tree tops. Flies flew circles, celebrating the feast. Death's stench hung heavily, clogging Finnbhear's nostrils, making the bile rise in his throat. He gagged.

No one wearing captain's colors lay among the dead. Finnbhear searched for anything, a rag or evidence they were slaughtered away from the main battle. Before he was done, he had already decided the outcome: No survivors. The dead, enchanted, marched toward Cnos Fada.

Grimly, Finnbhear checked the mirror which should have led him to these men. Its surface was just as black as before.

Picket stood in the trees, his hide resembling sunlight on autumn leaves, while Finnbhear pulled what wood he could into a pile. Exhaustion led to the use of his atma. Directed by his dancing fingers, tree limbs round as his waist floated to the growing mound. The sun had only moved an inch when Finnbhear set fire to his project. As flames licked upward, the Silver Fox turned his energies toward the grim task of burning the bodies.

It would be unwise to leave the dead as they were. Moirfenn's necromancers sometimes came back to old battle sites to find more bodies for their gruesome tasks. Any serviceable remains here had already been taken, but Finnbhear wanted to take no chances. An entire army of slain foes was difficult enough to fight without it growing larger every day.

The undead were hard to dispatch. The spell could be broken if the corpse were held by the head, forehead clapped by the heel of the hand with the proper words. But when in battle, there was no time to take such measures. Hacking cadavers to trembling pieces was usually the only way to survive.

It was exhausting work with few rewards. A severed limb could fight on without its host. Centuries ago, Finnbhear found a certain rhythm in severing the head first, grabbing it and clapping the forehead to end the spell. He got quite good at it, and this made him careless. An enemy's blade found his thigh while he stooped for an enemy's head. Finnbhear was lucky to get away alive that day. Since then he fought only the living, avoiding cadavers where possible.

The fire roared into the night. Finnbhear sat there with the sensible notion of staying near warmth and safety. He spitted a coney, roasted it by the bonfire's heat. Picket refused his offer to share with a disgusted snort. The Silver Fox shrugged to himself and ate every bite. Fire fodder was fire fodder, be it vegetable or mineral.

Flames still ate the bones of tree and elf when Finnbhear saddled Picket and took his leave. At first, they traveled without purpose. The path cut by Moirfenn's army was easiest to go by, but they hung back. Occasionally Finnbhear held up the mirror only to witness its constant darkness.

Too soon, he caught up with the enemy. Watching from the trees, he counted mentally. When he ran out of numbers he moaned, placing his head into his hands. Three quarters of the army were cadavers, tireless, and fresh from the field. Generals rode sentry around their charges, shouting cheerfully to one another. Fourteen necromancers clung to the rear in silent dignity.

There was nothing he could do against them alone. Picket eagerly, using his unseen stealth, was away faster than ever before. Finnbhear clung to his back like a burr to bear hide. Cnos Fada was only two days away.

Finnbhear and Picket camped a day away from Cnos Fada. Tempting as it was to press the issue and force the pooka to carry him with magic speed, the Silver Fox felt a reluctance to return to the city. His instincts told him there was something more to do; something the king would expect as par course. The Silver Fox found his eyes narrowing as he watched Picket graze.

"Picket," Finnbhear said on impulse, "can we not go to your people and ask their help?"

The pooka lifted his head, startled, and regarded Finnbhear with wild eyes.

"Well?" the Silver Fox prompted, undeterred.

Picket shifted slowly, as if by great reluctance. To Finnbhear's relief, he wore his kilt and the new shirt Aihn had given him. "Why go to them?" he demanded. "'Tis not one of your better ideas, Silver Fox."

"They have ways of dealing with trouble," Finnbhear reasoned. "Their help would be incomparable."

"Aye," Picket agreed softly. "And their scorn."

"Carry me to them," Finnbhear said. "We have to try. Who else can stop that dread army but the unseen people? Their cause should be the same, for it is their land that suffers the battles we fight to protect them."

"Protect them?" Picket practically whinnied with indignation. "Pompous Fox! Your kind destroys our forests the same as the mortals, then you come running to us. Help us, you say, from the consequences of your own actions. Then you have the nerve to claim such feats as that!"

"If MacKegan wins, all the land will look as his domain."

"Truth," Picket agreed, "but gives you no right to claim us under your boot!"

"All right," Finnbhear said, fighting a grin. "But you understand why we must ask their help."

Picket paused. "You might be able to gain their ear," he said doubtfully. "But I can only carry you so far. And you must make a bargain. What have you to give?"

Finnbhear opened his mouth to answer, but Picket held up a silencing finger. "Don't say anything!" the pooka warned. "I only asked rhetorically."

"You are willing to take me, then?"

Picket looked toward the trees with inner debate. After a long time he said, "'Twill help to balance things." He shifted, pawed the earth with a forefoot, then knelt for Finnbhear to mount. The Silver Fox regretted pressing the question as he left a half-cooked dinner for the offered ride.

The pooka almost threw Finnbhear with his sudden departure. The Silver Fox grabbed two fists of mane and clung with all his might. Tree limbs slapped his face and sides. Obviously enjoying himself, Picket frog hopped a few paces, thundered along trails that disappeared behind them, leapt streams and bushes, pranced when the mood took him. Finnbhear gritted his teeth as he held, wondering what he had gotten himself into.

When the pooka slowed to a sedate trot, Finnbhear dared to unscrew his eyes and lift his head. The path they coursed was broad and lined with flowers as if it were cultured frequently. A large weeping willow hung over the trail, shaping a natural door.

It did not look threatening, but Finnbhear knew better. Things of the Sidhe could be very deceiving. That portal might lead to Picket's home or off a cliff.

Another fey horse leapt from the bushes to bar their path. He was the black kind, with eyes fiery red and a square jaw. Snorting, he thrashed his tail and lay his ears back.

Picket froze. A rumbling sound in his throat tickled Finnbhear's hearing. The other pooka reacted by rearing, pawing the air and screaming a challenge.

"I entreat you," Finnbhear said, holding his palm outward, "to let us pass. Or call your kings and queens that I might speak with them."

The black pooka never moved. Picket's ears went flat. For an instant Finnbhear feared he would be brought into their fight the hard way; trapped on Picket's back.

"Thrice I ask you," Finnbhear said in desperation. "Seven times if I must."

The black pooka bucked wildly, screaming as he thrashed. Picket turned a roving eye to his passenger, also annoyed. Finnbhear's plea, coupled with such sacred amounts, required a response of some kind. Requirements did not include a favorable one, but Finnbhear was willing to take that risk. The cadaver army marched toward Cnos Fada now and could possibly reach it before the sun sank twice.

Finnbhear sat silently and waited for whatever came next. The black pooka continued to threaten them. Suddenly he subsided, leaping over some nearby hedges with a final squeal.

Picket slowly pricked his ears forward, snorting thoughtfully. Will-o-the-wisps glowed behind the willow, their light gleaming softly between branches and leaves. The branches rustled without a sound.

Finnbhear kicked Picket's flank, but the pooka did not budge. The Silver Fox dismounted, patted Picket's flank and nervously eyed the tree. If the pooka would not enter this domain, then neither would Finnbhear.

Something hopped down the twisted path. Finnbhear thought it was a frog at first, but the closer it got the more its features became something else. On gnarly legs it bounced past the tree and to Finnbhear's foot. The Silver Fox watched, mouth agape, as the ugly thing took hold of his pant leg and tugged.

"Why do ye seek us, cousin?" it asked with a voice both squeaky and deep.

"I have come to make a plea on the High King's behalf, friendly spriggan," Finnbhear said. The spriggan's hand was clammy through the cloth.

"Friendly spriggan," the creature cackled. "A plea on your king's behalf, also! What an ironic thing you be!"

"Kindly sprite," Finnbhear said with, he thought, incredible patience. "Would you carry my message to your leaders? Time is short, and Fion is in danger."

"From the nonliving in the field?" The spriggan hopped in place. "Horrible creations! They plow ask and ash, scar the earth without thought to the precious bluebells and cowslips. Your kind made them!" It pointed an accusing finger at Finnbhear. "And were it not for the wight you master here, we would not have allowed you this close." With its other hand it fingered an elf shot stone.

"I do not master Picket," Finnbhear said past a sudden lump in his throat. "He brought me here willingly."

Picket nodded his head. His powerful muscles shifted beneath Finnbhear's hand. The spriggan played with its elf shot, sometimes aiming at Finnbhear's head. The Silver Fox mastered himself and did not flinch.

"Willingly you say?" The elf shot lowered, then dropped to the ground as if forgotten. "P'raps that will make a difference." It turned and hopped back down the path, disappearing behind a clump of grass.

Finnbhear expected a fanfare or another angry wight. Nothing happened, no one approached them, the violet sky deepened with dusk. To stave off boredom, Finnbhear removed Picket's saddle and polished it. He could see his face gleaming in the silver trappings and was working on the straps when the air changed.

It was the mild feeling before a thunderstorm. Setting the saddle aside, Finnbhear quickly tried to brush himself clean. Picket tossed his mane but otherwise did not move. The white lady appeared by the tree.

Her platinum tresses, braided and coiled elaborately around her perfect face, trailed behind her as she walked. Everything about her was silver and white. Even her mantle was of white rabbit fur.

Looking at her, Finnbhear felt an odd tug at his heart. He thought of wild things, things his people had almost forgotten. So few, so few chose to remember the ancient ways. Even he, the Silver Fox, grew old with an elf's slow mortality and waited for death.

The silver maiden stopped a few feet from him. "I am Cliodna," she said simply. She extended a pale hand for Finnbhear's graces. "What is your request, cousin?"

Finnbhear bowed low enough to touch the ground with his forehead. She touched his shoulder, upon which he rose. Her smile was the only thing warm about her, frozen as she was in the icy embrace of white. Even her eyes were untouched by the otherwise friendly expression.

Haltingly Finnbhear spoke his request. Smile gone, the faerie's face never changed; no sorrow, anger, nor amusement. When Finnbhear had stopped speaking, her pale blue eyes bored into him for an eternity.

"Thrice, then seven times you asked to see us for this?" she asked. Did her eyes flash lightening anger, was her voice neutral or furious? This time Finnbhear did flinch. This lady's displeasure hurt him more than the thought of insanity by elf shot.

"I have," Finnbhear agreed slowly. "We sorely need your wisdom and skill to overcome this foe."

When her smile returned, it came from a wintry waste. "Perhaps we will give you aid," she said. "We cannot abide these unnatural monsters that destroy the sacred things without thought or regret. But you must pay a price, grandchild of Alainn."

"What must I do?" Finnbhear asked past his dread.

The faerie's eyes held no response. "Return to your place, cousin, and trouble us no more. You will see our answer when the times comes."

She waved a jeweled hand outward. Sparkling dust littered the air, gave the light reason to dance, landed in Finnbhear's eyes.

He blinked, tears forming, wiped his eyes with one hand. When his vision cleared, he was standing at his camp with Picket grazing nearby. The rabbit was charred black. Dark had completely fallen.

Disorientated, Finnbhear crept into his sleeping roll without complaint. He was trying to decide if his trip to Faery had been a daydream when he fell asleep.

***

Moirfenn's court held no trace of the cold dignity in Fion's halls. Pranks were played by visiting gentry with egregious and disastrous results. Slaves hurried to predict their masters' bidding, for to be deemed worthless meant death. Rough laughter as pranks turned toward sluggish slaves cruelly echoed around the room.

No one noticed the half elf in the green mantle until she stood mere feet from MacKegan's chair. A fell beast followed her on a chain like a docile dog. It snarled at any who came too near, foam dripping from its mouth, hands clenching as the desire to shift clenched its heart. But it dare not, everyone knew, for the chain was wrought of cold iron. The use of atma would cause it enormous pain.

"Who are you?" the dark lord demanded from his chair. The laughter died as all turned their attention to this new spectacle. The girl never let her eyes drop as befitting her age. Someone chuckled nervously.

"Uncle," the girl said, kneeling. The chain clanked as she went down, dragging the beast with her. "'Tis I." She swallowed from clear emotion. "Leannahn."

Chulain barked a laugh. "My niece is dead," he said. "Who are you, truly, and what dares you to come into my hall without invitation?" Not a sound could be heard but for the beast's quick breathing.

"I am Leannahn," the girl insisted in a clear voice. She stood again and pulled the beast closer to MacKegan. "I can prove myself."

She clearly had MacKegan's interest. Were it otherwise she would have been dead, or worse, before taking the first step. The dark elf placed his chin in one hand to contemplate this brave child. "Very well," he said. "Prove you are my niece."

Hope surged in the child's eyes. She began by recounting childhood memories; her first slave, a gift from MacKegan, and how he was captured. She spoke of times when her uncle had taken her alone to share the ways of his dark arts. Her voice faltered as MacKegan's expression of disbelief never changed. Still she braved on, moving to latter years when she served as part of The Six.

"I was trapped in the ley gate," she said finally. "Until Raori set me free. When I no longer needed his body I took this child the pooka would have fostered."

MacKegan affected a yawn. With the gesture, several swords were drawn. "Anyone would know those things," MacKegan said, "and could create a story of Leannahn's survival. Have you no other way to prove yourself, changeling?"

"Yes," Leannahn said. She jerked the chain. The Fell Beast choked and stumbled forward. "This creature obeys me," she said. "You yourself taught me that secret, and none other after me." She hesitated before asking, "Uncle, I must ask a boon."

"A boon?" MacKegan radiated annoyance.

"This beast," Leannahn rattled the chain of her pet, "is my comrade, Eahn. You control the sickness, Uncle. Is there some way that you can cure it as well? He gives poor service to you this way."

"So, this beast is the Northern Thorn." MacKegan almost stepped from his chair for a closer look. Obviously thinking better of it, he contented himself with leaning forward.

Leannahn's grin was mingled with pity and craftiness. "I am quite fortunate the Northern Thorn went Feral at the palace, where he could be kept until I claimed him. Very convenient."

Swords lowered as MacKegan, obviously intrigued, leaned back. "Eahn?" he questioned the air. At the name, the Fell Beast raised his eyes. "I did not expect it so soon. Life is just full of surprises. And now my long-lost heir has returned to me, revived in a halfling body. Practically glowing with power. How many have you killed, Leannahn?"

"Killed, Uncle?" the girl faltered. Her knuckles whitened as she clenched the chain in anxiety. Sensing her unrest, the Fell Beast glowered around the room, looking for a perpetrator. People shied away.

"Yes," the dark lord replied impatiently. "How many have you had to kill to survive, *niece*."

Her hair fell in a cloud around her face as, shamefully, she lowered her eyes. Then she looked up with fierce pride and determination. "Seven," she declared. "The first a northern lord, another a slave I took from your pens. The rest were brigands who thought to use me, and they got what they deserved!"

First MacKegan grimaced, then he erupted into hearty laughter. His servants and vassals waited in stunned silence. "Yes, I believe you now. That is very like you, Leannahn my darling," he said at last. "A pity you came to me this way."

He snapped his fingers. Sword bearers surged forward. Leannahn shouted a command and jerked the chain. It fell from Eahn, vanishing before it hit the floor. The attackers knew then that the chain was merely a glamour, that the Fell Beast was free, and they tried to turn. Eahn leapt on the first one, dispatched him quickly, and ripped into the second. He changed as he went, assuming the beast-like figure all Fell Beasts bore.

"To me!" Leannahn cried when Eahn ranged to far. The Fell Beast reeled back to her.

"Bring him down, or die trying!" MacKegan thundered. Reaching inside his billowy cloak, he pulled forth a dark blade engraved with bloody runes. Leaping down, he advanced on Leannahn.

Fear for their master overruled that of the Fell Beast. Six elves jumped Eahn, dragged him to the ground. Someone screamed in agony when Eahn bit his groin. The others grappled his arms and legs, straining, barely able to hold him down.

Leannahn calmly waited for MacKegan. He towered over her, raised his sword high, strained his muscles as he gathered himself for the killing stroke. She held no fear of him. Living weeks in Brighde's body, forced to take drastic measures for survival, had taught her things about her new existence.

She smiled demurely, placing atma in that smile by subtle measures. The sword above her faltered, then came whistling down to land at her side.

"Changeling," MacKegan spat accusingly. "Get out of my sight, before I find a woman to end your life!"

MacKegan's niece stared in shock at her uncle. Her bottom lip trembled for a mere second before she turned and fled the hall. Her choked sobs were drowned by cruel laughter.

Chapter Twenty-Four
"Siege by Cadaver"

Aramina fingered the scar on her ear, thinking of Gredber and the wolf pack she had left behind. Were they still alive? Had the hoard of half-alive beings trampled dens, muddied the water, chased away all the game?

"I can see the city walls," Raori said, shading his eyes with one hand, squinting against the morning sun. "Do you think they'll betray us, Priestess?"

Aramina had no answer. Bodb Derg's next move did not concern her as much as MacKegan's. He still held power over Raori and herself. Thus far he chose not to use it, gods only knew why, but soon he would. When he did, well, she just hoped to be free of the bond by then.

"What is that?" Duinn asked, pointing toward Cnos Fada. "Raori, use your blasted fey sight and tell me."

The mage smiled at Duinn's ire. He looked, frozen in place with his hand at his eyebrow. Impatiently Duinn and Aramina waited. Just when Aramina opened her mouth to demand a report, Raori spoke.

"It's an army," he said in awe. "I think they're moving around, digging..."

"Broken rings and twisted shards!" Duinn stomped in circles, raising his fists to the sky. "How can we get to the king with that in our way? It's impossible!"

Aramina looked at Raori, who still studied the far off field. She could not see the army he spoke of. He had to be using his mage's skill. Electing not to break his concentration, she turned to Duinn.

"If word of our defection has not spread," she said, "they will let us through."

"And if they don't know who we are?" Duinn demanded. "How do we prove ourselves, eh?"

"The Mark," Aramina said, surprised Duinn would not have thought of it. "We'll bare our shoulders to them if need be--"

"The Mark is gone from me!" Duinn wailed. Covering his face with his hands, he crumpled into the dirt. "Aye, they'll pike me and never will I repay my debt to my lord!"

Pity moved Aramina to lay a light hand on the dwarf's head. "Raori and I still have them," she said. "We can turn that to our advantage. And best done quickly, before MacKegan does something about us." The dwarf remained slumped, a picture of defeat. "Don't worry," Aramina said. "Have I ever let you down, old friend?"

"No." Duinn's voice was muffled by his hands but clearly to her favor. Aramina smiled to herself.

"Then let's get him," she jerked a thumb wryly in Raori's direction, "out of his trance. We'll need a glamour."

Three riders on grey steeds with eyes of deepest night cantered into the army camp. The horses were obviously conjured, and before long whispers of mages from Moirfenn were being passed from ear to ear. Their leader, a young-looking mage dressed in black and silver, haughtily rode in front. The woman had nothing but hatred in her eyes while the dwarf, ill-suited for his mount but mastering it, snarled at anyone who came near.

They rode past the gaping faces of undead warriors without a backward glance. Necromancers looked up from mending or creating new minions. Dark elves followed at a distance, slipping from shadow to shadow with their elf shot arrows. The riders remained unchallenged, but they were also watched. The three intruders never flinched, deigned not to notice the flash of silver eyes, urged their mounts forward like they owned the world.

"Unnatural," the dwarf grated into his chest. "Doesn't MacKegan have the honor to get the living to fight this war?"

"They're useful," the woman said coldly, looking around.

"They should stay in the ground where they belong," Duinn muttered.

The riders stopped in front of the largest tent, which was decorated with totem spears. Dismounted, they handed the reins to a silver elf who appeared from nowhere as if summoned. Raori motioned his companions to stay back as he stepped forward and scratched the door flap.

"Heffes, I told you to leave me in peace!" a voice roared from inside. "Now do as I say or I'll flay you alive!"

"Step outside and speak to messengers from MacKegan!" Raori commanded angrily. "And hurry, or you'll be the one flayed before the day wanes!"

The mottled face of an ancient silver elf looked out from the tent. He twisted his mouth before saying, "Who are you? How did you get here? Guards!"

"Hold!" Raori held his palms up. Atma flashed, bubbled around the tent. Guards ran into the fringes and bounced back as if they hit something solid. Raori grabbed the elf by his hair and hauled him out of the tent.

"How dare you threaten members of The Six," he hissed into his captive's ear. He threw the elf back. The elf made no movement to get back up again..

In days of old, Aramina and Raori played this trick on Moirfenn's outlying generals for sport. It had been amusing to see their victims' faces pale in horror while they stammered apologies and, sometimes, begged for their lives. This time was no different. "Apologies," the elf stammered. "With only three of you, and no word of your coming--"

"No excuses," Raori said, cutting the general off short. Aramina snickered into her hand. "You will cooperate fully with us, or we'll have you executed. Understand? I want a full report. Now. And," Raori mused into his hand, "your best wine. Immediately."

"Please, come inside." Without brushing himself off, the general stood and ushered them inside the tent. "I'll call for refreshments," the elf was saying nervously. He paused. The three companions looked at him expectantly. "My lord, if you would release your shield…"

Raori shrugged and flicked one wrist. The bubble disappeared with a soft popping sound. Looking relieved, the silver elf shouted for wine, cheese and fresh bread. "We must wait for my sorcerer," he said apologetically when the orders were received.

"You are not capable of telling me yourself?" Raori asked haughtily.

"Surely, lord," the general whimpered, twisting his mustache nervously, "but do you not want every detail? I cannot explain the things of sorcery as well as my compatriot."

Aramina lay a hand on Raori to calm him. "We can wait a few minutes," she said to the mage. "The result will be the same, regardless."

The general's sorcerer took his time coming. Meantime, the companions dined on MacKegan's food. They had not taken such luxuries for weeks and the meal was like a blessing from the gods. Raori polished off three goblets of dark wine, shared a fourth with Aramina and Duinn for friendship's sake, then took a fifth. With alarm, Aramina noted his eyelids were drooping sleepily as he lounged against the tent pole.

Someone stepped inside the tent, the flap rustling behind him. Everyone looked up.

"Impossible!" Aramina cried in spite of herself. "You're dead! I killed you!"

Astonished, Raori and Duinn could only stare numbly. Aes laughed, fingering the Mark on his cheek. Then he threw back his cloak to reveal his bare chest. It was laced with scars.

"You mauled me," he said. "But I'm a survivor. Like you."

Apprehensively, Raori shakily stood. Duinn stayed as he was, the blood leaving his face at a frightening rate. Aramina became determined to keep the sorcerer's attention on her. If ever they needed to keep the illusion of their purpose, it was now. She tossed her long hair haughtily. The movement caught Aes' straying glance.

"I told you before," she said, "you'll not keep me from completing my mission."

"So I recall," Aes said dryly. "Now you are here to complete it? I find that hard to believe."

Aramina said nothing. She lifted her chin to indicate stubbornness, but in actuality she had no idea what to say. This plan was weak to begin with. Now they were caught, with no way to pick the lock.

"MacKegan does not believe you capable of defiance," Aes said into the silence. "Even these scars on my body did not dissuade him." His eyes met and locked with Raori's.

Aramina could not tell what the two mages shared. Raori's eyes narrowed a warning, then lowered to the floor. Aes chuckled dryly.

"We've been punished enough by your report," Duinn said, regaining his composure. "Now do we serve MacKegan together or not?"

Aes thoughtfully ran a hand over his chin. "Aye, so he did call on the geis," he said. "Yet, there is something different about you..."

"By the gods," Aramina declared impatiently. She grabbed the shoulder of her dress and pulled. The cloth ripped with a loud sound. Turning her bare shoulder to the sorcerer, she demanded, "There! Still under MacKegan's thumb and working for his cause. Happy? Can we stop this senseless argument?"

Aes only look slightly mollified. "I cannot dispute the Mark," he said with a shade of disappointment. His eyes sought Raori again. "Remember, mage, what I told you."

Aramina turned to Raori. "What did he tell you?" she asked.

"Nothing important," the mage said. He dismissed her with the redirection of his eyes. "Very well, Aes. What have you to tell us?" He hardly looked sober enough to deal with this, but Aramina could no more get rid of him than she could Aes.

Aes took up the wine bottle and frowned at the small amount of liquid left within. "We're laying siege at the moment, obviously," he said dryly. "Without my comrades," he slipped a glare in Aramina's direction, "we do not have enough atma to break Cnos Fada's defenses." He downed the wine.

"Is that all you plan to do?" Raori asked sluggishly. "Not much of a plan. Aramina could think of better. At least her plans involve fire and something fun. This... this is outright *lazy*." He waved his hand in Aramina's direction. Despite herself, Aramina quirked a grin. The mage would kick himself once he sobered up for this.

"It works," Aes replied "Soon enough their food will run out. I've an apprentice searching for their underground water supply so we might poison it. Their days are numbered."

Yawning, Aramina stretched. "Why did we bother coming here?" she asked Raori. "I'm sure there are better things to do than sit around here, waiting."

"Where are the others?" Aes asked suddenly.

Raori opened his mouth, but Aramina cut in smoothly. "Abandoned us," she snarled. "Ungrateful traitors. The geis fell on Duinn one night and while he suffered, they took their leave. I wouldn't be surprised if MacKegan has them dead by now!" She crossed her arms as if to end the matter.

But Aes did not take the hint. "And here you are," he said. "What loyal heroes you are."

Raori grunted. "What smart servants," he corrected Aes mildly. "Just like you."

Aes ignored the gibe. "Word from Moirfenn is that your Northern Thorn went feral."

Everyone affected shock, even the silver elf who had slipped into a shadow to watch. The sorcerer grinned at a ready audience.

"He attacked the prince at his coronation," he crowed. "Loyal even until his end! I must admit it impressed me." Contemplating the empty wine bottle, he whispered, "How close are you three, eh? And where is the pooka now?"

"That is no concern of yours!" Aramina snarled, snatching the bottle from Aes' hand and hurling it across the tent. It rolled out the door flap. Someone shouted outside as they tripped on it. "Your concern, sorcerer, is aiding me with my mission! Now, you're hiding something. What is it?"

Aes blinked, but only long enough to regain his composure. He said, "In three days, MacKegan himself will be here to hear the upstart king's surrender. If Bodb Derg does not surrender then, we are ordered to bring the city down stone by stone."

"There's more than that," Aramina growled.

"I know nothing more!" Aes put his hands up in mock surrender. "Priestess, I have told you all we know. Anything else is MacKegan's sole possession."

"What a vain and useless gesture! MacKegan has gone completely mad!" Clenching her fists, Aramina forced herself to turn to her comrades. "Our lord will expect more than us to wait," she said to Raori and Duinn. "Tomorrow morning we must ride to the city gates and acquire their surrender."

"What?" Aes cried. "Take MacKegan's victory from him? Are you suicidal?"

"Quite the opposite," Raori said coldly. "We've served Chulain longer than you, Aes, and know what to expect. He cares not how Cnos Fada is taken, so long as it is done thoroughly."

"You're fools," Aes said. The thought tickled him. "Do as you will. I will wait for MacKegan's arrival." He exited the tent. The silver elf started to follow, but Raori stopped him.

"We will need a tent," he said. "This one will do nicely." Even Duinn chuckled at the general's discomfort.

"I can't believe you killed those sorcerers!" Raori cried later, when night had fallen. The tale of Aramina's confrontation with the three sorcerors had sobered him up considerably. He paced the tent tirelessly, alternately ranting and pulling anxiously at his bangs. Aramina sleepily curled into borrowed blankets and watched the mage with drooping eyes. For someone who not long ago had been deep in his cups, he was livelier than ever. She envied his energy.

"I can," Duinn muttered darkly.

"What's the fuss?" Aramina yawned. "It was to protect us. Not that it matters."

"Aye." Raori blew out in frustration, wiping his hair with one hand. "What do we do? We can't very well wait here for an all out siege, and we can't leave without confirming Aes' suspicions and having the entire army of Moirfenn hot on our heels. This is bad business, Aramina, and I don't like it!"

"Go to sleep," Aramina suggested with another yawn.

Obediently, Raori flopped onto his blankets. Duinn grumbled as he was forced to move over. Gratefully Aramina closed her eyes, breathed deeply

And opened her eyes to the dark. The tallow lamp had faded to a bare flicker. Raori and Duinn slept on, trapped in their dreams. It was the dwarf's snores that had awakened her. Kicking him lightly, to which he snorted once and turned over, she burrowed back into her blankets.

No good. She was awake now and must suffer the reality. Aramina stood and shrugged her ripped dress on. Before stepping outside, she smiled down at Raori's face.

The air was warm, summer being climaxed. Breathing in, Aramina shifted to all fours and walked out of camp. Ears turning in all directions, nose straining to catch the faintest scent, she still did not catch the other figure darting in the opposite direction.

Neither did her nighttime companion notice her. His cloak billowed dramatically as he walked. About a mile outside of camp, he reached a small carne of stones.

The place was a frequented area. Vegetation was sparse, except for offerings left by travelers. Aes stole the food, secreting it in his pouch. He lit a small fire, tossed herbs on it and chanted masterfully.

The enchanted face that formed in the smoke bore no patience. "State your business," the voice commanded irritably.

"Lord," Aes said, bowing to the ground. "I have news of the Six."

"I told you not to disturb me with your foolishness," the angry face, MacKegan's face, grated. "If you cannot handle them alone, then your demise is your fault."

"But lord," Aes stammered, "three of them are here--"

"Than killing them should be easy for you."

"They claim to be under your orders," Aes swallowed, "and that the others ran. The Feral one is among the missing--"

"I did not tell them to go to you," MacKegan nearly shouted, his face looming large in the wavering smoke. "Undoubtedly they think they can win back my favor. Well, sorcerer, I will take care of them. They will be weak as kittens by morning, by the Mark they wear!"

Aes cowered on the ground until the fire burned itself out. When he returned tc camp, he could not resist a gloating moment outside the tent his guests occupied.

Aramina did not know this, of course. Carefree, she danced among the hills with the will-o-the-wisps, rolled in the dust with glee, cavorted with an unfortunate mouse who found itself miraculously alive after she bounded away. It was a long time before she reached another, older carne of stones. She shifted to her human form.

Vines had almost claimed this carne, as had the bushes growing around it. That was the way she preferred it. Trying not to disturb the foliage, she bit a hole in her thumb and let her blood drop onto the top stone.

Lighting by itself, the fire was small. Aramina knelt and bowed her head. "Lord," she whispered.

"So you come back to me," the dark voice of her god chuckled. "I knew you would." The flame grew, shaped a hand, reached for her. She shrank back.

Another flame shot from the stones, surrounded the hand. A familiar voice berated Aramina's dark god sternly. "I paid the price," the voice said. "She is mine again. Upon your honor, you were to tell her."

The dark hand shuddered with anger, shrank back to the flame, disappeared into the rock. The new flame fluttered in its place. Aramina's mortal sight caught images of swans, harp strings, eyes in a handsome face.

"Mac Ind Og," she breathed. "How? Oh, what have you done?"

"Worry not for me," said the Harper. He appeared suddenly, the flame banished unnoticed. Cupping her face with her hands, caressing her hair, he kissed away her frown. "'Tis a small price and necessary to complete your mission."

"But--"

"Six months of a year is all. We spent less time than that when you were with me," the Harper interrupted. "And you'll be free again. The least you can do is be gratefully happy."

Aramina was too confused to feel joy. She shook herself from his light embrace. "You're a bigger fool than mortals think," she said. Tears sprang to her eyes. She wiped them away. "So you'll be gone, under *his* power for six months every year? Have you no consideration of others-"

"Consideration of others?" The Harper's laughter rang over the rocks and cut Aramina's ire short. "Such a jest! Consideration of others indeed. I'll not be under his power but my own. Just different."

Obviously he did not want to explain. Aramina turned her face away and looked into the dark. She could sense Mac Ind Og tuning his harp, which never needed it, then settling into a soft ballad. He did not sing.

"Aes has betrayed you," he said suddenly. Industriously, he packed the instrument away. "MacKegan knows where you are and will do something before the dawn."

Aramina turned to face the god, but he was gone. Frustrated, she picked up the nearest rock and threw it at the ancient altar. The rock bounced and clattered into the darkness. Aramina shifted back to wolf form. Her shadow streaked behind her across the land.

Dawn was still far away when she glided into the tent. Duinn was a rumbling lump in his blankets. Raori lay sprawled across the floor, his blankets tossed aside. He shivered in his sleep.

Aramina decided not to wake them. Running, as Aes surely was expecting, would only reveal them. The geis on Duinn was gone: MacKegan could not hurt him at least. But, she and Raori would need their strength for the trial ahead.

She lay her nose across Raori's chest and closed her eyes.

***

The wall around Cnos Fada was old, predating a time when civilized elves were not born architects. It resembled a humped mound of stones, huge, with rough stairways leading to the top along the inside. It was thirty feet thick at the base, tapering slowly to a ten-foot walkway along the top. Time and weather had worn it to rounded, bleached bones. Pieces of it had a tendency to fall on passers by.

Despite its inadequate appearance, the wall had stood against marauders time and time again. The people of Cnos Fada were proud of their wall and boasted nothing could get past. It was considered good luck if a crumb of mortar fell on your person. Babies were given the scattered debris as tokens of good health.

Picket mounted the wall slowly, pausing now and again to scan his surroundings. The once bustling city was deathly quiet. Everyone huddled inside their homes in fear of the army beyond the wall. Once, Picket thought the city emptied would be a blessing. Standing alone, surveying the eerie stillness, he changed his mind.

Once at the top, he squinted his eyes and looked around. His sight was not half as good as Raori's, but still he could see the undead standing below. They were impossible to miss. Four riders approached the great gates. Picket could only make out the dark color of their mounts. The riders sat tall and proud, save one who slumped.

Messengers from MacKegan, no doubt. What an ill wind! Picket dashed back down the stairs as fast as he could go. In his rush, he accidentally knocked a passing guard from his perch. Fortunately the guard's reflexes were quick enough to cushion his fall with atma.

Finnbhear met him at the bottom of the stairs. "What did you see, wight?" he asked nervously. It disturbed him to see the pooka running pell-mell down the wall.

"Messengers have come," Picket gasped. "They'll be at the gates by now."

The gate sentry hailed someone beyond the wall, listened to their reply, then shouted for someone to fetch the Silver Fox. Picket grinned, pleased at the timing, and followed Finnbhear.

Shoving everyone out of the way, Finnbhear slid back a bolt hole and peeked out. He looked a long time. Picket impatiently shifted his weight from foot to foot. Finally, he burst out, "Well?" The Silver Fox sighed and leaned back.

"They have Duinn tied to his horse," Finnbhear said in a flat tone. "One of your sorcerers rides with them."

Picket shouldered his way in and looked through the hole.

"Raori!" he shouted. "Priestess! What have ye done to Duinn?" He pounded the wood with one fist.

Haughtily, Aramina tossed her hair while Raori said, "It's the same you'll be getting, pooka. And t'others who turned against us!"

Picket leaned back in shock. Somehow he had expected Duinn to return triumphant. Seeing the dwarf slung over a horse like a sack of grain enraged the pooka. He wanted to dash out and cut his friend's bonds, maybe give his other teammates a slap or two for common sense on the side. Especially Aramina. Why, to think she would turn against them so completely--

"Let it go," Finnbhear said softly, laying one hand on Picket's shoulder. "Go tell the king while I see what these fools want."

Reluctantly, Picket backed away from the wall. He almost stayed, but one look from Finnbhear sent him in search of Bodb Derg. Finnbhear's voice, arguing with Raori, echoed in his ears. The king was in the storerooms listening to his head servants complain about dwindling supplies. He looked relieved when Picket stooped into the dark cell. Calling the pooka over, he silenced the others with a gesture.

"What news have you from beyond the wall?"

"Messengers from Moirfenn," Picket said, scratching his shoulder and ducking his head.

"Well," Bodb said jovially. "Can't keep them waiting, can we? Get those barrels in order," he commanded, pointing to various objects, "and report to me this evening."

Picket ignored the murderous glances from the servants as they bent to their tasks. Bodb left at a brisk pace toward the wrong gate. Picket called him, pointing the other way. Then, he shifted form.

"Of course," Bodb said, looking chagrined, before he settled onto the pooka's back. Picket proudly carried his lord through the city like a herald. People moved out of the way quickly. Those that did not felt the consequence when Picket 'accidentally' trod on their feet. The king looked a little flustered when they arrived at the gate. Picket regained his human form and snorted merrily to himself.

Bodb looked through the bolt hole a long time. "I might have expected this," he whispered to no one in particular. Snapping his fingers, he called the nearest elf within reach.

"Ready the archers, and be quick about it!. The mage is with them, so don't slip up! He and that sorcerer would know where you are and kill you before the slip was finished."

The elf saluted stiffly and backed away. While he passed the orders on, Bodb turned back to the bolt hole.

"You're not going to let them in," Finnbhear said in disbelief.

"No, but we at least have to open the gate," Bodb said unhappily. "Duinn trusted us to help him, and we can't leave him out there."

Finnbhear nodded, glancing quickly at Picket. The pooka shuffled his feet, unsure of what to say past his gratitude.

"Why are you here?" Bodb demanded through the bolt hole. "Other than to torment us, I mean. I see you have Duinn."

Picket found his own bolt hole. Finnbhear started to follow him, but thought better of it. Possessively, he fingered his sword as he remained at his master's side. The pooka grinned at the Silver Fox, relishing the freedom he now possessed.

"Yes," Aramina said with mocking satisfaction. "Twas Aes' idea. He wanted you to see what happens to even loyal comrades when they make the wrong choice."

"Barbaric," Bodb returned cuttingly.

Picket peeked out just in time to see Aramina's chin lift. There was something wrong with her eyes. The same could be said of Raori. Picket frowned.

"I think not," the Priestess said conversationally. Atma burst from her outstretched hand and flickered over Duinn's body. The dwarf moaned, twitched and lay still. "I will not claim it isn't cruel," Aramina continued.

Aes moved his horse forward impatiently. "You can have it back," he called out. "A peace offering, you might say, while you consider your surrender."

"Surrender," Bodb sputtered, so enraged he lost his speech. He placed one hand high on the wall and looked down in an effort to regain control. When he looked up again, his eyes had lost hope for the last members of the Six. "We will not bow to you," he said slowly, "We are not going to surrender."

Aramina barked a high laugh and turned her horse around, as if to survey the surrounding terrain. Raori leisurely turned in his saddle , apparently bored by the proceedings. Momentarily their backs were turned to the wall, and Picket's line of sight. They wore new clothing and sported the Mark on their shoulders. Aramina's shirt left her entire shoulder, and Raori's had an opening cut then decorated with fine embroidery. They had not dressed that way since the very beginning, before they burned the city. When they were proud of their lord and felt no shame.

How naive they had been, to take pride in a thing of cruelty! Were Aramina and Raori so set in their ways that even Duinn deserved punishment at their hands? To show the Mark, a symbol of their defeat, anguish, misery with such majesty– Picket shuddered.

"You have until MacKegan himself arrives to surrender," Aes cried. "We're giving you that long to get your affairs in order, if you have any affairs to bother getting in order. Consider MacKegan gracious!"

Bodb tried to stifle his laugh, which erupted with a few snorts and a choke. "MacKegan must be getting old," he said. "Are you distracting me for something bigger? This is hardly MacKegan's style. Where are your companions, his minions, and assassins to kill me? You are making this far too easy."

Aramina moved her horse forward. "Show respect when speaking to a sorcerer of Moirfenn," she said, her eyes sharp as the steel they reflected. "Else you will be too dead to come to terms!"

"Laugh while you can," Aes said stiffly. "But when MacKegan comes, you had better surrender. If you don't, he won't even leave the rubble intact."

"MacKegan stirring from his cesspool to come here?" Bodb laughed again. "Will wonders never cease. I'm only here for Duinn's sake. We'll not surrender, not now, and now when

MacKegan comes. I would never surrender to my family's murderer, besides!"

Aramina moved forward again. Part of Picket's view was cut off, but he thought she was clenching her fists repeatedly. She pointed at the king. "I'll make you surrender," she said. "Nothing MacKegan can do will match--"

"Priestess!" Aes fairly shouted. "Stand down!"

Picket bit his nails while Aramina and the sorcerer locked eyes. Raori made no move to protect her, as he would have in the past. His attention was on the city, as if waiting for something.

It was eerie, the way Aramina lowered her eyes. Aes turned back to the city, and Bodb. "Keep the dwarf," he said. He turned his horse about and guided it back the way he had come. Raori and Aramina followed; one sullenly, the other in a daze.

"Archers ready!" Bodb called when the trio were far enough away. "Open the gate!"

The great doors opened, slowly, as elves strained against the massive cranks which controlled them. A soldier dashed outside, grabbed the reins to Duinn's mount, and led it inside as quickly as possible. Chills sluiced Picket's body. Duinn was covered in blood, and the pooka was willing to bet that it was mostly his. The dwarf had been through a horrible ordeal.

"Get him to the infirmary," the king ordered and did not seem content until the dwarf was on his way. "Well, we know where they stand," he said doubtfully to Finnbhear. "They almost sound desperate. Or bored. One can never tell with MacKegan's ilk."

"Something isn't right," Picket said. Bodb glanced at him, unsurprised. "They act funny." Holding his shoulder, Picket stared at the ground as images repeated themselves in his mind.

"We have Duinn back, at least," Finnbhear said. He did not say what was on everyone's minds; why did they throw him out; was he going to live; had he turned again.

***

The moon was full again. Glad for it, the pooka danced a little before shifting back to human form. Full moon was a time of drunken power for Picket. Giddy, he clambered up the wall then jumped down the other side; forgetting the consequences. He crumpled on the earth, cringing where he fell, feeling sure his ankles were broken.

This was no way to live. How could mortals stand it? Even elves, with their crippled atma, lived better than this.

Such thoughts reminded the pooka of Aihn, waiting at home with her infant son. Already mourning for her lost daughter, she would be twice as protective for Liram. Picket needed to get the two into the city somehow, if they were not dead already. To do that, he needed to get up and going.

Picket slowly got to his feet, moaning as he went. Reality swam before his eyes, blurred and out of control. He moaned again for effect; he had heard a human in pain once. All the mortal had done was moan and groan. Picket thought perhaps there was something in the sounds that made the pain go away. Right now he would do anything for his ankles to stop hurting.

His eyes focused, then widened. He was face to face with one of Moirfenn's soldiers, a silver elf with unreadable eyes.

He was face to face no matter which way he turned. Deduction: Picket was surrounded. Struggle was imminent, if he chose to break free. What matter, though, if he reached the Priestess by fight or stealth? She often said the end was the same, despite the how.

Shrugging, Picket held his arms out. "Take me to your leader," he said.

They did not bring him inside the camp. Rather, their next stop was a small fire by which three generals sat. Dark elves, all of them, and hostile.

Shrugging loose from his captors, Picket strode forward until he could see the pupils of his enemies' eyes. He gritted his teeth, trying to ignore the pain shooting up his legs. "I've come to see the Priestess," he grated.

"Why?" demanded the oldest of his captors. His eyes were almost hidden beneath bushy eyebrows, but the glint of his ethereal gaze twinkled visibly. "Are you not serving the good king, now?"

"Perhaps I am spying," Picket said as aloofly as he could. "Should not your leaders decide, either way?" He stomped one foot imperiously, then almost cried out. Gods, that hurt! "Now, get her!" he demanded, letting the pain fuel to anger in his voice. "I came to see the Priestess, not three insomniac fools."

"Peace, Picket," said Aramina's voice from the shadows. The Priestess stepped into the light. She had been watching them the entire time. Her blank eyes cut through his soul, squelching Picket's hopes.

Beloved friend, desperate Sidhe; they looked at each other for a quiet moment. Aramina broke the silence with a delicate cough. "I anticipated your arrival," she said. "If they had taken you to my tent, you would have been seen and be dead. This is the most I can do to shield you and not for long."

"Come back with me," Picket said desperately. "Mina, you're the one who begged for our defection first. The Moonstone works! You could be free--"

Aramina's laughter held a note of sorrow. Shaking her head, she held up one hand as if to ward off Picket's words. "Free," she giggled. "Picket, you are the only one who ever understood what freedom means to me. I have to finish my mission first."

Feeling suddenly small and afraid, Picket turned his head away from the Priestess' unblinking eyes. Losing Aramina was suddenly a looming reality. He had hoped to she would listen and come with him. Not necessarily into Cnos Fada, but away from this war. Aihn would not mind, so long he was safe.

"Raori did this to you," Picket said suddenly, feeling futile anger stir in his breast.

"Do not blame him," Aramina said gently. "MacKegan holds us through the Mark." She seemed about to say more, but swallowed it.

"Mina--"

"I can think for myself," the Priestess said, cutting him off, not wholly aware of his presence. She was talking to herself, or her generals, and not paying attention to the pooka. "Thanks to Duinn, but MacKegan is strong. He sleeps now," Aramina returned to Picket, 'and will not know you came. But my poor mage sleeps also, exhausted by the things MacKegan has made him do today. His atma stirs in the bodies of the dead, swelling our ranks.'

Picket said nothing, knowing now how ineffectual his trip was. Aramina turned away, as if the sight of her friend bothered her. "Take him away," she said.

The pooka let his body to go limp, forcing his captors to drag him, heels through the dirt, head hanging low. The throbbing in his ankles began to subside. Picket used the moment to concentrate his atma and reinforce the bruised bones. When they reached the wall, he could stand without too much discomfort.

Almost gently, they released him and watched him climb his way back into the city. There were no handholds this side of the wall, but Picket could use cracks the size of a pinhead for purchase. He was halfway up when one of the soldiers hailed him.

"Tell your king," the elf said, "that he has allies."

Solemnly Picket nodded. Satisfied, the elf and his companion turned and entered the dark.

CHAPTER TWENTY-FIVE
"BINDINGS AND LOOSE ENDS"

Fire on his shoulder, fire eating his brain. He wanted to scream, but his jaw refused to open. Tears perched at the corners of his eyes but were not allowed to fall. Even his breath came only with permission.

This was life under MacKegan's command. Failure had its price, a higher one than he was willing to pay. Raori wept in his dreams, awoke dry-eyed, watched his body rise to begin a new day.

Exhaustion kept him from fighting back. Even Leannahn had been a gentler possessor, Raori reflected as he rode his smokey creation through the camp. The horse had been created from ash. Aramina and Duinn's mounts were gone, but MacKegan allowed Raori's to remain.

Aes was close by, watching while pretending not to. The dark elves also watched him resentfully, as if this entire war was his fault. And perhaps it was, in subtle ways. Maybe it began when he first helped to burn Cnos Fada, or when he failed to capture the Spear of Allen. Most assuredly when he had let Bodb Derg live. The prince-now-king's death would have deterred a lot of this destruction.

Aramina looked up from her place by a fire. She held a cup of brew in her hands, cradling it close against the early morning chill. Already the world held the faint scent of fall. Funny how he could notice those tiny things with his body constantly moving.

She set her cup near the fire and stood. Clearly she had been waiting for him. Her eyes were bright. Her half smile was full of trickery. Her walk was swaggered as she crossed the small distance between them. Without hesitation, she grabbed his horse's halter.

"Going to awaken more dead?" she asked. Raori wondered how she could enjoy their predicament. Ever since they both had awakened to MacKegan's angry voice in their minds, she had changed back to the hateful creature of early times. She seemed to enjoy what Chulain was putting them to.

It was always hard to predict Aramina's mood. Raori often wondered what drove her. Was she so crazy even the Feral disease could not touch her?

"There are no more bodies," Raori said heavily. MacKegan's touch did not keep him from thinking, and currently he could speak at will. The noose would tighten when the time was ripe, but for now all MacKegan wanted was to keep the mage under control.

And he was coming. Oh, Raori could feel it. MacKegan had made it plain that when he arrived, Raori would die.

"Then where are you going?" the Priestess asked, oblivious to his thoughts. "Might there be something I can put my own powers to?" Licking her lips, she looked hungry and a trifle bored.

"The new ones must be spelled to obey the commands of their leader," Raori said. "I could use your strength." His was scarcely repleted from yesterday.

"That's right," Aramina said as if remembering something forgotten. "They can only obey the command of one man, and you will be much too busy to tend to them. I hope we can trust the generals."

"We can," Raori said. The silver elves were bound to MacKegan in ways different from Raori's situation. They would not turn lest their families suffer gruesome deaths.

Gruesome deaths. His mind's eye brought forth the memory MacKegan had given him last night: Eahn's wife, burned alive in her house. MacKegan himself had been there, had put the burning faggot to the thatched roof... Her screams still floated in Raori's mind.

She had carried a child! Raori wanted to scream at his master. She was going to have a full-blooded child, so rare to the elves and more precious than the land MacKegan coveted.

This time the tears flowed freely down Raori's cheeks. Empty laughter echoed in the mage's mind. *What use is a helpless brat to me?* his venomous voice said. Then he was gone, lifting briefly from the mage's life while he diverted his attention elsewhere.

Aramina's eyes had never left Raori's face. He knew he must look a terrible sight, but he did not care. "Come when you can," he said, kicking his horse into motion. The Priestess let him go without a fight.

Moirfenn's grisly army had ten dark elf generals, and all were waiting impatiently by another fire. Aes was there, too. He twitched his cloak back nervously.

"This better work," he said in a hard tone while Raori dismounted.

The necromancers had done most of the work, but the main spell lay on Raori's shoulders. Raori was not sure he was up to the challenge. He had never worked such a large spell before, and after reviving so many bodies he doubted he had the energy.

"It has to," Raori said, trying to keep the weariness from his voice and failing. He instructed everyone to stand in a circle, gesturing to Aes last. "Aes, you can lend me your strength."

"Ha!" Aes crossed his arms defiantly. "I wouldn't make the mistake! Do it quickly, mage. When this spell is sealed, we attack."

Checking a sigh, Raori grasped hands with his neighbors. Hesitantly, everyone formed their linked circle. Their eyes went blank as each sought to tap his atma. The air began to hum with energy. It caught Raori up, sustaining him, making him drunk with power. He chanted the spell.

Not enough power, no. Halfway through the chant, his voice faltered. Faintness poured through his limbs. Darkness edged the corners of his mind. *Doom*, Raori thought wildly, *and death! I cannot hold it...*

Strength poured into him from outside. It brought him to new heights. He could see visions of things to come: A mound of stones. A horse carrying its rider home at last. A dress of silk, later cut into a small, soft blanket. A cradle rocked by loving hands. The smiling eyes of his firstborn child.

Back to the spell, gentle mage, someone said, beckoning him back down. *Why seek the future when it comes in its own time as the present?*

Chanting became the focus of his being. Never would it end, even as his voice grew raw with fatigue. Raori kept his eyes closed against what was happening around him. The undead were aware of their new masters and clustered near the circle. Their reek choked his breath.

Like wakening from a dream, his eyes opened to Aramina's smirk. She had slipped into the circle unnoticed. The two elves beside her blinked dazedly, adjusting to the dozens of dead minds now merged with their own. Aramina slapped one on the back. He stumbled forward.

"Hai, Raori, you'll make a master sorcerer yet!" she crowed.

Shrugging, Raori sought to hide his feelings in modesty. It was not he who had recaptured the spell. He felt cheated of his death, his release.

"Now, we must trust Duinn did his job," Aes said, stepping close. He wanted to be no nearer to the hoards of dead soldiers than Raori did.

"Oh," Aramina said with bright eyes and a toothy grin, "he did his job very well."

***

When Duinn awoke in the infirmary, under heavy guard and tied to bed, he bellowed for Picket, Finnbhear, the king, anyone. He bellowed until his voice was hoarse and his chest ached. His guards looked like they wanted to stuff a rag into his mouth.

One elf succumbed to temptation. Leaning into Duinn's face, he grabbed a fist full of beard. "None of those people can help you," he said. "They are at the wall preparing for attack. So shut up, or I will ram your beard into your throat, wrapping it around your tongue on the way."

Duinn subsided his yelling, but not his grumbling.

"Motherlorn pooka," he muttered, glancing at his guards a little fearfully. They ignored him again, but how long would it last? "Blasted Silver Thorn." He recited his father's favorite curses, stumbling over the ones he barely remembered.

"That's creative," one of his guards remarked. His tone of voice bellied their status of prisoner and keeper. "Know any more?"

Duinn knew plenty. He demonstrated.

"That's nothing," the guard said, settling beside Duinn like an old friend. "My uncle used those, and some he made up himself." The youth went into a bloodcurdling litany that could only have been created by a veteran soldier.

Despite the circumstance, Duinn grinned. "What's your name, boy?" he asked.

"Donnach," the lad said with an easy shrug.

"Honored, Donnach," Duinn said, "to meet someone with a family after my heart."

Donnach's laughter was warm sunshine. "To think I sit trading curses with one of The Six," he said, "as if he were family."

"Careful," Donnach's captain warned darkly. "He'll trick you, like he did the king."

Donnach's nod was respectful, yet disbelieving. "I don't think you tricked the king," he whispered loudly to Duinn. "Bodb is a man, like any of us, and prone to mistakes."

The captain grunted, refusing to be goaded by the spirited elf.

"He made no mistake in trusting me," Duinn said. "But to keep me from seeing him now could be a very grave error indeed."

"How so?" Donnach asked.

"Donnach," the captain said suddenly. "Back to yuir post."

With an apologetic smile, Donnach resumed standing with the other guards, all around Duinn's bed as if he were a badger hemmed in his hole. Duinn rejoined his mutters, but softly.

Shift change did not bring friendlier faces. Sour looks floated over him as the new elves took their places around the room, sitting together to play sticks and bones or lounging by a wall. No one else but Duinn was contained in the infirmary. The dwarf began to feel like a plague.

"Why keep me under such guard?" Duinn asked the nearest body. "You've got me tied as if for slaughter. Shouldn't that be enough?"

The elf chuckled. "Hear that, fellahs?" he asked his companions. "The Fell Beast wants to know why we watch him so tenderly."

Laughter erupted around the room. "It's because we care about you so much," another said.

"Aye. Every rope is tied with a love knot."

Duinn remembered Eahn. "Fools," he muttered. "Leannahn would not come back for me." The elves chuckled to each other, still trading comments, and did not pay attention. Duinn closed his eyes, seeking a brief escape from his tormentors.

"Should I wake him?" someone asked by his ear. Duinn's eyes fluttered open before he was completely awake. He tried to stand, get into the defensive, but found himself still bound.

"No," someone else said.

Bodb Derg's face came into view. His eyebrows drew down, resembling caterpillars meeting nose to nose. "Have you failed me, dwarf, or have you turned back to your master?"

"What?" Duinn roared. The king drew back in the face of Duinn's indignation. "Ye idiot, Bodb Derg, I should smite your face for such an accusation!"

Chuckling, Bodb drew a knife and began to saw at Duinn's bonds. "Even without the truth spell, I would believe you," he said jovially.

"Truth spell?" Sitting at last, Duinn felt light-headed. Biting back a groan, he said, "You truth spelled me?"

"It will wear soon," Bodb said offhandedly. "Donnach had the idea."

For the first time, Duinn noticed the youth was seated on the bed. "My word of honor was not enough for you?" he demanded weakly.

"I believe you," Donnach said, holding up his hands. "The others did not. It seemed necessary."

"And left me with no excuse not to see you," Bodb cut in. He sighed. "I'm sorry, but after what happened with Eahn I could not take the chance. I couldn't cage you, nor kill you. Leastwise, until I knew what you were about."

Duinn grunted, glaring at Bodb then Donnach. The elves took his manner lightly.

"I need to tell you what goes on in the camp," Duinn said. "Ye idiot."

Bodb said, "I think I liked you better a liar, Duinn." The caterpillars parted ways as his eyebrows lifted.

"Shut up, child, and listen," Duinn snapped. "Aramina and Raori have not turned completely. It's MacKegan. He caught them through the geis tangled in their Mark and holds their minds. I made pendants out of a piece of the Moonstone, but they do not wear them--"

"You broke the Moonstone?" Bodb cut in, aghast.

"I found a piece on the ground, whelp," Duinn said. "Shut up. I'm trying to tell you if we can get those pendants bound to them somehow, they'll be free again. Marginally." The last word was muttered, because he did not want to admit it even to himself.

"Except they're out there, laying siege to my city. The only mercy I can give them now is a quick death."

Duinn clutched Bodb's arm in sudden passion. "I can't lie here and let that happen. We have to find a way to help them!" He burst into tears. Embarrassment took hold, clenching his hands into fists as he turned away.

The elves looked at each other over Duinn's bowed head. "It's only the truth spell," Donnach said kindly. "It makes your emotions plain, as well as your thoughts. You should stay here until it wears off."

"No!" Duinn cried, bounding out of bed. Balance was hard to find in his giddiness, but stubbornness made up for the lack. "Give me a halberd and let me out! I will take care of them!"

"Duinn!" Bodb commanded, standing to tower over the dwarf. "So long as you are in my service, you will obey me! Now hie back to bed! There is nothing we can do for them right now. I will not lose you back to them, after so much trouble to set you free. And more trouble any would take for most, I might add. 'Twas my intuition that saved you, but even I will follow it only so far. Do not push me."

Grumbling, Duinn slid back into bed. Part of him was relieved for the excuse to sit back down. Another more rebellious part gave him more curses to recite. Donnach grinned as he recognized some of them.

"I promise," Bodb said softly, "if there is a way to help them, without hurting ourselves, it will be done."

The elves withdrew silently, as was their gift. Even the guards who had once teased him were gone. Duinn slouched in bed, rubbing his wrists, feeling very much alone.

***

Bodb chose a precarious position atop the wall, seated at the crumbling top and looking down. His fair hair, tousled by the rising wind, made a picturesque image of him. For a time he might have been a statue, so still was he while contemplating the army below.

"The dwarf is about," Donnach said, fading back to visibility as he approached.

"Now we will know why he was left here," Finnbhear said. Almost, he regretted the breakage of monotony. He was quite comfortable, leaned against the wall.

"Let us go then," Bodb said with a small smile. "Finnbhear, stay here and watch below."

The Silver Fox could have thought of better things to do than sit atop a crumbling wall and stare at an army of dead people. With a sigh, he obeyed the young king. His eyes wandered the field, lingering where horses stamped in their places and live bodies moved to and fro

Great catapults were pulled by straining horses, closer, yet closer to the city wall. One was already cocked. Finnbhear could see Aramina's black hair being whipped about in the wind as she directed its load. They were almost finished.

"'Ware the catapult!" Finnbhear shouted just as the rope was cut.

The missile swung upward, arching toward them. At first it was only a black object sailing through the sky, but as it neared its identity became unmistakable. Finnbhear cursed as it landed, softly, in the empty street below.

"Destroy it!" he ordered, brandishing his own sword. "Don't let it get away!"

Dull eyes looked around as the object unfolded itself to stand on bluish legs. Its stench was horrible. Teeth grinned through its face where the skin had rotted away.

"Gods," cried a young soldier nearby. "Father!" He doubled over to retch, moaning in misery.

Five youths sprang forward, swords drawn, ready for the kill. The cadaver silently drew his own sword and the battle was engaged. Finnbhear groaned, fighting to urge to leave his post. The lads stumbled over themselves in the effort to dispatch the foe.

"'Ware!" came a cry down the way. "'Ware!" cried another. The sky rained undead bodies, five of them, all curled in protective balls and landing with dull thuds.

Finnbhear looked back down, dreading the sight of another load preparing for the catapult. Aramina's flashed a grin and saluted him. She had sent six. There would be no more for now.

"Mina, you blasted heifer!" Finnbhear yelled. The woman below doubled over in laughter. Finnbhear turned back to the cadaver invaders.

One of the undead had been hacked to pieces. Its arms and legs quivered on the ground, vainly trying to fight on. Four more were surrounded by wary soldiers who hacked when they could, but dodged most times. Finnbhear did a quick calculation.

"Where is the other?" he roared.

"That way, sir," a soldier pointed the way. He stood to the side of the battle, waiting for an opening. "Last I saw, they had him hemmed in good."

"Back to the wall," Finnbhear ordered, leaving his own post to follow the indicated direction.

The last dead soldier had wandered down the streets toward the palace, but luckily not had gone far. Three young soldiers had it trapped in an alley, shouting encouragement to each other as they swung their swords at it. They had succeeded in cutting one arm from its frame, which had made it wary. It moaned, seeking escape.

A corpse worried for its life. Now that was something to behold. Finnbhear paused, marveling, before striding into the fray.

"Back," he ordered the others. "You'll get in the way. Watch my rear!"

His first swing was deflected by the dead's notched sword. He spun around, swinging his blade back, aiming for the middle. War instinct gave him that purpose, the intent to slice the opponents guts from his body. Again, Finnbhear's blade was deflected. Sparks showered them both.

"By the Morrigan," Finnbhear swore. Most undead only had enough sense to swing mindlessly. This one fought with skill and purpose.

Again and again, Finnbhear's blade was deflected against the defense of his foe. He was beginning to tire; he could feel it in his arms. Too old for this, he reminded himself. His blade was again deflected, ringing back, vibrating in Finnbhear's hand.

The cadaver lunged and scored. Pain cut him in the middle. With a gasp, Finnbhear fell back. The cadaver grinned, exhaling putrid breath, and stepped forward.

Three flashing swords cut into its path. The cadaver groaned, tried to retreat, but it was too slow. Its other arm fell to the ground, still clutching its sword. Shouting in anger, the three soldiers fell upon the dead one. Within minutes, it was cut into quivering bits.

"Lean on me, lord," one of the youths said, sheathing his sword. "We'll take you to the infirmary."

Finnbhear had not realized he was on the ground. He held his belly with one hand and supported himself with the other. Blood poured over his fingers. Numbly, he let the lads pick him up.

The pain worsened. He tried to cry out but could not find the strength.

"Easy," said the first lad. Together they took a small step forward.

Mercifully, Finnbhear fainted or he would have had to suffer through the length of the entire city.

***

"Ah!" cried Aramina, breaking contact. She was not going to kill the Silver Fox, but of course the soldiers had not known that.

It mattered not. Aes was ordering the silver elves to line their troops into formation. The time for attack was at hand. She could play with these dumb beasts later, after the field had been won.

She jerked her horse's reins and kicked it into motion. Her shouts of imminent victory echoed across the land.

***

Smoke spiraling toward the clouds, flames licking their grisly meal. Soldiers stood staring at it, too exhausted from their fight with the undead to do anything else. Duinn paused a moment to look with them and wonder what it was for. It provided a reason to catch his breath.

He knew someone was following him, but the elusive sons were invisible. It was annoying and forced him to delay his personal errand. No one but the concerned parties needed to know what he was about.

"Enough time for grieving later," a captain barked. "Get back to the wall!"

Duinn bowed his head and trudged with the soldiers around him. If he was lucky, he would lose himself in the shuffle and escape his unseen trackers.

Up the weathered stairway, jostled by his companions, Duinn ducked into a shallow alcove at first opportunity. He kept his back to the wall, breathing lightly, and waited. No soft step betrayed his trackers.

Duinn peered out of the alcove, his beard surfacing like a frightened cat. No one was there, but of course no one would be. They had chosen elven stealth; invisibility, silence, patience. So long as whomever they might be were around, the dwarf could not finish his errand.

Duinn leaned back into his corner. A peep hole, inches from his head, offered view of the outside world. Curious, Duinn stood on his tiptoes to squint against it.

Catapults, dozens of them, ringed the walls. Men, humans by the look of them, strained to cock their baskets. Aramina rode past on her mount, hair flying, shouting encouragement to MacKegan's army. The undead stood in formation, waiting their first commands.

"Come out and fight!" the Priestess was shouting. She reined her horse toward the city, facing Duinn with glittering eyes. "Come out or we will enter!"

No one answered her challenge, which suited her just fine. She wheeled her horse around and resumed her wild ride around the city.

"Thrice, yeah, thrice I shall ride!" she cried. "Three chances I give you, Cnos Fada, to fight honorably!" And she was gone from Duinn's view, her shouting echoing over the rocks. The time was near. Duinn growled curses to himself, turning back toward the stairs. Watchers or no, he had to hurry.

Dashing back down, he thought he felt someone or something brush by him. He paid it no heed, making for the barracks where Aramina had said his contact would be waiting. Running feet bespoke of his pursuers vainly trying to keep up. Few could match the pace of a dwarf.

His strength, frail since his return to Cnos Fada, faded quickly. Winded, Duinn leaned against a wall for support. He had lost those that tailed him, but he could not say for how long.

Stubbornly, Duinn lurched toward the barracks. Following mental instructions, he turned right, then left, right, left again. He reached the section where the silver elves shared their beds. A wooden door marked with the moon met the pound of Duinn's fist.

Must be at the wall, Duinn told himself when no one answered. Feeling like a fool, he turned back the way he came.

"You're that dwarf," someone said from the now open doorway. He was an aging elf, thickening at the middle but still in fighting shape. He was girded with a soldier's sword.

"I've come from your brethren," Duinn said. "Aye, you'd best let me in quick. The armies outside are readying for battle."

"I know," the elf said with an uplifted eyebrow. "Had you been a moment late, I would not have been here."

Already Duinn's keen hearing was catching the sounds of his pursuit. They had lost sight of him but not the trail, and they were coming fast. "Take this thing and be done," he said.

Duinn held up his hand, upon which an emerald ring sat on his first finger. The elf slid it off gingerly, held it up to the light to admire the beauty of it.

Palming the ring, he smiled. "My son's ring," he said. "He sent you."

Duinn started to speak, but at that time the king and Donnach came into sight. They saw him and shouted. Duinn cursed.

He was too weak to run again, and escape. "Get the gates open," Duinn hissed to the silver captain. "When the Priestess counts her third time." The king and Donnach were almost upon them. "You know what you have to do now," Duinn said.

The elf nodded, then drew his sword. "Traitor, double cursed!" he shouted. Then he slashed out, striking Duinn across the chest.

Even had Duinn wanted to defend himself, he was in no shape to do so. He staggered back, feeling the bright pain of the wound. "Fells," he cursed. "Did ya have to cut so deep?" Then his back met the ground.

Bodb was there, kneeling over him with worry etched across his face. "Damn you, and your comrades besides," the young elf said in disappointment. "Why must you betray every instinct I've ever owned? I wanted to trust you."

"By... following me... around?" Duinn managed to gasp.

"He came to speak for the Priestess, lord," the silver elf was saying. "He wanted me to join with those outside the gate."

Bodb vanished from Duinn's sight as he stood again. Duinn closed his eyes, taking what rest he could when he could. There was no telling what Bodb would do to him now.

"Truth spell him," Bodb was saying to someone, probably Donnach. "We'll see what went on here."

"I speak truth, lord," the silver elf protested. "The dwarf wanted me to open the gate--"

"Tell me when he's done," Bodb's voice said curtly.

The gentle sound of Donnach's chanting grew as the spell was cast. Even on the ground, Duinn could feel the warm glow of atma being released. It soothed his pain and relaxed his body.

"Now, tell me," Bodb said when the spell was done.

"I told you," the silver elf said. This time insult colored his voice. "The dwarf wanted me to open the gates when the Priestess counted the third time. I do not know what for, but he gave me my son's ring. MacKegan has him." The silver elf went into an obstinate silence, tinged with the hurt of betrayal.

"And you are loyal to Cnos Fada?" Donnach asked.

"Yes!" the elf shouted passionately.

Bodb sighed. "I am sorry, Chegh. But, understand with the Six involved I can not trust everyone."

Gentle hands lifted Duinn by the shoulders. Duinn groaned at the pain in his chest and wished they would not move him. He would be happy to die right there on the ground, in his own warm blood.

"Come, my friend," Donnach's voice said softly. "I will take you to the infirmary for healing."

"Would rather visit the dungeon," Duinn said through clenched teeth. He thanked the Morrigan, indeed any deity listening, that Bodb trusted his silver lieutenant enough not to ask for more. He allowed himself to be stood. His already weak form swayed, then steadied with Donnach's gentle touch.

"Perhaps you should put him in the dungeon, lord," said the silver elf. "We can hardly spare anyone to guard him."

"Nay," Bodb said. "That wound should hold him down at least for tonight. That and the company of an old friend. By the morrow, it may not matter where we have him."

***

Bodb reached the top of the wall just as the Priestess finished her third round the city. Dealing with Duinn left him barely enough time to prepare against her. By rights he should have given the job to someone else, but even kings had errands they preferred to do themselves. Besides, if he could not trust his captains to get the job done in his absence, then his city was done for.

He missed Chonnall. Chonnall had been more than a best friend; he had been adviser, teacher and someone who helped make sure other people obeyed with no question. Guiltily, Bodb wondered if he missed Chonnall more for his company or his efficiency. The lingering sorrow flared a moment, assuring Bodb that he merely missed his friend. It was no more complicated than that.

He pictured what Chonnall would have said about the situation; that Bodb needed to stop dreaming and take immediate action. Bodb's habit of letting his instincts guide him had made a mess of everyone's lives so far, but the king could not seem to help himself. For example, the issue with Duinn alone was subject to heated debate. The sensible thing was to never have let the Six back into the city, much less a second time to leave the dwarf behind. And yet, Bodb had made these mistakes... and he was not even sure why he had.

Blast it, but the dwarf had been truth spelled. Did he not say that he was loyal to Bodb? Perhaps MacKegan's hold over the mountain creature was strong and could not be compelled to break. But the dwarf had been to see the Moonstone. One could smell it on him; the cleanliness was like lye in a woman's wash. What was amiss?

Speaking of missing things, Bodb wondered how he could get word to the remaining troops in the countryside. Possibly they were all dead. It was possible they still patrolled their assigned areas, not knowing the threat to Cnos Fada itself. No one could get beyond the wall to carry a message. The troops had not magical implements with them for receiving a message.

The Priestess faced Bodb, her horse stamping and biting its bit. Her charcoal mount was not even lathered, but that might have been a trick in the waning light. Bodb could have sworn the beast was a conjuring, but no one remembered those magics anymore.

He shook his head, remembering how old Aramina was. Or at least, how long it had been since she made herself known in the world.

"Come out!" Aramina cried, jerking her horse's head sharply. Poor beast. Real or no, it would feel that.

"Come and get us!" Bodb yelled from his perch. Shouts rose behind him as his people cried insults and defiance to the enemy.

The wizard and mage rode from the ranks to flank the Priestess. They gave orders with their hands. Aramina galloped her horse to the end of the line, where silver elves and humans waited with ranks of undead. The catapults were cocked. The cadavers began to pile into them.

"'Ware the pult!" Bodb called below. "Undead coming!"

The burdens launched, missiled through the air and landed beyond the wall. Soldiers shouted to each other as they attacked the infiltration. The clashing of swords rang through the air. Picket was out there, somewhere, whinnying shrilly as he attacked the nearest foe. Bodb had chosen to allow the pooka his own mind, by which he seemed to better serve.

Someone ignited a cadaver with a torch. The creature flared brightly, being clothed in rotting material and mostly dry itself, but fought on. It presented a more difficult challenge. No one could get close enough to fight, yet it attacked doggedly. Elves dove out of the way.

"'Ware!" someone shouted above the din. More cadavers fell from the sky, rolling when they met the ground, rising on their putrid limbs to seek a foe.

Bodb looked back to the outside world, where Aramina sat her horse proudly and watched more cadavers climb into catapult baskets. Aes chanted a spell. Something made of fire was forming above his head. Raori hesitantly helped, wiping sweat from his brow every so often. The armies of human and silver elf waited patiently for their turn.

What to do? Bodb cursed to himself, pounding the wall with a fist. Everyone with experience was preoccupied with the undead invaders. There was no one to ask.

"Mages!" he shouted. "To me!"

Three came running awkwardly along the wall. It was not the fear of falling that made them clutch at anything stable. The mass surrounding the city was overwhelming from their height.

"Stop him," Bodb pointed at MacKegan's sorcerer. "By whatever means possible."

The flaming creature over Aes' head opened a mouth full of white-hot teeth in a silent roar. Soldiers shrank at the sight, muttering amongst themselves. "Dragon," was the word passed around. Bodb cursed again.

His own wizards linked hands and began to chant. Aes looked up, directly at them, and grinned. The dragon spread massive wings, raked the air with sharp claws, swelled its breast before soaring skyward. It circled the battlefield shrieking. The living winced at the sound, instinctively ducking. Men screamed as the distraction enabled the undead to score.

"Thing sounds like the Morrigan!" Picket cried merrily from nearby. He whooped, shouting praises to the goddess of war. "MacKegan has done us a favor, calling forth the goddess like that! She'll take these undead with her, for their heads, and that'll be less for us to fight!"

Bodb wished it were so. The dragon swooped low. Its heat washed the king's face, drying his eyes and lips. It took all his strength of will not to cower with the mages behind him.

"Stop it!" Bodb ordered, hauling one of the mages up. He was about to say more, but a roar of tumultuous shouts drew his attention away. There was a commotion by the front gate, where Aramina's commanders clustered in a surge. Something was happening, something they had expected--

"Close the gate!" Bodb shouted, letting go the mage and running along the wall. "Fells, shut it! Shut it!"

But the silver elves – his silver elves – continued hauling at the crank, widening the essential barrier further yet further. Aramina's merry smile flashed as she pumped her fist in the air, pointing her armies of undead, elf and human to new targets.

Bodb stopped running to watch the elves from his city pour through the gate. He saw his world being destroyed around him, and suddenly there seemed to be no hope.

Amidst the fray, Aramina and Chegh met and conferred. They clasped hands in greeting, grinning at each other. Bodb lay a hand on the wall and leaned weakly against it.

The Priestess made a sweeping gesture with her hands, then turned her horse back toward the catapults. Bodb followed her gaze, barely noticed the cadavers still piling into the baskets, launched over the wall, lining up to march through the open gate. His stinging eyes returned to Aramina and his silver captain.

They separated. Chegh's troops marched beyond the gate. The silver elf barked inaudible commands, guiding his troops along the wall to surround the city.

Aramina's mount pranced along them. She paused beneath Bodb's position and saluted him with heavy irony. Bodb fought temptation and failed. He spit in her direction. The Priestess only laughed and spurred her horse on.

Shouts still rang behind him as those left behind fought on. Many were dying, slipping in their own blood, wailing as the undead administered killing strokes. Some had laid the corpses to waste and hewed into new foes with vigor. Their battle cries were the names of their mothers, sisters and lovers.

Resolutely, Bodb drew his sword and took a step down to join battle.

A new commotion stopped him. In the fields beyond the wall, where MacKegan's armies had camped and waited, a battle had joined. At first Bodb thought his own loyal people left out the gate to fight the foe. Then Aramina rode past shouting commands, waving a sword of her own, careening into a silver captain with a flash of her blade.

Bodb Derg could not believe his eyes. He leaned on the wall and peered.

The catapults were the first to go. The cadavers, formally marshaling into the baskets obediently, now attacked those manning them. Undead came against undead. Silver elves, his and MacKegan's, flowed into the enemy camp. The humans stood against it, and new battle was joined.

"Hai!" Picket shouted. It startled Bodb, who had forgotten the pooka was nearby. "See, my king, the sacrifice she makes for you! Aramiiiinnaaaa!" He leapt from the wall: an impossible descent to the ground. Landing on all fours a horse, he galloped into battle.

The woman was crazy. She galloped back and forth, hewing anything down that got close to her blade. Her strokes were skillful, full of energy and fury. The flash of her teeth as she barred them sent chills up Bodb's spine.

Then the dragon roared as it swooped at him. Bodb was forced to forget about the Five, or Three, or whatever they were. He brought his sword up just in time to fend off a sharp claw. The blade bit into fiery flesh, passed through without causing damage, came out red with heat. Bodb cried out in pain as he dropped it.

He expected to feel searing agony as the dragon devoured him. He waited with closed eyes and tense muscles.

"Get to battle," someone said. "You do your people no good, standing here to watch them die."

Bodb cracked an eyelid. The dragon was precariously balanced on the wall. It looked at him with intelligence.

"You?" Bodb whispered.

"Never mind," the dragon said. "We'll talk later. I can't hold out against Aes much longer."

Then the dragon twisted back into the air, soaring over the ground. Dragons were presumed mostly gone. Yet, here was this dragon swooping down to burn anything in its path. It was there; a bit of old magic, a piece of Aes' mind real enough for the world to cower beneath.

Bodb shook his head to regain his senses. There would be enough time for speculation if he lived. As he picked his sword back up from the ground, it seemed to shimmer with bloodlust. Yelling, Bodb ran down the stairs to meet with the first cadaver he happened upon.

To his dismay, the cadaver backed away. He gave chase, determined not to be stood up by a walking corpse. The cadaver moved swiftly, weaving around fighting bodies. Bodb shouted his frustration at it.

The undead paid no heed. It slowed once, looking over its shoulder, before continuing its flight. Bodb shoved anything and everyone out of his way to get after it.

A different creature shuffled to him, raising its sword numbly to attack. Bodb wasted no time; he administered a swift cut across the neck, picked the cadaver's rolling head from the ground and clapped it to his thigh. The body went inert suddenly, crumpling to the ground and smelling of peat. Bodb rushed on to capture his prey.

It had escaped during the distraction. "Blast and be flamed!" Bodb cursed.

The battle was thin here; he was close to the gate and most were outside the wall. He took long strides toward the exit. Soldiers saw him and hailed his name. He nodded to them absently.

"Back!" someone was crying. "Back into the city!" A trumpet sounded retreat.

Bodb took advantage of the nearest stairs to climb the wall. From his new vantage, he was given a clear view of the battle. The dragon roared, sometimes snapping around it and other times at itself. Raori stood nearby, doubled over and clutching his head as he concentrated. Bodb could not see Aes.

"Back!" that resounding voice cried again. It was Aramina, astride her horse. A silver elf mounted behind her blew his trumpet. All that could began to turn, running for the gate.

Those that gave chase massed four times Aramina's surviving number. They trampled twitching bodies were they lay. The sight of it all made Bodb queasy. The Priestess stood by the gate, gesturing wildly as elves ran past. The pooka nudged some from behind before turning to defend himself against a human holding a halberd.

The dragon flamed the human, engulfing the pooka in its heat. When the flames faded, the pooka stood alone and untouched. Of the human there was no sign.

Bodb had all he could take. He ran back down the stairs only to end up fighting against the flow of refugees. Somehow he made it through to Aramina, who sat her horse like a queen. He grabbed the reins.

"What of the mage?" he yelled over the din around them.

"He battles Aes for the dragon and MacKegan for himself," she said absently. "Hai, Picket!"

The pooka thundered to them and slid to an impossible stop. Instantly the naked man stood before them, scratching his shoulder nervously. "Get inside," he ordered. "We have to close the gate. They're coming."

Bodb looked up, faced the hoard running for them. Their roar crested ahead like ocean froth. Their number was uncountable.

"Get inside!" the king commanded. "Quick! Close the gate!"

Picket swept Bodb up, onto his back, and galloped into the city. Bodb had not seen him change, but was glad for it. The Priestess was right behind them on her black mount. The gate shut behind them, then shuddered as MacKegan's army crashed against it. Elves struggled to bar the gate.

"Raori!" Aramina shouted, looking about herself. Somewhere beyond the city, the dragon roared. Aramina shoved the trumpeter from her horse, not heeding how he fell, and turned back to the gate. "Let me out!" she cried wildly.

"No," Bodb said. "That would let the hoard in, and the city would be lost."

"But, they'll kill him!" Aramina cried. Looking around herself in panic, "They'll kill him! Picket!"

"I can't," Picket moaned. "It would tip the balance."

"Cowards!" Aramina screamed. She kicked her horse into motion. For a fleeting instant Bodb thought she would attack the gate, but she mounted the stairs. Her horse never labored for breath as it climbed the steep a natural horse could not have attempted.

She reached the top. Without pause, she drove her horse over the edge. Bodb gasped in shock. He ran after her, taking steps four at a time. He reached the summit, nearly toppled completely over from inertia.

Aramina had plunged her horse into the masses. They attacked her as best they could, given the lack of room. She wielded her blade with abandon, urging her mount on.

Now Bodb saw what made the Six so special. Outside of being reckless tricksters, they were superb fighters. The Priestess received only nicks, minor injuries, while the enemy around her fell back with each blow. Most weapons bounced away; deflected by her force of atma as it shielded her. Bodb had never even heard of such prowess. In the back of his mind, he wondered if Aramina could be convinced to teach him that.

"She's practiced," Picket said beside Bodb. He leaned out and shouted encouragement.

"Practiced?" Bodb echoed.

"Of course," the pooka replied. "But she's still not very good. She might be able to beat Raori now, but the rest of us could still take her." His eyes never left the battlefield. Bodb was glad; he needed the moment to pull his chin up from the ground.

Aramina was a magnificent fighter, but such masses could fell an elephant. Halfway to her destination, she faltered against three humans. Exhausted, Aramina still brought her sword to bear. Arms groped at her from behind. Her blade was deflected against an opponent's axe. It spun away, lost, into the field. Aramina's horse reared, screaming.

The dragon landed with a loud *whomp*, flaming around it. Screams died suddenly as the attackers were incinerated. Aramina wiped a hand across her brow, regained control of her mount and urged it forward. Bodb blinked. He had forgotten about the dragon until now.

At last, Aramina reached the mage. He was slumped, alone, on his horse. MacKegan's men, thinking him their ally, had left him alone to fight or die. The Priestess tried to pull him into the saddle with her.

"He's too heavy for her," Picket cried, distressed. Raori slid to the ground and lay unmoving.

The dragon roared. Even from where Bodb stood, he could feel the sudden change in the creature. It swelled with ire and evil intent. Bounding on all fours, it landed in front of Aramina. Raori's horse, also released from the mage's mind, dissolved into fine ash and scattered with the wind of the dragon's approach.

Bodb looked wildly around, searching for MacKegan's sorcerer. He thought he spotted him, astride his own mount further up field. "Bowmen!" he shouted, beckoning to the nearest archers. "Shoot that horseman!"

Even were the archers still on the wall, Aes was out of range. The dragon snapped at Aramina, who raised one hand in puny defense. Her atma burst, noticeably dimmer, deflected his bite. Bodb cursed, unconsciously using Duinn's repertoire.

Picket grinned. "Ye've been a talkin' to the dwarf," he said thickly. Bodb blinked before he puzzled the pooka's ancient accent through. "Dinna worry, my king."

Bodb opened his mouth to shout. Worry, why should he worry? As denial touched his tongue, the pooka slipped over the wall. He shifted as he fell, landing on all fours.

At first, the pooka charged the dragon, bowling over any two-leg who dared to stand in his way. Suddenly he veered away, leaping impossibly over the heads of the enemy, straight at Aes. The dragon brought its head up, forgetting Aramina in light of this new danger. The enemy tried to dispatch the pooka, but none could touch him. He was too fast. There was a glow about the spotted horse as it made for its goal: fae magic.

With a roar, the dragon turned from its prey to chase the pooka. Men, elves and undead were literally burned out of the way. A path parted rapidly with some not making it out of the way quick enough. Picket bounded before it like a demented grasshopper. Aramina turned back to Raori, trying to summon the strength to get him onto her horse.

She did. Bodb breathed a sigh of relief. She vaulted into the saddle and sent her horse into another mad dash back to the gate. The dragon roared again. Picket landed before Aes, who was trying to regain his own senses.

The dragon, released now from Aes' control, gave one last, echoing roar as it melted from existence. Relief washed over Bodb. Without Raori, Aes would not be able to summon it again. And he could not count on help from MacKegan's necromancers, who were spent keeping the masses of undead animate.

Aramina and Raori were not in the clear. Making it back to the city was harder than leaving it. The enemy were prepared for her. Undead soldiers, linking in a large circle, surrounded them. Each dash for safety brought nicks from bristling weapons, forcing them back. Aramina was too exhausted to hold her atma shield for long. It was only a matter of time, and her captors knew it.

"Picket!" Bodb shouted, knowing the pooka could not possibly hear him. "Forget the sorcerer. Help your Priestess!"

Whether Bodb was heard or not, the pooka looked in Aramina's direction. Aes threw a ball of fire, but the pooka was no longer a stationary target. He had turned, bounding the way he had come. His hooves struck with deadly accuracy, always on the heads of the living. A path of dead and dying littered his wake.

Picket landed in Aramina's circle with teeth bared. Weeping, Aramina threw her arms around Picket's neck for a brief moment. Then they were fighting their way out together. Plainly, the support of her friend had given the Priestess new energy. One hand clutching Raori from behind, she threw bolts of fire with deadly accuracy. Cadaver bodies burned, crashed into others and spread the flame.

Somehow, they broke free and ran forward towards the gates. The enemy had learned respect and drew back a little. It was just enough. Had they battled an ordinary adversary, they would have won immediately. Weapons once again bounced away from atma shields. Aramina and Picket reached the gate.

"Open!" the Priestess commanded. Silver elves leaned on the levers. This time, Bodb did not waste his breath to command the gate be shut. The great gate opened just a crack, enough for Aramina and Picket to slip through. A small crowd of humans and undead slipped in with them before the gate could be shut again. The sounds of fighting once again filled the street.

Aramina reeled her horse to a stop when she was away from the battle. Raori slipped to the earth with a soft sound. Chest heaving, Aramina dismounted. Her horse dissolved to ash, banished from her thoughts as concern for the mage presided.

Bodb climbed down to greet them. The Priestess saw him, smiled, and crumpled in a faint. There was blood, too much blood.

She was no goddess, Bodb said to himself with small relief and felt guilty for doing so. No one could fight those odds, no matter how skilled or powerful, without taking some kind of loss. It would not surprise him if the wounds were deadly.

An evil thought. He could not understand why he cared about what happened to his enemies. It disturbed him.

He motioned for someone to help the Priestess. Slowly, he was obeyed. But not without many a misgiving glance.

Chapter Twenty-six
"Dragon's Blood"

Leannahn readjusted her mantle and stepped over the smoking body. Sounds of the man's rough laughter still echoed in her ears. He had thought her just another slave. Well, he had stopped laughing soon enough.

Here the dungeon was darker than at Cnos Fada. Thin groans came from almost every cell. Moans echoed from the pit, placed at the darkest corner. Stringy, furry arms groped for her between the bars. Leannahn skirted around, trying to ignore them as she passed.

The farthest cell was silent.

"Eahn?" Leannahn whispered, crouching as once before. No comforting presence stepped behind her. Regret, an alien emotion, closed her throat. The young lord in Cnos Fada had been a kind soul; she could feel it still within her.

The Northern Thorn was chained to the wall with iron chains and manacles of brass. Lacerations laced his body, white with infection, glaring madly in the dark. He remained human, although it was more difficult to reassume the form every time he shifted. One eye was swollen shut, branded. He might never see with it again.

"I am so sorry," Leannahn sobbed, burying her face in her hands. "Had I known they would provoke the changes– No. I should have known. This is where I grew up."

The Northern Thorn growled with frustration and hatred. Even were he free, he could not attack Leannahn. She still held the sway of command.

Leannahn leaned against the bars and wept.

***

I remember... training. Training, always fighting against others to be better for our lord. The flash of silver from the very beginning. They never used wooden swords. That would make them weak, and cowardly.

Duinn was the worst. His kind fight from birth, and sometimes they appeared too blood thirsty. Still, at times she managed to surprise him. Her lack of fear gave the ability to take risks. And the dwarf loved risk.

Even after they had been disbanded, Aramina spent her mornings practicing the art of war. Gredber had been most eager to help. It excited him, the smell of blood. After a while she stopped practicing with him; the price for his help was something she did not want to pay. Her body was her own. She had paid a high enough price to get it.

So, in secret she had practiced beneath the moon. Training.

Aramina opened her eyes.

Neither tent ceiling nor open sky greeted her. She looked around, frightened at first. Rows of beds in a large room surrounded her.

"Mina," a tired tenor said.

"Finnbhear?" she asked, turning over in her bed. The Silver Fox was bedded beside her. "What are you doing here?" She saw the bandages binding his middle. "Oh. Sorry."

"For what?" Finnbhear asked with a quirk of his eyebrow.

"Nothing," Aramina said with a small smile.

"Duinn is here, too," Finnbhear said, dismissing the matter. He gestured toward an inert lump across the room. "At least I was wounded in battle. He was cut on your behalf, or so he claims. Some errand you had given him."

"Poor Duinn," Aramina said lightly. "Where is Raori?"

"Not even concerned for the dwarf?" Finnbhear asked evenly. "How very like you."

"He'll be fine," Aramina said dismissively. "What about Raori?" Her last sight of the mage, before she fainted, had been of him lying on the ground.

"The temple, last I heard," Duinn grated, sitting up. White bandages peeked out from beneath his eiderdown quilt. "Midna came this morning to speak with you, but you still slept."

Aramina felt her mouth quirk. The tightness of bandages wound around her head pressed at her temples. She began working them loose, annoyed by their presence. "What did he want?"

Duinn's eyebrows became a straight line, low across his eyes. "You did bring him into the fold," the dwarf said. "It shouldn't bother you if he needs your guidance. As it is, he wanted to tell you how Raori fared. Why can't you leave those bindings where they are? You were cut deeply."

"Did Midna say anything?" Aramina slipped out of bed. The cool floor felt good under her feet. She wriggled her toes, relishing the feeling.

"Only that he hurts," Finnbhear said heavily. "From what I'm told, you and he accomplished godlike feats out there: Raori, fighting off Aes and MacKegan to control that dragon. You, fighting off hoards of undead and mortals."

"They were husks with no fight left to them," Aramina said uncomfortably. "A wee babe could have kept them away. And if it weren't for Picket, we wouldn't have made it alive."

"So he says," Duinn grunted. Aramina smiled. The pooka would be boasting to the dwarf everyday about his unusual deed. Duinn would never be allowed to live it down, if he had been wounded before the battle even begun.

"Well, I've got to see Raori." Mind made up, Aramina looked around for her boots. All she wore was a simple undergarment.

"Stay here," Finnbhear said. "It's a waste of time to go out. They won't let you near him."

"You said he was at the temple?" Giving up her boots for a lost cause, Aramina crouched. She let the wolf form take her, like the creeping of a vine. The two men were unsurprised but apprehensive.

"Midna will be here at sunset," Duinn said. "Why can't you wait then? You were wounded out there and should rest."

Aramina set her nose to the floor, diving into the pattern of scents. A mouse had made its way through the shadows by the beds. Unfamiliar elves had come through. If Midna's scent was there, it was too far tangled with that of others to be found.

Finnbhear said Raori was in the temple. As a safety precaution, Aramina wove an invisibility spell about herself. She left the infirmary without a backward glance, slipping past guards stationed outside easily. Keeping to stone areas, she resumed humanoid form only when crossing earthy ground. Wolf prints would show the way she had gone too well.

The streets beyond the palace were deserted. It was eerie, even though Aramina had seen a city under siege before. Troops patrolled the area. Defiant flags bearing clan colors hung out windows. There was not the roar of working voices, the noises of children playing. Even the filthy smells that normally accompany civilization were muted.

The temple was eerily empty, save for an old woman and a huddle of frightened orphans. Normally, the temple was packed with worshipers, all there to pay fealty to their chosen god. With death literally pounding at the city gates, no one dare leave their homes. Not even for the gods.

Aramina could not quite comprehend the need for a temple, at any rate. She could remember when there were no temples and few cairns, or altars made of piled stones, to be found around the countryside. Sometimes, she felt even Picket was a baby compared to herself. Of course, then he would look at her as if knowing her thoughts, and suddenly she was Mina the younger all over again. Not for the first time, she wondered why this was so.

Organized worship was from the mortal realm, and had quite polluted the elven way of being. Aramina wondered, too, what her homeland would be like had humans never discovered it. Or, if they had never been discovered. It would be a much wilder place, she decided. She would have liked that.

Aramina slipped by the old woman, pausing to listen momentarily at her silent keening. Her dark eyes sparkled a bit, and she grinned. "Shush, old bird," she said in wolf, her voice echoing a bit in the space. "He hears you. Listen, see?" And with that, the women fell silent. The children strained to hear, but whatever happened was beyond their senses. The old woman, however, suddenly smiled and burst into tears.

"Thank you," she whispered, wiping her eyes with one gnarled hand.

Aramina simply barked laughingly, as was her way, and resumed walking beyond the great hall of altars. Acolytes passed without taking note of the wolf slinking along the wall. Periodically, Aramina dipped her nose to the floor. Raori's sweat-mingled scent was weak, but still strong enough to lead her on.

A simple wooden door in the least traveled hall barred her way. Aramina whined to herself, turning back and forth in indecision. Finally she resumed her human shape, opening the door with still forming fingers. She shut it quietly behind her.

Midna sat near a bed. He looked up, surprised, but shrugged when he saw her. "I told them you wouldn't stay away," he said.

"How is he?" Aramina said. On the bed, Raori slept. He had been strapped down with thick straps of leather. His face was pale.

"He tries to wake," Midna said. "But then he falls deeper asleep. It's like--"

"No herbs have been given?"

"That's what I was saying," Midna said defensively. "We've given him nothing, yet he acts like he's had the year's harvest."

Sighing, Aramina made herself a place on the bed. Raori stirred then went inert as sleep reclaimed him. The Priestess pulled back his blankets.

"Where are his things?" she asked, scowling at the mage's naked body.

"Over there." Midna pointed to a small bundle in the corner.

"You didn't have to remove the blasted necklace, too," Aramina grumbled, going to the bundle and searching through it. The shard of Moonstone fell to the floor with a faint clatter. She picked it up. "Hasn't he been in enough pain?" she griped. "And then you remove the one thing to halfway shield him. Oh yes, I can certainly tell the temple's idea of medicine has really improved through the years..."

The leather strap the pendant hung from was broken, too short to mend. Aramina slipped the bit of stone free and examined it. Duinn had polished it to a sheen. He had probably been working on the piece nights as they traveled. Her own piece had been shaped like a pear.

"Open up, Raori," Aramina said, settling on the bed and grabbing the mage's chin. "Time for dinner." She pinched his jaw joints, forcing his mouth open.

"What are you doing?" Midna demanded, standing in alarm.

"Fixing Raori's problem." Aramina slipped the bit of moonstone into his mouth. His mouth muscles jerked. Aramina lifted his chin up and stroked his throat as one would do to their dog. The mage did not swallow.

"Bring me some water," Aramina said. Raori's head lolled when she let it go. The moonstone fell out of his mouth, falling to the floor and disappearing. "Blast. Midna, where did it go?"

"What?" the acolyte said.

"The stone."

"I didn't see it."

Aramina's eyes narrowed. She could feel herself growing fangs as she eyed the chubby elf. "Just get some water."

When Midna returned, Aramina had the bit of stone in Raori's mouth again. His teeth were clamped firmly shut. She had no doubt that was MacKegan's influence. Distractedly, she accepted the proffered glass.

Pinching the mage's nose soon forced his mouth open. Quickly, she poured the water into the cavity, grabbing his chin and jaw to keep him from losing the stone. Instinct forced Raori to swallow. He gagged briefly, eyes fluttering open with terror. When Aramina was positive the stone had been made a meal, she let the mage go.

"By BileEll, that's a horrible way to wake," Raori coughed. The mage sat slowly to look around. "Where am I?" he asked finally.

"In the temple," Midna said, attracting Raori's notice for the first time.

"How did I" Raori cut himself off as memory caught up with him. He put a shaky hand to his forehead. "Gods, what a fool I was... and an idiot. Moron! I might as well say feral, as well. To take on MacKegan and Aes' dragon! The pain!" He shuddered

"Had you obeyed my suggestion from the start," Aramina said smugly, "it never would have happened. Is he still with you?"

"How was I to know you really meant for me to eat that piece of rock?" Raori demanded. "I thought you were just as deep in MacKegan's spell."

"But, is he still with you?"

The world held its breath while Raori contemplated his mind. "No," he said. "Maybe a little, but like from far away."

"So, choking on a bit of rock wasn't so bad after all."

"Yes, Priestess, you've made your point." Raori sounded tired, not at all like himself. He swung his legs around, bracing himself to stand. Aramina stayed him.

"Where do you think you're going?" Even Midna put a hand forward to keep the mage down.

"Out of here," Raori said. "I'm no wounded babe."

Aramina caught Midna's eye, jutted her chin to the door in silent signal. The acolyte's face went carefully blank as he stepped for the door. "Let me get some fresh clothes and a meal," he said. "Then we'll let you out."

Raori relaxed with a wandering hand through his hair. "I'll compromise for that." He turned to Aramina.

"I'll stay," Aramina said with a wrinkled grin. She leaned forward to kiss the mage just as Midna closed the door behind him. After that Raori forgot food, and clothing would only have gotten in the way.

Later, the sated lovers emerged from their little room. Midna had never returned. Indeed, Aramina had not expected him to. Raori, on the other hand, complained loudly.

"Where is everyone?" he demanded as he walked down the hall. "How does Midna expect us to find food in this strange labyrinth? Follow our noses to the kitchens, I suppose," he muttered to himself. His cloak was torn and hung limply, but he insisted on wearing it. Aramina found his hand within the fabric and squeezed it.

"It's not as if we don't know the place," she said. "You'd think we never lived here."

"No, we haven't." Raori sniffed. "Maybe at this very spot, but not in this building."

"Shut up and keep going."

The hall seemed to grow darker with each step. Raori managed a feeble atma light, which he set to hover over his shoulder. He smiled ruefully, as if apologizing for his exhaustion. Aramina kissed his cheek, bursting energy through him with the touch. The glow brightened.

"It was you with the necromancers," Raori accused suddenly. He stopped walking to glare at her.

"What do you mean?" Aramina slipped past the mage, lightening her step so as not to disturb the dust.

"When I spelled the cadavers," Raori said, following.

"You saw me there. What's the problem?" Her back was turned, so she felt safe enough to smile privately. Raori should know her touch by now. Should have the feel of her atma signature memorized.

The mage stopped short again, grabbing Aramina's arm to turn her around. "You tricked us," he accused her.Alarm set Aramina's limbs to tingling. "Tricked you how?" she asked innocently, keeping her eyes wide and eyebrows up. She could not quite control the corners of her mouth, which tried to twist into her customary smirk. Instinctively, she started to fall into her mocking stance.

"Abandoning Moirfenn. You never wanted to kill the prince."

Aramina sighed. "Raori," she reasoned, "does it matter who was tricked by whom? I won't deny nor admit anything."

"Naturally." Raori released the Priestess, but slowly as if he forced himself to. "I wonder sometimes if you'll ever take any side but your own."

Aramina laughed lightly. Kissing Raori's cheek again, she danced down the hall, skipping to her own inner music. Something in the air charged her senses, made her want to run howling at everything. She settled for taking Raori's hand and curling into his shoulder. They had finally found the altar room.

He was not feeling himself, her mage, that much was obvious. The old woman had gone, the children too, and so they were alone but for the stray acolyte who tended the array of candles that lit the place. Raori reverently touched a nearby altar. It had been chipped recently from the furor. His calloused hands caressed the offering bowl thoughtfully.

"When the other temple stood here," Raori said, his voice carrying through the room with a cavernous echo, "no one came here to pray for relief. The city burned and no one came. And no one is here now. I wonder what it all means? They break their backs to build this altar, and when the time comes they have no faith in their work at all."

"I thought at the time it was because everyone was out fighting," Raori continued. "Remember, Aramina? No one came because they were out fighting. No one wasted time with self pity. Or so I thought... Which is just as well, because the temple was the first thing to burn."

"I made sure of that," Aramina muttered in satisfaction.

Raori said, "Moirfenn had Cnos Fada for a span of days. All our hard work was for nothing." Aramina barked a laugh. "No, really," Raori protested. "He couldn't hold it, because of those who thought their homes might be worth fighting for. And here we are, right back in the same situation. Only, now we're trying to stop it. It feels strange."

The silence was now filled with shame. "Let's go." Aramina's voice dropped into room. "I'm hungry. Besides, we need to find a couple of swords. If you actually want to fight for this place, that is."

***

Finnbhear and Duinn passed the time by trading war tales. Often, the stories were comparison of personal events during the same battle. It was interesting to hear what the Silver Fox had been thinking with each maneuver. Like having a window to the other side of the world.

New occupants were carried into the infirmary. A few died. Finnbhear did not seem to mind so much as Duinn, a dwarf and not meant for the same ethereal plane.

The pair's wounds were not as grievous as made out to be. Healer magic sealed the skin and sped the repair. Both feigned weakness when servants entered the room. Neither wanted to return to duty.

"Hai back to bed," Duinn hissed to Finnbhear, who was stretching his legs. "I hear someone coming."

Sure enough, just as Finnbhear had the quilts comfortably arranged, the door opened. Bodb, flanked by his guards, strode inside. He flopped himself into bed next to Duinn. The dwarf lifted an eyebrow. Bodb mopped his brow with one sleeve.

"I just found the mage and your Priestess in the kitchens," the new king said. "Had my head woman screaming in a corner, convinced they meant to cook her."

Duinn grunted into his chest and let his eyelids droop.

"I doubt the mage practices cannibalism," Finnbhear said.

"No? Tell my head woman that." Bodb motioned the guards away. They took position by the door stiffly. Duinn slumped further into his blankets, a sudden invalid seeking sleep.

The king irritably punched Duinn's leg. "Oh, get up. You've been here long enough, and the priests have others to care for."

His pretense shattered, Duinn struggle to sit straight. "Well, what do you want of me?" he growled.

"Council," Bodb said imperiously, pointing to both Duinn and Finnbhear. "Tonight. I want you and the rest of your little band, even the acolyte." The king stood, brushing invisible dirt from his knees. "I've already sent the mage to find Picket. You can rest until then." As abruptly as he had entered, he smiled and left.

"Feral Hammers and Spears," Duinn said. "Just when I was gettin' used to this."

Finnbhear chuckled, shaking his head ruefully. "It was nice." He slipped from bed and stretched mightily. "I was ready for my own quarters anyway. See you tonight."

Duinn burrowed back into his blankets. There was no way he was going to move until it was time. Sleep crept up and leapt on its prey. Finnbhear paused long enough to be sure the dwarf was comfortable, and he envied the dwarf's ability to find sleep so readily.

***

"Cnos Fada," Aramina said suddenly. The gleam in her eye was unmistakable. "Remember the fire?"

"We're discussing war against Moirfenn," Duinn reminded her impatiently. "Now is not the time to reminisce."

"No," the Priestess said with a giggle. "We can burn that army like we did this city."

The Six, formerly of Moirfenn, sat at council with Bodb Derg, the Silver Fox, and Cnos Fada's last living advisor, Caoimhin Long in the Arm. They nibbled on dainties while Raori explained Leannahn's miraculous reappearance. Before he was done, they pushed their food away, having lost their appetites. She was already gone, Bodb pointed out, and there was nothing to be done. Talk turned from that to the siege. Two hours later, they had not concocted a workable plan.

Cnos Fada had for available resources twelve small catapults, various barrels and other food storage supplies, and very little wood to build with. Even local buildings had very little to salvage, being mostly made of stone. The council was for the moment at a loss.

Aramina's outburst was her first complete sentence since the meeting commenced.

Bodb leaned across the table. "I've always wondered how you managed that," he said. "There was only the five of you, right? No one possesses enough atma to start a fire that size, but you did."

Caoimhin slammed his fist onto the table. "No! We'll never give you such a chance again." In days past, Caoimhin had been adviser to Bodb's father, and an expressive one. Now he sought to enforce reason in the same manner. He withdrew his fist when he saw Bodb staring at him.

"Be still," the king ordered. "I have them here for their ideas. Hear the Priestess out."

Grumbling, Caoimhin withdrew back into his chair. His burning eyes malevolently surveyed everything.

"We burned the city with dragon's blood," Aramina said.

"Dragon's blood?" Bodb repeated incredulously. "But, that stuff is rarer than gold. It would have taken, I don't know—"

"Barrels of it," Duinn intoned happily. "Wedding gifts donated by my cousins in the north."

Dragons' blood, exhuming noxious vapors known as dragon's breath, sometimes gushed from fissures deep in dwarf mines. It burned the skin and was highly flammable. Dwarves prized it highly for unfathomable reasons. *Leave it to a half-crazed werewolf and a dwarf to think of a use for it like that,* Bodg thought.

"It took us all night to wet down parts of the city," Raori mused into his seventh cup of win. "I swear the breath stayed in my nostrils for moons after."

"Do you remember the old woman?" Aramina rippled merrily.

"Oh, yes," laughed Picket. "And don't forget the merchant's cat."

"Made a comet all by itself," Duinn grunted.

Despite Midna's wide eyes and shocked expression, the original four chuckled. There was something unwholesome about it, like a naughty child's glee after the dog is found dead.

Bodb coughed gently into his fist. "How are we to get the stuff beyond our walls?" he asked after the chuckling had died down. "And, where are we to get it?"

"I can get it," Aramina offered.

"My lord, no," Caoimhin advised urgently. "We cannot be sure the stuff won't explode within the city walls. An accident might happen, or sabotage. We are not so desperate."

"So desperate as to what?" Raori asked in ringing tones.

"As to trust these feral intruders, perhaps?" Aramina's eyes never lost their gleam. She leaned her chin into one hand and grinned wickedly. "Were you never young, Caoimhin? Have you forgotten the thrill of danger, the scent of a challenge?"

"His blood has cooled, if it ever burned," Duinn grunted.

Bodb chewed his bottom lip to keep from snickering. The adviser's face was turning crimson as he struggled with his temper. His dislike of Bodb Derg's new allies was no secret. He made no attempt to hide it, although the young king wished that he would

"And how, again, are you going to get the dragon's blood?" Bodb inquired practically batting his eyes at the Priestess. She returned his look coyly.

"I suppose it doesn't matter if you know," she said at length. "It's here, in Cnos Fada. Right under your feet."

Bodb resisted the urge to pick up his feet.

"There is a secret tunnel from the temple to the palace," Duinn said. "The dragon's blood is down there."

"That is how you got into my palace the first time," Bodb observed.

"We're not here to reminisce," Aramina said with a smile.

"We'll need strong barrels," Duinn said. "Thin cloth, metal buckets. Hai, we can do it. Should've thought of it before!"

"And another mage," Raori put in.

"How can we trust you?" Caoimhin blustered. "How can we trust you? By my father, do you honestly expect us to forget how your treated this city in the past? What are you going to do? Tell me! You act so sure, but I have heard no discussion. How can you be sure this mysterious plan will work?"

To Bodb's interest, the Six regarded Caoimhin with sure expressions. "It's Aramina's idea," Raori said. "It will work."

"You haven't even worked out details."

"It will work," Duinn said.

Picket neighed a soft agreement. Bodb had to look twice to be sure the wight was wearing two legs instead of four.

"As far as trusting us goes..." Aramina let her voice trail away. The Six exchanged looks between themselves and shrugged. The center of attention shifted to Bodb.

The young king tried to turn inward, to tap his intuition and ask for the answer. If it said yes, he would tell the Six no. If it said no, well... The world was a crazy place no matter where he turned anymore. He would like to trust himself more, to trust his sense of knowing, but so many times the answers had seemed wrong.

His intuition nudged him to let the Six retrieve the dragon's blood. Bodb checked a sigh, chewing his lip still, and looked away. He did not even know why he felt this way.

"Finnbhear can gather volunteers to aid you," the king said. "As for barrels, check with the palace smith. He can provide everything else you need. When you are ready, I expect a detailed account of your plans. Whatever they are." He hoped they did not include feats similar to Aramina's rescue of Raori for sanity's sake, if nothing else.

"My lord, please reconsider." Caoimhin was practically on his knees.

"Too late," Aramina taunted. "We're getting the dragon's blood, and you can't stop us." She sing-songed the words, vacating her seat, skipping out the chamber door like a small child. Duinn bowed politely as he followed, with everyone else just behind.

Caoimhin and Finnbhear were the only ones to ask pardon as they left Bodb's presence. Bodb had not called an end to the meeting. The Six's departure had simply facilitated it. The king sat for a while at the table, fingers steepled, and contemplated the Six. Why in the realm had he given them permission?

He decided it was Aramina's influence. She was spirited and willful, somehow always getting her way without requesting it.

What a woman.

Late evening, three days later. Bodb sat atop his favorite place on the wall. The army below had not attacked again. Instead, things settled, waiting for Cnos Fada to starve. Half of the cadavers were gone, released from the bindings when their silver elf masters had turned against MacKegan. Odds were MacKegan never needed the dead. Humans made up other parts of the army. Necromancers, too.

In all that time, The Six had made no move to fetch their fabled dragon's blood. Bodb pressed them once about it and was told stiffly that the time was not ripe. Almost, he lost his temper. Almost. These ruffians had tried to kill him, but they also seemed to know what they were doing.

Bodb turned to survey the city.

As a child, he used to sit atop the wall and watch the activity below with fascination. Cnos Fada was like an anthill, he had told his father one day. His father had smiled, ruffled his son's hair, and agreed.

The city's deadness was strange, but not frightening. The men were armed for battle and waiting along the wall. The women and children stayed indoors. Some volunteered to help in the infirmary, a welcome thing. Women's magic could be the most beneficial.

Picket came from nowhere, approaching the king with head held high. He bowed with a flourish. "Aramina goes for the dragon's blood," he announced.

"Finally," Bodb exhaled. "Where are they now?"

"The temple."

"Take me to them," Bodb said, sliding from his perch. The pooka only balked a second before remembering his loyalties. He lead the way briskly, making it hard for Bodb to keep up.

When Picket opened the altar to reveal the tunnel, Bodb could not believe his eyes. For centuries a secret way to the palace had been hidden in plain sight as an altar. He did not know that the altar was there only because it saved the trouble of making a new one, and it was this chance of fate which had preserved the secret.

Eagerly, he slipped past the pooka to get inside. Once they were in, the altar closed and the darkness surrounded them. Bodb was created an atma light to see by, but the pooka did not seem to need it. Picket went ahead while the king took his time, pausing at the sun carving, examining every niche he found. Before long, he was alone in the passage. He worried about dead ends, but then where would Picket go? There was no way to open the altar from inside.

Aramina was waiting for him at the small door.

"Come along," she said, grabbing his arm and pulling him briskly through the cavern. Bodb wanted to stop and admire the wondrous element around him. The Priestess hissed when he balked. "Look later," she said. "We've business to do. Sometimes I wonder about your kind."

The last was snapped under her breath. Bodb ignored it.

The business Aramina had mentioned was watching four cadavers, including the one that had run from Bodb in battle, retrieve the dragon's blood. The werewolf grinned and directed the cadavers to the side so the king could see the source more clearly. Bodb looked because he was genuinely interested, but a part of his mind dwelled on Aramina and the cadavers. Now he knew why the cadaver had run from him in battle. Aramina was controlling it and did not want to lose her toy.

They shuffled in and out of a tiny alcove, bearing copper buckets full of acrid dragon's blood, pouring it into large barrels laced with metal. The stench made Bodb cough. Indeed, the living (Duinn, Picket, Aramina and Bodb) stood a space away from the working dead.

"We're very deep in the earth," Duinn rumbled. He looked around himself, taking pleasure in the dampness. The beautiful cavern was far behind them, a pale glimmer in the dark. "I could build my forge here, even, but for the dragon's breath. 'Tis peaceful here. '

Another bucket full of acrid fluid splashed into a barrel.

"Ha, I'd like to see you build a forge here," Aramina said. "The tiniest flame would send the entire city sky high. Now *that's* an idea." She put her fingers to her lips and openly mused the hypothetical disaster.

"What happens after we've, uh, gathered the blood?" Bodb asked tentatively.

"We burn it," Aramina said with a wicked grin.

"What she means," Duinn said when Bodb opened his mouth to protest, "is we'll use it to burn the enemy. This is why we needed another mage. Raori needs help charming the water skins to hold this foul liquid without it dissolving the sides and spilling everywhere."

"What water skins?" Bodb asked, feeling dumb.

"All the water skins," Aramina said. "Anybody wanting a drink will have to take wine until those skins are empty, or get it straight from the well. But, if the plan works there should not be a problem."

"Not a problem? Priestess, I don't take kindly to the idea of my people going without water."

"Worry not," Aramina said with a laugh. "This will work. The lad you gave Raori seems quite adept."

"Donnach likes the mage."

"Don't we all," Aramina said snidely. "Hah, except himself."

"Enough," Duinn said.

"Why put the dragon blood in water skins?" Bodb asked, heedless of the black look Aramina threw at the dwarf.

"Donnach and Raori will spell them to catch fire," Aramina said with growing excitement. "They'll burst into a rain of white-hot fury. Nothing will be able to stand against it, least of all that army camped outside yon gates. They'll be forced to withdraw. When the flames die, we can massacre the survivors. We shan't leave one standing. Kill them all, down to the lowliest mortal. Then MacKegan will have to--"

"Aramina," Duinn said urgently, pointing. One cadaver had spilled a bucket during Aramina's speech. With a frustrated sigh, the Priestess concentrated until the cadavers had the mess straightened out.

"MacKegan will have to do what?" Bodb asked when he felt it safe.

"Enough talk," Duinn grumbled. "Get her going again, and we'll have more than spilled dragon blood on the floor. I suggest you let her concentrate, My Lord."

"Duinn, you are no fun." Aramina tossed her dark mane, pouting.

Two barrels took their final load with faint splashes. Aramina directed her pets toward two more barrels. Looking at her unfocused eyes, the amused quirk of her mouth, Bodb shuddered. It must be a horrible thing, to allow dead men part of your mind. She must be feral to enjoy it so.

"How did you get these cadavers into the city?" Bodb demanded suddenly.

"By catapult," Aramina replied. "Weren't you there?"

Bodb was suddenly more interested in the cavern. He felt unneeded, just standing around as he was. With a shrug in everyone's general direction, he walked away. The glow of the cavern's walls made him blink: He was used to the darkness. He admired the scenery before turning to find his way outside. The place was beautiful, but he wanted a cup of mead and a comfortable chair.

Faint daylight, gray with dusk, made its way down the exiting tunnel to the palace. A black shadow fluttered near it: Possibly underground vermin.

The light in the tunnel vanished.

Alarmed, Bodb ran, scrambling up the tunnel fast as he could. The door, stone by the feel of it, was shut fast. He pounded on it, bellowing.

"Priestess!" he cried like a frightened child.

"What is it, my lord?" Aramina inquired testily, crossing the cavern. Bodb could hear the others following. The uneven shuffle of undead echoed softly.

"Someone shut the door," Bodb said wildly, shoving with his shoulder. "It's stuck!"

"Oh, let me see," she fussed, climbing up the small tunnel to shove Bodb out of the way. Moving around brought no results. She pushed, waited, and pushed again. She felt for an opening catch. Then, she pounded her fists against the barrier. "We're locked in! Duinn!"

Followed by Picket, the dwarf ran to them. Duinn scrambled up the tunnel, shoving Bodb out of the way. The king slid to the bottom and was helped to his feet by the pooka.

"I can't open it," Duinn said after a while. "It's sealed tight, with more than the lock."

"Someone wants Bodb to stay down here," Picket observed.

"No doubt," Aramina snarled, emerging from the tunnel. She paced back and forth furiously. "There is no other way out!" she howled after a minute.

"Calm down," Bodb said, daring to touch her arm. She whirled on him, eyes wild. Picket grabbed her fist just as it swung toward the king. Bodb spent an instant studying the pooka's knuckles up close.

"No call for that," Picket chided. "Now, ye do as the king says and calm yerself.'

The werewolf dissolved into Picket's arms, sobbing onto his shoulder. Her words were mostly unintelligible, but her companions were able to put things together.

"Gredber did what to you?!" Duinn demanded, reaching for the halberd he no longer wore.

"I wouldn't let him," Aramina moaned. The rest was garble.

"I don't understand," Bodb said.

"A living grave," Picket said, patting Aramina's hair. "Ye gods, the bat can be cruel! That is no way to treat a gift bride."

"Even one from MacKegan," Duinn growled. Raori, Duinn and Picket were protective of their female teammate, and it looked as if this Gredber had done something seriously wrong to her. Whoever Gredber was, Bodb had the feeling he did not want to see the dwarf anytime soon.

"Let me out! Let me out!" Aramina suddenly shrieked, pushing from Picket to fly up the tunnel. The men ran after her, pulling her back, holding her arms so she would not hurt herself. Aramina continued to scream, thrashing in panic.

It was a desperate and dangerous move, but someone had to try. Bodb knocked her across the head, thrusting his atma into the blow. The Priestess jerked once, then went limp. Favoring his hand, Bodb eyed the others for signs of hostility.

"Thank the Morrigu for that," Duinn said, dropping her arm. "She can be a handful, eh?"

"We can't knock her out every time she wakes," Picket said, cradling her into his lap. "Dear sister," he whispered sadly, "to think you were hurt so deeply."

"You're a dwarf," Bodb said to Duinn. "Do something! Can't you burn the door with the dragon's blood?"

Overlooking Bodb's inadvertent insult, the dwarf stroked his beard in thought. "Good idea, even coming from an elf." He cast Bodb a sly look. "Picket, drop her and follow me!"

With Aramina unconscious, the cadavers merely stood as silent witnesses and would not help. The men were forced to hold their breath and roll a barrel up the tunnel themselves. It stuck fast just as it reached the door. Picket and Bodb stumbled back, coughing, while Duinn stayed. After a few whispered spells, he asked for their shirts.

Ripped into shreds, the cloth was tied end to end until they had a makeshift rope. After soaking it in the dragon blood, Duinn tucked one end into the barrel, trailing it after him as he retreated. The rope barely made it to the end of the tunnel.

There was a spark as Duinn lit the end of the rope with his flint and tender. Soaked with the volatile liquid, it ignited with a burst. "Down!" yelled Duinn while the flame ran up the line, into the tunnel. Bodb thought he saw crude paintings on the tunnels wall before Picket shoved his face into the dirt. Something roared, sending hot air searing through the cavern. Bits of rubble landed on them. Sand flew into Bodb's mouth.

Spitting, Bodb lifted his head. "What was that?" At least, that was what he thought he said. It was difficult to tell past the ringing in his ears.

"An explosion," the dwarf said with a grunt. He cast about, then swore. "The cadavers got blown up, too. Aramina is going to be mad for weeks."

"There's no way we can put them back together?" Bodb asked in momentary panic. Something groaned beneath a pile of rubble. Aramina's head emerged, and she scanned the room muzzily. The rest of her came forth, shaking dirt down. The men cringed.

"Are you alright?" Picket ventured.

"What did you blow the door up for?" the Priestess demanded. She staggered to her feet, holding her head. "What happened? We were getting the dragon's blood…"

Turning in a slow circle, she took in the damage. The tiny tunnel had opened into a gaping hole. Faces peered down as castle inhabitants examined it. No one ventured down yet, but they would soon enough.

When Aramina regained her senses, she whirled on the men. "Where are my cadavers?" she demanded.

"Well," Bodb said, patting Picket's shoulder. "We'll leave you to it. She seems right enough. Everyone will be wondering where I am."

Nodding cordially to the slightly confused Priestess, he made for the opening.

"Wait for me, Lord," Duinn called from behind. "Better not leave you alone with whomever locked the door running about."

Behind them, the shrill tones of Aramina's anger echoed across the cavern. Bodb winced and started running.

CHAPTER TWENTY-SEVEN
"MAGES AND MACHINES"

Raori heard the explosion, felt it vibrating through the ground. He paused in his work, reached with his mind, searching. Picket and Duinn were dull points of concern.

At first he could not find Aramina, then suddenly she flared to life with anger. Shaking his head, he turned back to his project.

"Hold that rope steady," he said to Donnach. The lad nodded, perspiration beading on his brow. His fingers moved faster than lightening, creating cat cradles and lady feathers, sustaining levitation spells and bindings. He was really talented, albeit mostly self taught. Raori wondered if he would like to be apprenticed.

At first he was disappointed that Donnach was the only passable mage available in Cnos Fada. After the first day working with him, Raori was pleased with the lad. Donnach bent his back to everything and had even taught Raori a few new tricks.

Besides, he was easy to get along with.

"That should hold it," Donnach said tightly, releasing his bindings and stepping back.

Raori ran his fingers through his hair, eyes tracing every curve and tangle before him. Donnach beamed with pride.

The result of their labor, a pile of waterskins that were both enchanted and waterproofed with wax and grease, mounded inconspicuously on the ground. All they needed now was the dragon's blood. With a few placed catapults, victory would be not only in their grasp, but cuddled to their breast like a newborn babe.

"Well," he said. "Let's see how my friends are doing." Donnach was practically jumping with excitement.

"I can't imagine," he said as the pair made their way from Raori's impromptu workshop toward the temple, "that your tunnel was not discovered all this time! How did you do it? A glamour?"

"No, just a simple disguise. It used to lead to a cellar," Raori said. "But the back caved in one day." He smiled at the memory, which involved a small cask of dragon's blood and the cover of night.

The temple was not crowded as Raori's last visit. Genuine worshipers ignored them. The Trickster's altar maintained an air of solitude, ignored even by servants carrying bowls of soapy water.

Raori cradled the Trickster's bowl in his hands before kneeling. He remembered a day, so long ago. Aramina had been scrubbing the bowl and singing a litany of curses...

"Are you worshiping or just crazy?" he wanted to ask. Instead, "Can I help with something?"

The girl dropped her cloth into a bowl of water, blowing a stray hair from her eyes. The sparkle in their depths intrigued him. He wanted to lean into them, reach for the brightest spark.

"Ha, only if you can convince that fat priest to quit overlooking me," she exclaimed angrily. "Nine times, now! And for what?"

"Wha—"

"I'll tell you," the girl continued. "Pubescent nothings who flash their legs for a bit of attention. Eager, the priests call them. Ha!" Angrily, she squeezed her rag until the fabric screamed, the water rushing onto the floor. "Oh, I'll say they're eager. Eager for a little--"

"Aramina, that will be enough!" a priest exclaimed, striding hastily across the room. To Raori, "My pardons, if this ingrate has been troubling you."

"No trouble," Raori said with a laugh. "Just getting to know a fellow student."

"Ah, so," the priest said with a nod, "you would be Harrel's boy."

Raori smiled quietly. His master had sent him to the temple for a season of outside training. Honed the mind, the old man had claimed. Privately, Raori suspected it was to escape his apprentice's clumsiness. The great seashell bowl would never be same, and that just the latest fiasco.

The priest did not take stock in Raori's silent despair, but perhaps the girl did. Her eyes gleamed for a moment, and she blew him a kiss. Then she was scrubbing the altar, a dutiful servant, and he was following the priest to his new room.

He forgot her in the following days. His schedule was packed with classes, errands, classes, contemplation meetings, and classes. He went to bed early, rose before cock crow, repeating the process everyday. When for the first time he was left alone, by a fountain in order to contemplate the source of atma, she appeared suddenly. Only then did he remember her.

She was wearing a brown dress, embroidered along the skirt bottom, and carried a basket. Pausing as if surprised, although the twinkle in her eye belied it, she stepped toward him.

"Hello, Harrel's boy," she said. "A moment of your own, at last?"

"My name is Raori," Raori said. "And no. I'm contemplating atma." His eyes scanned her curvatures, sparking contemplations of a different kind.

She snorted, tossed the basket to the ground and sat beside him. "What's to contemplate?" she said airily. "It comes from your will and belongs in your head."

"Really?" Raori had different conclusions, drawn from lengthy talks concerning gods and the touch of their father.

"Really," the girl said seriously. "I'm Aramina."

"Lovely. I mean, nice name." Raori swallowed, realizing how uncomfortable he was around women. When apprenticed to self-contained mages, a boy does not get much exposure to feminine elements. Raori never was at ease around women to begin with, except for his numerous sisters. The creature before him was definitely not his sister.

"Come on, you know the answer now. Let's go." She stood, picked up her basket and slung it over one arm.

"But, why? I mean, I don't think I should ..."

"Live a little!" Aramina said with a laugh. "You won't be missed, you know. Who's going to come looking for their dutiful boy, who reports on time with each duty done? I promise you'll not get into trouble. If so, I'll take the blame. You saw how eager the masters here are to punish me.

"Where are we going?" Raori half whispered, looking fearfully about. He had horrid visions of priests swooping in to hand her more soapy water and send him home in disgrace.

"The fields," Aramina said. "To gather herbs."

Raori was a youth of fifteen. This girl, so much older and yet just as young, could not be resisted. The sparkle in her eyes, dancing motes of light, called him on.

The fields the first day, the woods the next. The woods again under the full moon. Sneaking away evolved into Raori's obsession. He reported to his teachers later and later from his contemplations. No one seemed suspicious. If anything, they patted his shoulder and remarked what a deep-thinking soul he had.

If only they knew what he thought about during those times. They never asked, a favor Raori thanked the gods for every day.

There came a night when Aramina practically herded him to the forest. She said only that she had a surprise, something that would show his old master how good a mage he could be. Did he not want to go proudly home with skills to be envied? Curiously, Raori allowed himself to be led.

Then a dark shape loomed dangerously at them. Aramina squealed and scooted back. Raori dodged, rolling in leaves *and wet grass. As he stood, the shape addressed his fellow conspirator.*

"I thought you would be here tonight."

"So?" Aramina planted her feet apart and glared. "Should it matter to you? Why don't you go back to your wife, and leave us alone!"

Atma light flared, and the intruder was revealed. A handsome face looked down on Raori, smiled a little, seemed sad in a way. Silver was this man, like metal or animals from the frost. He turned to Aramina.

"You're only hurting this boy."

"Am not!" Aramina practically screamed. "He wants this. Say you do, Raori!"

"I..." Raori swallowed, quite overwhelmed. "Yes, I do."

"See?" Aramina took his hand triumphantly.

"I can't let you go," the man said. "Mina, you're courting doom. I can see it all around you. Please, don't do this. The others bring ill luck with them."

Aramina shouted, "Leave us!"

Raori expected this silver man, whom he later learned was a soldier, to argue. Perhaps even pull his sword and force them home. At the very least, he could threaten to tell the priests where the couple was. Instead he backed out of sight, disappeared into the shadows.

And Aramina's eyes, visible even in the dark, beckoned with their dancing lights. Onward into the dark, through the forest, to the place where Duinn waited with a bowl and knife. Onward.

Raori shook from his reverie and focused on Donnach's merry face. The lad was recounting memories of his own childhood, happy times every boy should have. His voice fell short when he saw Raori's solemn expression.

"I followed those merry lights," Raori said, because he felt he should explain his guilt. "I leaned forward and caught one. And this is where it took me."

Donnach lifted one eyebrow, wanting to ask yet reluctant to do so. Then they stepped through the door, into a cavern with a gaping hole. Aramina was there, furious, complaining loudly about lost cadavers. Picket wilted in her fury and cast Raori a hopeful glance. Raori could only smile. He still saw the angry girl by the altar. Her pointed chin, her black hair, the lights in her eyes. Ah yes, those merry, lively lights. He wanted to lean forward and catch one.

***

Finnbhear alternately gaped at the hole and watched Aramina direct volunteers in collecting dragon blood. She had no time for him, indeed seemed annoyed by his lingering presence. He was off duty and felt no need for company, anyway, ~~so he~~so he left. A secluded spot in the garden, hidden by a large tree, gave him shelter. He curled in the hollow of the tree's large roots and played his silver flute.

At first he played the newest tavern rounds, but after a while he let his fingers wander. Sometimes he played fast, other times slow and sad. Before long, he was playing a song his mother had taught him. Cliodna's Scald, she had called it: a woeful tale of the Sidhe's love for Keefe, a poet of Éire.

Most things she had taught him were fae born. Upon reflection, she had seemed almost fae herself. Her eyes had sparkled, much like Aramina's, as if she held secrets and could see invisible things. She used to laugh about having ten brown thumbs, yet their garden was the best in the village. Not so good as her father's, she used to say. Not so good.

Finnbhear knew he took after her. His father had died in a chieftain's skirmish when he was young, and with only his mother to raise him…

He was no longer alone. Busily, as if oblivious to the danger, Finnbhear stopped playing. He took the flute apart and began to clean it. His eyes searched for some sign of the intruder. His sword was propped by the tree, his knife in his boot. If he rolled quickly enough, he might make it up alive and armed.

"About time ye learned t'play the thing," a piping voice said above him. "I wondered sometimes. If it hadn't been for your mother, I might have cut off me ears!"

Finnbhear froze in motion. Mouth agape, he looked up. A merry brown face grinned at him, half hidden by leaves. Without warning, the face's owner leapt at him.

Blinded by the proximity of brown rags, Finnbhear rolled, trying to pull himself lose. Skinny arms and legs wrapped around his neck. A mirthful laugh rang in his ears. Then he was released to stand sputtering, wiping his mouth against the taste of dirt.

"When is the last time you bathed?!" Finnbhear demanded.

His attacker was a brown lad, dressed in rags from head to toe. He swung a hairy belt—a troll's tail, Finnbhear's memory supplied—and danced in place.

"What kind of greetin' is that to give me, your best friend?" the boy wight said. "I maun leave now, as you don't want to see me."

"What are you doing here?" Finnbhear asked in shock. "I thought I'd never—I mean, how did you find me. Uh, how have you been? You haven't changed a bit..."

Kegal snorted a laugh, slapping his knee. Then he walked up to Finnbhear, punching his arms and thighs. "Well, look at you," he said. "You've changed all over. Ye've gotten taller, but I suppose that couldn't be helped with a tree lover. But, ach. What's this? Your hair is grey!"

"And you stink more than usual," Finnbhear countered, wrinkling his nose.

The two burst into easy laughter. Then they pummeled each other as best can be done between man and boy. Before long they were sharing the hollow of the tree, recounting adventures and tall tales.

The brown lad was Finnbhear's boyhood friend, of course. Finnbhear thought of him frequently, but had never thought to see him again. Now he was there, and it was like Kegal had never left. Finnbhear wondered how he let his friend go in the first place, when they were so comfortable together.

Yet, he was acutely aware of the time since he had seen his boyhood friend. How long? Ten seasons or two thousand?

"Kegal, what are you doing here?" Finnbhear asked, interrupting one of Kegal's enthusiastic rambles. "I haven't seen you since I was a boy, when you traded me the flute. But it's good to see you. Very good."

Kegal reached out a dirty hand, to which Finnbhear tentatively grasped.

"How do you greet old friends these days, Finnbhear?" he said seriously.

For the first time in ages, Finnbhear erupted with an easy laugh. "We'll play it my way, then. And I'm suddenly curious. What happened to you? Why didn't you stay?"

"How could I, me friend, when you made such a commitment to growing up? But life treated you well, that it did. Five children, a pretty wife AFTER seducing her flesh sister! A war general, and now a diplomat."

"Diplomat?" Finnbhear scratched his beard.

"Didn't you come to my folk seeking help? And here I am, your answer, and all you can do is complain about a bath!"

"I never seduced Aramina," Finnbhear said suddenly.

"Ach, no. She seduced you!" Kegal laughed again, rocking in his seat. He was so like Finnbhear remembered, down to the rip in his shirt sleeve. Yet he was real. He had to be. Nothing illusionary could smell so musky.

"Forget Aramina," Finnbhear snapped. "What do you mean, I sought help and here you are? You can't be the answer Cliodna promised! Can you?"

Kegal winked. "You cannae think I'm here just to see ya. Ye were my favorite lad, my boy o, but you're a lad no longer. My magic for you is faded and needed elsewhere besides. Although," and he twirled his grisly belt, "I have things to thank ye for yet."

It was too easy, Kegal reappearing and making Finnbhear forget their years of distance. Too easy to sit underneath a tree, like ages long past, and forget the world. He should have known. Finnbhear stood to mask his disappointment.

"Dinnae take it so hard," Kegal said kindly. Finnbhear faced the boy, who could seem so wise and then just as foolish. "She sent me, knowing I was missed, and that just a sign of favor. No, she'll require other things in balance for worthy deeds. You'll know it when the time comes. Be ready, old friend."

There was something wrong with Finnbhear's vision. The world had a golden quality. A white mist clouded his eyes. He rubbed them, then blinked.

He was sitting underneath the tree, still holding his flute. Of Kegal there was no sign.

***

"Oh dear," said Midna. He stood before what had once been a neat pile of waterskins. What greeted his wandering gaze was a pile of rubbish, if it could be called even that.

No one else was about. The crime would have to be reported by himself. Midna sighed wearily. Since stumbling upon Aramina, he had been frightened, starved in her search, and now he must witness this setback. Although Raori was extraordinarily patient for a mage, Midna had no desire to find out just how patient.

Almost, he looked skyward to ask what foul thing could happen next. He thought better of it. The gods were having enough fun as it was. It was best not tempt them.

It turned out, there was no need.

"Gods, what happened??!?" Raori's voice echoed. The mage, followed by half a dozen servants with barrels and sick expressions, had just turned a nearby corner. Aramina was with him. She surveyed the wreckage with what could only be the first stages of shock.

"Midna," she gasped. "Even My Lord would think this was a prank gone too far."

"I didn't do it!" Midna cried in panic. "I found it this way! I was finding the pooka for the king, and I didn't do it!!!!"

Raori stamped to the shredded mess and kicked it. "What is this nonsense? Who cares? Can't you see we've been sabotaged? Blasted Fell Beasts! It has to be someone who knew what we were up to. But, who?? Blast!"

"Sir Mage," a quiet voice interrupted. "The catapults are ready, as per your instructions." A young soldier stood a few feet off, holding his leather helmet under one arm. He picked a bad time to report the next part of their plan complete. Though twelve catapults were now positioned around the wall of Cnos Fada, their ammunition was ruined. Midna waited for Raori to explode.

Instead, Raori waved the soldier away and ran his fingers through his hair. Midna poked at the ruin. Aramina crossed her arms, apparently waiting for what her lover had to say next.

"There's no use to the catapults, now," Raori moaned into his hands. "Donnach bespelled them for nothing! Without the waterskins, we have no escape. Unless we can come up with another plan, but I doubt we have time. MacKegan, if he really is coming, will be here any day."

"Couldn't you fix the waterskins with magic?" asked one of the servants. Raori whirled to glare at him, but was unsure which one it was.

"I couldn't fix them with magic, even if I wanted to!" Raori cried. "I have trouble boiling eggs! This is horrible! We took every waterskin in the city, on faith that we could end the siege. Now we have no ammunition and fewer ways to store water. Everyone will thirst to death! Or kill each other fighting over the wells! Us, included, only His Highness will have us executed first! Blast!!"

Aramina clucked sympathetically and placed a hand on Raori's arm. Midna picked up a piece of waterskin and examined it thoughtfully.

"What about wineskins?" he asked.

"...wineskins?" Raori went dangerously quiet. Aramina removed her hand. "You want me to use wineskins?? That's heresy! Feral Beasts! What is wrong with you, ye under bloated god loving northern..."

As the mage was yelling, the waterskins shuddered on the ground. Midna dropped his piece in time for it to collide with another, and then another. Miraculously, the waterskins began stitching themselves back together.

Raori was last to notice. His string of curses, now extending to Midna's forebears, halted. He watched, mouth slack, for a few minutes before sputtering in Aramina's direction. "Show off," he accused. The servants had already dropped their cargo and run.

"I'm not doing it," she said with a laugh.

"Then who?"

"Best concentrate on them," Aramina said, grabbing Raori's chin and forcing him to look at the jumping skins. "They're starting to unravel."

It was true. The instant Raori's attention went elsewhere, the waterskins started to sag. Once he refocused on them, they returned to their dance. One after one, whole waterskins plopped to the ground as if never hurt.

Raori let out a whoop. "We'll be burning the siege before dawn!" He hugged Aramina, kissed Midna's cheeks, danced a little jig. Behind him, the waterskins jerked in sympathetic motions.

Midna caught Aramina's broad wink, a signal meaning 'job well done.' Congratulating himself, he walked away. He could get used to this trickster business, with practice. It was rather fun.

No one saw the shadow, and its owner, slip away.

Chapter Twenty-Eight
"Battle of Fire"

Mornnacht cursed himself, pausing now and again to listen. No one saw him leave, but there was no room for carelessness. And right now, he was in such a rage it was difficult to see straight.

The Mark on his arm burned with foreboding coldness. It had moved higher up, a sign Mornnacht was unsure about, and pulsed. Evidently, he was on borrowed time. MacKegan liked to slip into his head sometimes. If MacKegan found out Mornnacht had failed again, he was done for.

How could he know the mage was so highly skilled, even as part of the fabled Six? The Mark on Raori's shoulder (Funny how the mage seemed untroubled by it. Could he really have escaped MacKegan's influence?) ranked him only a third class magician, besides being a member of The Six. It was his fighting skills that had kept him alive, mission after mission.

Not even MacKegan's sorcerers could repair waterskins like that. It was almost as if he was being helped by some outside influence.

Mornnacht hoped only to delay the mage's plan and give MacKegan time to arrive. If Mornnacht killed a few of the enemy as well, that would be all the more to please MacKegan. Chulain had made it very plain he wanted The Six dead by the foulest means possible. Mornnacht had not had the opportunity to catch one of them alone, but he was bound to eventually. For days he had skulked in dark corners, crept the palace halls at night, sat on rooftops, watching his prey. Gauging their patterns, gleaning their plans. Waiting for just the right moment.

Like other quirks in Mornnacht's behavior, this pusillanimity was uncharacteristic of the typical black assassin. Another assassin would make the right moment, somehow, before the second dawn. They believed in fighting to the death, anybody's death. If your opponent mastered you (not uncommon amongst lower ranks), then you died. It did not matter how.

Hence the suicide in Finnbhear's room, when the black assassin had crept in to kill him.

Mornnacht, however, had made a momentous decision. While those in Tech Danaan died by their victims' hands, he had slipped away to safety. Someone was going to die, he resolved, and it would be The Six. For that, Mornnacht had to live. So he did.

***

The old man stood next to Raori for a long time. The mage ignored him. Soon, the catapults would be loaded. MacKegan's army massed below, positioning war engines of their own. Cadavers waited to pile into the catapult baskets. A giant battering ram was being carried to the front gates. If Cnos Fada did not fire its catapults before MacKegan's army attacked again, they were sure to lose the race.

"Now, what's the matter?" the old man asked when Raori sighed.

"Nothing, elder one," Raori said miserably. "I was just thinking how much easier my life would have been had I died sooner." He gestured below.

"That," the old man said while leaning out and squinting, "is definitely a problem."

"And you didn't notice it before?" Raori ran his fingers through his hair. "Better off dead because we're going to be dead, unless we can get ourselves prepared before. Any time now, MacKegan will attack. What can we do then but defend ourselves, and only unto the death?"

For some reason, Raori's thoughts fled to Moire. He wondered if she knew what was happening, or even if she was alive. How long had Moire been with him? Ten years? Twenty? Come to think of it, the gentle human had been much younger when he bought her. She must be in her late twenties now, at least.

Raori suddenly felt guilty, remembering Aramina.

"Silly fool," the old man said. "Don't you know beauty when you see it? Is she lovely because she's lovely, or because she changes? You craved change, and you got it. What did you do? You spurned it for immortality, and now look at you. There's beauty in everything, but mostly what does not last. You have everything to fight for. Remember that, and you will win over those below."

Raori's jaw had dropped before the second sentence of the old man's lecture was uttered. He watched numbly while the old man turned and made his slow way down the wall. Just before he turned a corner, he turned back to Raori.

"Tell my blasted son, when you see him, to stay out of this. Your wolf may be tangled in this mess, but its not our place to choose sides. Leastwise, not the way he has done."

Raori swallowed three times before finding his voice. "Who is your son?" he called weakly. Had he just been visited by the fae, or something else? Was it even safe to ask?

"The harper!" the old man snapped, then he was gone. He did not walk away, nor fade out with a convenient puff of smoke. He was simply gone.

Raori, having seen a myriad of fantastic things in his lifetime, blinked a moment in astonishment before shaking it out of his mind. He watched the cadavers below a while longer. He did not see them. His mind was on the harper and moving quickly. After centuries of dealing with magicians of every caliber, he should be used to strange old men disappearing at whim. It turned out that he was not.

"I thought worrying was my job," Bodb said. He had come unnoticed.

"By all means." Raori made room for the young king. Bodb settled against the wall, took one look down, and groaned.

"How long before we launch our own catapults?" he asked. Raori merely shrugged. "Well, do it now. Find your fellows, launch our counterattack. Right now I don't even care how you do it. Just go! Report to me immediately."

Raori dashed away, skirting soldiers as they ran to their stations. He could practically hear the army outside Cnos Fada thrumming with purpose. He shifted into cat form for better speed.

Aramina was in the garden with Finnbhear. Unnoticed and forgetting his errand, Raori climbed a nearby rose tree. Aramina looked right at him. Then, she cuddled to the Silver Fox. Suddenly, Raori forgot his errand.

"Aramina-"

"Hush, Silver Fox. In an hour we might be dead. Don't you feel it?"

Raori's claws dug tiny trenches in his tree limb.

"Mina, I–"

She kissed him full on the lips. Raori hissed softly, his ears lay flat against his scalp. Finnbhear's arms found Aramina's waist, her back. His hands discovered her hair. Raori discovered how to fly.

Aramina yelled as Finnbhear threw her back. Raori was in the Silver Fox's face. He managed several good swipes across the old elf's brow before Finnbhear grabbed him by the scruff of the neck. Howling, Raori struggled. Then he shifted. His man form was too large for Finnbhear to hold. He came at the Silver Fox with fists balled.

Aramina dove between them.

"Stop it!" she yelled. "I won't have this! Raori, get away from him!"

Raori only stopped because the Priestess was in his way. She threw herself into Finnbhear's arms and glared over her shoulder.

"Wicked mage," she snarled. "Why can't you mind your own business? He was my friend long before you knew I was alive. Just go away! Leave us alone!"

Finnbhear pushed Aramina away. "I won't be a jealousy tool," he said roughly.

"And why not?" Aramina whirled on the Silver Fox, who stepped away from her sudden fury. "You married my sister, didn't you?!?!? You're worse than he is! At least he's willing to fight for me!"

Raori blinked stupidly. "I–"

"Shut up! Be quiet! Silence! Do you understand? I won't be owned, not by Finnbhear, not by you, not by anybody! If you don't like what I do, or with whom, you shouldn't eavesdrop!" She wiped her face, then looked at her fingers in shock. They were wet with tears.

Raori had never seen the Priestess cry before. He tried to hold her, but she shoved him roughly away. "Don't touch me!" she screamed. "Never touch me again! It's your fault! Both of you!" She wiped her face again before dashing away.

"And she said I was going feral," Raori said in shock.

"Are you?" the Silver Fox asked with interest. He dabbed absently at a scratch across his brow.

"I suppose so." Raori shrugged. "She and I are not completely free of him, you know. Or didn't you know?"

"No, I didn't."

The men stood silence. Finally, Finnbhear patted Raori's shoulder. "Come, mage. Let's drink on it. We'll never understand women, but wine is no mystery."

Yes, a drink would be perfect right about now. It had been just before noon since last he had a cup, and what time was it now? Just afternoon? Too long a time. Yet–

"No time," Raori said. "MacKegan readies his catapults. Bodb has given the order to counterattack. Quickly."

"I will find Picket," Finnbhear said with an uplifted eyebrow. "Duinn is holed up in that gaping cavern. Posted a sentry. Won't let even Aramina in."

As a cat, Raori made a bee line for the cavern. He leapt a few bushes past the garden, climbed Finnbhear's tree and spent a minute trying to get down. He always forgot how high everything looked to a cat.

He was breathless when he reached the one time secret cavern. Two guards paced resolutely before the gaping hole. The cat made it past them without being challenged. He would have to talk to Bodb Derg about that. Not every elf had forgotten the art of shape shifting.

Duinn sat at a makeshift table with something resembling a bellows. He chuckled to himself while examining his handiwork. Then he placed the thing under one armpit, spoke the magic formula for fire, and squeezed it. Fire roared forth in a thin line. Raori crouched and felt every hair on his body stand on end.

Duinn then did a strange thing. He threw the bellows away and crouched behind a large rock. It was fortunate Raori was near one himself. The bellows exploded with a loud rushing sound. Pebbles scattered around the cavern.

The guards looked inside the cavern, but Duinn waved them away. "I'm fine!" he shouted. Raori stood on two legs and brushed himself off. He was at a loss for words at the moment, but Duinn would say something soon enough.

"What are you doing in here?!? How much did you see??"

"Enough," Raori said quickly. "Interesting weapon. A shame we have no time to use it."

"Hammer Fells," Duinn muttered. "MacKegan is here? Now?"

"I can't say to that," Raori said. "But their catapults are loading. And they have a battering ram. Bodb has issued the order and wants us now."

Duinn stumped outside and grabbed a guard by the arm. The tall elf cringed before the dwarf, apparently intimidated. "Load the pults," Duinn ordered. "Now! And stand ready for my command."

"Aye," was the murmured response, and the elf dashed away. His partner hesitated, then followed.

"Finnbhear went to find Picket," Raori said, leading the way back to the wall. "Midna, I have to assume, is at the infirmary. That's all he's good for. We'll have no time to mother him, besides."

"What of Aramina?"

"Well," Raori shrugged, keeping eyes to the ground. "I'm sure Finnbhear will tell her. She's the smartest of us, I think sometimes. She'll be there."

"What did you do this time?" Duinn growled.

"Nothing, I just–"

"Never mind," Duinn said suddenly. "We're at war, and I prefer to worry about that." Around them, soldiers ran toward the gates. It was difficult to get up the wall, but they managed. War cries resounded from below.

Bodb was screaming something to the enemy army. It sounded like insults, but he cut himself off before Raori could comprehend it. The young king half grinned.

"I had hoped to hold one last council before this." He shrugged boyishly. "Ah well. Here comes the Silver Fox. Just in time."

The Silver Fox was followed by Caoimhin Long in the Arm and seven handpicked messenger boys. Finnbhear looked around blankly before forcing himself to focus on the king. "I could not find Picket," he said. "Nor Aramina."

"We will have to fight without them," Bodb said.

"They are here," Raori said, adjusting a sleeve. Something boomed. The cries from below turned into cheers as the battering ram thundered into the gates a second time.

Around him, the messengers were sent with orders to launch the catapults. Finnbhear left to direct his army waiting at the gate. But Raori experienced the eternal moment of battle; the time when the world slows and every minute detail must be catalogued.

For what seemed like five years, he stretched his fingers wide and summoned wind to blast against the battering ram. Duinn screamed, "Cast the spell, Raori! Cast the spell! The pults are launched! Cast!" for six weeks. Days later, Raori obeyed and threw his arms to the sky, where the bespelled skins sailed beyond the city walls. He spoke, and the words rang around him like bells. The world rushed forward-

-and exploded. The water skins literally rained fire as each burst into lethal splatters. The jeers from below turned into screams. The battering ram was abandoned as everyone fled the flaming rain. Fire made a second wall around the city.

"They're running now, by the Morrigu!" Caoimhin shouted gleefully. "Ha!"

"Not such a bad plan after all, eh?" Raori could not resist asking. The old elf narrowed his eyes but did not respond. "Of course," and he gestured to the roaring fire below, "our army can't get out to fight what's left of the enemy because of the fire. Quite ironic." A waft of smoke made him cough.

"We need Aramina," Duinn declared. "And did you get her? No. Of course. You chased her off." He punched Raori's arm. "Now we're besieged by fire rather than the dead. I can see how well our circumstances have improved."

"What?" Bodb demanded softly. "Please don't tell me you didn't plan this far."

"Then we won't," Duinn said.

"Your Highness," Raori explained quickly, "things have too much of a tendency to change from point to point. Besides—"

"It's much more fun this way," Aramina said.

Dressed in soldier's vest and leggings, she stood mere feet from them. Her entire face was swallowed by a helmet. She carried a lance.

"The pooka will battle beside Finnbhear, My Lord," the Priestess said to the king. "And I will be joining them, by your leave."

"But, Aramina—" Raori's protest was cut short by Aramina's curt look.

"You forget," Aramina said coldly, "I have as much reason, if not more, to fight down there."

"I don't care how you do it," Bodb said dubiously, "so long as it's past that fire wall."

Duinn grinned. "We'll get out with your help, mage. You've more tricks than petty fire spells in your head, if you'll care to remember."

"Then we attack," Bodb decided.

"As Milord commands," Aramina said softly.

It was Bodb's command, but Aramina led them to the gate. Raori walked just behind her, although her very aura rejected him. He recalled every water spell he knew and rejected each singularly. He had spells to encourage rain, roll in the mist, summon water sprites. None of these were appropriate.

There was a blizzard spell, he decided, that would work. He did not like working with ice – it froze his fingers – but blasting the gates with ice would kill the fire and destroy any stray enemies. With Donnacht's help, he could do even more than that, but there was no time to find the elf.

"The fire rid us of half of 'em," Duinn was saying, "but we'll have the rest to fight. If we're lucky, the humans spooked and ran for their lives."

"I can get us out," Raori muttered.

Aramina glanced at him, mouth open to speak. Then she remembered she was angry and looked away. It was tantalizing.

Finnbhear's army was small but crowded the gate nonetheless. The Silver Fox pranced his mare before them, lifting a hand to deflect the sun's waning glare. "Where is the king?" he asked. "Will he be at the wall? Rather that than losing him in battle."

"What do you mean?" Duinn said, looking around.

"Huh," grunted Aramina.

"He was right with us."

"Oh, my." Raori squinted the way they had come.

Aramina threw her lance to the ground. Her helmet followed with a bounce. "If it's not one of you men ruining my fun, its another somewhere else!" She started to unlace her shirt with vicious movements.

"What are you–"

"Going to get your stupid king!" she shouted. "Meanwhile, you might want to get out there and fight while the enemy is too afraid to fight back!"

"Here, Aramina," Finnbhear protested, "without Bodb's order–"

"*I'm* ordering you!" she snarled. "Did that sound like a suggestion?!?" She left her clothes in a small heap and, as a wolf, ran back to the wall.

"Right," said Duinn after a moment's awkward silence. "Raori, get us out of here."

Raori heard Finnbhear stuttering his protests as he walked away. Apparently, the Silver Fox had never seen Aramina's will exerted before. Of course, he had also never been on the same side with her before. It was almost amusing.

He was tempted to stand before the great gate but knew he could better serve his team atop the wall. The battlefield was hushed, but for the crackling of the fire, when he finally stood on the rise.

The first spell he cast was a rain shower. Water came down in heavy sheets. The fire was not cowed. Indeed, Raori knew it would not be. In his brief experience with dragon's blood, he had learned the stuff could burn for days and nothing known would douse it. No, the rain was for the army's benefit. Let them think themselves protected. MacKegan's army, too.

Through the flames, Raori saw silhouettes as the enemy came closer, feeling more secure. The fire stayed the same as before; water could do nothing against a dragon blood flame. The silhouettes jumped and moved.

They were fools to trust a rain storm summoned by the enemy. No doubt, they thought the Cnos Fada's mage was trying to save the city. Steam drifted up in clouds over the field. MacKegan's men trusted the heavenly source and waited.

It was now or never. Raori swept his arms outward. The summoned wind whistled over Cnos Fada and down the wall. The fire was pushed before it. Once again, MacKegan's army screamed.

Knowing smugly that he was doing something no other atma-user had done or could do, he switched spells in mid-chant and sent torrents of snow and hail pounding to the earth below. The fires began to die, but Raori would not relent. What was left of the enemy grouped out of reach on a distant hill and watched. Some turned their horses and slunk away, but the rest appeared determined to stay. Raori sent a final blast of white in their direction. It died feet from them without leaving a mark on the ground.

"I can't do anymore!" Raori gasped. Exhausted, he fell back against the wall. The wind died as he lost grip on the spell until it was gone. "The rest is up to you," he panted, staggering up to Finnbhear.

"Then we go." The Silver Fox sounded almost excited. "Perhaps we'll die, but we'll never surrender!"

The great gate was opened, and the army rushed to leave the city. The earth rumbled with thundering hooves and marching feet. Finnbhear charged in front, but suddenly reined his mare to the side. The marching mass from behind slowed. "Hold!" he cried. Picket, four-legged, whinnied shrilly. Men shouted complaints.

"Halt, I said!" Finnbhear roared. Around him, the tide of combatants fought to come still. He ignored them. Across the field from them stood a lone woman in white. Raori blinked. He did not know her, but it was obvious that Finnbhear did. The Silver Fox dismounted, motioning for everyone to stand at attention, and began to walk towards her.

Raori rushed from the wall, conjuring a grey stallion to wait for him at the foot of the stairs. As quickly as he could, he mounted it and kicked it into motion. He drove his horse past the soldiers and beyond the gate where Finnbhear goggled this new development.

"Who is that?" someone asked.

"You expect me to know? Where the hell did she come from?" This entire business smelled of fairy magic, and Raori was none too sure he wanted to trust it.

The woman walked to towards Finnbhear. She did not look threatening, but she did not look happy to see him either.

CHAPTER TWENTY-NINE
"PRICE FOR A FOX'S PELT"

Bodb Derg decided that he was not in a good mood. Not only had the Six (or Five, he was still a little confused) practically taken over his authority, he ended shuffled at the end of the line while descending the wall stairs. The Priestess led with Raori second in line and giving her doting looks with slumped shoulders. How these people managed to do the things they did was beyond the young king.

One minute he was shuffling behind the dwarf, the next he was grabbed and thrust into a dark corner. He lost his wind. Gasping, he could see nothing although he tried. Then a leering face filled his vision.

It was the face of an insane man. Brown spots graced his forehead, splattering down like splashes from an especially bad burn. He grinned a filthy grin full of broken teeth. The cold edge of a knife touched Bodb's neck.

"We could do this the easy way," the crazy elf said, "but I'm not after you." He tittered.

"If you're not after me," Bodb whispered, "then why do this at all?" His voice went high as the knife began to cut his flesh.

"I'll get the wolf first," the elf was saying. He laughed again. "First her, oh yes, that damnable woman. She always thought she was so special, and now she's no more special than dirt under MacKegan's feet!"

Bodb Derg decided that not only was he not in a good mood, he was not having a good day. Somehow it all centered on something Aramina was doing or had done. He was tempted to help the crazy man kill her.

Kidnapper and victim lay silently in their dark corner. Screams floated to them from outside. Someone was shouting. Feet thundered past. Bodb hoped someone would stop, but no one did. It was just as well. He was getting tired of being rescued from certain death all the time. Maybe this time he could save himself, or die and not have to worry anymore.

Time passed painfully. Bodb began to get a crick in his neck. He opened his mouth to complain, thought again and shut it. His attacker never moved, as if listening with his entire body.

Over the faint screams and rushing of passing soldiers, Bodb could hear the faint clicks of nail against stone. Apparently, the crazy man heard them, too. He shifted his weight, gathering his feet under him. The knife withdrew.

Bodb twisted, shoving a fist out and hitting solid flesh. The man grunted, slid back and landed against the wall. He started to gather his feet beneath him, glaring at the king with glassy eyes. Viciously Bodb kicked the man's neck. Something cracked. The man lay still.

"It's about time you fended for yourself," Aramina said, slinking into the shadow. She was nude. Bodb averted his eyes, although he did not know why.

The Priestess ignored his discomfort. "Come on, king," she said. "By now, Raori has routed MacKegan's men."

"What of this fellow?" Bodb said, nudging the crazy man's body with his toe.

Aramina sighed with frustration. "I dare say you killed him," she said. "No small feat, Milord, as that was a black assassin. The spirits either like you, or you're unusually lucky."

"A black assassin?!" Bodb edged away. "The old women say that when a black assassin dies, his body becomes a werewolf–" Aramina's gaze was steady. "Well, I suppose that's just a myth," the king finished lamely.

"He won't come back from death," The Priestess said. "But, if you must be sure."

She semi-shifted. The wolf arose from her like a fog, insubstantial yet there for the world to see. She nosed the kidnapper, wagged her tail, then melded back into her elven body. "He's dead," The Priestess announced. "Poor Mornnacht. He only wanted some attention, too." And she turned away.

If Bodb had not seen it, he would never have believed it. He knew The Six, and Finnbhear, could change shape. He had even seen it once or twice; a quick transition from one form to another. It happened within the blink of an eye.

But Aramina's shifting was leisurely, purposeful. Bodb had seen the beating of her heart, the growth of fur on her smooth skin, the lengthening of her canines. The change looked entirely painful.

Bodb himself could not shift form. Not many elves could anymore. With each human immigration came human values and customs. The elves became less fae everyday, but with few regrets.

He followed The Priestess down the wall, trying not to study the dimples of her behind. The screams outside had stopped, and the gate opened by the time they got there. The army jostled, but went not forward. Bodb and Aramina pushed their way through, occasionally getting poked by the stray lance, until they emerged past the gate.

"What is going on here?" Bodb demanded. "Has MacKegan been routed so soon?"

"Ha, I doubt it," Aramina said. She grabbed the nearest soldier, who could hardly have been older than sixteen summers, and put the question to him.

"We don't know," the boy trembled. "We come through the gate, and they were over there." He pointed. A figure in white stood on a hill with another figure in grey. "My captain don't know if we should attack or wait. The general, he went up there. They've been there a long time."

Bodb grimly walked toward the hill.

"And just where do you think you're going?" Aramina demanded, grabbing his arm and pulling him back.

"To do my own negotiations." Bodb jerked his arm away, then regretted it. To his surprise, Aramina backed off a pace. He resumed walking.

"Listen to me, young king," The Priestess was saying breathlessly as she struggled to keep up with his angry strides. Bodb's legs were longer than hers, and she was almost running. "There are more diplomatic ways to walk into peace – or bargain – negotiations–"

"I'm through with diplomacy," Bodb grated. He was the one who should be bargaining with MacKegan or welcoming an ally, whichever the general on the hill was doing. Indeed, he was the one who should have led the fighting.

But, he did not. Some feral idiot with disease colorations on his face had to play games. He probably looked like a fool to his men or a traitor for allowing the Five (Six?) to take over the war. Enough was enough. Whoever the wearer of white was—

"Stop!" Aramina hissed, jerking Bodb back again with surprising strength. "How many times must I save you in a day? You trusted my counsel in war, now trust my counsel in this. *Do not interrupt them!*"

They stood feet from the couple on the hill. One was the Silver Fox, who had his back turned. The other, the one in white, was a woman. She turned ice blue eyes toward them and stared. She did not acknowledge their presence, and suddenly Bodb Derg was glad. Something about her perfect face, those silver braids, and the entire whiteness of everything around her was chilling.

Bodb nodded unsurely and turned slightly away to indicate he would wait. From the corner of his eye, he saw the woman nod. Finnbhear turned. Aramina let out a breath, slowly. She squeezed Bodb's arm and let go.

The woman stepped, nay, glided down the hill. Bodb was entranced by her grace and almost forgot to bow when she reached them. Finnbhear did not follow, the young king noted, but disappeared down the other side of the hill. Aramina gave a nervous giggle, grabbed Bodb's arm, and half hid behind him.

"You may call me Cliodna the White," the woman said with a breathy voice. She did not extend her hand, to Bodb's relief. With Aramina hiding behind him, an eerie sensation in itself, he had no desire to insult this fair vision by touching her.

"My lady," Bodb said, managing a bow despite Aramina's tight grip. "To what do I owe the pleasure?"

"The Silver Fox," the woman said plainly. Her eyes never blinked. It was disconcerting. Aramina's grip tightened with a sharp intake of breath.

"My Lady?"

The woman sighed impatiently. "Your kind have become so deaf! Can you not hear? The Silver Fox has won your city for you."

"I see," although he did not. Aramina punched him.

"Follow me," the woman said, beckoning. Bodb, with Aramina in tow, followed her up the hill. As he topped the rise —

The army had been camped below for some time. Elves made weapons, exercised their horses, or sat by fires relaxing. They were the men Bodb had left outside with no way to get word to them. Somehow they had come together and to Cnos Fada's aid.

Walking toward the nearby forest, Finnbhear was accompanied by a small man dressed in brown. Bodb opened his mouth to call his general, but Aramina pulled his hair. He dare not retaliate because of the white woman's stare, although he knew not why. Finnbhear disappeared into the trees.

"Finnbhear has a favor to perform," the woman said.

"My Lady," Bodb sank to the ground, "you have my eternal gratitude. I am lost in knowing how to repay you. You have brought my men and rid Cnos Fada of MacKegan's filth. Any boone I can grant shall be yours."

"Your gratitude yes, but eternity is not something your people possess any more than the humans do. You are mortal yourselves now. Get up." Bodb stood, again confronting those cold eyes. "I have my boone, little king. And this one," she touched Aramina's arm. The werewolf looked like she might faint. "I will have her again, too. In time.

"You rid yourselves of MacKegan's siege with the help of MacKegan's vassals. I admire that. All those below us did was kill those that ran from the fire. And, of course, my own called the sorcerers away in the night."

Bodb blinked away sudden tears. He looked around wildly. The woman was gone.

***

The army entered Cnos Fada with quiet triumph. There was some revelry in the streets, but over all the mood was somber. The siege was ended, but now MacKegan had made his move. They could not hope to retaliate. Cnos Fada was just one small city in the vast lands of Northern Fion.

The sun rose six times. Finnbhear the Silver Fox did not return.

Raori rode in the fields daily on his grey steed. He never had to let it rest, being a creation of magic. Picket ran with Raori when he was not with Moire and baby Liram. However, Raori spent most of his time alone. Aramina avoided everyone, even as a four leg.

The first band of refugees arrived on the seventh day. Covered in dust and half starved, they limped through the gates at dawn. Bodb Derg met them halfway into the city with a basket of food and a table. This he traded for news of the world beyond the fields, sitting in the street and pouring the wine.

Bodb Derg had no supporters so much as acquaintances, many of whom attended his coronation just to look at the last of Fion's blood heirs. MacKegan punished them now for that tiny betrayal. Most were hung on the spot. Very few were taken to Moirfenn. Any who sympathized, indeed were known to in the past, shared their fate. The landscape was littered with smoking homesteads and empty pastures.

"They came for us," one of the refugees, an old woman, said around a scrap of bread. "If it had not been for Fend, oh poor Fend." And she wept, bowing her grey head with shaking shoulders.

"Fend was my older brother," the woman's son said. "He pushed us out the back and cast a glamour so MacKegan's soldiers would not see us. But he wasn't very good."

"No one is very good at the magic anymore," the old woman said, wiping a tear from her eye. "He couldn't cast on himself, my dear, and perished fighting while we escaped. We waited for him in the woods. We waited as long as we could..."

It was something to ponder while atop the wall that evening. There was a little niche even the king did not know about. Raori had confiscated it for himself. Picket left to bring his bride and her son into the city. Even this close to Cnos Fada, the pair were no longer safe.

Inevitably, Raori's thoughts were turned to Aihn's lost daughter, Brighde. Picket's new wife never mentioned her, but a cloud of sorrow hung about her just the same. The pooka was at a loss. He had no experience comforting grieving mothers. He must have been more lost knowing that his former lover lived on in Brighde's body. If ever a Sidhe could find a flux to live in, Picket had found the best.

It was an especially chilly hour of the day. Winter had settled firmly into the ground. Snow clouds billowed slowly toward them on the horizon. Raori knew seventeen spells that would hold them off, but he decided not to use them. The city could use a little snow.

Seventeen spells. He could remember them all, curse his memory, with the clarity of still water. Raori wondered if he were the only one who knew those seventeen spells. He doubted it.

Mage elves found no use for keeping a grimoire, a log of their spells, because of their fantastic memory. This was something humans did, those that could read. Now Raori wondered if he should take their example. Were he to die in battle, those seventeen spells might die with him. Sometimes it cost many lives to find a spell that worked. If he were the only one with his knowledge, its salvation could be in his hands.

Of course, that meant finding an apprentice and teaching him or her to read. Raori shuddered. Such tasks were for old men.

However, he still pondered the thought two days later. He was breaking his evening bread atop the wall, wondering at the cost of parchment, when someone shouted at the gate.

Four riders were admitted, all astride dancing steeds of fine breeding. They were not travel-worn as other refugees, but some refugees were using the ley lines and did not have to travel very far. Their arrival was nothing new, so Raori went back to his bread. The soft sound of paws on stone did not make him pause eating, but he slowed. For a while, he was silent.

"Have you chosen at last to forgive me?" he said without turning around. For a while he received no answer.

Then, "Don't I always, my dear Raori?" Aramina slid into his arms, toppling the food and wine to the ground.

"Yes," Raori said softly. "We'll never learn, I guess."

"Of course not." His beloved grinned a toothy grin. "We're young."

***

Finnbhear the Silver Fox returned to Cnos Fada late that same night, after the moon set and even the night critters were sleeping. The guard at the gate was relieved to see him. Rumors ranged from Silver Fox being dead to transformed into a fish. Finnbhear only corrected half the tale.

It felt strange to be in Cnos Fada at last. Cliodna the White explained he was gone from Fion only eight days, but in her realm he had stayed twelve seasons. He wondered what had happened during this time. How was he to avoid the questions that were sure to be asked about his disappearance?

It felt like he had just closed his eyes when a shy maiden came to his bed with summons from Bodb Derg. Finnbhear groaned, forcing his body into motion. It was damn hard to face the real world this morning.

Or had he left reality to come here? Finnbhear groaned again and put philosophical thoughts behind him.

The great table was cleared from the hall and replaced with elaborate rugs. Bodb sat in his chair, holding his gilded scepter. Finnbhear had forgotten how young the lad was. He greeted the Silver Fox with a cry of pleasure, rising from his chair to grab the elf in a bear hug.

"You should have told me when you'd returned," the young king said testily, sitting again. He motioned for Finnbhear to stand at his left side.

"My pardons," Finnbhear said. "I did not want to wake you."

"Well, I know you're here now. I suppose that will do since I cannot change the past." Bodb smoothed his clothes and twirled the scepter. "I know better than to ask of your adventure. I was told it was you who won the day. Strange woman." He never looked at Finnbhear, but the Silver Fox felt the scrutiny just the same.

"Aramina is just different," Finnbhear said unsurely.

Bodb Derg choked on his laughter. "No. The woman in white."

"Ah," Finnbhear said wisely as he dared.

"Never mind." Bodb laughed again. "You're here to stand while I congratulate our allies. I'm quite glad you came when you did, actually. I would have had to continue this morning without you otherwise. Old Long Arm, Caoimhin, has declined my invitation. Such a surprise, eh? Do they know you're here?"

"Who, milord?" Finnbhear asked before catching on to his lord's disjointed, if jubilant, train of thought. It was a struggle to remember what was happening around the palace after three years. "No, Milord." Finnbhear coughed self-consciously. He wore nothing but plain clothes. The king never took notice, but it would do well if he dressed appropriately next time.

"All the better to surprise them," Bodb said with relish.

At that moment, The Six were ushered into the room by a small hoard of servants. They looked around, mildly confused, before lining up to approach the throne. It was a practiced move, one they must have performed for MacKegan; No mistakes were made. They barely spared Finnbhear a glance, as if afraid to take eyes off their king.

Bodb motioned his allies to bow, which they did. It was a perfect motion, save Midna who sank a second late. When the group arose, Duinn stepped forward.

"We are here at your command," he said, bowing again. The company nodded their heads.

Clearly Bodb was impressed. He hesitated a minute before pointing to Duinn with his scepter.

"Approach me, Blacksmith," he said.

But they hesitated. Picket's eyes looked wild for a second. Even Aramina cringed. Just as Bodb started to frown, Raori spoke. "Forgive us," he said. "Milord, the last time we were given that command was not a pleasant experience."

"I am not MacKegan," Bodb practically thundered. His face grew livid, briefly. "Blacksmith, approach me!"

Duinn obeyed, his back stiff and head held high. When he reached Bodb's feet, he kneeled. Bodb touched his shoulders with the scepter and bade him rise.

"You have my protection for as long as you need it," Bodb said. "In gratitude for what you have done for Cnos Fada, I grant you a boone. A name, if you desire it, and land to start a new life."

Duinn's eyes were suspiciously bright when he rejoined his companions. Bodb called Picket before him. The pooka approached slowly and accepted his boone, which was the same offer of protection and land. From there, the others calmed enormously, and the proceedings were much happier.

Bodb Derg honored all of the companions, even Midna who wanted only to return to his temple. With the ceremony done, Bodb cast all formality aside and ordered food and wine. Even Midna hugged Finnbhear while servants set the table. Before long, the companions were seated and eating heartily.

"It is my hope," Bodb said around his wine cup, "that all of you stay and take positions in my court. I know Finnbhear has his own home – "

"And my roses," growled the elder elf. Bodb chuckled.

"And your roses," he agreed, "but the rest of you do not. MacKegan has only been driven back; he'll be a threat to us so long as he remains in power. I could use you,, all of you. Picket, I will give you and your wife whatever you need. More land, more sheep, just name it. Raori, I am in dire need of a real mage. I hear you are the only one left in Fion. And Aramina – "

"No," she said.

Bodb blinked.

"I am sorry," she said gently. "The others will be happy here, but not I. Not now. Remember Eahn and Leannahn."

The comrades looked uncomfortable. Picket scratched his shoulder, looking down. Raori cleared his throat uneasily while Duinn looked away with pressed lips.

"We have two in MacKegan's clutches," said Aramina with spread hands. "My lord, we were a team once. They were my family. Even Eahn."

Silently, Finnbhear struggled with himself. He wanted to convince her to stay and forget the other two, but it was hopeless. Apparently her goals were not met. And she was not one to give up easily.

Bodb watched him sidelong in expectancy. The young king appeared to be considering the situation, but Finnbhear suddenly knew what the boy wanted. He cleared his throat.

"We're going to save them," he said more for Aramina's benefit than the king's. The king's smile flickered briefly before he adopted a serious, and somehow entirely put on, expression.

"If you survive," Bodb said, "you will find a place waiting for you here. Always. Just," and he took a deep drink of wine, "don't find yourselves on the wrong side of this again. At least, not anytime soon."

***

It was agreed they would wait two days before leaving Cnos Fada. Aramina rejoiced by running in the hills all night. Her friends, the tiny voices, ran with her. Even the wind rejoiced as she bounded from bush to bush.

She returned at dawn with sore paws and an incredible urge to curl in the road for a nap. Raori found her by the big tree in the garden. He spent the day unsnarling tangles in her coat with his fingers. If she were a cat, she would have purred.

"I say we take the ley line to Moirfenn," he was saying. "We never told anyone, except Finnbhear, why we stopped riding the line. MacKegan wouldn't expect us that way, if at all."

Aramina groaned and rolled over, exposing her underbelly. Raori's fingers crawled over her chest. She sighed happily.

"I suppose I should be telling all of this to Finnbhear," Raori said. "He'll be expecting to lead us along. He's a lot like Eahn in that respect, you know. Don't tell him I said that."

Aramina opened one eye.

"I mean it," Raori said. "Would you like to be compared with the Northern Thorn like that?"

She yipped her reply, but the mage was not listening. Someone had wandered into the garden, quite unaware of its current occupants. That someone was human, a young female. Rolling out of Raori's reach, Aramina sat. The movement startled the human.

"I'm sorry," said the young female shyly. "I didn't know there was someone here."

"No, stay," Raori said as the girl backed away. "It's quite alright. I dare say only the king can keep people out of here."

The human fidgeted where she stood, looking around her in obvious awe. Aramina lay her ears back and laughed a little. She remembered what it felt like to be in a new place.

"You act as if you've never seen a tree before," Raori said casually. He scratched Aramina's ear, but distractedly. The scratching was brief because he had to lean over to reach her.

"So I haven't," the girl responded. "I mean, nothing like the trees here. And this village has so many houses! It's a wonder there's room for the people. We have nothing so big in Éire."

"Oh, there are places," Raori said. "But so far away from your island, they might as well be faerie themselves. They have towers with pointed tops, carpets that fly, little spirits they keep in glass bottles, even graves tall as the sky."

"Why would anyone want a grave to fill the sky?" the girl asked incredulously.

"I'm not sure," Raori said with a laugh.

"I never knew the world was big as this." Sure Raori was safe to be around, the girl sat under the tree by him. Aramina let the girl scratch her ear. "Good dog," she said.

"She's not–" Raori began. Aramina barked, cutting him off. The mage did not argue.

"I always thought this place was just a story," the girl continued. "And suddenly, here I am!" She shook her head a little.

Aramina knew the girl was the one kidnapped on Bodb Derg's sluagh ride. The entire city had been alive with gossip for days after it happened. Many had been in favor of seeing her returned, especially after it was reported she wept constantly for her lover. To look at the girl now, one could safely say she meant to stay.

Raori was thinking of his servant, Moire. Aramina could read it on his face, almost hear his thoughts. She laughed another silent lupine laugh. While the two talked, she slipped away. Neither of them noticed.

She was still laughing the next morning. Her companions readied their mounts, who stamped against winter's chill. Someone suggested she conjure herself another horse of ash. She curled up, tail to nose, as if to say her present form suited her. In actuality, she did not want to admit how exhausted she was from their battles. Any horse she conjured would not hold her.

Picket also rode a horse. It was an ironic sight. Aramina snickered at the pooka. His mount misunderstood her intention and spooked. The company spent the next few minutes collecting Picket's belongings from the ground. Midna grumbled but did not whine. Duinn wheezed with laughter.

"Now behave yourself, wicked animal," Raori admonished with a grin. "Picket is only human."

"A better-looking one," the pooka sneered. "Look you, turning gray before your time even! I should be so lucky!" He barked a laugh, urging his mount forward. Raori ducked his head, raking fingers through his bangs. They were indeed lined with grey.

Aramina's laughter faded. That was something she had forgotten about. She wondered if Raori had noticed the change in himself before. It explained a good many things she had seen in him lately, including his tendency to worry about the future. She decided she liked it. Maturity suited the mage well.

Bodb Derg saw them away with a casual farewell. It was too cold for anything else. Midna moaned a little in his furs, huddling on his horse's back and shivering. Aramina laughed again and bit his horse's heel. Their journey from Cnos Fada began by chasing Midna's horse down.

***

True to Raori's prediction, Finnbhear assumed leadership almost immediately. He led them into the forest, where even Picket preferred not to go. It was dark and cold, but not scarey as simple folk believed. All was silent but for the snorting of the horses and their steps in the dead leaves. Aramina disappeared in the trees, returning only to check their path. Duinn mumbled curses at his horse, although he handled it superbly.

Finnbhear's felt inside his shirt automatically. His silver flute was gone, as he knew it would be, but habits died hard. He had been forced to leave it behind in the land of fairy. Now it was where it belonged, with the Sidhe. He must live without music until he could get another.

The loss made him sad. Kegal's flute, a gift when they parted as children, had been his only link to those happy days. Cliodna said he must let go. Who was he to argue with she, a queen of Faery?

Darkness comes faster in the forest. When twilight approached, the company camped between three oak trees. Aramina surveyed the site with a snort before digging a shallow den. Picket looked around nervously, but did not comment. The others did not care or did not notice. It was a quiet night.

As usual, Finnbhear took first watch. Truthfully, he did not feel it necessary. While the others slept miraculously through Raori's snores, Finnbhear leaned against the smallest tree. He thought of his flute again before turning the thought away. A small hand touched his shoulder.

Finnbhear jumped, half drawing his sword. It was only Aramina, who grinned at her mischief. The Silver Fox relaxed.

"I wish you wouldn't do that," he complained.

"Hai, you'll miss it when I'm gone," Aramina retorted.

"Maybe." Finnbhear turned his eyes to the darkness around them. Aramina was close, but he was not tempted.

"What's wrong, Finn?" she asked, touching his chest with her fingertips.

"Him." Finnbhear jutted his chin toward the snoring lump of Raori. "He doesn't understand your free spirit. I don't want to fight over you."

Aramina huffed. "Our passion, that of Raori and myself, is a flame. It will burn out, like every other love in the universe. Like yours did for me." Her smile was kind; the gentlest expression yet with their past mentioned.

"I never stopped loving you completely," Finnbhear said wistfully. "I wish you could forgive me for marrying Llondha. This next time we part, we may never see each other again. At least let me live with a little less regret."

"Oh, Fox." Aramina tossed her ebony locks carelessly. Her fingers caressed her ear. "I never really left you. Haven't we always come back together, despite the odds? You thought me dead, and here I am. After this final adventure, there will be another time."

"Can you say for sure?" Finnbhear pressed, feeling boyish. He was being selfish and immature. He did not care.

"You will see me again," Aramina said. "I promise." She kissed him. He lost his breath, but she gave it back before releasing him. She settled next to him on the tree and tilted her eyes upward.

"You named that cluster the Limping Dragon," Finnbhear said, pointing. "I still remember the story you made up to go with it."

"Oh yes," Aramina laughed. "How could I forget. We made your idiot cousin the victim, don't forget, and Llondha the poor helpless maid!" They laughed softly.

"Why did you turn from me, from all of us?" Finnbhear asked after a silent pause. "I never understood your decision. I would have married you. Given you the world. The temple wasn't everything."

Her recovery was nothing short of a miracle, so all the healers said. The unhappy spirit did not understand, but she nodded and smiled anyway. She would understand in time. Meanwhile, she had to learn how to eat, walk and other complicated things. It was very overwhelming.

Friends and relatives came to visit. Once they learned she did not remember them, they appeared to lose interest. Only Llondha, the body's sister, paid regular visits. Llondha faithfully believed Aramina would remember her in time. The spirit within smiled often, taking selfish delight in this fleshly relationship.

She was still weak when the northern king, Morc of Fomor, paid the temple a surprise visit. The priests had left her in the sunlight that day. Sunshine warmed her, relaxing her muscles. Sleepily, she barely lifted her head to acknowledge the man standing nearby.

"Who is this woman?" the man demanded. The harshness of his voice opened Aramina's eyes wide. She had not encountered such negativity since arriving.

"She was injured in the hills," a priest fawned, wringing his hands, "and has come here to heal. She is very weak and needs help just to move about. If the sight of her offends you, Milord, we can have her moved–"

"Yes," the man said. "Move her to my sleeping chamber. I'll join her there later."

"But, Milord," the priest protested. "She is hardly ours to treat as such, and not well–"

"Do it," the man said. "I am king, and every maiden is mine. She I will have." With that, he turned with a dramatic swirl of his cloak and walked away.

The priest moaned to himself. "I am so sorry," he said to Aramina and helped her to stand. "If we disobey, he'll have this temple burned and all of us killed. He thinks we're an abomination and blames the loss of druidry on us."

"I don't understand," Aramina said as they walked into the temple. "What could he possibly want from me?"

"You do not know? Oh, poor innocent child." The priest moaned again. "If only you were strong enough to run away."

The king found out just how strong she was that night. And many nights after. Aramina was confused at first, then angry. After the king was gone and she, soiled in the eyes of those around her, was given menial chores to earn her keep, Aramina began to get her first taste of bitterness...

Finnbhear sighed happily. His arm was draped around Aramina's shoulder, but suddenly she did not want to be touched. She slipped away. Finnbhear let go, oblivious to her distress. The werewolf shifted, a dark shadow seeking her makeshift den.

Chapter Thirty
"Into Moirfenn's Dark"

They reached the ley gate before the morning mist left the ground. It was a large structure, larger than any other, and in reasonable repair. Solid oak trees, heavy with mistletoe, shaded the clearing where the gate was built. To one side was a large stone table, its purpose mostly forgotten.

"The king's path!" Aramina exclaimed in delight. She dismounted and ran forward to caress the giant stones.

"I thought this place destroyed," Duinn rumbled.

"Not everyone has forgotten how to use the gates," Finnbhear explained, dismounting. He opened his riding pack and withdrew a bundle of rags he had packed for just this occasion. Riding a horse into a working gate was like trying to control a hurricane. The light frightened them, making them unmanageable. Even Picket's mount had to be blinded, so he would not see the gate in action.

Picket whispered reassurances into his horse's ear. It was an untrained animal. There were advantages to being an equine, especially of the enchanted persuasion. Picket could do more than train, he could communicate. Thus far, his horse had learned all it needed to be a lady's mount. The pooka planned to gift his steed to Moire as a late bridal gift.

Finnbhear was first into the gate with Picket bringing up the rear. The ancient ring of stones lit with a soft whoosh. Dead leaves were stirred by the rush of power. They danced away as dustless devils. The horses, blinded, took no notice. Midna, however, shied from them until Aramina took his hand.

The other side of the gate was only worn nubs poking out of barren earth. The light left them all partially blinded. Picket rubbed his eyes, sure the spots would never go away. Aramina sat desolately on a stone.

"Coming here always depresses me," Raori said while unbinding his horse's eyes. "Surely the gates can't have fallen into such disuse in a couple of hundred years. Even humans can remember things longer than that."

"Are you certain it's only been a couple of hundred?" Finnbhear asked with arched eyebrows.

"No more, surely," Duinn said. "Why, the young king is only the old king's grandson, right?"

"Which old king," Midna said confusedly.

"The king you knew," Finnbhear said wisely, "has been dead five generations hence. I could not begin to say how old you are."

"You're still here," Raori said confidently. "Don't tell me you took the path we did."

"My family lives long lives," the Fox replied ambiguously.

"Oh, stop worrying with the past," a new voice interrupted them. "You'll be sitting by the fire cackling like old hens before you know it. Especially you, Raori MacGuinnan."

It was the bard. He had been watching their discussion all the while, seated on a small log nearby. Aramina rushed to embrace him, which he returned fervently. Picket glanced sidelong at Raori. The mage only shook his head, uncaring.

"Paying graces to MacKegan's court?" Finnbhear asked.

"Not until next spring," Oenghus said. "No, I'm here to warn you." He reached into his shirt and withdrew Aramina's medallion. Aramina took it, smiling.

"Eahn was right! The medallion is cursed!" Duinn exclaimed.

"The medallion has nothing to do with this," Oenghus said with an easy laugh. "This was left carelessly in the wild. I found it. I'm returning it to Aramina." He kissed the werewolf on the cheek.

"Then speak your warning," Finnbhear growled. "MacKegan must have felt the power of the gate. If he doesn't know we've arrived, he will soon. I'd like to leave while we can."

"There is a danger in Moirfenn," the harper said.

"I should say so," Picket snorted.

"Shush, fairy, and mind your manners," Oenghus snapped. One look into the bard's cold eyes and Picket obeyed. He wanted to cross this bard no more than he wanted to cross Cliodna the White.

"Well, what is it?" Raori asked, heedless of Picket's uncharacteristic respect.

"I can only say that MacKegan is no longer a threat. He hasn't been for a long time. How else do you think you got as far as you did or that things fell the way they have? You should mind the reasons why." The bard picked his harp off the ground, where it had lain unnoticed until then. "Now I must be off. I wish you well."

"But–" Finnbhear stammered.

"No buts!" Oenghus kissed Aramina on the lips. "I shall see you soon, my love."

"Truly?" the werewolf said happily.

"Dung," Finnbhear swore when he realized the bard meant to take the gate, explanations untold. He mounted his horse, jerking the reins. "We ride. Hammer this bard to the ground; we've got your friends to rescue. If they can be." He rode off a pace and sat waiting, his horse pawing the ground.

Duinn, his mount flanked by Aramina the wolf, followed Finnbhear. Raori was slow mounting his horse. Curious, Picket lingered nearby.

"I think the Fox is jealous," the bard said.

"Everyone seems to be," Picket said blithely.

"So I've noticed," the bard laughed.

"You know, your father doesn't want you involved," Raori said, casually leaning forward in his saddle.

"He told you that?" Oenghus asked. At Raori's nod, "Well, I can't go against him. Pity." He shrugged.

"I suppose not," Raori said, raking bangs with fingers. The bard activated the gate and stepped through. It wasn't until the light had dimmed, taking Oenghus with it, that Raori turned his horse toward Finnbhear. Picket followed closely.

Led by Raori and his memory, they walked old, mostly forgotten roads to avoid confrontation. Aramina and the mage grew increasingly agitated the closer they got to MacKegan's keep, which according to Raori was only two days away.

The two were the only ones uncured by the Moonstone in Tech Danaan. Picket worried ceaselessly, but he kept his thoughts to himself. If the others were as concerned, they made no mention.

The only place to make camp that night was in the open, devoid even the shelter of brush. Trees did not grow in Moirfenn. MacKegan had used all the lumber for war machines long ago. Most cooking fires were fueled with waste or bog peat.

Neither option was available to Finnbhear's company. Raori employed his most exotic fire spell to create their campfire. It fed on a small pile of stones, as any normal fire on wood. The mage grinned into the multicolored flames and looked entirely haunted. Aramina clapped her hands in delight before huddling close to the eerie blaze.

"You must be the only one alive who remembers that spell!" she exclaimed.

Blushing, the mage looked at his feet. "I wonder where to buy the best parchment," he said.

Picket volunteered for first watch. Like Finnbhear, he could stay awake for days and not feel the fatigue. He wore his kilt, but over leggings so he looked entirely confused of his background. It was warm, for all that the wind howled urgently around them. Raori staked his cloak down with rocks so it would not blow away. Aramina, four legged, curled beside him. They were the only other ones awake.

It was apparent the two were doing more than keeping warm. Picket waved his freckled hand by Raori's nose. The mage never budged.

"He struggles against MacKegan still," Aramina's voice said. Picket leapt back, thinking he faced a Feral Beast. The werewolf had semi-shifted so that she appeared as an extremely hairy woman. Picket knew they all could do that, but it was an uncomfortable way to be. The body warred against itself until you went nearly mad with confusion.

Smiling, Aramina let go her twisted form. Her fur faded before Picket's eyes. Slowly, her naked flesh was covered with the black robes she had worn when facing MacKegan's sorcerers down. She huddled closer to Raori, who never noticed.

"You can't tease me," Picket said. "I don't see you as the others do."

"I know," Aramina said. "But practice makes perfect."

"You should do that to Midna." The pair snickered wickedly. Picket relaxed again, grateful for the fire's warmth.

"You're worried," Aramina said. "I can smell it on you. Don't. It's difficult, mostly for Raori, but we'll be fine. MacKegan's influence grows strong the closer we get, but we devoured the Moonstone and are now a part of it. Or it is part of us. Either way, we have our inner strength and each other."

"What were you doing just now?" Picket asked.

"Wards," was the answer. "If you had been doing your job instead of spying on us, you would have noticed the threat that surrounds us. Look." She pointed.

Picket obeyed. At first he saw nothing, then something flitted to the right. It was joined by two others, then the three split up and disappeared again. There was no sound.

"Feral Beasts," Picket said in dread.

"You can't have thought MacKegan was going to let us walk to his door like old friends? We're lucky, though. He truly must not be the threat we feared months ago if this is all he has to send against us. I don't know why he let us live so long, or even why he never showed at Cnos Fada. I do know that from here on, going will be less easy." The werewolf stretched her fingers toward the fire. Her eyelids drooped tiredly. "Between you and I, my brother, I am much weaker since we battled the siege outside the gates. I do not think we will be able to perform those same miracles. This will be a hard fight for all of us."

Picket nodded somberly. "I noticed," he said. "But we can't tell the mortals. They are fragile in their belief."

"Don't wake the others," Aramina said when Picket moved toward Finnbhear. "Raori and I can handle them for a while yet. They'll need to be rested when the beasts do break through."

The night wore on. While Finnbhear, Duinn and Midna slept, the Feral Beasts trotted around the camp. Occasionally, one would attempt to pass Raori's wards. The smell of burned fur wrinkled Picket's nose. The bodies piled around them, but the Feral Beasts remained.

When Raori sagged, face to knees, Picket roused the sleepers. Duinn was on his feet instantly, groping for his halberd. It was smaller than his first, but good enough for the fight. He swung it experimentally just as the ward failed.

Fighting Feral Beasts was always different from other battles. The weakest of the beasts, those who went Feral early in MacKegan's service, rushed headlong. They threw themselves on the companions' weapons; a suicide attack to weaken the foe. The stronger beasts hung back, conferring. They need only wait until the group tired.

Picket lost his sword early in the fight. He shifted to four legs and stomped anything furry that moved. Aramina and Raori stood together by the fire. Raori sagged, too exhausted to stand. Aramina's fingers blazed with atma as she defended him. More burned bodies piled around them.

Picket bucked and sent two beasts flying into the darkness. A large beast landed on his back and ripped into his mane with fierce claws. Picket screamed and rolled. He felt the body crush beneath his weight. He rolled over the beast a second time before seeking a new foe. It was not a long search.

Aramina's cry caught his attention. Raori had been snatched from her. Two beasts dragged him by the feet away into the darkness. He lived only through his atma shield which weakly bubbled around him. When it failed, they would rip him to shreds.

Aramina tried to follow, but other beasts kept her at bay. Picket also tried to reach him, but three beasts grappled his legs. Enraged, Picket bit one's ear off. The creature howled and let go. His leg freed, Picket crushed the skulls of the other two. They were quickly replaced. Before he was trapped again, he summoned all his energy and leaped. The momentum carried him into the piles of bodies.

Finnbhear somehow managed to reach Raori and his captors. The beasts were unwilling to release their prize and snapped menacingly at the Silver Fox. The old elf sighed visibly, raising his sword and shouting a single word. The sword glowed, slashed out seemingly on its own, and Raori was free. The heads of the Feral Beasts rolled a few feet away.

Picket refused to feel incredulous. He knew Finnbhear knew some magic. Knew it, but somehow it had never registered. The Silver Fox had never used magic in battle against him, why would he now? Finnbhear, attempting to get Raori to his feet, slipped and sagged himself. Picket had his answer: Finnbhear's resources were very limited.

Aramina fought to reach Raori and Finnbhear, but beasts still blocked her way. The Silver Fox could not leave the mage, who weakly tried to summon enough atma to fight. Duinn fought a large beast alone. Midna cowered behind the dwarf. The field was littered with bodies.

His latest foe trampled, Picket galloped to Finnbhear and Raori, shifting to two legs just as he reached them. He grabbed Raori's shoulder and sent atma into the mage. Raori suddenly stood straight and thrust his arms out. Atma poured from his fingers and struck the beasts attacking Aramina. With a final howl, they were reduced to cinders.

"You should do that more often," he complained to the pooka.

Picket muttered weakly, "No, I shouldn't."

Duinn dispatched his own foe a second later. Its blood sprayed across Midna's robes. The acolyte shuddered but did not complain. Everyone stood ready, but no more beasts came.

Picket found a clear spot of ground and sat. He was suddenly very tired.

"Why couldn't you have done that in the first place?" Finnbhear asked Raori.

"There is no way I could've killed all those Feral Beasts like that," the mage said weakly. "If the wards had not killed so many before, we would probably be dead by now. If Picket hadn't… hadn't..." He fainted.

A wild howl cut through the waning darkness. An answering howl echoed to them. The sun was rising, but light was no protection against Feral Beasts. Aramina wiped gore from her face with her robes. They were ripped, abused from the battle. She looked like a banshee.

"Hurry, grab everything," Finnbhear ordered. "They're coming."

All the horses except Raori's smokey creation had bolted during the fight. It looked at them with drooping eyes, as if bored by the entire situation. Desperately, the companions loaded everything possible including Raori, who seemed to be recovering, onto its back. Distant howls echoed closer to them.

Picket hopped from foot to foot. Another howl reverberated through the air, crawling his back. With a shiver, he shifted to four legs. He slapped his back with his tail and felt slightly better..

Midna mounted behind Raori while everyone else shifted to their animal forms. They were just in time. Two beasts appeared over the nearest hill.

The companions ran for their lives. Raori's horse galloped speeds to match the pooka's, never stumbling over pits and rocky terrain. Aramina matched their pace, but never seemed worried. In that shape, she was safe from Feral attention. She smelled like one of them.

Finnbhear fell behind, but not for long. Picket turned, dashed behind, and scooped up the little fox by the tail with his teeth. Bristles of fur tickled his sensitive nose. Trying not to sneeze, Picket rushed to catch up with Raori's mount.

A small area of brush stood against the barren terrain. The companions collapsed there. Finnbhear set his strongest protective wards while Picket, on two legs, made a camp fire. Raori slept where he collapsed on the ground. Aramina curled by him, warming him as best she could with her fur.

Duinn remained in his boar shape even though he usually discarded it soon as possible. His reasons were his own and soon revealed when, rutting, he produced truffles. Midna pounced on them with a glad cry and, with the only cooking pot they had saved, started cooking their meal. Duinn grunted once before retaking his two legged shape.

"About time you earned your keep," Picket murmured.

The dwarf snapped, "What did I do while you were leaping about in the battle? I rescued the miserable acolyte's hide!" Midna wisely ignored the remark and concentrated on the soup.

·"Ha... and what were you doing while I rescued Aramina and Raori from MacKegan's army? Sleeping!" Picket grinned, careful to avert his face from Duinn's view.

"Why," the dwarf blustered, "I was wounded, ye idiotic wight!"

Finnbhear stepped between them, grabbed Picket's arm and looked him in the eye. The Fox's hazel eyes had a glint to them, something that reminded Picket of Cliodna. Whatever had passed for Finnbhear beyond reality's veil, it showed. Picket felt himself shrink away, awed by of this mortal elf.

The mock fight ended without a word. Picket retook equine form and paced the wards' edges, watching the land around them.

***

Raori opened his eyes because he had to. Someone was shaking him quite roughly, and his neck was beginning to hurt. His assailant was Aramina, who smiled fleetingly before disappearing. The mage sat, holding his spinning head. He could not remember swallowing a tavern's wealth in drink, but his body swore he had.

"Eat," someone said, shoving a pot of soup into his hands. Its aroma was delicious. Raori devoured the soup then licked the pot clean. Done, he searched for wineskins. There were none.

"We left the wineskins?!?" Raori cried. Everyone laughed.

"Now that you're with us," Finnbhear said, "we can go. The Feral Beasts haven't found us yet, but they will if we don't move."

"Do you know where we are?" Duinn asked, handing the mage a waterskin. Raori wrinkled his nose, but drank the vile stuff. At least his thirst was killed.

"No," Raori said, "wait. Yes. That's a burial mound over there. The Hedinach place."

"I remember him," Aramina said, wrinkling her nose prettily. "He wanted us to help him assassinate MacKegan."

444

"That's the past, and he's dead," Finnbhear grunted. Raori felt the wards release; like a bubble popping. That was their cue. Everyone but Midna shifted forms.

Raori, tingling with the feel of being a cat, perched in front of Midna on the horse. It was easier on him that way. The heavier the load on the horse, the greater the strain on his atma. He was surprised the horse still existed after his collapse that morning. Well, it was there. The companions moved on.

Through the day, they saw only one Feral Beast. It was at a distance and ignored them. Raori knew it was the company's animal shapes that protected them. Midna, despite his normal appearance, was unknown and masked by his friends' odors.

Evening deepened. Howls, sounding like desperate cries, pierced the air. They were not hunting calls, just pack communication. Raori wondered if they remembered their former lives.

MacKegan's mental presence increased the further they traveled into Moirfenn. Raori could feel the old elf trying to take control in the same way Leannahn had done. Ironically, Leannahn's cruelty had been a kindness. If she had left him alone, Raori would not know how to keep MacKegan away. Privately, Raori thanked his former friend. Wherever she may be.

They camped in the open again, this time in animal shape behind triple wards. Midna lay encircled by the unusual pack, kept warm by fur and hide. When morning was light enough, they broke camp swiftly.

MacKegan's keep loomed from the morning fog. There were no lights around it, nor any other sign of life. The company, in human form, stared for a while. Raori raked his bangs with his fingers.

"We should have been challenged by now," Duinn said uneasily.

"Maybe someone beat us to the old weasel," Raori said, straightening his cloak. "Come on." He did not wait to see if he was followed. The path ahead beckoned. MacKegan called him on, almost begging. Well, Raori would come. What happened when he got there was another matter.

The gates were open. Four guards lounged outside beside a small green fire. They looked once at the group, then huddled back to the flame. It was almost as if they were afraid. Raori pondered that while they passed down the silent halls of the slumbering fortress.

Inside the dank halls, a lone human replaced guttering torches with fresh ones. She dropped her load at the sight of them and ran.

"Are you always greeted this way?" Finnbhear asked. The fresh torches sputtered against the cold floor.

"I didn't expect a warm homecoming, but this is eerie," Raori said.

The doors to MacKegan's great hall stood ajar without the customary guards. Everyone looked at each other. Aramina became a wolf to dip her nose to the ground. When done, she whined.

"Hai!" Duinn shouted to the darkness. A slight figure bolted from the shadows and down the hall. Immediately, Finnbhear's group gave chase. The dwarf's speed left the others behind. His shouts echoed back to them.

Raori was the first to catch Duinn. The dwarf had someone cornered in a dark shadow. A flash of green caught his eye.

"Come out," the dwarf said patiently. "Have we killed you yet?"

"You might," a feminine voice whispered.

"Only if we have to," Raori said. With the pounding of feet, the others finally arrived. Raori waved them still and Duinn back. Aramina growled softly. Edging forward, Raori lit a small atma light.

A young woman looked at them with widened eyes. Her clothes were ripped and dirty. She covered her face with her mantle, the green that had caught Raori's eye.

"I promise I won't hurt you," Raori said softly. "Can you tell us what happened here?"

Something rumbled behind him. It was Picket. His ears might well have been laid back, if his human form allowed it. Raori turned back to the girl, who no longer hid her face.

Brighde.

Or was it Leannahn? In either case, Raori could not believe his eyes.

"Don't look at me that way!" the woman-child cried with a familiar stamp of foot. "Just leave me alone. Go away!" She burst into tears and covered her face again.

"What happened to you?" Raori asked incredulously. She looked starved. Even MacKegan's slaves were healthier. Compassionately, Raori gathered the girl into his arms. Aramina barked a warning, too late.

At first touch, Raori knew who he held in his arms. There was no mistaking her atma resonance, especially after hosting her in his body. She was stiff at first, then relaxed. The tears flowed freely.

"I took Eahn home and asked my uncle to heal him," the girl once called Brighde sobbed, "but... " When her voice trailed away, it left a sense of horror. "He's in the dungeon. They provoke the changes. I... I think it's too late for him."

Raori watched the girl in the ripped green mantle cry with ever-narrowing eyes. For all she had been friend and companion, she was a changeling now. The sickness would fall on her more swiftly, if it came at all.

He knew not to trust her, but he could not leave her like this. Picket backed away, his eyes nearly white with emotion. Aramina's ears were flat against her head. Even Midna's face showed lines of disapproval.

"The king knew better than to believe your excuse for coming here," Finnbhear said neutrally. "As usual. He was sure you meant to kill MacKegan instead, but could not hold you to him. Well now, you've found one of your lost comrades. What do we do with her?"

"Kill her," Duinn said flatly.

"You can't!" Leannahn screeched, flinging herself away. The only place to go was the wall. She huddled there like a cornered mouse.

"No," Raori said.

"How can you say that after what she's done to you?" Duinn asked. "After everything you told us–"

"You can't possibly know everything she's done," Raori replied, remembering a frightened woman's face in a dark alley. "But still I say no. It's not completely her fault."

"You're right," Picket said slowly. He came forward, clearly forcing himself. "This is MacKegan's doing. He knew what would happen if we took that spear. He might even have helped her, his only kin, but I'll bet he laughed. Didn't he?"

"Yes," sobbed Leannahn. She crumpled to the floor.

"The death of my Brighde was just an accidental benefit," Picket rumbled sadly.

"Where is everyone?" Finnbhear asked gently.

"Most went to fight Cnos Fada," Leannahn said. "The rest either sleep or are still passed out from the night's drinking. We have few servants."

"You can still control the Fell ones, can't you?" Raori asked, lifting Leannahn to her stolen feet. "We can free Eahn and escape before the household wakes completely."

Leannahn nodded shakily. Raori exchanged a wise look with Finnbhear. There was something the girl was not saying.

"The dungeon is this way," Leannahn was saying, straightening her clothes. She started to lead, but Aramina hung back.

Raori knew why Aramina came to Moirfenn. Only now did he stop to think about it. He should have done so before. Was standing in the jaws of MacKegan's mouth worth it?

Yes.

"MacKegan first," Raori said, scratching his beloved's ears. "Then we worry about Eahn. He's in a dungeon cell. Where is the Northern Thorn going to go?"

Aramina barked then trotted down the hall. First, Raori followed. When everyone else fell in behind, Aramina turned and growled.

"We might need help," Raori said. Aramina would not be moved. She did not want the others coming.

"Looks like we worry with Eahn first after all," Finnbhear said easily. "Very well, Leannahn. Lead the way, won't you?" With a jaunty wave from Duinn, Raori's teammates turned with Leannahn into the darkness.

Raori was not comfortable splitting the team, especially since that meant he and Aramina had to face MacKegan alone. Arguing with Aramina was pointless, so he held his reservations. They walked the hall in silence, almost creeping. It was tempting, but Raori did not take animal form. Aramina was animal enough for both of them.

The door to MacKegan's great hall was still ajar. Aramina slipped in like water, but Raori was too big. The door creaked when he moved it.

"There you are," MacKegan said from across the hall. Wrapped in otter fur and ermine tails, he was alone, and the tables were devoid of food. Shock struck Raori numb. The proud lord was a shell of himself; frail, weak and suddenly old. "Where are the others? I know where the werewolf is, by the way, so you might tell her to come out now."

Aramina stepped from the shadows a woman. She wore her brown dress. Where it came from, Raori could only speculate. She had a way of doing things others thought impossible.

"And you," MacKegan cackled. He slumped in his chair uncharacteristically. "Well, my dear, I give you permission to leave your forest and this is your thanks. Are you the only two with the graces to pay your former lord a visit?"

"They are with our companions," Aramina said before Raori could speak. Her warning look silenced him. She meant to handle this alone.

"Come to free the Northern Thorn?" MacKegan laughed again, a high pitched sound. "I should like to see it when they find him. If they can."

"Leannahn helps them," Raori said despite himself. Aramina barred her teeth in his direction. MacKegan laughed again.

"My niece is a survivor." MacKegan snapped his fingers. A small child holding bottle and cup approached from the shadows. The old elf took the bottle and offered it to Raori. The mage shook his head. "He can't help it, my dear," toward Aramina's flashing eyes. "Even though you ate those shards of Moonstone (yes, I watched you all the while), I hold you still. I wanted to know, and the mage told me." He cackled again. "You were too far away then for me to stop you, not that I cared, but now you stand before me."

Aramina growled. Clearly, she wanted to attack but held back. Raori walked to her. At least, he tried. His legs refused to work. Chulain MacKegan continued to laugh.

"Your essence within me," the elf said, "also protects me. You cannot harm me without harming yourselves. Your spirits know this. You, lovely Aramina, I want to thank. It has been you keeping me alive while my niece," he snarled the word, "crept in to feed. Yes, I know your secret. Your essence, so unlike anyone else, told me. Perhaps Leannahn doesn't know yet, but she will. Unless I can kill her first. Perhaps you will help me, my lady, when you see what she does to your friends. You don't want to see your dear old lover, Finnbhear, an empty husk, do you?"

"No," Aramina spat. "But I will not help you. I've come to regain myself, Chulain MacKegan. I will see this through!"

"Very well." Standing was a struggle for him, but MacKegan managed it. He clapped his hands.

The largest Feral Beast Raori had ever seen leapt at Raori from the shadows with a wild snarl. The mage ducked and rolled just in time. He could credit MacKegan with this: the old man liked a good fight enough to release them. The beast howled and turned on Aramina.

She met him in like shape, a powerful beast of fur. They grappled, snarling. Aramina became a wolf and leaped for the beast's throat. The beast turned aside and gouged Aramina with a blow from his claws. The werewolf yelped, thrown to the floor, and struggled to her feet. The Fell beast advanced.

Desperately, Raori raised his hands to call lightening. He froze in the position, unable to move again. MacKegan's voice cackled near his ear, although the elf was feet away.

"Let them," the voice said. "They've been wanting to fight for centuries. Stay, stay. I'll wager twenty shells and a silver cup that my Thorn wins."

"Aramina, it's Eahn!" Raori cried just before MacKegan froze his lips. The beasts battled on, rolling as each sought the right shape to win over the other. Aramina was human, then lupine, then somewhere between. She scored occasionally against the Northern Thorn, but the wound in her side bled heavily. She was slowing and he, Raori, could do nothing but watch.

Aramina was thrown. She made no sound as she regained her feet, human, and called forth an atma shield. The Northern Thorn's claws glowed as they scratched the magical surface. Aramina stood firm, but could not move without releasing the shield.

Raori felt MacKegan in his mind; a blanket controlling everything but his breath and senses. If he could run, escape, MacKegan would lose control again with distance. But that would leave Aramina alone. And first, he had to break free.

Aramina released her shield, rolling to stand on all fours. She dodged another swipe by Eahn. Blood trailed the floor.

Raori searched his memory, trying to find the key. He remembered Leannahn and her former control over him. This was a lot like that, only worse because Leannahn would not have forced Raori to watch Aramina die slowly at Eahn's hands. .

Aramina's ribs heaved as she gasped for breath. Her last dodge had been slow. Another wound bled along her flank. Raori closed his eyes. He could not stand to watch.

Deprived of the visual world, Raori's trained senses automatically cast around him. That was how he found the thin atma cord connecting him to MacKegan. He could feel MacKegan's influence pulsing down it. Almost without thinking, Raori pushed himself up... and could move his arms.

Aramina yelped again.

With a wild yell, Raori thrust all his atma through the cord. He opened his eyes just as it hit and blew MacKegan back. The elf yelled from pain and collapsed on the ground. Raori cried out, too, as did Eahn and Aramina. MacKegan's pain was their pain. It hit Eahn the hardest, for Feral Beasts were the closest bound to their master.

Aramina did not let the pain stop her. While Eahn crouched on the ground, moaning, she made her final leap into Eahn's throat. The fight, and Eahn's misery, was over. She made her final shift, tossed her black mane over her shoulders. Blood coated her bare body. At least the bleeding was slowing.

"You did it," she said breathlessly. "I always said you'd make the world's greatest mage!" They embraced, forgetting for the moment where they were.

MacKegan groaned, struggling to sit. His legs were burned nubs. Despite that, he glared at the pair.

"You'll return it now," Aramina crooned, stepping to the dark lord.

"No!" MacKegan shouted, flaring atma from his hands, sending it out in destructive bursts. It washed over the werewolf, blew her hair back, but otherwise she was unharmed. He prepared another atma blast.

Raori sprang forward, alarm energizing his limbs. There was no need. Aramina reached MacKegan unharmed, caressed his cheek with one hand. MacKegan's hands fell as the dark elf succumbed to her seduction.

It came out of him in a rush; the glow of her stolen atma. Aramina sighed and let her hand drop. MacKegan, weakened further, collapsed in a charred heap.

"Free," she whispered, tears choking her voice. "Ah, how can your kind stand it?"

"What?" Raori asked numbly. Before his rounding eyes, Aramina's wounds knit together and disappeared. She never even noticed. Rather than voice his amazement at her latest spectacular feat of magic, Raori contented himself with knowing she was alive.

"Take yourself back while you can," Aramina advised. "He'll die soon."

Unsure how to proceed, Raori touched MacKegan's sweaty brow. His atma greeted him of its own. It was the sweetest feeling in the world. Raori's mouth fell open, he sat enraptured.

Something else touched him. MacKegan's force, entwined with Raori's, also poured into the mage's limbs.

"See, uncle?" the child laughed. The wine goblet floated shakily, but it was a superb achievement for a small child. She promised to be a strong mage. "I can do it all by myself!" And she hugged him.

"Wonderful," Chulain said. "It must run in the family, eh?" And, smiling, he looked into those precious eyes...

Alarmed at first, Raori fought it. Then he realized what he had gained. The foreign knowledge told him this was inevitable. Touching souls took from each other when parting.

Aramina touched his arm. Raori looked at her and knew what she was. He knelt and kissed her hand.

"Oh, get up," she said irritably. "As if it makes a difference now. We need to find Finnbhear before Leannahn strikes."

Chapter Thirty-One
"A Final Foe"

To reach the dungeons, Finnbhear and his reduced band had to leave the keep. The dungeon entrance was a large door in the earth behind the larder. Stairs leading down waited. Either things were darker than usual, or the small band remembered things differently. The dwarf could not decide which. Only small torches, spaced far apart, were lit. The companions stumbled over each other. Duinn cursed at them, for he was the shortest and easiest trod on.

"Where is he?" Finnbhear asked when they finally reached the line of cells. No moans came from the pit, nor arms reaching through the bars. Leannahn closed her eyes, trying to forget that harvest.

"In there," she said, pointing to Eahn's former cell. She stood to the side and let the others pass.

"It's too dark in there to see," Finnbhear complained.

Duinn, who held no interest for spying dark dungeon cells, hovered near the stair entrance. "Just get him out of there," he growled. "Knock him senseless, I say, and Leannahn can teleport us to Raori and Aramina."

"I can do that," Leannahn agreed readily. The acolyte looked at her askance. She ignored him.

"Very well," Finnbhear agreed dubiously. He gave Leannahn a strange look before melting apart, with atma, the lock to Eahn's cell. The show of strength was lost on Leannahn, who never knew how rarely he used his power. Duinn, on the other hand, grunted appreciatively. The door swung open soundlessly. Finnbhear and Picket stepped inside together, prepared to grapple with the Feral Beast.

Swift as sunlight, Leannahn slammed the door behind them. She melted the door together with her own atma. Finnbhear and Picket slammed into the door too late. The acolyte yelled, stepping forward. Leannahn put him to sleep with a quick touch. Duinn charged her. She dodged nimbly. The dwarf smashed into the cell door and slumped.

"Idiot," Leannahn said. "You should know I would be prepared for you. You'll be my first, then."

Daintily, she knelt by her former companion and reached a hand to him. She was trembling from exhaustion; the use of her atma had drained her reserves. Picket reached a hand through the bars and grabbed her wrist.

"Don't," the pooka pleaded. His grip was firm, but not painful. He could hurt her, and Leannahn knew it. She struggled to pull free.

"If you hurt this dwarf, I can safely swear that Bodb Derg will have you hunted until the end of your unnatural days," Finnbhear said. Leannahn shrank from him. The Silver Fox's eyes glinted like cold stars from the shadows.

"Picket, let me go!" Leannahn cried. The pooka held tighter, yanking her close.

"Finnbhear, go away," Picket said without turning his head.

"But," the Silver Fox protested,, only to be cut short when Picket shouted, "Go!" To Leannahn's horror, Finnbhear walked to the farthest corner of the cell and sat with his back turned. Involuntarily, Leannahn squealed.

"What are you going to do to me?" Leannahn faltered. Her heart stopped. Picket's face was very grave, very long.

"Hush," Picket admonished in a whisper. "I'll help you, and you can leave Duinn alone. But you'll have to let us go."

His face was burned from touching the iron bars. Leannahn had forgotten what touching dead metal did to the Sidhe. Stabs of remorse brought tears to her eyes.

"Picket," Leannahn said, "I'm so sorry. I can't let you out. The lock is melted, and my energy is almost spent. If I don't," she gulped, "feed soon, I'll die."

"Hush," Picket said again. His smile was for her. "Here." Then he closed his eyes. Despite the iron between them, his hand pulsed with life. Leannahn tried to recoil from it, but survival won. She had to feed. Reluctantly, she allowed herself to dip into Picket's offering and take it. Every inch of her body was soon suffused with Picket's life. Finnbhear was somewhere in the background, shouting for them to stop. Hands were shaking Picket's shoulders.

"Picket?" Leannahn wavered. The pooka's grip released, Picket lay on the ground. He did not answer her. "Picket? Oh no!"

Leannahn ripped the cell door from its place without effort and threw it to the side. Finnbhear was by Picket. He tried to keep her away, but she blasted him down with her new energy. Picket moaned softly when she rolled him over.

"You can't die!" Leannahn cried. "Take it back. Please take it back!" She willed herself into the pooka, but the energy would not go. Weeping, Leannahn collapsed over her ex-lover's body.

"So you have a heart after all," Duinn said groggily. Holding his head, he staggered into the cell. "What happened to Picket?"

"My fault," Leannahn choked.

"I think Picket fed your changeling," Finnbhear said. "But I'm not sure." He fumbled for his sword, clumsy from grief and shock. Duinn snarled something inaudible. Leannahn waved the Silver Fox's weapon away in distraction.

"Just go," Leannahn said, withdrawing from Picket. "Take him and go. Eahn is with my uncle. He knows you're here and waits in his great hall. I would hurry." She wiped the tears from her eyes. "Duinn, you know the way."

By rights, the men should have cut Leannahn down. She waited for them to, but they only lifted Picket in silence and withdrew. The acolyte awoke with a touch. He was only too eager to help carry the pooka up the stairs.

She did not watch them go. Her tears blinded her.

***

Picket was a heavy load. There was not enough room on the stairs for Midna to help. He went ahead to watch the entrance.

Even in human form, Picket weighed as much as a fat horse. Duinn cursed often on the way out of the dungeon. He had Picket's feet, the heavy end, and struggled not let them drag.

"Put... him... down," Finnbhear gasped. Duinn was more than happy to obey. Picket thumped to the floor.

"This is insane," Duinn said. "We should go back and kill that creature before she does this to anyone else."

"No matter now," Finnbhear said. "She'll be gone. Didn't you pay attention to her? If Eahn is with MacKegan, then we should hurry to help your living friends."

"We'll never get there dragging Picket like this," Duinn muttered. They dare not leave Picket behind, but Aramina and Raori needed them.

"Well," Finnbhear said, grabbing Picket's shoulders. "Come on."

It was starting to rain when they emerged from the dungeon. Midna was already soaked from waiting outside. Duinn found more curses. He hated water of any kind.

The rain splashed into Picket's eyes. The pooka blinked, kicked and grunted. The movement made Duinn's hands slip. Picket landed roughly.

"What are ye doin' wit me?" the pooka said. He sat, apparently none the worse for wear, and wiped his eyes. "Ye threw me in the mud!"

Duinn crowed. "You're alright!" He patted the pooka's shoulders. The rain was falling harder, but the dwarf no longer cared. All was suddenly bright in the world.

"We thought Leannahn killed you," Finnbhear said, helping Picket to his feet.

"It takes more than that to end one of my kind," Picket said with a grin. He wobbled on his feet, but refused Midna's offered shoulder. "I maun admit, you'll not see the horse of me for a while, though."

"This is enough," Duinn said happily.

"Quiet!" Finnbhear hissed. "Someone comes!"

The team dove back below ground, just beyond the dungeon doors. Duinn peeked through a crack. Picket prodded him from behind.

"What do you see?" the pooka hissed.

At the moment, Duinn saw nothing. He indicated such with a swift kick. Picket grunted.

Two elves, male and female, came around a corner. The man wore a long grey cloak against the pouring rain. The woman was dressed in blue gossamer and stepped lightly beside her companion. She was dry.

"It's the Priestess and Raori," Duinn said before opening the doors. Picket nearly trampled him to get out.

"Hai!" Raori called when he spied the approaching friends. Everyone embraced. Midna kissed Aramina's hands. The werewolf blushed happily.

"Where is Leannahn?" Raori asked, looking around for her.

"We left her in the dungeon," Picket said. Duinn opened his mouth and got elbowed in the ear. "She told us about Eahn."

"We met," Aramina said. She looked radiant. "MacKegan is dead."

The news was met with astonished silence. "Dead?" Duinn said, the first to break the silence. "Hai, won't His Highness be glad to hear it! And here he was worrying about further attack!"

"Well, I'd say we're finished here," Finnbhear said with satisfaction. He clapped his hands together. "We've done more than we came to do, I'd also say." Aramina's grin was nothing short of mischievous. "Let's go home before some loyal idiot decides to take revenge."

"Fair enough," Raori said. He snapped his fingers. Six whirlwinds erupted around them, widened and settled into brown-grey horses. The largest stamped once and snorted.

"And Leannahn said you couldn't magic dust from a desert storm," Duinn laughed.

***

Although it did not seem necessary, the Five wanted to camp as far away from Moirfenn as possible. This turned out to be a good distance, for Raori's conjured steeds walked faster than any horse. They stopped near a mound of large rocks. The rain had stopped, but the clouds were threatening the world with snow.

One solitary howl sang through the air. Aramina assured the company that it was only a wolf. The night passed uneventfully. It was relaxing after all the action they had seen.

It did snow lightly the next day. Those that had thought to bring them donned heavier clothes. Raori conjured furs for those that did not. Aramina disdained all such garments. She and her blue dress rode haughtily onward. She appeared perfectly warm, from her rosy cheeks to her bare feet.

They reached the stone nubs of the ley gate late that evening. Relief washed over the group. Their journey was over at last.

Raori banished the horses one by one. He apparently enjoyed the task, as if he had never shown his power off before for anyone. Finnbhear waited impatiently by the stones with everyone else. Aramina sighed and paced the area. Taking her medallion out of her bodice, she admired it in the waning light.

Later, no one could decide just how MacKegan's surviving sorcerer got so close to them. Raori swore that he would have felt it if magic had been involved. Duinn argued that point, as there was no cover to hide behind.

However it was done, Aes managed not to be seen until he grabbed Aramina from behind. Everyone stumbled forward until Aes pulled a knife. The werewolf relaxed in Aes' grip.

"We can talk about this," Finnbhear said shakily. "Let the girl go." He remembered the sorcerer from their meeting in Cnos Fada. His knees went weak, seeing Aramina in his clutches.

"Aes," Raori pleaded, "MacKegan is dead. This is pointless–"

"I warned you," Aes screamed, jerking Aramina's head back by the hair and brandishing his knife. "Watch her die, traitor!"

Raori chanted fast as he could, throwing the spell forward with cramped fingers. Aes' knife cut its path, leaving a red trail, before the mage could reach his target. Raori's atma shoved into Aes, the icy blast of his spell catching the sorcerer full in the chest and throwing him back.

"Mina," Raori sobbed, lifting the werewolf's limp body. He buried his face into her chest, getting blood on his arms and cheek. Aramina's eyes watched him unblinkingly, the light slowly fading out of them.

Aes coughed, rising to his feet. Picket was on him, holding his shirt with a spotted hand and snorting softly. His fist punched the elf into a dazed stupor.

Like a stalking panther, Raori dropped Aramina's body into her blood and rose to approach the dazed sorcerer.

"Stop him," Finnbhear commanded, even as he knelt beside his sister-in-law's body. "Raori, come to your senses!"

But the others, even Midna, stepped aside as the mage let loose his rage. Fire, snow, wind, even glowing spears barbed with poison pierced Aes' body and buried him in a heap of glowing elemental weaponry. The sorcerer tried to fight back at first, but he could not surpass Raori's speed nor equal the power of Raori's grief.

Finnbhear closed his eyes to the scene and reminded himself that he was dealing with former minions of Moirfenn. Aes was getting only what he deserved. It did not make the elf's dying screams of agony any easier to hear.

No one noticed the skulking shadow that crept to Aramina's body, gasped in dismay, and ran away. Away to the ley gate, jumping into the light, taking the first direction offered.

No one was there when the shadow stepped into the mortal world. It was the way Leannahn wanted it. She sank to the ground, choked with guilt and sorrow, and wept until nightfall.

***

They took Aramina's body with them through the gate and buried her near the forest edge. Raori wept bitterly over the mound of stones that was her grave. He sat there until dawn, when Finnbhear came and touched his shoulder. Raori looked up, and the Silver Fox handed him two full bottles of wine.

And two large goblets.

***

Duinn and Picket were gone ahead to Cnos Fada. One went to grieve with his wife. The other went to grieve with his friend. Midna went with them because the pair insisted. Picket had an arm thrown around the acolyte's shoulders when they disappeared from view.

Raori and Finnbhear passed out leaning on each other. Two bottles of wine had not been enough. Raori had conjured two more barrels. Only one was half full. In their stupor, they did not hear the soft approach of someone out of the mist. Had they been awake, they still might not have seen her, although Raori stood a better chance at it than Finnbhear.

It was just as well.

She hovered near Finnbhear for the time it takes a butterfly to choose the next flower. A second entity approached her, nearing with the ease of dominance. She was smaller but not intimidated. Her greeting was distracted.

The smaller entity stooped over Raori and touched his cheek. Her glowing essence reflected hues of blue, green and yellow. The blessing lingered on his skin for half a second before absorbing into his flesh. The mage sighed and smiled.

Sliding forward, the large entity took the smaller in a light embrace. "He will miss you," the larger reflected.

"It's best this way,' said the smaller. Facing the wilderness around them, she flickered, "How wonderful to be finished with that dreadful mission at last! Are you coming with me?"

"At last," the larger echoed. "Mortality has given you a new sense of time."

"Will you come?" repeated the smaller.

"I have another place I must be," the larger said regretfully. "But we will meet again, when the seasons change."

"I will wait," said the smaller. She drifted away toward the trees. Her light flickered bright enough for the mortal eye to see it. Just beyond the crowded branches, will o' the wisps collected around her, welcoming her home.

The larger entity touched earth, found form, adjusted the straps to his harp case and started walking. He did not shift again until he had to, and then he winged toward his island. The waters of Tech Danaan greeted the swan with tranquility.

It was not a bad way to spend the seasons. Oenghus did not mind so much anymore.

Chapter Thirty-Two
"Circles of Seasons"

Memories reside in the holder's heart, and in essence Aramina lived on with them. Each of Aramina's former companions never thought to see her again, but they did in their own special ways.

For Duinn, he recalled her face while working in his new forge just north of Tech Danaan. She danced in the flames of his furnace, graced the sculptured statues he made for leisure. He heard her clear voice in the ringing of his hammer. Walked his memories beside her when recounting events to his new wife and children.

As dwarves are creatures of stone, and stone no matter how old can last forever, she possibly lives with him still today.

***

Midna attained high priesthood and lived in the temple at Cnos Fada until his death centuries later. He cleaned the Trickster's altar daily, prayed there and encouraged new servants to his god's service. A lock of hair, the one Aramina had placed on the altar, was kept at his breast until the end. Every morning, before his prayers, Midna would hold the lock and look, just look…

***

Leannahn last thought of the Priestess when she walked a strange shore. Lost, afraid, cold from the winds that battered her tired body, she envied Aramina her death. How lovely it would be to lay down and die. Try as she might, Leannahn could not spurn the instinct to live. At some point, she collapsed near the onrushing tide.

Mortal hands lifted her from the wet sand, carried her to his hut, fed her warm milk and bread until she was stronger. Language was a barrier between them at first. Leannahn struggled to overcome this handicap and won.

Locals held her in awe. She looked through you with ancient eyes, never knew wrinkles when babies born had children of their own. It was whispered she was Sidhe, kidnapped by the kind fisherman who had saved her. Even he, after they were wed, sometimes put the word in conjunction with her name.

For many years she controlled her spiritual hunger with success. Grief killed that newfound ability when her aging husband died at sea. She took many lovers after that, sometimes revisiting Fion for them with tales of inspiration. Always they died before she loved them.

It did not stop her from trying to rekindle her peace.

***

The last time Raori saw his beloved's grave, he was returning home from a short errand for the king. This was only six moons after Aramina's death and his first homecoming. It was chance, coming upon the weathered pile of stones. Were it not for his infallible memory, Raori would not have known where he was.

He placed a wreath of heather on the little mound of stones. Grass was growing between the cracks. He started to pull it, then changed his mind. His mare snorted, butting his back with her nose.

"Alright, Mina," he said to the horse, taking the reins and stepping back. Somewhere in the evening a wolf sang to its mate. Raori listened until the answering call had faded. He swung into the saddle and pointed his horse home.

Moire was waiting. She had received his message to reopen the house with joyous returned tidings. In his saddlebag, Raori had a gift of gold and a silken wedding dress.

He had missed her; her smile, the smell of eggs when she cooked for him in the evenings (Never the mornings. He always slept those through). She had been someone to talk to and, he knew now, the perfect eternal companion. He would bless her with youth and time so that they could grow old together.

Touching heels to his horse's flanks, his adventure ended how it had begun: The thunder of hooves and Moire's loving eyes watching for his return.

***

The king only thought of Aramina the day his first daughter was born. There was just something about the way her little eyes looked at him as she suckled her mother's breast. The babe was named Grian, his impression quickly forgotten.

***

Picket forgot everything, as was his habit, except for his wife and adopted son. On Liram's twenty first year, the pooka waited at the edge of the forest for something he could not quite recall. When the will o the wisps accompanied his parents to welcome the wight home, Picket only shook his head human fashion and grinned.

"Soon enough," he said. Then he returned to his family. They say he spent many happy years there, as was his due.

The sheep, it is well known, spent their days wandering the fields past broken fences. The fences were repaired, but they never stayed that way. Nor the fences of nearby homesteads. Which was just as well, for a fence is a boundary and a means to confine.

***

Finnbhear was ancient, too weak to sit, when next he saw Aramina. He, looking at his roses, lay on his couch in the sunshine. The garden was now tended by one of his loving granddaughters. She did a splendid job and even coaxed the flowers to bloom in unusual shades.

A busy personality, this granddaughter who shared his love for beauty. Her smile was quick, her mind sharp. Nothing was safe from practical jokes around her. Sometimes she fell into quiet moods, during which she wrote poetry and thought about the universe.

He had loved a girl like that once. So thinking, his eyelids drooped in the warmth. Everything had been brighter then, when he was young and she met him daily in the fields. Whatever had happened to her?

Oh, yes. She went away and he had married her sister. How could he have forgotten?

"Hello, Finnbhear," said the girl. She stood by the couch as if she had been there all along. Finnbhear smiled and wondered if she were a dream. Things were so confused lately.

"Mina," he said. "You're here. I can't believe it."

The smile she gave him was like a rainbow on a stormy day. It lit her eyes. Her hair fell in dark clouds around it. Reaching with a hand that had not aged a day since last they met, she tenderly touched his brow.

"I had to come," she said. "I promised. And it is good to see you, dear Fox."

With strength he had not possessed for too long, he reached up and grabbed her hand. "I love you," he said.

She whispered, "I love you, too."

They talked of unimportant things. Falling into the most restful sleep he had ever known, Finnbhear eventually stopped talking and only listened. When his last breath sighed forth, Aramina leaned down and tenderly kissed his lips.

Even after passing to the next world, Finnbhear never knew if her statement of love was a lie. Whatever he chose to believe, he was content.

Katrina Joyner

ABOUT THE AUTHOR

Katrina Joyner doesn't get to write and create as much as she likes, but when she does it's usually along the lines of fantasy. She's also been known to write academia, science fiction, for children, and regular boring fiction that has no magic in it whatsoever. She can't help it. It's probably because she likes to hear herself talk.

She lives near a big forest with her cats, dogs, husband and hamster. Her hair is a meter long. The rest may change, but you should never ask a lady her weight.